Also by Laurance L. Priddy

*SON OF DURANGO*
*WINNING PASSION*

# CRITICAL
## EVIDENCE

# CRITICAL
# EVIDENCE

A Courtroom Suspense Novel

Laurance L. Priddy

SUNSTONE
PRESS

The events, people, and incidents in this story are the sole product of the author's imagination. The story is fictional and any resemblance to individuals living or dead is purely coincidental.

Printed and bound in the United States of America. No part of this book may be reproduced in any form or by any electronic or mechanical means including information storage and retrieval systems without permission in writing from the publisher, except by a reviewer who may quote brief passages in a review.

Sunstone books may be purchased for educational, business, or sales promotional use. For information please write: Special Markets Department, Sunstone Press, P.O. Box 2321, Santa Fe, New Mexico 87504-2321.

FIRST EDITION

10 9 8 7 6 5 4 3 2 1

Library of Congress Cataloging-in-Publication Data:
Priddy, Laurance L., 1941–
    Critical evidence: a courtroom suspense novel / by
Laurance L. Priddy.—1st ed.
        p. cm.
    ISBN: 0-86534-306-3 (harddcover)    —ISBN: 0-86534-365-9 (paper)
    1. Texas—Fiction.  I. Title.

    PS3566. R559  C75  2000
    813' .54—dc21                                    00-058783

Published in

SUNSTONE PRESS
Post Office Box 2321
Santa Fe, NM 87504-2321 / USA
(505) 988-4418 / orders only (800) 243-5644
FAX (505) 988-1025
www.sunstonepress.com

# ACKNOWLEDGMENT

I thank my wife, Kim, for putting up with the hassle that goes with having a writer in the family, Jim Smith, of Sunstone Press, for his excellent editing, and my friends and colleagues at the DFW Writers' Workshop for their invaluable critiques over the many months it took to complete this book.

# 1

Officer Albert Wilson sat parked in his squad car at the side of an access ramp on a hill overlooking Interstate 30 in the west part of Fort Worth. The compactly built black man sipped the coffee he had bought at a Stop 'N Go. On the highway below, heavy traffic slogged through driving rain brought by a late summer tropical storm that had come up from Mexico.

Wilson hadn't wanted the duty today. His son was having a birthday party and he wanted to be there but he hadn't been able to arrange a shift change.

On the interstate a dented black Ford truck approached, traveling well under the speed limit in the left eastbound lane. A load of watermelons swelled its rickety sides. Wilson noticed that the truck had lost power. As it slowly coasted to a halt the driver turned it partly onto the narrow median next to the fence dividing the highway but it came to rest with its rear still in the driving lane.

Wilson slipped his car into gear and pulled onto the access ramp. He was westbound and would have to go up to the next crossover and come back on the other side to get to the truck. As he pulled onto the freeway a blue pickup speeded around a line of traffic on the opposite side of the road and clipped the protruding rear of the watermelon truck.

The pickup spun on the wet pavement, hitting two cars in the center lane. The tailgate of the larger truck tumbled open and shiny green watermelons cascaded onto the roadway. Oncoming cars swerved right and left, sliding out of control and crashing into each other. In seconds, a tangle of seven or eight vehicles clogged the eastbound lanes of the freeway.

Wilson's blood raced. "God damn!" He reached for his microphone. "West Sector, this is Car 450!"

"Go ahead Car 450."

Before he could reply, a large Alamo Oil Company gasoline tanker westbound on the highway next to him veered left across the pavement, crashed through the dividing fence, and careened into the cluster of disabled vehicles in the eastbound lanes. With a flash of heat and light and a low-pitched roar, the tanker exploded, covering the scene with blazing fuel.

Forgetting his radio, Officer Wilson jammed on his brakes and jerked his car off the road. He got out, facing the flaring mass on the other side of the median. The heat stifled him.

He cast useless shouts to heaven. "My God! My God!"

Figures ran from the flames, covered with fire. Their high-pitched screams surmounted the roar from the burning vehicles. Two ran in circles, arms waving, and finally collapsed into burning heaps on the roadway. Others stumbled to the grassy strip along the far shoulder and rolled over and over until their flames were out.

But no screams came from the heart of the conflagration where the gasoline truck and its consorts burned fiercely. Traffic on both sides of the freeway had come to a halt. People were getting out of their cars and running toward the scene.

"Car 450, this is West Sector. Are you there?"

Wilson got a grip on himself, opened the car door, and grabbed the microphone. He skipped the usual protocol. "This is 450. Get everything you can out here fast. Fire trucks, ambulances, all the cars you got. A tanker truck's just exploded in the middle of the freeway."

"Where is it, Car 450?"

"3300 West Freeway, just east of the loop, in the eastbound lanes."

As the dispatcher started calling up the dozens of units that would respond, Wilson turned on his lights and siren and headed his car over the curb to the access road where he raced to the next crossover several blocks away, sped across, and moved east on the interstate to the scene. He steered along the grassy shoulder past the cars that had come to a stop behind the accident and pulled his car across the driving lanes thirty yards short of the burning vehicles.

He spotted other police cars arriving from several directions and heard the wail of many sirens. An ambulance pulled past Wilson's car and stopped. Paramedics spilled out and ran to the still living burn victims on the shoulder. A crowd of people from the stopped cars had gathered in the downpour, observing the carnage with sick, fearsome faces.

Wilson motioned them away. "Move back folks. There's nothing you can do. Fire department's on the way."

The people turned slowly back toward their cars. Several held their fists clenched as they cried tears of frustration and sorrow. A fire truck eased along the shoulder past Wilson's car and swung into the roadway. Firefighters pulled hoses from the truck and started laying foam on the fire. Another truck pulled into place on the far side of the wreck and its firemen attacked the blaze from that position. The flames began to diminish.

Other officers joined Wilson and other police cars sealed the freeway in both directions. The police routed the cars up the embankment to the service road. Soon the freeway around the accident was clear of cars except for the seven or eight ruins clustered around the hulks of the burned out gasoline and produce trucks.

Watermelons littered the area, many split open from the heat. Their mushy red interiors clashed with the slate grey pavement. Paramedics escorted those who had survived to ambulances and put the smoldering bodies from the roadway on stretchers.

Wilson and tall, blond Sergeant Crow walked together to the tangled vehicles where firemen were prying open the blackened door of a Ford Taurus with the Jaws of Life, a hydraulic device. Not an appropriate name this time, Wilson thought. An acrid stench of burned flesh hung in the air, overpowering the pungent odor of gasoline.

The door of the Taurus popped open. Wilson's stomach turned at the sight inside. The fire had destroyed all semblance of their features but the charred forms were inescapably human. The larger adult body lay protectively over the corpses of two children.

The face of his son smiling as he opened his birthday presents flashed through Wilson's mind. He turned from the pitiful sight.

From the top of the roadside embankment a big man in a suit came running through the diminishing rain. At the edge of the road an officer tried to restrain him but he broke free and hurried to Wilson and Sergeant Crow. He stared at the still-legible license plate of the burned car.

"My wife! My kids! Oh, my God! My God!"

He started forward but Wilson and Sergeant Crow grabbed his arms and turned him around.

"You can't do anything sir," Crow said. "Come away."

The big man's shoulders slumped. He put his hands to his face, sobbing. Wilson and the sergeant gently led him to the side of the road where they turned him over to two paramedics. Wilson, overcome, stumbled to the grassy shoulder, vomiting time after time as if his stomach could purge his soul of the evil he had seen. Finally, he straightened.

Sergeant Crow took his arm. "You okay?"

Wilson nodded. "Yeah."

"Did you see the wreck?"

"Yeah, I called it in."

"I got to write the accident report."

"I don't envy you."

"It's a mess all right. What happened?"

Wilson described what he had seen. "It wouldn't have been much of a problem if the tanker truck hadn't got involved," he concluded.

"What caused it to go out of control?"

Wilson shrugged. "Don't know. I couldn't see any reason for it. He just suddenly veered across the median. He couldn't have done a better job of hitting 'em if he'd aimed for 'em."

"Did you see what happened to the driver?"

"Probably still in the cab."

Both men turned toward the tanker, looming oppressively over the other vehicles.

"Maybe we oughta check it," Sergeant Crow said.

Wilson shook his head. "Let's let the fire boys take care of that. I'm sure he's in there."

"Guess you're right. Can you help me with a diagram?"

"You bet. Let's get started. I need to get out of here."

❧

The next day, lawyer Jim McSpadden sat at his desk reading the *Star-Telegram*. Nine Killed In Pileup, ran the headline. According to the story the drunken driver of an Alamo Oil Company tanker had veered across the median into a wreck that had just occurred on the other side of the road. Nine people had died on the scene and two of the eleven injured remained in critical condition. The dead trucker's blood alcohol had tested at double the amount that classified him as intoxicated in the eyes of the law.

Jim pushed the paper away and got up. He walked to the window and looked out at the summer day, bright and hot after yesterday's storm. Untold human misery came from an accident like this one, he thought. The psychic wounds of the survivors would never heal, however much money the Alamo Oil Company paid them. The money was important, though, and here was an opportunity for some lawyers. He could sure stand to be one of them.

At forty-three, his fine blond hair had thinned and his grey-specked beard made him look older. Tall and thick through the middle in spite of his jogging program, he wore ready-to-wear slacks and a red, open-necked sports shirt. No point in wearing a suit when he wasn't going to court.

He still wasn't used to his small, one-lawyer office. Until last year he'd been in a partnership with Bobby Toricelli and Gene Burns. They'd had a big volume worker's compensation practice until the Texas Legislature had changed the law to make it almost impossible for lawyers to work in the compensation field. The change had come several years earlier but there had been enough unresolved cases under the old law to keep them busy for a while.

They'd struggled to hold on as their income dropped but eventually had to dissolve the partnership. Bobby had gone back to work for the District Attorney's office and Gene had opened a small office doing divorce and criminal law work. Jim had stuck to personal injury work, surviving on what car wreck and construction accident cases he could get. It was tough. Many months he couldn't pay his bills.

A shot at even one of the death or injury cases from the West Freeway accident would give him hope for the future.

His secretary, Susan Rawlins, stuck her head in the door.

"Coffee's ready. Want a cup?"

"Sure do."

She brought him a large ceramic mug. Jim had hired Susan when he'd opened the office. In her mid-fifties with two grown children, she'd found it necessary to go back to work as a legal secretary after the failure of a twenty-five year marriage. She had a solemn, skinny triangle of a face, wore glasses with fake tortoise shell rims, and had an unflappable, no nonsense approach to the legal business.

Jim took the cup, nodding toward the paper on his desk. "See the story on the big wreck?"

"I sure did. What a shame!"

"No one's called about it, have they?"

She smiled, shaking her head. "Not yet."

"Somehow I didn't think they had."

At noon Jim went down to the deli on the ground floor to get a sandwich. He ate alone most days now and missed the exchange of banter and lawyer talk with Gene and Bobby. They had taken long lunches to discuss their cases, bitch about judges and insurance adjusters, and exchange the latest courthouse gossip. Now, with a reduced case load and no lawyers in the building he wanted to lunch with, Jim usually ate in fifteen or twenty minutes and went back to the office.

He stayed caught up on his work and usually went home before five. He lived alone in a town house near Ridglea Country Club. The three-bedroom brick ranchstyle on five acres west of town had gone to his former wife, Ellen, in their divorce settlement. Thoughts of Ellen, their son, Travis, and the house he had loved ran through Jim's mind as he slowly ate his pastrami on rye. Were they watering the grass enough and had anyone ever fixed the leaky wellhouse roof?

Susan was wiping lunch crumbs off her desk when Jim walked back into the office.

"Any calls?" he asked.

She nodded. "Several."

"Anything important?"

"There was one about that accident."

"You're kidding!"

"I'm not."

Jim's pulse skipped a beat. "Who was it?"

"Some preacher. Said he needed to talk to you about it."

Susan handed him the number and Jim went into his office to make the call.

A church secretary at Saint Stephen's Episcopal in the Wedgewood area put him through to Reverend Goodall.

"I had a message to call you," Jim said.

The reverend had a deep, throaty voice, full of confidence and compassion. "That's right. I got your name from Jack Corcoran."

"That's my pastor. What can I do for you?"

"We lost three members of our congregation in the wreck yesterday. A woman and two daughters. I'm sure the surviving husband's going to need some legal help."

"Have you talked to him about it?"

"Not yet. Right now he's in no shape to make decisions. He came on the scene and saw the bodies still in the car."

Jim drew in his breath. In his gut he felt the anguish of the distraught husband and father. "That's terrible. Does he have any other children?"

"There's a surviving son. He's taking it hard, too."

"How old is he?"

"Around twelve."

"When do you want me to talk to the man?"

"The funeral's tomorrow and he'll need several days after that before trying to do anything."

"I understand. What's his name?"

"Al Richaud."

Jim scribbled the name on a legal pad.

"Call me when he's ready. But don't wait too long. Even though it's hard, he needs to move fast. You can bet the insurance company investigators are working day and night on this one. If I'm gonna get into it I'd like to be able to look over their shoulders."

"I'll talk to him about it after the funeral. What do you think about the case?"

"All I know is what I've seen in the paper. From that, it looks like Alamo Oil Company's clearly liable. There's probably a good case on the drivers of the

14

watermelon truck and the pickup, too, but I doubt if they've got much insurance."

"Maybe Al should just wait and see how much Alamo will pay before getting a lawyer."

"I wouldn't advise that. They'll probably try to throw some money at him and it'll sound like a lot but there's not much chance they'll make a really fair offer right off the bat. And they may try to wiggle out of it. They could claim Alamo isn't liable because the driver deviated from the course and scope of his employment by getting drunk."

"Isn't their insurance still responsible?"

"Maybe. But the coverage on this truck and driver may not be adequate for all the deaths and injuries involved. The umbrella coverage and reinsurance on the whole company needs to be brought into play and if they can get the driver out of the course and scope it may exclude those larger layers of coverage."

"I guess it's pretty tricky."

"It sure is. That's why Mr. Richaud needs a lawyer right away."

"I understand. I'll call you in a few days, Mr. McSpadden. Thanks for talking to me."

Jim put the phone down and walked out to Susan's desk. "We may get a shot at one of the cases."

"That's great. Who would we be representing?"

Jim told her about the claim.

Tears shone in her eyes. "How terrible for that man to see the bodies!"

"He'll never get over it."

"When will you know if we get the case?"

"The pastor's going to call me in a few days."

"I sure hope we get hired."

"So do I. Lord knows, I need a break."

Back in his office, Jim stood with his hands behind his back looking out the window over the tops of the full-foliaged trees. It had been nice of Jack Corcoran to think of him. Jim hadn't darkened the doors of the church much since the divorce.

This case could make things work for him again. Excitement and exhilaration mingled with his sympathy for Al Richaud. He knew he could do a good job. But he didn't have it yet and you shouldn't count your birds before you have them in hand.

∞

Rollin "Rolly" Sullivan had seen the story in the *San Antonio Express-News* about the wreck. This case was right up his alley but he couldn't work on it if no one hired him. Over the last ten years he'd become one of the brightest lights in the Texas personal injury bar with a score of multimillion dollar verdicts and settlements to his credit. A small man of fifty-six, he had an angular Irish face and wore his greying red hair short. In his last big case he'd convinced a South Texas jury to award a woman eight million dollars for injuries sustained in a traffic accident. She'd been rearended by an A-1 Moving Company van traveling through town at a grossly excessive speed and had suffered a ruptured disc. As a result of her injury and surgery, she had permanently lost all interest in sexual relations with her husband. At least, that was what she'd testified.

Rolly had his own opinion of why she'd lost her libido. He'd been around her husband a lot while working on the case. But in the end the jury had found her problem was grounded in the psychic effects of the accident.

It had taken expert opinion testimony and a slick argument from Rolly to convince the jury of the connection. The expert testimony had come from psychologist Nadine Graves, an imposing lady with a wide forehead who wore her glasses secured behind her neck with a cord. She had been based in San Antonio but had recently moved her office to Fort Worth.

Remembering this, Rolly dialed Nadine's number and a secretary quickly connected them.

"Rolly, baby! How you been doing?"

Nadine's enthusiasm recalled the physical relation that had developed between them as a result of their work on the last case. Rolly thought of her thrusting large white breasts, the roll of her wide hips, the labored creaking of the motel bed. He could stand some more of that. Maybe this new case would give them a chance. Of course, their respective spouses mustn't know. "I'm doing great, Nadine! We miss you here in San Antone."

"I'd love to be there, sugar, but when Bill got transferred, I had to move too."

"I understand."

"What can I do for you?"

"We're too far away for that."

She laughed. "You know what I mean."

"I'm gonna get involved with the litigation on that big wreck up there."

"The one yesterday?"

"Yes."

"Who do you represent?"

"No one, right now. That's where you come in."

"What do you mean?"

"Don't you think the wreck victims and their families could stand a little grief counseling?"

"Sure. No doubt about it. But none of them have called me."

"I was thinking you could send them letters."

"I can't solicit clients like that."

"But you can offer them services for free."

"It'd be pretty tricky. What did you have in mind?"

"I'll get the names and addresses through a contact my investigator has in the Fort Worth police department. You can write them letters offering free group grief counseling to help them deal with the aftermath of the accident. What would be wrong with that?"

Nadine hesitated. "Nothing, I guess. A session like that could do them all a lot of good. I could offer it as a public service. But where do you come in?"

"I'll pay your charges for the session. I'll rent a meeting room at the Worthington for it. At the end, you can introduce me and I'll talk to them about being their lawyer."

"Is that ethical?"

"I think so. You're providing them a free service and I'm giving them a chance to hire the best lawyer they can possibly get."

"But isn't that kind of solicitation illegal? Isn't it...what do you call it?"

"Barratry? No, I don't think so. The court decisions allow us a lot more latitude to promote our services than they used to. I think what I'm talking about is commercial free speech, protected by the Constitution. These folks are going to get referred to a lot of pissant lawyers who don't know shit about handling a case of this magnitude. The recovery could be huge but it won't be if these people get tied up with the kind of incompetents their preachers and friends will send them to. I need to get in on the ground floor to make sure they don't get screwed."

Nadine laughed. "And to give yourself a big piece of the action?"

"That, too."

"Well, you're the lawyer. When do we start?"

"Right away. Times a'wastin'."

"Fax me those addresses and a draft of the letter."

"I'll have them to you this afternoon."

"I'll get the letters right out and shoot for Friday for the counseling session."

"Perfect. I'll have my secretary call you this afternoon with the arrangements for the meeting room."

"Sounds good, Rolly."

"Of course, there's a bonus in all this...."

"Yes?"

"It'll give us a chance to get together again."

"Yes it will. Timing's perfect. Bill's out of town for a week."

"Till Friday, then."

∽

Seventeen people showed up. They sat in padded hotel chairs lined up in rows before a podium in a meeting room in the Worthington Hotel in downtown Fort Worth. The hotel had done a good job on the room, closing off a section of a large ballroom into an intimate space.

The subdued mauve covers of the chair seats matched the carpet. The lights had been turned down to a pleasant level. Arrangements of cut flowers in vases sat on small polished tables along the sides and coffee, soft drinks, and snacks were available at a buffet table. Rolly sat at the back of the group as if he was one of them.

He had hoped for more. How many of the killed and injured did they represent? They sat solemn-faced in small, aloof groups, talking little.

Nadine suddenly entered from a door behind the podium. With her high forehead, substantial bust and clear eyes, she projected an air of authority and understanding. Leaving the mike on its stand, she moved in front of the podium.

"Good afternoon, folks," she said. "I'm Nadine Graves. I'm a psychologist and a counselor. My office is out on Camp Bowie Boulevard. Let's start this session by rearranging the chairs in a circle so we're all facing each other."

They got up, moved the extra chairs to the side and brought their chairs into a circle. This simple act of cooperation broke the tension and the men and women smiled at each other and exchanged remarks as they worked together. Rolly helped, moving more chairs than anyone else. When the rearrangement was complete, Nadine took a seat near the center. Rolly parked himself across from Nadine.

She then favored the group with a bright smile. "That's better. If this session is to do any good, we have to be able to talk to each other. I invited you to come here today because I thought it might help to talk about what you're going through. Too often, in the aftermath of tragedy, people bottle up their feelings, try to go on with their lives, and defer dealing with their grief.

"Although most of you don't know each other, you have something in common in your loss from this accident. I believe talking about it can be helpful and I'd like to invite all of you to share your feelings with the rest of us."

Nadine looked over the group, her eyes projecting invitation. A thin woman with a flushed face held up her hand. She was seated with two men and another woman. They had a solid, middleclass look.

Nadine nodded. "Please tell us your name and share your experience."

The woman looked around. "I'm Rhonda Carter and this is my husband Joe, and my sister LaVerne and her husband, Dick.

"Our mother was in right in the middle of the pileup. The doors of her car were jammed and she never had a chance to get out. We lost our father to cancer a year ago and we're having a lot of trouble accepting this second loss so soon, especially with the way it happened. I keep thinking of mother trapped in that car while the fire closed in on her. I wake up in the middle of the night thinking it's all a bad dream and then I have to realize it really happened and that I've lost her for good."

Tears ran down Rhonda Carter's cheeks. She put her hands to her face and quickly sat down. Her husband put his arm around her shoulders.

Rolly made a mental note. The mother would be Ruby Walthall, the seventy-two year old lady in the old Lincoln that had ended up between the tanker and the watermelon truck.

Nadine nodded with an expression of sympathy. "You're among friends, Mrs. Carter. These other people are here for the same reason as you."

A small man with greying, curly hair held up his hand and Nadine nodded to him.

He spoke with a shaking voice. "I'm Roger Lombardo. My daughter and her husband couldn't get out of their car, either. They were going out to dinner for their fifth anniversary. My wife and I are keeping the granddaughter. She keeps asking about her mother and father. It's really hard to handle."

Several people started sobbing. Rolly dabbed away his own tears. He knew this man was the surviving father of Doreen Baer who had died with her husband Kurt in the small Plymouth caught between the blue pickup and the BMW.

A thin black man in a blue suit stood "I'm Odell Wyatt," he said "My daughter got out of the van she was riding in but she was all afire. The doctors think she'll live but it's gonna take years of plastic surgery and rehabilitation and she'll never be the same."

That would be Demetria Wyatt, Rolly thought. She and two other black teenagers had been riding in a Dodge van that had spun away from the center of the wreck. All three had survived but were terribly burned.

A woman with her face swollen from crying raised her hand. Her unmarried daughter, a promising young doctor, had been in the BMW on her way to her hospital rounds. She had suffered broken bones in her face and a broken shoulder along with serious burns. She would be in the hospital for several more weeks.

Over the next hour, many others in the room stood to share their stories of injury and bereavement. Nadine played the role of compassionate listener and guide, letting the people interact in mutual revelation and support. When all had spoken who wanted to, Nadine turned to Rolly.

"Folks, it's important to open up as you have today and I hope the process will continue for all of you. In addition to dealing with your grief, there's something else you'll all have to deal with and that's the legal aspects of the accident. It takes a lawyer to adequately advise you in this area so I'd like to introduce one of the best personal injury lawyers in this state, Rolly Sullivan from San Antonio, who will speak briefly about your legal rights."

Nadine spread an open palm toward Rolly. He slowly looked around the circle, studying the people for signs of hostility. What he would say in the next few minutes was critical. No one was smiling. Lines of tension and uncertainty marked many faces. He knew they had all assumed he was one of them and had not yet adjusted to his new identity.

"Ladies and gentlemen, I'm glad to be here and I thank Nadine for asking me. This is a grief counseling session but we both thought it would be helpful for you to know your legal rights. These deaths and injuries happened because of wrongdoing on the part of the Alamo Oil Company. Without the criminal negligence of the drunken Alamo truck driver, no one would have been killed or seriously hurt.

"You don't have to be passive victims of Alamo's negligence. Bringing this guilty corporation to justice and making it pay for the devastation it has caused will help all of you put the affair behind you and go on with your lives. Even now, Alamo's lawyers and investigators are working to minimize their exposure. To fight back you all need a lawyer of your own.

"I'm not here to make a hardsell pitch to be that lawyer. That would be inappropriate at this time. But I do think you need to know something about the process involved in a case like this so you'll be prepared to deal with Alamo and its adjusters and lawyers when the time comes."

Rolly outlined the procedure he thought Alamo would follow in dealing with the claims. He said they could expect the adjusters to contact them very soon and that they would be very sympathetic and would want to settle, but to beware of the early offers; they were almost certain to be too small. Only by employing someone who knew the process inside and out could victims get truly fair treatment. He asked if there were any questions.

Suddenly, small, grey-haired Roger Lombardo stood, face red and hands shaking.

"What kind of charade is this, anyway? You get us here to talk about our sorrow and it's all just a pretext for a pitch by a goddamn greedy lawyer."

Rolly wasn't surprised. He'd known some of them would feel like Lombardo. He put on a sorrowful face.

"Don't think badly of me, Mr. Lombardo. Mrs. Graves asked me here as a public service to make sure you were aware of the legal aspects of the accident."

"Sure she did. You think I'm fool enough to believe that?"

"It's the truth."

"Bullshit!"

Abruptly, Lombardo turned and headed for the door, but no one followed. So far, so good, Rolly thought.

He waited until Lombardo was out the door. "Seriously, folks, I'm here mainly to ask you not to be lulled into a false sense of confidence by slick-talking insurance adjusters. Remember, however sympathetic they may sound, they are not your friends. All I'd ask is that you get legal advice of your own and get it now. It doesn't have to be from me but if any of you want to talk, I'll be available at the close of the session."

Rolly flashed a friendly smile, his way of letting them know he was a good guy just trying to be helpful. He couldn't help it if some mistrusted his motives.

Nadine took over. She thanked them for coming, reminding them to confront their losses by talking.

"If any of you need further counseling, please get it promptly from a mental health professional of your choice. I'm leaving some of my cards here on the podium. If you don't have someone in mind, I'd be glad to talk to any of you."

The meeting over, some turned immediately to the door while others clustered around Nadine. Rolly walked quickly to a table at the side of the room where he had placed a thick scrapbook. A few in the group followed him, led by a big, black-haired man in slacks and a sports shirt. He had not spoken during the counseling session.

The man stared at Rolly for a moment, unsmiling, then spoke. "It's pretty obvious this whole deal was staged to get your foot in the door but I don't mind that. I'm ready to talk to a lawyer. What makes you think you're the one?"

Rolly motioned toward the chairs around the table. "That's a fair question. Ya'll sit down and I'll try to answer it."

Rolly opened the scrapbook and showed them newspaper clippings from the case of the lady who lost her libido, then turned the pages back to some of his other impressive victories. Rolly Sullivan Strikes Again, ran one headline in the *San Antonio Express-News*. The story described the tactics he had used to win a twenty-two million dollar class action lawsuit for hundreds of people across the country damaged by rototillers that had climbed up their legs when placed in reverse.

Other clippings detailed his success in a bad faith damages case against Hercules Insurance Company. Rolly had proved to the satisfaction of a jury in Houston that the company's agents and adjusters had been retroactively canceling property damage policies after accidents in order to avoid paying the claims. The award was ten million in actual damages and fifty million in punitive damages. No matter that the court had reduced the punitive award to thirty million, Rolly had collected a total of forty million plus interest for his clients and himself.

He pointed out a few more cases and then slammed the book shut. "Folks, these are my credentials. I don't believe I'm being immodest in saying you can't get a better lawyer for a case like this."

The big man put out his hand. "Mr. Sullivan, I'm Al Richaud. I lost my wife and two daughters because of Alamo's negligence. No money award can bring them back but I'd like to send the bastards a message for what they did, and I'd be proud to have you for my lawyer."

Rolly gripped his hand. "I'd be proud to represent you."

An hour later, after everyone had gone, Rolly and Nadine toasted each other with soft drinks from the buffet table.

"To our success," she said.

They clinked their glasses and drank. The session had ended well. Rolly had signed up Richaud, Rhonda Carter and her husband and their inlaws, and Odell Wyatt. Yvonne Shaw, the mother of the injured doctor, had promised to introduce Rolly to her daughter Mary in the hospital. This group represented four of the nine fatalities and two of the eleven injured. Rolly thought his contract with Wyatt would lead to his representing the other two badly burned teenagers in the car with Wyatt's daughter.

He would have liked to have everyone, but that was too much to expect. It was just as well not to have the families of the drivers of the watermelon truck and the blue pickup. Both had died in the wreck. Since their negligence had contributed to the accident, representing their heirs would conflict with his representation of the victims who were guiltless.

All the claimants he had signed up were as pure as the driven snow and he had them all on contracts providing a one-third attorney's fee, contingent on the outcome. All things considered, he had done a good day's work.

For her part, Nadine now had five new clients who had made appointments for further counseling. It was understood she would also earn fees for the psychological evaluations Rolly would have her perform in connection with his trial preparation.

They finished their soft drinks and put the glasses on the table.

"We ought to be toasting each other with something stronger," Nadine said.

"That's for sure. Let's grab a couple of drinks at the bar and get a bite at the Star of Texas Grill."

Later that night, well-greased from the bar and mellow from their good meal and after-dinner drinks, Rolly and Nadine took the elevator to the top floor of the hotel. Pulse thumping in anticipation, he preceded her down the hall. They quickly entered the suite he had booked and Rolly fastened the security chain.

As he turned around, Nadine moved into his arms. Taller than he was by several inches, she pulled him against her and covered his mouth with hers. Large, gelatinous breasts pressed against his chest. She pulled her lips away.

"I want your body, little man," she whispered.

"I'm all yours, Nadine."

He took her hand and led her to the window where he pulled back the drapes of the still-darkened room. Below them Main Street ran south through downtown Fort Worth to the Tarrant County Convention Center ten blocks away. Hundreds of small lights in the trees along the street lent a touch of magic to the scene. Passing cars left red and white trails along the street.

Rolly put his arm around Nadine's waist. "It's pretty, isn't it?"

"Yes it is. You picked a room with a view."

"That's not all it has."

"What do you mean?"

"There's a spa with a hot tub."

"Let's try it out."

They took off their clothes. Nadine had lost any claim to a girlish figure long ago. Large white breasts hung pendulously, capped with dark, elongated nipples. Her midriff, generous but still taut, merged with wide, flared hips. She wouldn't win any Miss Petite contests but her big body excited Rolly.

She looked down at his throbbing member. "I never could understand how a little guy like you could have such a big pecker."

"It's one of my most loveable attributes."

They soaked in the hot tub for half an hour, then toweled off their reddened bodies and headed for the bedroom. She lay on her back and he moved over her, tugging gently on her nipples with his teeth. He trailed his tongue to her navel where he explored its inner recesses.

Her breath came harder. "Hurry, Rolly, I can't wait."

Spreading her legs, he entered, and they began a rhythmic pumping as he rode her pudendum like a cowboy on a bronco. She took his buttocks in her hands and forced him down, harder into her. Suddenly, with a cry, she thrust herself up and he penetrated deeper as she shuddered in a long spasm that he instantly reciprocated, fiercely fulfilled.

Later, relaxed, they lay atop the covers as the air conditioning cooled their heated bodies.

"You know what?" she asked.

"What?"

"I'd say it's been a pretty good day."

# 2

Seven days after the freeway wreck, Jim McSpadden called Reverend Goodall at Saint Stephen's Episcopal.

"I hadn't heard from you so I thought I'd follow up on our conversation. Do you think Mr. Richaud is ready to talk to me now?"

The reverend paused, then answered in an embarrassed tone. "The reason I didn't call you is that he already hired someone else."

A breath caught in Jim's throat. "Who did he get?"

"A lawyer named Rolly Sullivan, from San Antonio."

Jim suppressed a curse. The news wasn't really surprising. Sullivan had a statewide reputation for soliciting big cases. He'd been before bar ethics committees for his tactics and had almost been indicted for barratry, but the only penalty he'd ever drawn was a reprimand.

"How did Mr. Richaud come to hire Sullivan?" Jim asked calmly.

"He didn't go into details."

"I'm sorry he didn't wait to talk to me."

"So am I. I didn't even get a chance to ask him about it. I was giving him some time. He called me several days ago and told me. I told him about you, but he'd already hired the other guy."

"Well, that's that. I sure appreciate your thinking of me, Reverend Goodall." Jim kept disappointment out of his voice.

"I know you would have done a good job. Jack Corcoran recommended you highly."

"Keep me in mind in the future."

"I'll do that."

Jim hung up and sat staring at his desktop, black thoughts charging through his brain. Susan came in with the morning mail.

"What's eating you?" she asked. "It can't be that bad."

"It damn sure can. That guy Al Richaud hired Rolly Sullivan."

Susan's angular face softened. "I know that's a letdown. Who's Rolly Sullivan?"

"A goddamn, unethical case-running crook of a lawyer from San Antonio."

"That's a pretty strong description."

"No more than he deserves. To give him credit, he's also one of the best personal injury lawyers in this part of the country. But why did he get the one client I had a shot at?"

"It doesn't seem fair."

"I learned a long time ago that fair doesn't have much to do with our business."

Several days later, a big headline in the *Fort Worth Star-Telegram* served notice that Sullivan had filed suit in Richaud versus Alamo Oil Company against Alamo Oil on behalf of six victims of the wreck and their families. It made Jim feel worse that Rolly had named Al Richaud as his lead plaintiff. In the story, the paper quoted Alamo's lawyer, Arthur Kurtz of Dallas. Kurtz expressed regret that Sullivan had not joined in a good faith effort to settle the case without litigation. He said he planned to file an early motion for court-ordered mediation.

That night, the Fort Worth and Dallas television stations ran footage of the press conference Sullivan had called in response to Kurtz's remarks. At home in his town house, Jim leaned back in his easy chair sipping a beer as he watched the show. Rolly appeared before the cameras on the ground floor of the Tarrant County Government Center in a plaid suit, two-tone dress shirt, and tie with bold yellow stripes.

He squared his small shoulders and set his pugnacious face in a look of righteous anger. "I'd like nothing better than to have settled this case without litigation," he said, "but ever since I was hired several days ago, I've been trying to get access to Alamo's burned tanker truck and the results of their investigation.

"I'd like to know what business they had turning a drunken driver loose behind the wheel of a fully loaded gasoline tanker and where he'd been to get in that condition while on duty. But they won't answer my questions. I've got nothing but stonewalling from them. I'm compelled to file this lawsuit so I can ask the court to enter a protective order against spoilation of evidence. If I mediate with Alamo first, it will be too late, and all the evidence will be gone before the case even gets started."

Rolly then screwed his face into a sincere expression. "I agree with Mr. Kurtz that this case should be mediated but only after all sides have equal access to the facts. Mediation on an uneven playing field won't get us anywhere. I'm fully prepared to mediate as soon as I have all the information I need and I join with Mr. Kurtz in the hope the case can be settled that way."

In a way, Jim had to admire the man. He had balls. He'd got the whole world's attention with his fanfare. How many more victims would now hire him as a result of this publicity? Jim's style would have been to call Art Kurtz on the phone and make a deal for an exchange of information, then try to settle without filing suit. He knew Kurtz from other cases and was sure he could have worked with him.

The case seemed cut and dried. Jim doubted there was much way for Alamo to change the facts to its advantage. Under Texas law, you had two years to file suit for a traffic accident. A few months of delay for presuit mediation wouldn't have hurt anything. But Sullivan hadn't got where he was by being a shrinking violet and he'd probably get paid double for his brashness. He had raised a good question about the wreck. What was that driver doing double drunk on duty?

The next day, Jim got to the office a little after nine. Susan had already written up the messages from the voicemail on slips of paper and put them on his desk. He got his first cup of coffee and shuffled through them. Several lawyers and adjusters had returned his calls about pending cases late in the previous day, after Jim and Susan had closed up.

Some people always returned calls after normal hours. That way, they could take credit for returning them without actually having to talk to anyone. The only other call was from someone named Laura Marcus who wanted to discuss a potential new case. He'd call her first. He could sure use some new cases.

He dialed the number and waited while the phone rang.

"Hello?" a woman answered.

"Hello, this is Jim McSpadden. Is this Laura Marcus?"

"Yes, it is."

"What can I do for you?"

"I need a lawyer, Mr. McSpadden."

"How did you get my name?"

"Sally Wilson told me to call." She named one of Jim's former clients.

"What kind of case is it?"

"My husband was killed in that big wreck on the freeway ten days ago."

The connection flashed like lightning in Jim's head. Danny Marcus had been the driver of that tanker truck. Of all the death and injury cases resulting from the accident, Mrs. Marcus was calling about the only one where a lawyer probably couldn't do much good. The whole thing was Danny Marcus's fault. What does his wife think I can do, Jim thought. He had to speak gently, though. Like the others, she'd suffered a terrible loss.

"I'm familiar with that case. What kind of help do you need?"

"I'm sure you've read the papers. They're all claiming Danny was drunk but I don't believe it. He didn't do things like that."

Jim hesitated. How could he let this loyal, grief-stricken wife down easily?

"The blood test is usually pretty conclusive."

"I know that but there must be some mistake. He had no reason to get drunk in the middle of the day."

"It's a mighty tough case, Mrs. Marcus."

"I know that, too, but couldn't you at least talk to me? You're the sixth lawyer I've called, and the others wouldn't even make an appointment."

It was nice to know he was so high up in the hierarchy of desirable lawyers. Choice number six for a loser of a case that wasn't going anywhere! But he was a sucker for sad situations and the desperate intensity of Laura Marcus's voice compelled him to at least listen to her.

"It wouldn't hurt to talk about it," Jim said. "Could you come in tomorrow?"

"What time?"

"Ten o'clock."

"I'll be there. Where are you?"

Jim gave her directions, then hung up and walked into Susan's office.

"Do you know who that was?" he asked.

Susan shook her head. "She said she had a case."

"That she does and what a case it is! That was the widow of the truck driver from the freeway accident."

Susan frowned. "What does she think you can do for her?"

"She doesn't think her husband was drunk."

"Why did he swerve across the median, then?"

"That's a good question."

"Can you help her?"

"Probably not, but I made an appointment."

∽

Jim studied Laura Marcus sitting across the desk from him. A tall brunette with an attractive, rangy figure, she had her lips set in a hard, grim line, projecting a spunk that Jim admired. Her handshake at the door of the office had been firm and no nonsense. She wore a cotton blouse of subdued lavender, and a light beige skirt. He had expected her to have the seedy, disheveled look that came of too many kids and not enough money. Instead, she appeared organized and crisply competent in spite of the grief in her brown eyes.

"Do you have any idea why your husband would have been drinking on the day of the accident?" Jim asked.

She shook her head. "None whatever. He never drank on the job, as I said on the phone."

"Did he drink at all?"

"Sure. He loved his beer. Especially at the Ranger games. We'd all sit together and Danny would drink maybe four or five but never more than that."

"How many in your family?"

"There were four. We have—I have—two kids."

"How old are they?"

"Eddie's fifteen and Kim's twelve."

"How are they taking it?"

Laura bit her lip. "Not good. I had to pick Kim up at school yesterday. She was crying so much she couldn't stay in class."

Jim turned away, blinking at tears. "Sounds like you had a close family."

She nodded. "We did, Mr. McSpadden. And I knew my husband. That's how I know he wasn't drunk."

"Was there anything unusual about that day?"

She shook her head. "No, there wasn't. Danny left for work around six in the morning like he always did. He didn't act any different."

"What did his job involve?"

"He made deliveries to local gas stations and convenience stores. Every morning he went to the Alamo terminal between here and Weatherford and got the truck and the paperwork showing where he was supposed to deliver that day."

Tears streaked her face. It was brutal to make her relive the day that had destroyed her happiness but Jim had to have the facts.

"Did he load the truck himself?"

"No. Someone else would do that before he got there. He'd just get in and make the deliveries."

"How many places did he go?"

Mrs. Marcus looked down, eyes narrowed. "I'm not sure. It varied a good bit."

"Where was his route?"

"That varied, too. Sometimes he stayed in Tarrant County, but he also went to Denton County and Wise County."

"Do you know where he was going on the day of the accident?"

"No, I don't."

"When did he usually get through?"

"Late in the afternoon. Sometimes he ran as late as six or seven but he'd usually be through by five."

Plainly, Mrs. Marcus didn't know much about the circumstances. Jim would have to get his information from other sources.

"Have you seen the police report?"

"Yes, I have a copy."

"Let's see it."

She opened a brown leather purse, pulled out a folded paper, and handed it to Jim. He unfolded it.

"This says the accident was around six o'clock. What time did he usually get home?"

"Anywhere from six-thirty to eight depending on how much he had to do."

"He must have been almost through for the day, then."

"That's what I'd assume."

"Have you talked to his supervisors about what happened?"

"I talked to his boss at the funeral."

"What's his name?"

"Marlin Reeves."

"What'd he tell you?"

"He didn't know much. Told me no one knew how Danny came to be drunk."

"Did he know where Danny had been that day? Surely some of his customers remember seeing him. It would be good to know if any of them are going to claim he was under the influence."

"I tried to talk to Marlin about that and he clammed up. Said he had instructions not to discuss the details."

"What kind of guy is he?"

"I thought he was a good man. He and Danny always got along fine. Now, I'm not so sure." Mrs. Marcus spoke with a bitter tone.

"I think Alamo owes you some information."

"So do I. And I'm not getting any. That's one reason I'm here."

"If I got into the case what would you want me to do?"

Laura Marcus leaned forward locking her eyes on Jim's. "Help me find out what happened and help me collect worker's comp benefits."

"Are they contesting comp?" Jim asked.

She nodded. "The insurance company says they don't owe anything because Danny was drunk."

Jim understood the problem. "I'm not surprised they're saying that. In the usual situation worker's comp pays benefits regardless of who's at fault but if the death or injury is caused by intoxication comp doesn't have to pay anything. Who paid for the funeral?"

"I did. I had to borrow the money."

"If your husband wasn't drunk, worker's comp should pay. What carrier is it?"

"Houston Beneficial."

"That's a tough outfit. Who's the adjuster?"

"A butthole named Joe Bob Savage."

Bob smiled. "I know Joe Bob. He's got all the compassion of an alligator."

"I'm not getting anywhere with him. I went to the Worker's Compensation Commission and filed a claim but he's already told me Houston Beneficial will contest it."

"How are you paying family expenses?"

"We had a few thousand dollars in savings. Once that's gone I don't know what I'll do. I've got a job but I don't bring in enough by myself to cover everything."

"Where do you work?"

"I'm a teller at Texas Guaranty Bank on Hemphill."

"That's not a bad job."

"No, but it doesn't pay enough to support a family."

"Those lifetime comp benefits would sure make a difference."

"They sure would. But I can't get them without a lawyer."

Jim looked aside, letting his eyes focus on the long view to the west of streets and buildings marching to the horizon. Laura Marcus couldn't get her benefits without a lawyer but he wasn't sure he could do her any good. Lawyer or not she'd lose unless she could prove her husband wasn't drunk.

And the worker's compensation process wasn't favorable to lawyer involvement since the rewrite of the law several years earlier. He wouldn't get paid unless she won and then his fee would be twenty-five percent of her benefit checks as they came in. He hated to collect fees that way. Not only did he not get paid right away, the only way he could get paid at all was by taking money the client needed to live on.

Jim turned back to Laura. "I have to be honest with you. There's almost no chance unless we can explain that blood alcohol test."

"I know that."

"I'd like to get a medical release from you and get the autopsy report, then do some preliminary investigation. If I don't find something encouraging I won't get into the matter."

"What about your fees?"

"If I take the case I'll have to charge twenty-five percent of all the comp benefits, subject to the approval of the Worker's Compensation Commission, but you don't pay unless I get you the benefits."

She smiled wanly, easing the lines of tension in her face. "Seventy-five percent of something is better than nothing."

"I'm not promising anything."

"I understand. Could you do one more thing?"

"What's that?"

"If you can prove Danny wasn't drunk, try to figure out what caused him to swerve across that median."

"I'll sure do that. If we can prove something was wrong with the truck or that someone else caused the accident, the case could be worth a whole lot more than the comp benefits."

"What would your fee be then?"

"If some third party's responsible I'd handle that part of the case on a one-third contingent fee. But that's a long shot. Even if Danny wasn't drunk the accident still looks like his fault at this point."

Jim got out the papers for Mrs. Marcus to sign, authorizing him to represent her and her children, and to obtain the autopsy report and medical records.

"That's it for today, Mrs. Marcus," he said when they had finished. "I'll try to let you know something later this week."

"Thanks, Mr. McSpadden. I'll wait to hear from you."

They both stood. Jim followed her to the door and into the waiting room. At the outer door they shook hands and she left, leaving the subtle smell of perfume in the air. He watched through the glass door as she walked down the hall, a tall, graceful woman, dignified in her sorrow.

The next day, he picked up a copy of the autopsy report on Danny Marcus from the Medical Examiner's Office. It described in cryptic medical terms the charring burns over his entire body and reported that, several hours after the accident, his blood alcohol was more than double the level that made him intoxicated in the eyes of the law. Yet Laura Marcus was sure Danny hadn't been drunk.

Jim noted a doctor named F. Morgan Sutter had signed the autopsy report. He'd need to talk to Dr. Sutter, but first he'd try to get right to the heart of the matter by talking to Alamo Oil's lawyer, Art Kurtz.

"How you been doing, Jim?" Kurtz asked when his secretary put Jim through. "Haven't seen much of you lately."

As always, Art had plenty of volume. Jim moved the receiver away from his ear. "Oh, I've been doing okay. Not as busy as I used to be after all the changes in the law."

"They're hurting us, too. We've let seven lawyers go in the last two months. I hate to turn these young guys out on the street, but there's no choice. We just don't have the business we used to."

A big, affable, white-haired man, Art headed Kurtz, Jacobs and Silverstein, a firm of over one hundred lawyers located in palatial quarters near the top of the Dallas skyline. He and Jim went way back to when Jim had been a young attorney just starting out and Art had been the chief litigator for Gruen and Stillwell, one of the old, premier Dallas firms.

"It's been a while since we had one together," Jim said.

"That's a fact. I can't remember the last one."

"We may be gonna have another."

"Good. I need the business. What case are you talking about?"

"The big freeway wreck last week."

"You mean something got through Rolly Sullivan's clutches?"

"This one did. I've been contacted by the widow of the truck driver."

Kurtz laughed. "Christ, Jim! You don't want that one."

"I'm not sure I'm gonna take it. She wants me to help her get worker's compensation and to investigate the accident to see if there's a basis to file suit for her."

"That's a mighty tall order. 'Course, I don't have anything to do with the comp claim but there isn't much doubt Marcus was drunk. I'm just trying to keep the damages down on the liability case."

"Are you gonna pay Rolly without a fight?"

"I like to pick my fights and this would be a good one to settle early."

"I know what you're saying. You're pretty sure it was all Marcus's fault then?"

"No doubt about it."

"Mrs. Marcus says no one at Alamo will talk to her about it."

"I told them not to discuss it. With all the media interest we don't want a bunch of speculation flying around."

"Why does that matter if you're gonna settle?"

"I just don't want a bunch of loose talk making grist for Rolly's mill."

"But you don't mind talking to me?"

"Of course not, so long as you don't expect too much."

"Would it be all right to bring an engineer out and look at the truck?"

Kurtz hesitated, then answered with an edge to his voice. "Sure. Why not? Nothing much to see there. It's just a burned out truck. Rolly's made such a fuss I've agreed to let him look at it Thursday afternoon. Can you come at the same time?"

"Do you think the great man will tolerate my presence?"

"He won't have any choice."

"That's fine, then. If I get in this case, I'll have to meet the asshole sooner or later. I'll clear the time with my engineer."

"Sounds good. Confirm it with my secretary, and she'll give you directions to the terminal."

∞

On Thursday afternoon, Jim drove out the West Freeway toward Weatherford with automotive engineer Nick Stavros. Jim had been a little ashamed to pick Stavros up in the three year old Ford pickup he drove these days. Stavros was used to high-priced sedans. His taste for luxury was reflected in his bills. When he flew out of town on cases he demanded first class tickets.

About fifty with curly black hair and a handsome Mediterranean face, Nick hailed originally from Albany, New York, and had a degree in automotive engineering from Rennselaer Polytechnic Institute. He had come to Texas to work at the General Motors plant in Arlington but had run his own consulting engineering outfit for the past fifteen years. Today he wore well-fitted grey coveralls and heavy duty work shoes instead of the Italian suit and loafers he usually favored.

Jim had borrowed two thousand dollars from his bank to pay Nick the retainer he had demanded to look at the Alamo Oil tanker. Jim couldn't afford it and wouldn't have paid it except that Stavros was one of the best in the business. If anyone could find something wrong with the truck, he could.

"How much further?" Stavros asked in the superior upstate New York accent twenty years in Texas had not moderated. It was a wonder Texas juries could relate to him, but they did. It was almost as if they expected someone with his credentials to be abrasive.

"It's about halfway between here and Weatherford."

"At least we got good weather, except it's too damn hot."

Jim nodded. It was a scorching summer afternoon with the temperature over one hundred degrees and the view of distant trees and buildings distorted by the heat haze. They drove west from the downtown area, past the exit for Camp Bowie Boulevard and the Ridglea Mall. As they approached the intersection with Loop 820 Jim pulled into the right lane and slowed down.

"The accident happened over there on the left," he said.

Repair crews had patched the gap in the fence along the middle of the road where Danny Marcus's truck had veered across. Marcus had been going west. Did that mean he had been headed back to the terminal? The pavement still bore the black smudges and blotches of the fire.

"Have you had a reconstructionist look at that yet?" Stavros asked.

Jim shook his head. "I just got the case a few days ago."

"You better get one pretty fast. Those marks will be hard to interpret in a few more weeks."

"You're right about that," Jim said, not wanting to commit to another charge he couldn't afford. He'd just have to rely on the police report for the time being.

West of the city Interstate 30 ascended a wide, sweeping prairie of short grass with long views to the horizon to the north and south and the downtown skyscrapers in the rearview mirror shimmering in the distance like a child's block city. White cattle grazed on one of the huge ranches that still stood guard against the city's development to the west.

This stretch of road lifted Jim's spirits every time he drove through it although he knew time was against this remnant of frontier Texas. How long would it be before subdivisions and shopping centers swallowed the big ranches and all they stood for and covered the far vistas of the prairie with the dreary stamp of development?

Nick yawned, covering his mouth with his hand. "This place is really out in the sticks."

"It's not too much further now," Jim said.

They came down from the elevated stretch of prairie at the cutoff for the town of Aledo and drove into the bottoms of the Clear Fork of the Trinity. On the right a maze of pipes and silver storage tanks marked the multiple acre site of Alamo Oil Company's North Texas terminal. Jim exited to the access road and drove along it to a driveway leading to the office. Inside a bored blonde secretary gave them directions to the tanker.

Three vehicles were parked near the gutted truck. The grey Cadillac probably went with Art Kurtz while the green Jaguar was more Rolly's style. A maroon Dodge van rounded out the trio. A black-haired man in an maroon jumpsuit was pulling equipment from its rear door. Jim parked next to the Cadillac and he and Nick got out. Stavros got his camera bag and other equipment out of the pickup bed.

Kurtz approached smiling, his hand extended. It had been several years since Jim had seen him but he hadn't aged much. He still had the same head of thick white hair. Jim thought he might have added a few pounds to his substantial midriff. Otherwise, he looked the same.

Jim took Kurtz's hand. "How you been doing, Art?"

"Just fine, Jim. It's sure good to see you again."

"Is Rolly here?"

"Can't you tell?" Kurtz nodded toward the Jaguar.

"I figured that was his. Where is he?"

"Over looking at the truck."

"Who's this guy?" Jim jerked his head toward the man at the van.

"That's Professor Karl Abelmeyer. He's Rolly's engineer."

"Where's he from?"

"Isn't it obvious?"

Jim realized the significance of the maroon van and jumpsuit. "Oh my God! An Aggie!" Graduates of Texas A & M University advertised their alma mater with the color maroon.

Nick walked up carrying bags in both hands. He nodded to Kurtz. "Hello, Art. Excuse me if I don't shake your hand."

"It's good to see you again, Nick. Guess the last time was on that headon crash over east of Tyler a couple of years ago."

"Yeah, that was it."

Professor Abelmeyer walked over from the van, loaded with equipment. He nodded curtly to Nick. "Look what the cat drug in."

"Go screw yourself, Karl," Nick said, with a derisive twist to his mouth.

Kurtz laughed. "I see you two know each other."

"Can we get started?" Abelmeyer asked.

"Sure." Kurtz started toward the truck and the others followed.

Jim studied the tractor trailer combination as they approached. The grim remains evoked a sense of sick horror. Danny Marcus and eight others had died because of this vehicle. Several feet separated the cab from the shell of the tank trailer. The fire had burned the paint from both units. Remnants of burned tires clung to the wheels.

Jim caught up with Kurtz. "How'd Alamo get the truck back out here?"

"It took a crane and a couple of flatbed trailers."

A narrow-shouldered man with greying red hair came from behind the tank trailer as Jim and the others walked up. He wore slacks and a Mexican style sports shirt with broad black and red stripes. Rolly Sullivan looked smaller in person than he did on television.

He stopped short, staring at Jim and Nick. "Who the hell are these people?" he asked Kurtz.

"Didn't my secretary tell you?"

"Tell me what?"

"That some other folks would be here."

"She damn sure didn't. I don't want anyone looking over my shoulder."

Jim stepped forward, blood pumping in his temples. "I'm Jim McSpadden, Mr. Sullivan. I represent the widow of Danny Marcus. I don't have any intention of looking over your shoulder."

Sullivan frowned. "Why are you even here? The Marcus family doesn't have a claim."

God, what a bastard, Jim thought. "Maybe not, but we have a right to look at the evidence."

"I'd rather you did it another time."

"I'm sorry for the mixup, Rolly," Kurtz said. "My secretary was supposed to tell you. I don't want to have to do this twice."

Rolly shook his head. "You should have cleared it with me." He studied Nick's face. "Don't I know you from somewhere?"

Nick nodded. "I'm Nick Stavros."

"Oh, yeah! You were on that Jimenez case in Corpus Christi."

"That's right."

"You're the engineer who said that Mustang was completely crashworthy."

"That's what I said."

"The jury didn't agree with you, did they?"

Nick's face darkened. "Not that time. They bought Karl's pack of lies. There are other juries, though."

Karl had set his equipment down. He shot Nick the finger.

Rolly laughed. "Any jury with any sense would see that case the same way. But enough of this bullshit. I don't like being cramped like this but let's get on with it."

For the next several hours Nick Stavros and Karl Abelmeyer inspected the cab and trailer, studiously avoiding each other. For his part, Jim made a point of staying away from Rolly Sullivan. Whenever Rolly walked to one side of the truck, Jim went to the other. Rolly held his mouth in a line of grim contempt and wouldn't look at Jim or Nick. Art Kurtz stayed to the side, surveying the activities from the thin shade of a mesquite.

Jim held the end of a tape measure while Nick recorded the critical measurements. Nick crawled under the cab to inspect what was left of the steering system then started making notes and photographs. Jim had brought his own small camera and started snapping away to record useful views of the vehicle. He made detailed notes on a legal pad.

Harrigan Motor Corporation of Chicago had manufactured the cab. Although Harrigan had been in business since the thirties it had remained one of the smaller manufacturers of diesel tractors for semi rigs. You didn't see many HMC's among the Peterbilts, Kenworths, Macks, and Freightliners that crowded the highways.

Jim ran his hands along a jagged gash in the side of what had been a silver tank trailer with the words Alamo Oil Company painted in big red letters on the sides. The odor of scorched paint hung in the air. Most of the lettering had burned away and the top of the tank had been torn back and mangled by the force of the explosion. Should it have been able to withstand the collision without rupturing? The manufacturer's plate on the end said it had been made by Triton Trailers of Nacogdoches, Texas.

After more than two hours Karl Abelmeyer put away his camera and other equipment. Without a backward glance at Jim and Nick, Abelmeyer and Rolly Sullivan headed for the cars. Kurtz walked with them. Nick rolled up his tape measure and put it in his tool box.

"Are you finished, too?" Jim asked.

"I been finished for half an hour. I just didn't want to leave before those bastards."

"Obviously, you've seen them before."

"Yes, I have. I testified for Ford in a case three years ago in Corpus Christi. The jury bought Abelmeyer's argument that the Mustang involved should have been built so it wouldn't explode on impact."

Jim shrugged. "Sounds reasonable to me."

"Usually, I'd say so too but this involved a car that had just been filled with gas and then got hit by a freight train. The driver didn't see the crossing lights. Just about any car would explode under those circumstances."

"How much did Ford have to pay Rolly?"

"Millions and millions."

"Maybe this case will give you a rematch."

Nick shook his head. "I don't think so. At least, not at this point."

"Why not?"

"I was thinking maybe something had come loose and caused the truck to veer but the steering mechanism's intact."

"Any chance someone's messed with it?"

"No. If they had there'd be evidence of bolts being screwed, marks where things had been put back together. There's nothing like that."

Disappointed but not surprised Jim studied his notes.

"What about the tank trailer?" he asked." It sure did blow up easily."

Nick smiled, shaking his head. "Not really. It's actually very well made, but hit something that put a rip in the side. There's no practical way to design against that kind of impact."

"What do you think Abelmeyer will say?"

"Probably the same as me. He's just ruling out a malfunction in the truck. Rolly doesn't need one if the driver's negligence caused the accident."

Jim nodded. "That's true. Are you giving the truck and trailer a clean bill of health then?"

"That's how it looks to me."

"What would it take to change your mind?"

Nick looked down, poking the toe of his work shoe into the ground. "There's one area I'm not sure about and that's the power steering. That unit was heavily damaged by the fire."

"Is there any way to know if something was wrong with it?"

"Not from what I can see here. I'd like to have the maintenance records from Alamo and the manufacturer's technical manuals. Maybe they'll tell me something."

"I'll try to get them for you."

Jim shouldered one of Nick's equipment bags and Nick took the other. As they walked back toward the cars, Rolly's Jaguar pulled away from the parking area in a flash of shiny green with Abelmeyer's maroon van right behind it.

Kurtz was waiting for them next to Jim's pickup. "Ya'll see everything you needed to see?"

Jim nodded. "Yes we did."

"Anything else I can do for you today?"

"I'm gonna need to look at the maintenance records and shop manuals on the truck."

"Rolly wants them too."

"Who gets them first?"

"Ya'll don't have to fight over them. I'll get copies for both of you. I'll send copies of Harrigan's brochure, too. But don't expect much. There weren't any problems with this truck."

"Thanks for sharing that with me, Art. When can I get the stuff?"

"I'll have it couriered over tomorrow."

"I'll appreciate it."

As Jim and Nick drove back toward Fort Worth through the lengthening shadows of late afternoon, a futile feeling settled over Jim. He wasn't surprised Nick hadn't found some dramatic proof that the truck had malfunctioned and he didn't doubt that Art was telling the truth about the maintenance records but he had allowed himself hope that some evidence would vindicate Laura Marcus's belief.

So far that hadn't happened. It looked more and more like he was going to have to tell Laura he couldn't do anything for her and he really didn't want to tell her that.

# 3

The next day, Jim poured over the documents Kurtz had sent. Art had furnished copies of the shop records and the maintenance manual and a slick descriptive brochure. The truck had been a two-year-old M-5000 Loadmaster, powered by a big Cummins Diesel engine. The picture of a shiny new example on the cover of the brochure contrasted sadly with the burned, twisted wreckage Jim had viewed the day before.

The inside cover displayed a picture of Harrigan's CEO, Gerald Forbes. Clad in an expensive-looking tan suit, he sat at a desk of dark wood with a view of downtown Chicago through the window behind him. He appeared to be in his fifties. Styled blond hair, grey at the temples, offset a haughty face and a contrived, chilly smile. Bright, ice-blue eyes stared at the viewer. The blurb under the picture advised that Forbes, an automotive engineer, had personally supervised the design of the M-5000 Loadmaster.

In the brochure, Harrigan Motor Corporation bragged about all the truck's state of the art features: computer controlled antilock brakes, computer monitoring of all engine functions, and power steering that applied force in proportion to the speed of the vehicle measured against the rate of turn of the steering wheel. Jim laid the brochure aside and glanced through the maintenance records looking for evidence of problems, but he saw nothing.

Jim had Susan box the material up and dictated a letter transmitting it to Nick Stavros. It would be best to let Nick analyze the records with his trained eye.

After lunch Jim dictated a second letter to the Personal Injury Lawyers Exchange in Philadelphia. Known by the acronym PILE, the exchange served as a repository of technical information for product liability and negligence cases. Lawyers like Jim sent the exchange information on defective products involved in their cases.

If any other lawyer who belonged to the exchange had registered any information about a case involving HMC trucks, PILE would send it to Jim. He could call the other attorney and talk about the situation. Any other cases involving steering failures on Harrigan trucks would probably be registered with the exchange. Having the benefit of the experiences of others could be the key to the case.

Jim had done all he could with the records until he heard from Nick and the exchange. He pulled the autopsy report on Danny Marcus, called the medical examiner's office, and asked to speak to Dr. F. Morgan Sutter.

"He's very busy, sir," said the protective-voiced secretary.

"It's very important that I talk to him," Jim said. "Can I make an appointment?"

The girl hesitated. "Is that really necessary?"

"If that's what it takes."

"What is this about?"

"I represent the family of the truck driver who was killed in the big wreck on the West Freeway several weeks ago. I need to talk to Dr. Sutter about the blood test."

"I'll see if he can talk. He really doesn't have any time for an appointment."

"I understand."

Jim held for several minutes. He expected to be put off. Most doctors preferred not to talk to lawyers, especially when hard questions might be involved. It was easier to claim to be busy and defer the interview for another day.

The girl came back on the line."Doctor Sutter asks if you have a medical authorization from Mrs. Marcus."

"I sure do."

"Can you fax us a copy? He can't talk to you without one on file."

"Sure. I'll fax the authorization and call back in a few minutes."

Jim had Susan send the authorization, then called back, and the secretary put him through.

"This is Doctor Sutter." The good doctor's voice projected irritation and hostility.

"Thanks for talking to me, doctor," Jim said, sugarcoating his words. "I represent the family of Danny Marcus."

"I know the case. What do you want to ask me?"

"I had a question about your autopsy report."

"What is it?"

"There's a finding in there that says Danny was drunk at the time of the wreck. I was just wondering how you determined that."

"It was based on a chemical test of the blood taken from his body."

"But how was it done? How did you ensure the accuracy of the test?"

"I didn't."

"What do you mean?"

"The blood test was done by the lab at E. M. Daggett Hospital."

"You didn't test it yourself?"

"No. They do our blood work for us."

"That means you just relied on what they told you?"

"That's right. We do it all the time."

"Then you can't personally say the blood test was accurate?"

"That's right, except I have no reason to doubt it. They've never screwed anything up before."

"Never?"

"Not that I can recall."

"Who would I talk to about the testing they did?"

"I'm not sure. Call the hospital lab. They'd know."

Jim wasn't getting anywhere with this guy. "Thanks for your help, Doctor."

"You're welcome," Dr. Sutter said, and hung up.

Jim made a call to the hospital lab and made an appointment to talk to the lab supervisor. That afternoon, he drove out South Main to the E. M. Daggett Hospital complex, the hectic beehive where the poor and uninsured of Tarrant County got their medical care. He parked on a crowded lot inside a chain link fence and followed a line of other people to the main entrance.

The complex had been added to many times over the years and presented a confusing maze of passageways, doors, and elevators. After several wrong turns, Jim found the lab where a weary looking receptionist ushered him into the office of Lab Supervisor Delbert Dillow, a natty little man in his fifties with wire-rimmed glasses and a bright bow tie contrasting with his white lab coat.

Dillow motioned Jim into a seat across the desk from him. "How can I help you, Mr. McSpadden?"

Jim assumed a sincere tone. "I'm involved in litigation coming out of that big freeway accident several weeks ago. A question has come up about the blood test on the truck driver."

"What kind of question?" Dillow asked, his voice full of suspicion.

"I was just wondering how you verified the accuracy of the test?"

"Does someone say it wasn't accurate?"

"Oh, no. But that blood test is an important part of the evidence. All the lawyers are going to want to know how it was done."

"Well, it's sure no mystery. The medical examiner's office sent a blood sample to us and one of our technicians tested it according to our usual procedures."

"Who was the technician?"

"Elaine Jones."

"How did she determine the percentage of blood alcohol?"

42

"That's a very technical question."

"The answer's important to me."

"Talk to a toxicologist. One of them can tell you how it's done."

"But I need to know how ya'll did it."

"Look, Mr. McSpadden, I don't want to have to go through this with half a dozen lawyers. You can subpoena Ms. Jones to testify at trial. She can tell you all about it just one time and that will save a lot of trouble."

Jim started to argue but what was the use? He'd revisit this issue later when he knew more. "Thanks so much for your cooperation, Mr. Dillow. I'll be back in touch with you later."

"I'll look forward to hearing from you."

Jim walked quickly through the halls toward the exit. "Worthless asshole!" he muttered.

He had an innate distrust of bureaucracies like the medical examiner's office and the hospital lab. They handled a great volume of material, were chronically short-handed, and employed many who were not the conscientious public servants the taxpayers had a right to expect.

Their procedures presented many opportunities for mistakes, and they made lots of them but they'd never admit to one unless you got the goods on them and that was one thing Jim didn't have. For his part, he'd keep an open mind about Danny's condition and hope for something positive from PILE or Nick Stavros. In the meantime, it was time to talk to the police officer who had witnessed the accident.

The next day, Jim waited for Officer Albert Wilson in the day room of the Fort Worth Police Department. Jim had called and made an appointment to meet Wilson when he came off his shift. He could have talked to the officer on the telephone but that wouldn't have given him a feel for what the man was like or how much he could be believed.

Jim sat on a hideous sofa of green Naugahide next to a scarred blond coffee table holding overflowing ashtrays and a dogeared stack of magazines about crime, guns, and ammunition. Several officers sat across the room watching a mid-afternoon talk show hosted by a sincere black-haired young man, lank as a cadaver, who was asking two squirrely brothers why they had not reported their father's sexual activities with the family livestock to the police when he forced them to become involved. How much were these nerds being paid for this nauseating performance?

One of the double doors at the end of the room opened and a black officer of medium height with powerfully muscled arms entered. He carried a file folder. Jim got up and walked over to the man.

"Officer Wilson?"

"That's me. Are you Mr. McSpadden?"

"Yes, I am."

"We can talk in here." Wilson nodded toward a conference room.

Inside, Wilson closed the door, shutting out the talkshow drivel. They sat opposite each other at a round table.

"I understand you witnessed the accident," Jim said.

"I sure did. I don't want to see anything like that ever again."

"I'd think you saw lots of bad things in your line of work."

"I do, but this was different."

"Why?"

Tears clouded Wilson's eyes. "All those people burning to death and I couldn't do anything about it."

"I see what you mean. I've got the police report so I know most of the story, but I wanted to talk to you in person about what you saw."

"What do you want to know?"

"I represent the widow of the driver of the tanker. She tells me he never drank while he was working and she's sure he wasn't drunk. How did you know he was drunk?"

"I didn't at the time. I relied on the blood test."

"You didn't see how he was driving before the accident?"

The officer shook his head. "All I saw was the truck suddenly swerving to the left. It went right through the barrier fence and the barricades and ran into that mess in the oncoming lanes. Marcus burned up with the truck. I didn't even try to look at him afterward."

"I can sure understand why. How long after the first pileup did he come along?"

"Just a few seconds. When I saw those watermelons going all over the road I called for help and started to drive around to the other side but before I could do anything the truck got involved."

"Was there anything in the road to make him skid?"

"Well, for one thing, the pavement was covered with water from the storm."

"Was there anything other than that, though? Any oily place, or defect in the pavement?"

"Nope. Sergeant Crow and I went over there and looked at every foot of road for a hundred yards. Even with the rain Marcus should have been able to keep it under control."

"I've got the witness list from the accident report but it doesn't tell me where they were or what they saw. Did any of them see the tanker before you?"

"One of them."

"Who was that?"

Wilson laughed. "Just some crazy old guy who called in the day after the accident."

"What'd he say?"

"He claimed he was driving behind the tanker in a bobtail truck and it was like the hand of the Lord just suddenly reached down through the clouds and pushed the tanker through the barricade."

Jim laughed. "Did you see anything like that?"

Wilson shook his head. "I sure didn't. I'd have noticed that for sure."

"Did you get a statement from this guy?"

"Yeah, but it doesn't say much except that he did see the truck before the accident."

"Can I look at it?"

"Sure." Wilson leafed through his folder.

He handed a sheet of paper to Jim. It said the witness, L. T. Tinsley, had been driving behind the tanker truck when it suddenly swerved to the left across the median. The statement ended with a telephone number and an address on the North Side.

Jim looked at Wilson. "Is it okay if I talk to this man?"

"Sure. Be prepared for a Bible lesson, though."

"Thanks for the warning. Can I get a copy of this?"

"That's an extra you can have."

As Jim drove back toward his office, he sifted what Wilson had told him. He rated the officer a straight shooter and a good observer. The jury would believe his version of the accident. There was no reason not to.

Jim didn't agree with Wilson's assumption that L. T. Tinsley's statement wasn't important. Tinsley had been driving behind Danny and apparently hadn't noticed any reckless driving until Danny swerved to the left. Wouldn't a man as drunk as Danny have been weaving all over the road? Jim would talk to Tinsley as soon as possible.

"Call Nick," Susan said, as Jim walked into the office.

"What's he got?"

"He's found something in the maintenance records."

Jim went to his office and put in a call to Nick.

"What's up?" Jim asked.

"It's not much but it's about the best we're gonna be able to do for now."

"What is it?"

"There's an entry in the records about a week before the accident where Marcus took the truck into the shop with a complaint the steering was erratic."

"What does that mean?"

"I don't know. All the records say is the mechanic couldn't find anything wrong."

"There's no description of the problem?"

"No there's not. I'd like to talk to the mechanic. You think they'll let me?"

"I'll call Art Kurtz and ask him."

"Let me know what you find out." Nick hung up.

Jim got a cup of coffee, savoring the bitter fluid as he considered his new information. He was still a long way from having a case. All he had was a couple of new rabbit trails to check out. Danny Marcus's drunken driving still provided the most logical explanation of this accident. But at least, Jim now had something to go on.

∞

Rolly Sullivan left Loop 410 on the west side of San Antonio and drove the green Jaguar onto the Bandera Highway, heading toward his office in the hills west of the city. He'd spent the night in Fort Worth at the Worthington after inspecting the tanker. Nadine had come to the room around ten. She said she'd told her husband she had to get a few things at the grocery store.

Rolly didn't like to be rushed in his lovemaking but he and Nadine had it down to an art. In twenty minutes she had her clothes off and back on and left Rolly with a quick kiss and a promise of another session. The whole thing had taken about the same time as a trip to the grocery store. Rolly had driven back that morning, dumped his suitcase at the huge Tudor mansion he'd bought in Alamo Heights five years earlier, given his wife, Rae Jean, a peck on the cheek with a complaint of how tired he was, and headed for the office.

With that complaint he'd laid the groundwork for begging off any demand for marital performance that night. Rae Jean was a thirty year old redhead with strong passions. Usually, Rolly kept pace with them but after the session with Nadine it would be best to wait a night. Sex was a kind of hobby with Rolly, the only one he had other than his work, and it required thoughtful management. After a night's recuperation he'd be ready for Rae Jean again.

He'd considered taking the rest of the day off but decided against it. Karl Abelmeyer had told him he didn't see anything wrong with the truck. Rolly would get the shop manuals and maintenance records for Karl but it seemed unlikely they'd point toward any problem. It was ninety-nine percent certain the wreck was the fault of Danny Marcus.

Who did that big stupid-looking ass, Jim McSpadden, think he was, pretending he might have a case for the Marcus family? He shouldn't delude them that way. Rolly had some sympathy for them. It was rough to lose a husband and father especially when his negligence had caused so much grief to others.

McSpadden ought to have enough sense to know he couldn't do anything for them. He should tell them to forget it. But the Jim McSpaddens of the world never knew their limits. They'd get in over their heads and try to make a case where there wasn't one just because they were so desperate for success.

McSpadden's presence in the case didn't worry Rolly. He could handle McSpadden. But there were some troubling aspects of the situation. He needed to have a straight talk with Art Kurtz about them so he could decide what to do next. Kurtz didn't have to give Rolly information at this early stage in the case but he was enough of a pro he probably would. He'd give Rolly anything he knew Rolly could get eventually unless there was a tactical advantage in holding it back.

Rolly pulled off the Bandera highway onto a two lane county road. He drove several blocks and turned onto the drive that spiraled around a small hill to his offices on the top. He'd been in this location for two years and had more than three million dollars tied up in the place. He deserved a nice office. He'd paid his dues.

Born and raised in San Antonio, he'd graduated from Saint Mary's University School of Law and started out as a personal injury lawyer more than twenty-five years earlier with a storefront office on Zarzamora Street among the barrios of the west side. He spoke halfass Spanish, but didn't rely on his own faulty knowledge. He'd always been associated with Spanish speaking lawyers, paralegals, and secretaries. Rolly had always made good money from his base of Hispanic clients but in the last ten years, his practice had taken off as he'd gained a reputation.

He didn't need the Mexicans any more but they'd been with him in the old days and he still considered himself a lawyer of the poor and disadvantaged. His new office lay beyond the city limits to the west in a rural area but not so far from Zarzamora Street that his old clients couldn't still find him.

He rounded the final turn and pulled into his reserved parking space by the front door. His architect had designed the office to look like a Spanish colonial building Rolly had admired in Guanajuato, Mexico. It had thick outer walls plastered in white and a roof of red tile. Envious local lawyers referred to the place as Fort Sullivan.

Rolly's personal office lay on the east side of the building and commanded a grand view of the San Antonio skyline through a huge picture window. Outside, the hill fell away in a sheer drop to the first loop of the entrance drive a hundred feet below. That picture window was the building's only break with the Spanish colonial tradition.

All the other windows were narrow, recessed deep into the thick walls to keep out the hot Texas sun. Rolly pulled open one of the massive double oak doors and entered the reception area. The receptionist, Mary Lou Rodriguez, dark and placid-faced, raised her hand.

"Hi boss. Did you have a good trip?"

"Sure did, Mary Lou. Is Pedro here today?"

"He's in his office."

Rolly walked through the inner garden of banana trees and other tropical plants. It resembled the courtyard garden of a Mexican house except that a roof of thick glass let in the sunlight while keeping out the heat. Air conditioning kept the garden at the same temperature as the rest of the building. The plants imparted moisture to the air and gave the garden a fresh smell of lush vegetation.

He knocked at the door of his partner, Pedro Ávila.

"Come in."

Rolly opened the door and walked in.

Balding and mustachioed, Pedro sat behind a desk piled high with papers. He'd been with Rolly since the early days on Zarzamora. "I didn't expect you back today," he said, smiling.

"I've got some work to do. How're things going with you?"

"Pretty damn busy. Judge Merritt set a hearing on the motion to dismiss in the DeLeon case for next Monday."

"You ready for it?"

"You bet."

"You oughta win that one."

"I think I will. How'd it go in Fort Worth?"

"Fine. That case is shaping up to be a good one."

"That's great. Let me know if I can help."

"I'll do it."

Rolly walked down the hall to his own office. His longtime secretary, Maria Fuentes, sat at her desk in the anteroom. Tall, dark-eyed, and good looking, she served Rolly with singleminded efficiency, screening calls from insurance salesmen and stock brokers, irate clients and opposing lawyers, and all the camp followers his success had generated.

"How's it going, Maria?"

"Pretty good. No problems."

"Any important messages?"

"I don't know how important they are but there's a lot of them." She handed him a thick stack.

He sifted through them as he walked past Maria into his office. Nothing that wouldn't wait. He'd return some of the calls later that afternoon but first, he needed to call Art Kurtz.

"How you doing, Rolly?" Kurtz answered, in his deep, folksy voice, hard as nails in its undertones.

"I'm doing good, Art."

"Did you see everything you needed to yesterday?"

"Sure did. When you gonna send me those technical manuals?"

"They're on the way."

"Good. I'll have Karl look at them but at this point it doesn't look to him like anything was wrong with the truck."

"That's how it appears to me, too," Kurtz said. "I wish there was some way to put what happened off on the truck manufacturer. It would get my guys off the hook."

"It looks to me like the negligence is just about one hundred percent on your driver."

"I agree with that. Are you ready to talk settlement?"

"It depends on how much you can pay."

"How much do you want?"

"It's gonna take a lot."

"That's gonna be a problem for you," Kurtz said in a condescending voice. "We don't have a lot."

"What do you mean?"

"The policy on the truck's one million with a five million umbrella."

Rolly tightened his grip on the phone. He'd been afraid Kurtz would take this tack. "Christ, Art, Alamo's bound to have more than that."

"Alamo does, but Alamo's not liable."

"What the shit are you talking about?"

"Only the driver's liable. He was out of the course and scope of his employment when the wreck happened. The only insurance that covers him is what was on the truck itself."

"The hell you say. Just the fact he'd been drinking doesn't take him out of course and scope."

"Our investigation shows there's more to it than just drinking. He'd completely abandoned his work for the day and was on an excursion of his own."

Rolly hesitated. He had expected Kurtz's argument but had no ammunition to counter it.

"I thought you wanted to settle this case."

"I do, Rolly. But I'm not gonna tell my company to pay beyond what it's liable for."

"You were singing a different tune a week ago. 'Come, let us mediate', you said. You acted like you could pay what the claims are worth."

"That was before we finished our investigation of Danny Marcus's activities on the day of the wreck."

"What was Marcus doing if he wasn't working?"

"I'm not quite ready to share that with you, Rolly."

"How can you expect me to settle, then? You know I can't settle this case for six million dollars."

"I can't help it if you signed up too many clients."

"You don't leave me much choice," Rolly said. "I'll have to take some depositions from your people."

"Be my guest. After that, you might give some consideration to whether you've sued the right party."

"I see I'm wasting my time."

"Don't look at it that way. I think after the depositions you'll see what I'm talking about."

Rolly affected a tone of resignation. "Okay, Art. I need to depose Marcus's supervisor and whoever knows about this excursion Marcus was on. Can you give me some dates?"

"I'll get back with you on that."

After Kurtz hung up Rolly walked to the picture window and looked toward the distant downtown. Beyond the older office buildings highrise hotels stood along the San Antonio River catering to the tourists who flocked to the city at all seasons. The slim needle of the Hemisfair Tower, topped by a revolving restaurant, rose beyond the hotels.

Rolly considered the situation. Kurtz's position presented a dilemma. Under the legal doctrine of Respondeat Superior, Alamo was not automatically responsible for the negligence of its driver. Danny Marcus's actions subjected Alamo to liability only if he was acting in the course and scope of his employment—doing his employer's business—at the time of the accident.

Being drunk didn't take Danny out of the course and scope, so long as he was still on the job, but if the jury found he had abandoned his work, Alamo wasn't liable for his drunken driving. What evidence did Kurtz have that Danny was off on a joyride of his own? Kurtz was sure being coy about it.

Even if Marcus was not in the course and scope the insurance on the truck would still pay. Usually six million dollars would be enough, but not in this case. Rolly had signed up Al Richaud, Odell Wyatt, and the family of Ruby Walthall at Nadine's counseling session. Later, he'd contracted with the families of the two other teenagers who had been riding with Wyatt's daughter and with Mary Shaw, the young doctor who had been so terribly burned.

Several more clients had called Rolly after his press conference. He now represented all the accident victims or their families except for the families of Danny Marcus, Doreen Baer and her husband, and the drivers of the watermelon truck and the blue pickup. Doreen Baer's father, Roger Lombardo, had been so offended by Rolly's tactics the Baer and Lombardo families would probably hire someone else.

Jim McSpadden had the Marcus family and someone would probably join the lawsuit on behalf of the families of the watermelon truck driver and the driver of the pickup. In all, Rolly represented nine who had been seriously injured and the survivors of four who had been killed. The combined value of these claims could easily top a hundred million dollars or even two hundred million. With its layers of umbrella coverage and reinsurance Alamo could cover the claims but the six million on the truck alone was woefully inadequate.

Kurtz had taunted Rolly with the fact he had sued only Alamo Oil and not the estate of Danny Marcus. If Rolly tried the case against Alamo alone and the jury found Danny was not in the course and scope of his employment, Rolly couldn't even recover the limited insurance on the truck. To do that he'd have to sue Danny's estate.

Rolly didn't like the idea. Suing Danny's estate would be bad public relations. It would look to the press and the jury like Rolly was picking on a family that had already suffered enough. But he didn't have any choice. To go forward with the lawsuit the only safe thing to do was to get Danny's estate into the case.

Rolly returned to his desk and started dictating an amended petition to sue Laura Marcus as the community survivor of the marriage. Her joinder would trigger the truck's insurance coverage on Danny's behalf. Once the truck coverage had been assured Rolly could start ferreting out the facts that would make Alamo liable as well, and trigger its huge layers of insurance.

He hoped to hell Kurtz was bluffing and the claim Danny Marcus had deviated from his employment would fall apart under close scrutiny. All Rolly's carefully laid plans would be for naught if scant insurance coverage made a mockery of his claims.

∽

Jim opened the legal-sized manila envelope that had come from the Personal Injury Lawyer's Exchange and was surprised to find only a few pages. The cover letter informed Jim that PILE had only located two other inquiries regarding the steering system on Harrigan Motor Corporation trucks and copies were attached.

In the first letter a lawyer named Walter Ellis in Billings, Montana, asked if the exchange had any reports of steering problems with HMC trucks. Ellis didn't elaborate on what had prompted his letter but the summary included his address and telephone number. Susan put a call through.

"Mr. Ellis?" Jim asked.

"That's me." Ellis had a high-pitched, humorous voice.

"This is Jim McSpadden in Fort Worth."

"What can I do for you?"

"I was calling about this inquiry you made to PILE about HMC trucks."

"That was sure a waste of money."

"Because the report was negative?"

"Yes. PILE charged three hundred dollars to tell me they didn't have anything."

"What kind of case do you have?"

"Doesn't look like I have a case at all. I haven't been able to develop any evidence showing liability."

"What happened?"

"I've got this client who's a truck driver. He's based here in Billings but drives coast to coast, mostly through the northern part of the country. Last year he was making a run from Seattle to Chicago when he left the interstate coming down a mountain pass west of Missoula. The truck rolled over and threw him through the windshield. He ended up with a bunch of broken ribs and one leg shorter than the other."

"Was he driving a Harrigan truck?"

"Yes he was. The state police report cites driver inattention as the cause of the accident, says he may have fallen asleep. But my client swears he lost control when the steering froze up on him."

Jim straightened in his chair. This might be interesting.

"Have you filed suit?"

"Are you kidding? I don't have anything to go on. I had an engineer look at the truck and I wrote that letter to see if anyone had turned up something wrong with the HMC steering system. I drew a blank on everything. All I have is my client's passionate belief something went wrong with the steering. That's not enough to justify a products liability suit."

"Have you contacted Harrigan?"

"Yeah. I had an investigator write 'em a letter claiming he was a customer having trouble with the steering on a late model Harrigan and asking if there'd been any problems or recall notices."

"What kind of response did you get?"

"A one-pager from some customer service rep saying they haven't had any steering problems and recommending a visit to the local Harrigan dealer."

"That's about par for the course."

"Yes it is."

"At least you have a truck driver that can talk to you." Jim told Ellis about his case. "I'm in worse shape than you are. I can't prove anything was wrong with the steering, the driver was killed, and the blood test shows he was intoxicated."

"Not much you can do with those facts," Ellis said.

"The guy's wife says it was out of character for him to drink while he was working. And I don't really trust the hospital lab or the autopsy report."

"I don't blame you. Whatever they say, you really don't have a way to refute it."

"I'm just about to the point of calling it quits."

"You may not have much choice."

"I've still got a few more things to do. If I get a breakthrough, I'll give you a call."

"I'll do the same for you but don't hold your breath."

Jim hung up and turned to the second letter. A lawyer named Ernest Starns in Tupelo, Mississippi, claimed his client had been injured after the steering locked on a Harrigan Loadmaster. The truck left the road and crashed into a culvert leaving Starn's client with several ruptured discs in his back.

Jim called Starns's office and a secretary with a low, seductive voice put him through to her boss. If she looked as good as she sounded, she'd be a knockout.

"What can I do for you, Mr. McSpadden?" Starns asked in an affable Southern drawl, so friendly, yet with an undertone of reserve and suspicion.

"I wanted to talk to you about your PILE inquiry on the Harrigan Loadmaster," Jim said.

"You got a case like that?"

Jim outlined the facts.

"That sounds a lot like what happened to my guy," Starns said, "except he wasn't killed."

"Did you figure out what happened?"

"Nope. Sure didn't. State police said it was the driver's fault. PILE only had one other inquiry and that guy couldn't tell me anything. Harrigan says there haven't been any recalls and no problems with the steering system."

"It's sure funny for there to be three cases in a couple of years that are so similar and no explanation."

"It sure is, Mr. McSpadden. I smell a rat. But I don't know what to do about it."

"I know what you mean. Will you call me if you get any more information?"

"Be glad to."

"I'll do the same for you."

Jim hung up and walked into Susan's office. She raised her eyebrows. "Any luck?"

He shook his head. "Not really. Two other lawyers have cases for drivers who claim the steering locked but no way to prove why."

"What's next then?"

"I need to get some investigation done up at the Harrigan headquarters. I don't know how I'll pay for it but I need someone to snoop around and see if any of the Harrigan employees know anything. I'm also intrigued by this witness, Tinsley, who was behind Marcus. I guess I'll try to talk to him this afternoon."

After lunch Jim drove to the North Side and parked in front of the address Officer Wilson had given him for L. T. Tinsley. Jim set his briefcase on the cracked sidewalk and surveyed the decrepit house. Two Dobermans came running up to the rusted chain link fence, snarling and showing their teeth. Could he make it to the front door before they tore him to pieces? No, he decided. Even if he got there, he'd have to wait for someone to open the door.

A two-story frame from the early part of the century, the house faced the mean North Side street with a villainous, weatherbeaten facade. A full-length front porch cluttered with old washing machines and refrigerators kept the weed-grown yard at bay. Get right with God! declared a large sign in the front yard, freshly painted in black and white in contrast to the predominating decayed look of the place. An old truck with faded red paint and dented sides parked in a patch of weedy gravel by the front door looked as though it had grown up from the ground. L. T. Tinsley Used Appliances, read scratched and faded lettering on one of the doors.

The front door of the house slowly opened and a small old man in a grease-stained grey jumpsuit came onto the porch.

He yelled at the Dobermans. "Molly! Ben!"

The dogs left off their barking and ran to the man. "What do you want?" he called to Jim, suspicion in his voice.

Jim cupped his hands around his mouth. "Are you Mr. Tinsley?"

"Maybe I am and maybe I ain't."

"I'm looking for L. T. Tinsley."

"What you want him for?"

"I need to talk about that bad accident several weeks ago."

"Who are you?"

"I'm the lawyer for one of the people involved."

"Just a minute." The man Jim took to be Tinsley went to the side of the house where he opened a gate and put the dogs in another area. He walked slowly toward Jim, shielding his eyes against the sun.

He came to the gate. "I'm Tinsley, all right. Don't like to give out my name till I know who I'm talking to. The city inspectors are always hassling me."

"Why's that?" Jim asked.

"They think they have a right to tell me when to cut my grass and what I can keep on my front porch."

Jim wanted to be agreeable. "The bastards!"

Tinsley frowned. "No bad talk around here, son. The Good Lord don't like it." He peered closely at Jim with watery grey eyes athwart a bulbous nose covered with a patchwork of red lines. "Are you a Christian?"

"I like to think so."

"Thinking so don't get the job done. You got to know. Have you been born again?"

That experience wasn't part of Jim's Methodist upbringing. "I guess I haven't."

The old man's face assumed an expression of pity. "Know your maker, before it's too late. No man knows the day or hour."

"I'll work on it."

"Don't just work on it. Get your business straight. Your soul's too precious to waste. Would you like a glass of tea?"

"Sure," Jim said, relieved at the abrupt change of topic.

He came through the gate briefcase in hand and followed Tinsley to the house. A dank, moldy smell pervaded the interior. Ratty overstuffed furniture crowded old vacuum cleaners, radios, and television sets. Several scrawny cats bounded away.

Tinsley turned toward Jim, his meager smile showing bad teeth. "You'll have to excuse my housekeeping. Don't keep the place as straight since my wife passed on."

"Looks fine to me," Jim lied.

The old man motioned toward one of the ruinous chairs. "Have a seat. I'll bring the tea." He walked from the room.

Gingerly, Jim sat down. An acrid cloud of dust floated up as he sank into the cushions. Tinsley came back carrying two grimy glasses filled with ice and amber liquid. He handed one to Jim. Jim took a sip. It tasted like oversweet, stale tea, but he didn't trust it. He'd only drink a little to be polite. He set the glass on a dusty coffee table.

He smiled. "This really hits the spot."

"Nothing like a glass of tea on a hot day." Tinsley flopped onto an overstuffed couch, raising another cloud of dust. "What'd you want to ask me about?"

"I understand you were driving behind the tanker when the wreck happened."

"That's right.'Vengeance is mine, sayeth the Lord', and I saw the Lord's vengeance but I been livin' right so I didn't get sucked in."

"I'd like your version of what happened."

"I'll be glad to oblige."

"Do you mind if I record this?"

"What do you mean, record it?"

"Just make a tape recording of what you say."

Tinsley shrugged. "Seems like you could remember it without that but it's okay with me."

Jim pulled a pocket recorder out of the briefcase. He'd skip any preliminary statement. It might annoy the old man.

"Just tell me what you saw," Jim said.

Tinsley leaned forward, eyes narrowed. "I seen the hand of the Lord sweep that tanker through the barrier into all those other cars and trucks."

Hairs raised on the back of Jim's neck. Tinsley had holy fire in his eyes. "Can you take me through what happened?"

"Sure. I'd been out in Wedgewood pickin' up a coupla washin' machines and I was on my way out to Weatherford to get a refrigerator when the storm hit. I was going slow 'cuz I wasn't in no hurry and it was rainin' so hard. The tanker passed me on the left. When he was about four or five car lengths away the hand of God pushed him into that mess on the other side and the fires of the Lord burst forth. There must 'a been a lot 'a wickedness in that bunch."

"What did the hand look like?"

Tinsley looked beyond Jim, eyes distant and fearful. "It was like a dark shadow in the rain but I seen it swat the side of the tanker and send it through the fence."

"How do you know it was the hand of God?"

Tinsley drew back, his face defensive. "That's what it was all right. There's no other explanation for it."

Jim hesitated. Should he press Tinsley for a better description? No, wouldn't do any good. He'd just get mad. Best to get back to the facts.

"How long was it after the tanker passed you before it went across the median?"

"Oh, I dunno. Maybe five minutes."

Not very likely, Jim thought. Witnesses to accidents usually overestimated time. "What about in terms of blocks? How many blocks had he been ahead of you?"

"Maybe two or three. It was right around the last exit that he pulled ahead."

"And he was in the left lane?"

"Yep, and he stayed there until he went through that fence."

"Was he doing anything unusual?"

Tinsley shook his head. "Nope, he sure wasn't. He was just goin' straight down the road a little faster than I was."

"Wasn't speeding?"

"No way."

"What'd you do after the accident?"

"Pulled to the shoulder and went over there but there wasn't nothin' I could do."

"The police report says the driver was drunk."

"I read that in the paper. You couldn't prove it by me. But then my daddy could drink a fifth of whiskey and then drive as straight as you please so the man mighta been drunk all right."

"Is there anything else you remember?"

"Nope, that's just about it."

"Would you be willing to testify in court?"

Tinsley drew back, eyes narrowed. "What would it involve?"

"Just coming to court and telling what you just told me."

The old man scratched his grizzled chin. "I guess I can so long as I don't have to swear to nothin'. My religion don't hold with swearin'."

"The judge'll let you affirm to tell the truth instead."

"I'll do it then. I'd need to be paid for my lost time."

"That can be arranged."

Jim took a final sip from his glass, then set it down. "That's all I need today Mr. Tinsley."

"Would you like some more tea?"

"No thanks."

"You sure? Your ice's all melted. I'll get you a fresh glass."

"No thanks. Really. It sure was good, though."

After the interview Jim digested what Tinsley had told him as he drove back. The witness had disappointed him. From what the old man said, Jim could argue to the jury that Danny Marcus wasn't driving like a drunk man but Tinsley's belief that the hand of God had swept Danny across the median and his general appearance and demeanor would cast great doubt on his credibility. Had he really seen something or was it all his inflamed imagination?

# 4

$B$ack in the office Jim started doing some hard thinking. L. T. Tinsley would testify Danny hadn't been speeding or weaving on the road but the jury probably wouldn't believe a man who thought God Almighty had swept the tanker into the pileup to punish Marcus and all the other victims. Tinsley's testimony wouldn't help.

The key to the case was the truck. There had to be something wrong with it. Even though PILE only had two inquiries besides Jim's about the steering on Harrigan trucks and no information indicating any defects it seemed unlikely the cases were coincidences. In both situations, truckers had been seriously injured when the steering jammed for no apparent reason.

The police had discounted the drivers' stories and assigned human error as the cause of the crashes. The fact Danny Marcus had reported problems before his accident tied in with the stories of the other two drivers. Jim believed in his gut some common problem with the truck steering had caused all three accidents but Harrigan claimed there was no problem. It was time for some investigation at Harrigan headquarters.

In palmier days Jim would have called an investigative agency in Chicago and asked them to snoop around but such a move would require the investment of money Jim didn't have. Besides, an investigator might not ask the right questions. He could go up himself for the price of the airfare and a few days in a hotel. He mapped out a plan of action in his mind, then called Susan on the intercom.

"Get me plane reservations for Chicago for tomorrow. I'd like to get there before noon."

"What's in Chicago?"

"Harrigan's headquarters. I've got a few questions for those folks."

"How about hotel reservations and a car?"

"I'll use taxis but get me a hotel reservation as close to the Harrigan plant as the travel agency can find. Shouldn't be a fancy place. Just good enough it won't have bedbugs."

"When are you coming back?"

"Probably in two or three days but leave it open. I'll schedule the return flight when I get there."

The next day Jim drove his pickup to the DFW Airport, parked it in the remote parking area, and rode an automated train to one of the American Airlines terminals. He checked his suitcase, went through the metal detector, and bought bacon and eggs in a cafeteria near his gate. As part of his plan he was wearing his shit-kicking outfit: jeans, scuffed boots, western shirt with red and blue stripes, snaps instead of buttons, and a V design down the back.

He crowded onto the 737 with a full load of other passengers, then shoehorned himself into a window seat near the rear of the plane. An amorphous mass of a man who must have weighed over three hundred pounds took the next seat. He bulged over the armrest like an overstuffed cushion. Jim kept his arms close to his sides.

The plane taxied to the end of the runway and pulled to the side. The captain came on the address system informing them they'd have to wait ten or fifteen minutes for clearance. With the air conditioning not fully functional the plane started heating up. It wasn't going to be a comfortable flight.

Finally the plane taxied into position and took off. Always a nervous flier, Jim pressed his right foot hard onto the carpet as they gained speed as though this could slow the plane down. He felt better as they pulled away from ground and the buildings, roads, and other terrain features took on the look of a topographic map.

His seatmate suddenly became garrulous. "You stopping in Chicago?"

"Sure am."

"What kind of business takes you there?"

Jim thought he might as well get into character. "I gotta go out to Harrigan Motor Corporation and talk about a truck."

The man turned to look at Jim, rearranging himself in the process. "You a trucker?"

"Yep."

"How many trucks you got?"

"Just one. Been having some problems with the power steering. I wanta get some technical advice."

"Don't they have a local dealership?"

"Sure. I've tried going through them. They don't know nothin.' I'm going right to the top. It's the only way to get anything done."

The big man nodded. "I sure find that to be true in my business."

Jim took the bait. "What do you do?"

"I got an insurance office out in Garland." The man stretched his arm across his stomach extending his hand, and introduced himself.

Jim shook the offered hand. "I'm Billy Don Hickson."

"Nice to meet you, Billy Don. Are you covered with life insurance?"

Without thinking, Jim shook his head. "Nope. I'm sure not."

"You really oughta protect your family with a policy."

"I'm not married."

"Then you oughta have insurance as a retirement plan. What are you gonna do when you're too old to work?"

Jim shrugged. "Live on social security I guess."

The insurance man's face lit up. "Social security'll be bankrupt by the time you retire. I'd like to make a few suggestions."

He launched into a description of the merits of life policies as investments. Jim shrank down in his seat and endured the assault. He would have been happier thinking his own thoughts, but his big seatmate wouldn't be denied.

When the stewardesses came around with drinks Jim stopped the spiel long enough to get a Bloody Mary. He didn't usually drink in the mornings but he had to anesthetize himself against the onslaught. After two hours, the plane descended, then landed at O'Hare Airport. As the two of them shuffled to the exit, the salesman handed Jim a business card.

"It's been nice talking to you," he said "I'd sure like to discuss your insurance needs further. Give me a call and let's talk about it."

"I appreciate all the info," Jim mumbled. "I'll call when I can afford something."

"Don't wait too long. Let's get that money working for you now."

The salesman turned into the first restroom they came to. With a friendly wave of his hand Jim started walking faster. He used a facility a little further down the concourse then headed toward the main terminal. A sign advised him to go down an escalator for ground transportation. At the bottom he saw the exit leading to the taxi area and walked toward it.

A man in a brown suit wearing a billed cap like a bus or taxi driver accosted him. "You going downtown mister?" Dark-skinned with a calculating, clever face, he spoke with a heavy mid-eastern accent. He wore a name tag identifying him as Jamal El Ibrahim.

Jim shook his head. "Nope, I'm going out to the south side."

Jamal's face brightened. "I drive to south side. Real cheap."

"How much?"

"Forty bucks."

Jim had no idea whether the price was fair. It seemed high, but this was Chicago. "You a taxi driver?" he asked.

"No, mister. I got a better car. A Lincoln. We'll go in style."

"You got a taxi license?"

Jamal looked around, then stepped closer. "No license. But I'm a good driver."

This jaunty black market entrepreneurship appealed to Jim. "I gotta get my suitcase."

Jamal smiled. "I'll carry it."

As they walked toward the luggage area Jamal took off his hat and name tag. He slipped the name tag into his suit pocket and put the hat in a cloth sack which he carried under one arm.

"Cops see hat, they'll stop me," he explained.

The luggage was just coming out on the moving carousel when they got there. Jim identified his suitcase and Jamal swung it off the platform. Outside, they bypassed the line of waiting taxis and walked to a parking garage. Jim wiped the sweat of the muggy late summer Chicago day from his forehead with his shirtsleeve.

On the third floor Jamal opened the trunk of an old but decent red Lincoln and put Jim's suitcase inside. The rear window displayed a decal of a scimitar underwritten with an Arabic inscription.

Jamal opened the door on the passenger side. With a deep bow he motioned for Jim to get in. The car had been re-upholstered in a cowhide pattern and black and white shag carpet covered the floor. A tassel of golden thread hung from the rearview mirror. The interior reeked of strong tobacco. Jamal got under the wheel and put his hat back on.

He drove to the cashier's window of the parking garage. The woman cashier took his ticket and put it in a time clock.

"That's five dollars," she said.

Jamal turned to Jim. "You got five dollars?"

Jim drew back. "Isn't that covered in the price of the trip?"

"No," Jamal said, shaking his head. "Forty bucks just for ride."

"A regular taxi wouldn't charge for parking."

"This is not a taxi."

The logic was unassailable. Jim reached for his wallet. Free from the parking garage, Jamal headed toward the airport exit. "Where we headed, boss?" he asked.

Jim pulled his itinerary from his shirt pocket. "Economy Ritz, on 71st Street."

"Which way do I go?"

Jim had an uneasy feeling. "You don't know?"

"No boss."

"Don't you know the town?"

"I know downtown."

"But we're going to the south side."

"Don't know south side."

Jim waved his hands in exasperation. "How are we supposed to get there? I sure don't know the way."

Jamal turned, grinning. "Take it easy boss." Pulling to the side of the road he opened the glove compartment, pulled out a map, and handed it to Jim. "You tell me the road."

"Christ a'mighty," Jim muttered, unfolding the map. He located 71st Street and saw that it intersected Interstate 94 about eight miles south of the downtown.

"Drive like you were going downtown," Jim said, "but stay on 94 and go south. I'll tell you where to get off."

Jamal nodded. "That's good boss."

After they pulled on the interstate spur leading from the airport Jim relaxed. He could handle being the navigator. They would just stay on I-94 until they got close to 71st, then exit and find the street address of the Economy Ritz. He studied the map and located the Harrigan Motor Corporation plant. Only a couple of blocks from the motel, it would be easy walking distance.

"Where you from?" Jim asked.

Jamal turned, flashing a smile. "Palestine."

"How long you been here in this country?"

"Six months."

"Where'd you get this car?"

"I buy from my cousin."

Jim felt a grudging admiration for Jamal. He had a lot of hustle to him and a lot of balls palming himself off as an expert driver in a huge city he didn't know well. Jamal switched on the tape player and a blast of mideastern music filled the car. The skyline of Chicago, dominated by the Sears Tower and the Hancock Center, filled the windshield. Here was a skyline that put Dallas's to shame.

As they drove toward the southside Jim told Jamal he was a truck driver, trying to get technical help on his truck. Jamal said he'd like to be a truck driver or at least something besides an unlicensed taxi driver.

He turned to Jim with an elaborate shrug. "But what can I do boss? I got to work what I can get. Got a wife, three children. Maybe someday I'll get something better."

Jim had Jamal take an exit just before the point where I-94 intersected 71st Street. They negotiated several blocks of heavy traffic and pulled into the drive of the Economy Ritz, an undistinguished prefab concrete conglomerate with the bright red doors of the rooms lined up on two levels in equal-spaced monotony.

Jamal parked the Lincoln and got Jim's suitcase from the trunk. Jim handed him two twenty dollar bills.

He frowned. "You no like how I drive?"

Jim pulled out a ten.

Jamal smiled as he accepted the offering. "When you go back?"

"In two or three days."

"I drive you?"

Jim hesitated. It would be easier to get a regular cab but despite the shakedown, Jamal had an appealing charm.

"Can you find this place again?" Jim asked.

"Sure boss. I go one time, next time I know." He reached in his pocket and handed Jim a card. Jamal El Ibrahim, Chauffeur, it read. "You call me night before you go, I be here," Jamal said.

As his new chauffeur drove away Jim lugged his suitcase into the motel office where he gave the gum-chewing girl on the desk his American Express card. The accommodation would run sixty dollars a night, a third more than it would have been in Fort Worth. He put his suitcase in the room then ate a hamburger and french fries in the restaurant attached to the motel. Just after one he went out on the street to walk to the Harrigan plant.

Strident traffic crowded the streets of the rundown residential area he walked through. Turn-of-the-century houses of stucco and brick with sad, neglected yards stood together in dreary unison. The late summer sun made a steam bath of the humid air. Before Jim had gone a block sweat soaked his armpits.

He came to a commercial corner with a filling station, a convenience store, and several bars. Beyond them several large buildings of dull red brick stood in a line behind a chain link fence topped with barbed wire. A smaller building of the same material as the others fronted on the sidewalk.

Jim crossed the street and walked to the steps leading up to the double doors of the smaller building. Corporate Headquarters, Harrigan Motor Corporation, Home of Handmade Quality, proclaimed a large sign over the doors.

Jim walked up the steps and went in. A welcome blast of refrigerated air engulfed him. An attractive blonde sat at a deeply polished desk of dark wood on an expanse of thick tan carpet with a group of thickly padded chairs of the same style to the side. Lighted color photographs of different models of Harrigan trucks decorated the walls of the waiting area.

"May I help you sir?" the girl asked.

"I bet you can," Jim said. "I'm Billy Don Hickson from Fort Worth. I got a Harrigan Loadmaster and I need to get some technical information on it."

The receptionist smiled. "The publication department's down the hall to the right."

Jim nodded. "Thanks a lot."

He walked down the hall and turned through a pair of double doors. A tired-looking brunette sat behind a long counter. She stood as Jim approached.

"What can I do for you sir?"

Jim shuffled his feet and looked down at his boots. "I got a two year old Loadmaster and I wanted to get some technical material on it."

"What kind of technical material?"

"I need the most recent maintenance manual for one thing and any technical bulletins that have come out on it."

"Let's see what I can find."

The girl turned and walked across the room to a set of shelves filled with books and pamphlets. She gathered up several items and returned to the counter.

"Here's everything we have," she said. "You're welcome to look through it and see if it's what you need."

"Thanks, ma'am."

The girl sat at her desk while Jim went through the literature. The largest item was a thick maintenance manual. Jim checked the publication date and thumbed through it. It appeared the same as the one Art Kurtz had previously furnished him. Nothing new here, which was just as well since it had a price tag of a hundred and ten dollars.

Jim turned to the other literature, a series of bulletins advising service personnel of problems that had been encountered since the M-5000 Loadmaster had come on the market. Kurtz was obligated to furnish any bulletins that might affect the operation of the truck but Jim had no confidence he'd get the material that way. Art was a good guy and one Jim genuinely liked but that didn't mean he'd necessarily be forthcoming with information that might hurt his side of the case. Besides, Harrigan might withhold the information from Kurtz.

One of the pamphlets advised of a problem in the heating system and another described an oil leak that could be fixed by replacing a gasket. Jim flipped through the series quickly and found nothing relating to the truck's steering. One dealt with a brake malfunction. Could it have been locked brakes instead of locked steering that sent Danny Marcus across the median? Jim needed time to study the material.

"Any charge for these bulletins?" he asked the girl.

She shook her head. "Those are free. You don't need the manual?"

"Nope. It's same as the one I got. I thought there might be an update."

"That's the most recent we have."

"Have there been any recall notices on this truck?"

The girl smiled. "No sir. We've never had anything like that."

"I'll just take the bulletins then."

Back in the motel room Jim read the pamphlets. Most dealt with routine problems that were easily fixed. The one published in response to the brake problem described circumstances under which the brakes might fail to automatically adjust under usage, as they were designed to do. Replacement of one particular spring on each set of brakes would fix the problem.

It didn't seem to Jim that kind of failure could have had anything to do with Danny's accident. To be sure Jim would take the bulletin to Nick Stavros for his expert analysis but there probably wasn't much there for Nick to get excited over.

Jim called Susan and checked his messages, then took a nap. At three-thirty, he walked back toward the Harrigan plant. At the corner across from the corporate headquarters he studied the two bars he had noticed earlier. One of them, spic and span with a white brick facade and pink shutters, declared itself to be The Love Pit with foot-high red letters along the roof line. He walked along the sidewalk until he came to the padded red front door.

An engraved bronze plaque mounted at eye level set out a pointed message: Gay bar. Straights welcome. Enter not those who take offense. This obviously was not the right place. Harrigan probably employed a number of gays but they wouldn't do their drinking so close to the work site. Besides, Jim didn't want to send any wrong signals.

The other bar held more promise. Atop a rustic front a wooden sign in the shape of an eighteen wheeler carried the name of the place on the side of the trailer: Slim's Truck Stop. Jim pulled the front door open and went in. A long bar stood along the far wall with shelves of glasses and liquor bottles behind it. The room smelled of stale beer, whiskey, and cigarette smoke.

Several men were playing pool at a table under a shaded light suspended from the ceiling. Pictures of Harrigan trucks like those in the corporate office lined the walls. Five or six people sat at tables and booths. A thin man in slacks and a white shirt stood polishing glasses behind the bar. Jim took one of the stools.

"What'll it be?" the bartender asked.

"What ya'll got on draft?"

"Bud and Miller Lite."

"Gimme a Bud."

The man drew the beer and Jim took a sip. "Do a lot of the Harrigan workers hang out here?" he asked.

The bartender nodded. "Place'd go broke without 'em."

"You the owner?"

"Yep."

"You must be Slim then?"

The man laughed. "No, I'm not. Slim was the last owner. I'm Joe. I just kept the old name when I bought it. No point in changing something the customers were used to."

"Makes sense to me. When do most of 'em come in?"

Joe looked at his watch. "In about fifteen minutes. The shift changes at four and I got a bunch a regulars who drop by for a few rounds before they go home. What's your interest in Harrigan?"

"I'm the proud owner of a Harrigan truck. I been having some trouble with the steering. I got some technical bulletins today from the corporate office but they didn't help me. Have you heard about any problems with the steering system?"

Joe shook his head. "No. Sure haven't. As far as I'm concerned, they make a super truck."

"I sure think so. I've been real happy with mine except for this one thing. Do you think any of the guys that come in here could give me any suggestions?"

"Why don't you just go to the office and ask for a technical consultation?"

"I'm gonna do that tomorrow but sometimes you get better information just talking to the people who work on things."

Joe laughed. "That's for sure. There is one guy who might know if they've had any trouble. He's one of the quality control superintendents. I'll point him out if he comes in."

"Thanks. I'll appreciate it."

Joe turned to wait on other customers, and Jim sipped his beer. Just after four Slim's Truck Stop started filling up with men in working clothes. Some wore sports shirts stuffed into blue jeans, others grey or khaki coveralls. A few women filtered in. Wearing jumpsuits or jeans, they had the hearty appearance of assembly line workers.

Jim ordered another beer, then turned on his stool toward the incoming crowd. Layers of cigarette smoke and a confusion of voices saturated the room.

Joe whispered in his ear. "The guy I was talking about just came in. He's the fella in the red and black sports shirt. Name's Doug Spivak."

Joe pointed to a medium-sized man of about forty-five with a fiery red face and thick arms. He was headed for the now-vacant pool table.

He turned toward the bar. "Who wants a game of pool?"

Quickly, Jim slid from his stool and walked over, carrying his beer.

"I'll play you," he said.

A small young man with coarse brown hair had followed Jim to the table. He wore garish orange coveralls. "I'll make it three," he said.

Spivak bent a disparaging look at the small man. "I can always beat you Rusty, but we got fresh meat today." He put out a hand to Jim.

"Doug Spivak."

Jim shook his hand. "Billy Don Hickson. Good to meet you."

He shook hands with Rusty. Spivak racked the balls and paid Joe for the game. They played rotation pool. Spivak obviously had pride in his pool-playing abilities but Jim quickly saw that he wasn't as good as he thought he was although he was much better than little Rusty who regularly missed even the easy ones.

Spivak leaned across the table for a bank shot, sinking the nine in one of the corner pockets. He chalked his cue before moving to the other side of the table for his next try.

"Haven't seen you around before, Billy Don. You work around here?"

Jim shook his head. "Naw, I'm a trucker, just passing through. What do ya'll do for a livin'?"

"Rusty and me both work for Harrigan Motors."

"I thought you probably did, bein' in this bar. I went by ya'll's office today to get some technical bulletins on my truck."

"You from Texas?"

"You bet."

"I thought so. What kinda truck you have?"

"It's a M-5000 Loadmaster."

"That's a good one."

Spivak missed and Rusty stepped up. A little drunk, he rattled his cue on the side of the table, took doubtful aim, and scratched on a straight in shot on the ten. Spivak spotted the ball and Jim took aim and sank it in a side pocket. He missed the next try and Spivak came forward again.

Jim picked up his beer from a nearby table. "I sure like my Harrigan," he said, "but I been having some trouble with it. That's why I came by for the bulletins."

"What kind of trouble?" Spivak asked, bending over the table.

"Nothing much. Just every now and then, the steering gets a little stiff for a second or two. You got any idea what might be the problem?"

Spivak's cue hit the ball with a dull crack and he scratched. He straightened, eyes suddenly wide, but he recovered quickly. He shook his head.

"No Tex, that's a new one on me. Must be something binding on your unit."

"My local dealer can't find anything wrong."

Rusty raised his chin, eyes animated. "Didn't you tell me there were some problems like that Doug?"

Doug whirled toward Rusty, locking eyes with him. "There wasn't any problem Rusty. No problem at all. We got a couple of complaints about accidents involving the steering but when we got the police reports it was plain that good 'ol driver error was the culprit."

"Oh, I see," Rusty said, his voice doubtful.

Jim shrugged. "I don't guess it's a big deal. So far, I've always been able to control it."

"Don't worry Tex," Spivak said, "it's probably just a maintenance problem. Take the truck back to your local dealer. They're bound to be able to fix it."

"I'll do that."

They finished the game and played two more without talking about the truck steering. Jim knew Spivak would deflect any attempt to get back on that subject. He wasn't going to allow any loose talk about Harrigan's problems, whatever they were. Rusty kept getting drunker until he could hardly line up his cue stick.

Spivak stayed in control of himself, drinking very little and winning two out of the three games. He kept referring to Jim as Tex, in the condescending way northerners have when confronted with a rural-talking Texan. That suited Jim just fine. He sure didn't want Spivak to know he was really a slick personal injury lawyer fishing for information.

At the end of the third game Spivak hung up his cue. "Gotta get on home. Wife'll be expecting me. Come on Rusty. I'll give ya a ride."

"I got my car," Rusty protested.

"You'd best leave the old crate here. I'll come by for you in the morning."

"I'm not drunk Doug."

"And the Pope ain't a Catholic. Let's go." Spivak turned to Jim. "It's been good meeting you Tex. You'd be a pretty good pool player if you could make those bank shots."

Jim laughed. He could have won all three games if he'd tried. "I 'preciate that Doug. I'll keep practicin'."

"You do that. And get that truck in to one of our dealers down in Texas. I'm sure they can fix it."

"I'll do that for sure."

Rusty allowed Spivak to herd him out the front door. Jim went back to the bar and got another Bud.

"Doug help you out any?" the bartender asked.

"Naw he didn't, but he's a pretty fair pool player. Did he take that little guy to raise?"

Joe laughed. "When Doug says jump, Rusty says 'how far?'."

Jim stayed in the bar another hour but other opportunities to talk to Harrigan workers about Billy Don's truck didn't materialize. The workers from the eight to four shift gradually drifted away and the bar emptied. At seven Jim hit the street in the long shadows of early evening and walked back to the Economy Ritz where he had a steak and baked potato in the restaurant.

In the room he lay on his back thinking. Spivak's reaction to his questions seemed to confirm a problem with the truck steering. A problem Harrigan wasn't sharing with the public. How could he get the truth? He'd see what he could find out by going back to corporate headquarters in the morning. Didn't seem to be much else he could do tonight.

He turned on the TV and brought up the menu. It offered over fifty television channels, five conventional movies, and a selection of seven or eight adult movies. One of those might be interesting. Should he watch *Patsy's Passionate Plaything*, *Fruit Salad*, or *Sex Squad*? Not liking the implications of *Fruit Salad*, he entered the code for *Sex Squad*.

In the movie's rudimentary plot, a seedy looking police detective was gathering evidence on an auto theft ring by sending out a series of lascivious female cops to inveigle the ring members into intercourse. Although the sex was simulated, the girls' nude bodies presented considerable prurient appeal. After an hour of the inane production he turned it off and started considering the inadequate state of his own love life.

He was in Chicago, a city of many opportunities. The night was still young. He could hit the bars and see what action was available. Since his divorce he'd picked up women that way in Fort Worth and Dallas.

Only trouble was, most of them had been prostitutes who provided sexual services with the clinical detachment of emergency room nurses. Even with the few lonely women who had not wanted money he'd had no real pleasure. With the exhaustion of passion he'd thought of nothing but escape from their company.

Jim turned the television on again and found an old movie channel featuring a Roy Rogers western. Better to be amused with memories of his childhood than waste his time with a sterile quest he'd regret later.

The next morning he slept late, then walked to the Harrigan headquarters around ten. He asked the girl in the publications department if there was anyone he could talk to about his problem. She made a phone call and made an appointment for him to talk to a technical representative that afternoon. He frittered away the rest of the morning in the motel room, had a hamburger for lunch, and walked back to the plant at the appointed hour.

In a conference room on the second floor of the headquarters he met with a congenial young man who seemed to be more of a public relations person than someone with technical knowledge. The young man reassured Jim that there couldn't be anything serious wrong with his truck, that Harrigan had the most sophisticated steering system in the industry, and that Billy Don's local dealer in Texas could surely set things right.

"But I've heard some rumors there was a problem with the steering. That's why I wanted the consultation," Jim said.

The man flashed a condescending smile. "We here at Harrigan don't put any stock in rumors Mr. Hickson. We'd rather rely on our experience and technical knowledge. Believe me, there's no problem with the design of our steering system."

Jim thanked the representative and left. As he walked along the hall on the first floor of the building he passed the entrance to a cafeteria and decided to get a cup of coffee. He sat at a Formica-covered table, almost alone in the large, brightly lighted room as he pondered whether he had any additional options.

A blond man in a blue suit came through the cafeteria door. Jim recognized Harrigan's CEO, Gerald Forbes, from his picture in the brochure Kurtz had sent. He looked just as insufferable in person as he did in the photograph. The ice-blue eyes scanned the room, locking onto Jim for a long moment with a look of haughty superiority.

Jim stared back with all the insolence he could muster. Surely this asshole knew what was wrong with the Loadmaster steering. With an irritated jerk of his head, Forbes turned to the serving line. He bought a piece of pie and headed for the door.

As he left the room little Rusty from Slim's Truck Stop came in. He nodded deferentially to Forbes then went through the line and got a cup of coffee. Jim waved to him and he came over and sat down.

"How's your head?" Jim asked, grinning.

Rusty put on a face. "Awful. I'll be glad when this day's over."

"Was your car still there this morning?"

"Sure. No one'd bother a junk heap like that. What brings you back this way?"

Jim sipped his coffee then set the cup down. "You remember I said I was having trouble with the steering on my truck?"

Rusty nodded. "Yes."

"Well, I came back to talk to a tech rep about it."

"What'd you find out?"

"Nothin'. The guy said there's no problem."

"That's the same as what Doug says."

"But I thought you'd heard there was something wrong."

Rusty looked down at the table, eyes troubled. "I did hear something like that."

"What was it? I need to know real bad."

Rusty looked around the room, then leaned forward. "I don't really know anything. Just that there is some sort of problem. I heard Doug and some of the other guys talking about it."

"What was it Rusty? Think hard."

Rusty shook his head. "I've told you all I know."

At that moment Doug Spivak came through the cafeteria door, spotted them, and headed for the table, face reddening more with each step.

"Well look what the cat drug in," Spivak said. "It's good 'ol Tex. I thought you'd be long gone by now."

Jim put on a go-to-hell smile. "I'm still trying to find out about my steering system."

"Well Tex, you came to the wrong place. There's nothing wrong with your steering and you'd best be going."

"Who says so?"

"I do."

A beefy uniformed security guard came through the cafeteria door and headed for the serving line.

"Bill!" Spivak called.

The man looked toward them.

"Can you come over here a minute?"

The officer ambled over. "What's the problem?"

Spivak jerked a thumb at Jim. "This butthole doesn't work here. He's snooping around asking questions and won't leave."

The guard's face turned stern. "You'd better come with me, sir."

Jim stood. "Keep your shirt on. I'm tired of this place anyway."

Spivak thrust his chest out like a banty rooster. "Then get your ass back to Texas."

"Thanks for the suggestion. That's the very thing I'm gonna do."

With a downward wave of his hand to Rusty Jim followed the security guard. Spivak had made his blood boil but he wasn't about to show it. The guard ushered him onto the street and he walked toward the motel. He'd done all he could for now.

That evening after another supper in the motel restaurant he pulled out Jamal's card and dialed the number.

"Hello?" a voice answered.

"Is Jamal there?"

"This Jamal."

"This is Billy Don Hickson. Can you pick me up tomorrow morning and take me to the airport?"

"Who?"

"Billy Don Hickson. The south side guy. The Economy Ritz guy."

"Oh sure. How you doing boss?"

"Just fine. Can you come tomorrow?"

"What time?"

"Nine."

"I'm coming boss."

Jim hung up, unsure if he could trust Jamal to make it. He called and made reservations for a flight at eleven. That way there'd be plenty of time to call a cab if Jamal was late. He needn't have worried. When he toted his bags to the front lobby at eight forty-five the next morning, Jamal was already there, sitting in an easy chair eating one of the donuts the motel provided for its guests.

He jumped up as Jim entered the door. "Ready boss?"

"Just a minute."

After Jim checked out Jamal grabbed his suitcase and loaded it in the Lincoln. They drove back to the airport in bright sunny weather. At the terminal that served American Airlines Jamal opened the trunk and hefted the suitcase to the sidewalk. Jim handed him fifty dollars.

Jamal viewed the bills with disappointed eyes. He shook his head. "Not enough boss."

Jim laughed. "What do you mean it's not enough? It's the same as last time even down to the tip."

"My cousin tell me should be sixty dollar."

"Did I hire your cousin to drive me?"

"No boss."

"That's right. I hired you and we made a deal. Forty dollars plus ten for the tip. That's all you're getting."

A policeman had come out of the terminal. He viewed Jamal with a critical eye and started toward the car.

72

Jamal headed for the driver's door. "Okay boss. Fifty dollars okay. Next time you call me again."

He started the engine and pulled away just as the cop arrived. "You shouldn't do business with that guy, mister," he said. "He doesn't have a license. I wrote him up twice last week."

"Thanks, officer. I'll know better next time." Jim grabbed his suitcase and headed for the terminal.

# 5

The next day at the office Jim faxed the report on the brake problem to Nick Stavros who told him the bulletin did not describe a problem that could have contributed to the accident. Jim added up the money he had spent on the Chicago trip. More than twelve hundred dollars of his own funds. And he hadn't really gotten any useful information.

Nothing was going gone right on this case. It was time for Jim to face facts: he was beaten. He knew in his gut something was wrong with the Harrigan steering system but that was beside the point.

The fact truckers in Montana and Mississippi had been involved in similar accidents wouldn't count for much in a court of law without something to connect those accidents to Danny's. Why should Jim delude Laura Marcus any longer? He should tell her she didn't have a chance and get out of this loser.

He buzzed Susan on the intercom. "See if you can get Laura Marcus on the line."

Several minutes later, Susan connected them.

"Mrs. Marcus?"

"I'm glad you called Mr. McSpadden."

"What's up?"

"I just got served with some papers signed by Mr. Sullivan."

"What kind of papers?"

"They say something about I'm being sued because the wreck was Danny's fault."

Gears meshed in Jim's brain. Rolly hadn't sued Danny's estate at first. Now, for some reason he'd joined Laura to the lawsuit. Not really a good idea. Rolly would look like a bully. It was best just to sue the employer, even when the wreck was the employee's fault. Juries got mad when you sued the little guy. What was going on? Now wasn't the time to tell Laura she didn't have a case. First, Jim needed to advise her on this new development. He'd tell her he was getting out afterward.

"Can you bring the papers in?" he asked.

"Not today. Kim's home sick. Otherwise I'd be at work."

"I'd better come over and get them then. I can't tell what they mean without looking at them."

"Doesn't the bastard know I don't have any money?"

"He's not really after you. He's only after the insurance."

"Does he have to sue me to get it?"

"He seems to think so. How do I get to your house?"

Laura gave him directions. Thirty minutes later Jim pulled up in front of a white frame with green trim in an older neighborhood in the Arlington Heights area on the west side of Fort Worth. He parked at the curb and walked up the sidewalk to the front door. How many times had Danny Marcus lovingly mowed the immaculate green lawn and who was keeping it in such good condition now that he was gone?

Laura met him at the front door. Her hard, bitter look had softened since her first visit to Jim's office but her brown eyes still held a pensive sadness. She wore white shorts and a white blouse, contrasting with the healthy tan of her arms and legs. A simple band held her brown hair in a ponytail.

She smiled, holding the screen door open. "Please excuse how I'm dressed."

"You look just fine."

Inside a girl of around twelve or thirteen with her mother's slim build and brown hair lay on a couch in a housecoat watching an afternoon sitcom. She regarded Jim with unsmiling, curious eyes.

Laura stepped forward. "Honey, this is Mr. McSpadden, our lawyer."

The girl sat up. "Nice to meet you."

"This is Kim," Laura said.

Jim nodded. "I understand you're sick."

Kim smiled. "I'm better now."

Laura put her hand on her daughter's shoulder. "Why don't you go on back to your room and rest so Mr. McSpadden and I can talk?"

"Sure mama." In a listless movement Kim rose from the couch and left the room.

"There's really not much wrong with her," Laura said. "Sometimes she just can't stand to go to school."

"Has she had any counseling?"

Laura shook her head. "I'd like for her to, but we don't have any insurance."

"You could go to E. M. Daggett Hospital."

"That madhouse? It might make her worse."

"I know what you mean."

Mrs. Marcus motioned toward the couch. "Sit down. I'll go get the papers."

Jim sat down and Laura went down the hall. The mantle above the fireplace beyond the television held a family photograph in a polished wood frame. Laura and Kim sat side by side next to a proud-faced boy with curly brown hair. Behind them stood a large man with a broad, weathered face and humorous smile. Tears rose in Jim's eyes. The Marcuses had made an attractive family.

Laura returned carrying a sheaf of papers. She handed them to Jim and sat next to the couch in an easy chair.

"I didn't stay home from work so some damn constable could come around hassling me."

"Don't worry about it. He was just doing his job."

Jim scanned Rolly's amended petition. As Jim had suspected, it named Laura as community survivor of her marriage to Danny and claimed she was liable to Rolly's clients in that capacity for the deaths and injuries resulting from the accident.

Jim looked up. "This is no big deal."

"What should I do?"

"Nothing for now. I'll take care of it. The insurance company on the truck will furnish you with a lawyer and pay any damages assessed against Danny, up to the policy limits."

"I thought you were my lawyer."

"I am but not for this part of the case. The insurance companies always get their own counsel to defend them in cases like this."

"You'll still be on the case won't you?"

Jim hesitated. He'd planned to bow out, but somehow he just couldn't do it now. The Marcus family needed him. Laura needed him. Why did he keep shooting himself in the foot by getting into impossible situations?

"Yes," he said. "I'll still be on the case."

"Are you going to file suit for me?"

He nodded. "I'm not sure I can do anything with it, but since Rolly's sued you you might as well bring a cross-action against Harrigan Motors. We'll try to prove the truck was defective."

He told her about the trip to Chicago; that he had a gut feeling Harrigan was hiding something but he didn't know what.

"How can you make them tell the truth?" she asked.

"I can ask them some questions on the record and see what they say. But right now I don't have any way to prove they're lying if they withhold information."

"What about Alamo?"

"The accident might be due to faulty maintenance on their part but you can't sue them since they carried worker's comp on Danny."

"But comp's not paying."

"They aren't but they should be."

"Can't you make them pay?"

"Not right away. I'll have to ask the Worker's Compensation Commission to set the claim for a hearing against Houston Beneficial. And there's no point in doing that until we can prove your husband wasn't drunk. We'll just have to put it on hold until we see what happens."

Laura compressed her mouth in a thin line. "Why not go ahead and sue Alamo for negligence?"

Jim leaned forward, spreading his hands. "Do you think Danny was working when the accident happened?"

She nodded. "There's no doubt about it."

"Then there's no point in suing Alamo. If Danny was on the job, Alamo's protected from a suit for negligence by their worker's comp policy with Houston Beneficial. Our only choice is to sue Harrigan in Rolly's lawsuit and try to make Houston Beneficial pay comp death benefits by going to court on the comp claim in a second lawsuit."

"It all sounds pretty complicated."

"It is."

Laura smiled. "Well you're the boss. I'm glad we got you."

The warmth in her eyes confirmed Jim in his decision not to quit. What the shit! The practice of law wasn't supposed to be a bed of roses. He'd do the best he could for Laura and her family in spite of the obstacles. If things didn't pan out he could always take bankruptcy.

Thirty minutes later Susan raised her eyebrows as he walked back into the office. "Are we off the case?"

He shook his head. "Nope, we're still hitched."

"What happened?"

"I just couldn't say no. They need my help."

Susan smiled. "Somehow, I'm not surprised. What's the next step?"

"I gotta call Art Kurtz." Jim headed for his office.

Kurtz answered with his customary deep growl. "Hello?"

"Art, this is Jim McSpadden."

"How you doing Jim?"

"Not so good. Rolly's joined my client to the lawsuit against Alamo, and I can't figure out why."

"Maybe I can enlighten you."

"What's going on Art?"

"I told Rolly I have proof Danny Marcus wasn't in the course of his employment at the time of the accident. The insurance on the truck's all he has a shot at and he has to sue your lady to get it."

"What kind of proof are you talking about?"

"Well, for one thing one doesn't usually get double drunk driving around town delivering gasoline."

"Oh come on Art. You know that's not good enough."

"There's more but I'm not prepared to discuss it right now."

"Why not? You'll have to tell me sooner or later."

"You're not even in the suit at this point."

"Yes I am. My client's been sued."

Art laughed. "But you don't get to represent her on that part of the case. I've already lined up a lawyer to defend her."

"Good 'ol Art! Who'd you get?"

"His name's Al Hildebrand."

"What firm's he with?"

"Gruen and Stillwell."

"That's your old firm."

"That's right. I know this guy and he's good."

"Does that mean you get to call the shots on the defense of my client?"

"No sir! I think you'll find that Al is pretty independent."

"I'll give him a call. There's one more thing."

"What's that?"

"I need to talk to the mechanic who made the note about the malfunctioning of the truck steering."

Kurtz paused. "I don't recall a note like that."

"It was in the records you sent me."

"Oh, *that* note. Marcus was the one who said the steering was erratic. The mechanic didn't find anything wrong."

"Then you shouldn't mind my talking to him."

"I'm afraid I do."

"For Christ's sake why? What are you hiding?"

"Nothing," Kurtz said with studious calm. "It's just that from here on out I'd like to do everything on the record."

"You're gonna force me to get into the lawsuit just to find out if I've got anything."

"That's your decision."

Jim composed himself. "All right Art. If that's the way it's gonna be I'll file a cross-action against Harrigan and then take your mechanic's deposition."

"Sounds like a good plan to me."

Jim hung up, got a cup of coffee, and sat at his desk, thinking. Just a few hours ago he'd planned to get out of Laura Marcus's case but now he was hooked good. He couldn't win unless he could prove Danny wasn't drunk and that something else caused the accident.

To top it off, he wouldn't even get paid for representing Laura Marcus as Danny's survivor. Kurtz represented Alamo's insurance company, United of Rhode Island. The company had a duty to defend Danny under the truck policy even if he was drunk and to pay any judgment up to the six million dollar policy limits.

Kurtz couldn't represent Laura on that part of the case because of the conflict of interest caused by his claim that Danny wasn't working at the time of the accident. Of course there was no possibility that United of Rhode Island would hire a plaintiff's lawyer like Jim to represent their interests. He represented Laura Marcus and her position was potentially adverse to theirs.

Besides, insurance companies didn't trust plaintiff's lawyers. They'd rather be represented by one of their own. That was why Art had lined up another insurance defense lawyer to defend Laura. Would Al Hildebrand be Kurtz's puppet or would he go to bat for the Marcus family like he was supposed to?

Taking the suit papers to Hildebrand would be a high priority but first Jim would draft the cross-action to get Harrigan Motors into the case. He'd make an appointment to talk to Hildebrand early next week. For the time being it was time to relax and unwind. This was his weekend for visitation with his son, Travis, and they were going camping with Travis's scout troop.

He picked up the telephone and dialed his parents' number at Possum Kingdom Lake sixty miles west of Fort Worth. Both retired, they lived in a small house on the lake. Lloyd McSpadden had been a history professor at the University of Texas at Arlington and Jim's mother, Rose, had served as an elementary school principal in the Fort Worth school district.

"Hello?" Jim's father answered in his rich, full-toned voice.

"Hi dad. It's me."

"It's good to hear from you, son. When you coming out to see us?"

"It's gonna be a while dad. I'm going camping with Travis this weekend and I've got involved in a new case that's gonna take a lot of time."

"What kind of case?"

Lloyd always wanted to know about Jim's cases. A passionate admirer of Franklin Roosevelt and the New Deal, his strong feeling that the law should be an instrument of social justice had influenced Jim's decision to be a lawyer. Jim described the litigation.

"You're always getting into the tough ones," his father said.

"I'm hardheaded just like you. How's mama?"

"Okay. Her blood pressure's been up a little but the doctor's got it under control again."

"Is she there?"

"Naw. She went into Mineral Wells to get the groceries."

"Tell her I'll call next week."

"Okay."

"And I'm gonna get out there in about a month."

"That's good. Why don't you and Travis come out for the weekend?"

"We'll do that the next time I have visitation."

They hung up and Jim went to the hall closet and started pulling out his camping gear.

Early the next morning he turned south off Interstate 20 onto the farm to market leading to Cottonwood Springs. The land sloped away to the south in the fenced pastures of large ranches, their tall grasses golden in the Saturday morning sun. The first Canadian cold front of the year had raked the country, moderating the unseasonably warm weather.

A low range of hills in the distance marked the far side of the valley of the Cottonwood Fork of the Trinity. In Cottonwood Springs Jim drove slowly down the main street. With its single row of nineteenth century stores, it looked like a set for a western movie but change was coming.

A brand-new McDonalds on the corner heralded the many new businesses to come, in service of the displaced city dwellers who were putting big brick houses on acreage tracts all over the Cottonwood Valley. Jim turned onto the bumpy, poorly paved county road leading to the house he and Ellen had bought twelve years before.

He looked at his watch. Six-thirty. He and Travis would be at Worth Ranch by eight where they'd meet the rest of the troop. The others had gone out Friday afternoon but Jim had worked late at the office getting Laura Marcus's cross-action ready to file. He'd take it to the courthouse the first thing Monday morning.

He rounded the final curve and the house came into view, a red brick ranchstyle atop a gentle hill covered with range grass, prickly pear, and yucca. He had hated giving it up in the divorce settlement. He parked in the wide gravel driveway, walked to the front door, and rang the bell. It still seemed strange to have to ring for admission.

Ellen opened the door. "Come on in, Jim. Travis is almost ready."

She looked better than ever: trim-figured, determined green eyes, blonde hair in an immaculate wave. She must be using a color rinse; there was less grey this time. He walked past her into the living room. She turned, following him.

80

"Sit down." She motioned toward the blue, corduroy-pleated couch they had picked out at Edmond's Furniture the year before the divorce.

Jim parked himself on the couch.

"Would you like a cup of coffee?" she asked.

He shook his head. "I grabbed one on the way out."

She sat across the coffee table from him in an antique-looking chair he hadn't seen before.

"Nice chair," he said.

"I'm glad you like it."

"Where'd it come from?"

"I got it at an estate sale in Weatherford."

"You always did like things like that."

"It doesn't go with the couch."

"Doesn't look bad to me."

"I'm looking for a new couch. I'm going to furnish the whole room with antiques."

He looked away with a pang. The next time he probably wouldn't recognize the place. She would get rid of everything they'd picked out together.

"How're things going?" he asked.

She beamed. "Just great. Travis's making great grades so far this semester and the real estate business is really taking off."

Ellen had celebrated their divorce by getting a real estate license and had been capitalizing on the boom in sales in the Cottonwood Valley. She had a pleased, prosperous look. She had to be making more than he was these days. That was a good joke since she'd been awarded the house partly because of her supposed lesser earning capacity.

He still didn't know what had gone wrong between them. One day out of the blue she'd asked for a divorce. He'd thought there must be another man but, so far, no one else had made an appearance. It seemed Ellen had just grown tired of him and taken a different path.

Travis walked in from the hall dragging a pack and a bedroll. Sandy, curly hair set off a sour face. "I guess I'm ready," he said.

Jim stood. "Don't you want to go?"

"Not really. I wanted to go to the movies this afternoon."

"But you'll go camping with your 'ol dad won't you?"

"I guess."

"Let's go then."

Ellen followed them to the pickup where Jim threw Travis's things on top of his own in the bed. "Give your mother a kiss," Jim said.

Without enthusiasm Travis pecked Ellen's cheek.

She hugged him. "See you tomorrow."

They drove back to the interstate and headed west. "How's school going?" Jim asked.

Travis shrugged. "Okay, I guess."

"You don't sound very excited about it."

"What's there to be excited about?"

"You should like school."

"It's okay."

"Your mother says your grades are good so far."

"They're okay."

Jim shot a look at his son. "Come on, Travis. Lighten up. I only get one weekend a month."

Travis smiled for the first time. "Just let me wake up and I'll be all right."

Separation from this tall son with the springy build was one of the hard byproducts of the divorce. They made the most of the time they had. Scouts and fishing trips in the fall, then basketball season. Jim went to all the games. He hoped Travis's talent would land him a scholarship in a few years.

At Palo Pinto west of Mineral Wells they turned north and drove several miles along a two-lane highway running through scrubby mesquite country. Just short of the Brazos River Jim turned on the gravel road leading to Worth Ranch. The venerable Boy Scout camp spread over hilly terrain between the river and Kyle Mountain, a several hundred foot flat-topped hill covered with cedar.

They bypassed the parade ground surrounded by military-looking buildings of native sandstone and drove down the steeply slanting drive to the river bottoms. Mesquite and cedar gave way to large oak, elm, and pecan. They found the Troop 401 campsite at the end of the rough road on the banks of a dry creek that ran to the river.

Scoutmaster Pete Malone, tall with a silver-tipped beard, walked up as Jim and Travis got out of the truck. "You're just in time for breakfast."

Jim shookPete's hand. "You sure picked a good day."

"Yeah, it's pretty weather all right. That cold front last night took the edge off the heat. It's sure gonna be good sleeping weather."

At the campfire Jim spoke to several other dads who had come along and helped himself to bacon, scrambled eggs, and a cup of coffee from a blue enameled pot. Travis went to eat with his patrol.

The campout had been billed as a relaxed affair with plenty of free time. After breakfast Jim and Travis got their rods and tackle boxes and went down to the river. The Brazos ran fifty yards wide between a long sandbar on the far side and a grove of willows on their side. Opaque with silt, it flowed in a slow, lazy current, riffling over submerged rocks near the middle. Beyond the river, the winding curve of Shutin Mountain rose in the distance against a bright blue sky.

By midmorning they had landed a few small bass and channel cat. Heavy fishing by the scouts didn't make for much of a catch along this stretch of the river. It didn't matter. They hadn't really come for the fishing. They'd come to be in this place, still wild and free after one hundred and fifty years of settlement.

Jim laid his rod down and took a drink from his canteen. "How're things really going with you and your mother?" he asked.

Travis looked down, solemn-faced. "Everything's okay, but I miss you, dad."

"I miss you too."

"I wish you and mom hadn't got divorced."

"What's done is done. We all have to make the best of it."

"I know."

That night after the campfire and the jokes and tall stories of the men when the boys had gone to bed, Jim lay awake in his tent listening to the wind in the branches of the big trees of the river bottom. A barred owl passed through the campsite with its peremptory challenge of all comers. Hoohoo-hoohoo.

Camping and fishing trips helped him forget himself for a while but the problems always returned when he had time to think. Things had sure changed the last several years. He'd thought he had a marriage and career for life. Now the marriage was gone and he doubted his ability to continue in the legal profession.

At least his son still needed him. He'd fight to hold onto that. And he'd fight to hold onto his law practice, too. There were still people who needed his help. People like Laura Marcus and her family. He drifted into sleep confirmed in his resolve to do a good job for the Marcuses, whatever the cost.

∽

The Dallas skyline loomed ahead beyond twisting lines of early morning traffic. Soaring structures of steel and glass vied with each other for greatest height and most unusual shape. Downtown Dallas represented massive levels of investment and raw financial power. Jim pulled around a line of cars waiting to get on the Stemmons Freeway and exited the freeway system to Commerce Street. Laura Marcus sat next to him, her pretty hands folded in her lap.

"Have you ever met Mr. Hildebrand?" she asked.

He shook his head. "No. I've just talked to him on the phone."

"It still seems funny to me that I need two lawyers."

"That's just the way it works on a case like this."

"What will he ask me about?"

"He mainly just needs to meet you, to see what you're like."

They drove over to Main Street and pulled into a parking garage in the guts of a tall building covered with panels of green glass. Jim took a ticket from a machine and parked several levels down. They rode escalators up to the building's elevator lobby where Jim checked the computerized building directory.

Gruen and Stillwell had the forty-fifth through the forty-seventh floors. Jim and Laura squeezed in with a crowd of other people and the elevator took off like a spaceship, bypassing all the floors up to the fortieth level. On floor forty-five the elevator door opened directly into the firm's waiting area.

Shiny hardwood floors decorated with rich-looking area rugs and hemmed by solid oak baseboards set the tone. Impressive landscapes graced the walls. The dry smell of reams of paperwork subtly infused the air. Laura sat in a deep-cushioned chair while Jim approached the receptionist's desk.

"May I help you sir?" asked the smartly groomed black girl.

"I'm Jim McSpadden. We have an appointment with Al Hildebrand."

"Have a seat Mr. McSpadden. I'll tell him you're here."

Jim sat next to Laura. In several minutes, a young man entered the room from a hallway. Jim took his measure: about thirty-five, round build, tenacious wide-set brown eyes. He wore the usual big firm uniform—subdued blue suit with a starched white shirt and trendy tie—but his clothes didn't fit neatly as protocol demanded. The shirt puffed out over his belt, one of the buttons on his button-down collar was undone, and the tie hung backward down his shirtfront.

He walked up to them. "Mr. McSpadden?"

Jim stood, putting out his hand. "Yes, that's me."

"I'm Al Hildebrand."

They shook hands.

"This is Laura Marcus." Jim nodded toward Laura.

She stood. "Nice to meet you."

Jim and Laura followed Hildebrand into a conference room with a dark wood floor and a conference table with a thick top of polished glass. Outside, beyond the downtown, Dallas rolled away to the west. In the distance the buildings of the Fort Worth skyline clustered on the horizon.

They got coffee from an insulated carafe on a sideboard and sat at the conference table, Hildebrand on one side, Jim and Laura on the other.

Hildebrand leaned forward, looking directly at Laura. "Mrs. Marcus, first I want to tell you how sorry I am for the circumstances that bring you here.

84

There's nothing I can say or do to change the tragic nature of this case but I can try to ease the process as much as possible. I've been hired by the United Insurance Company of Rhode Island to represent your interests. I'm sure Mr. McSpadden has explained how I fit in. Do you have any questions about my role?"

Laura raised her chin. "Yes I do Mr. Hildebrand. I thought you represented the insurance company. How can you represent both their interests and mine? And what about Mr. Kurtz? Doesn't he represent the same insurance company?"

"Those are good questions. Under the law my sole duty is to you even though I'm paid by United of Rhode Island. But there is a certain conflict. The insurance company's only liable up to six million dollars so far as the policy on the truck is concerned and they have a right to settle for that amount at any time.

"Mr. Kurtz was hired by them to represent Alamo Oil and Alamo has a conflict with you because it claims your husband had abandoned his work at the time of the accident. They're trying to settle the case and get out although I don't think Mr. Sullivan will let them. Such a settlement may not be in your interest and that's where Mr. McSpadden comes in. He can't stop the negotiations but there are certain things he can do to discourage them."

"What are those?"

"He can write letters opposing settlement and can continue with the cross-action he's filed against Harrigan Motors even if United of Rhode Island settles. That will make it very hard to settle the case if you don't want to."

Laura shook her head. "It's all too complicated for me."

Hildebrand nodded. "It is complicated all right, even to lawyers. Rest assured I'll work with Mr. McSpadden in every way possible." Hildebrand turned to Jim. "What about that course and scope issue? What's your take on it?"

Jim leaned forward, arms on the table. "For one thing, the autopsy report shows Danny was drunk."

"That's not enough to take him off the job but it does raise an interesting question: why was he drunk?"

Laura's face reddened. "He wasn't drunk Mr. Hildebrand. I'm sure he wasn't."

"I'm sorry Mrs. Marcus," Hildebrand said. "I shouldn't have made that assumption. But how do we explain the report?"

"Some mixup at the hospital," Jim said. "They insist their report's right and wouldn't discuss it with me but I think they made a mistake."

"Where had Danny been that afternoon?"

"We don't know," Jim said. "Kurtz claims he has some evidence about that but he won't share it with me."

"In that case, we'd better start with some interrogatories and production requests to find out where Art's coming from and then take some depositions."

"You want to do them or should I?"

"Let's work on 'em together, and send 'em out over my signature."

"Sounds good to me. Has Rolly Sullivan called you about settlement?"

"Naw, sure hasn't. He's not interested in my six million dollars. He wants all those layers of coverage Kurtz controls."

"Sullivan needs to know what evidence Art has as much as we do."

"He sure does. Tell me about your cross-action against Harrigan. Do you have any evidence of a truck malfunction?"

Jim shook his head. "Nothing, except a report Danny had trouble with the steering. Once they answer I'm gonna send Harrigan some interrogatories and see what they'll tell me about steering problems. I wrote 'em a letter about it and they claimed there haven't been any. Several days ago I even went up to their headquarters in Chicago and snooped around but I didn't really find out anything. One guy said there'd been a problem but he didn't know what it was."

"You're just shooting in the dark then?"

"Pretty much, at this point."

"Well, we know what we have to do. Let's get on with it."

For the next half hour they traded ideas for strategy. At the end of the session Hildebrand walked with Jim and Laura to the elevators.

He shook hands with Jim, then Laura. "Remember, Mrs. Marcus, I may be hired by the insurance company but I'm on your side."

In the car, Laura asked, "Is he being honest with me?"

"In what way?"

"In saying he's on my side."

Jim nodded. "He's walking a tightrope since the insurance company's paying him but I think he's a straight shooter. I think we can trust him."

"He's funny looking guy. His clothes go every which way."

"That's one thing I like about him. He's a maverick. Doesn't fit the big firm mold. That's good, as far as I'm concerned."

"What are these interrogatories and production requests y'all kept talking about?"

"The interrogatories are questions you send in the mail to the other side to find out what they know. Under the rules of procedure they're required to answer them. With the production requests you can compel them to give you documents and other physical things connected with the case."

"Do you get much information?"

"They try to hide the ball but you always find out something you didn't know before."

Forty-five minutes later they stopped in front of Laura's house. A tall boy with curly brown hair marched behind a lawnmower with a spray of grass flying to the side.

"I'd like you to meet my son," Laura said.

They got out and walked toward the boy. He killed the engine and stood waiting.

"Eddie, this is Mr. McSpadden." Laura nodded toward Jim.

Jim put out his hand. "Nice to meet you."

"Good to meet you," Eddie mumbled, suspicious-eyed. They shook hands.

"You're sure doing a good job with this lawn."

Eddie's face tightened. "I'd better get back to it."

He pulled the starter rope and marched away behind the lawnmower.

Laura shook her head. "He used to argue about yard work."

"It's rough on a boy to lose his dad," Jim said.

Laura looked down, blinking away tears. "It's rough on all of us."

Jim put his hand on her shoulder. "I know it is."

She raised her head. "We'll come through it all right." She looked at her watch. "I'd better get started on supper."

He walked her to the door.

"When will you know something?" she asked.

"It'll be about a month. In that time we should get the answers to our initial interrogatories and production requests and get an answer from Harrigan Motors."

"Let me know what you find out." With a parting smile over her shoulder she went inside.

Jim drove toward his town house thinking of Laura. What an impressive woman she was, valiantly supporting her family in adversity. Her loneliness compared to his own and he imagined himself holding her and comforting her. Best not to think of her that way. She was a client and entitled to his professional judgment and assistance unfettered by emotional involvement.

∽

Rolly contemptuously flipped the letter from the State Bar grievance committee onto the desk in front of him. Roger Lombardo, the little sorehead from Nadine's counseling session, had complained that Rolly had acted unethically in using the session as a subterfuge to get clients from the wreck.

The letter from the committee informed Rolly that the matter was under investigation and might result in disciplinary action.

Rolly's old enemy Ronald Hobbs had signed the letter as head of the committee. Hobbs had presided over the last grievance filed against Rolly when Arturo Fonseca, an irate San Antonio bail bondsmen, had complained Rolly had not paid him the fifty thousand dollar referral fee that had been promised on a case Rolly had settled for ten million dollars.

Payments to laymen like Fonseca were illegal and amounted to barratry. Fonseca cared nothing for the legality; his beef was that he hadn't been paid but he had vented his ire with a complaint that Rolly had acted illegally in even offering to pay him. Rolly had responded that there had been no deal; Fonseca was the one trying to promote the breaking of the law.

After several hearings amid much fanfare the committee had dismissed the charge. They'd had no other choice. Fonseca was too sleazy to be credible and had nothing in writing to back him up. Rolly knew Hobbs and a majority of the committee members had believed him guilty even though they had dismissed the charges. Now they had another shot at him. So be it. He'd done nothing wrong.

Nadine had a right to offer the counseling service and Rolly was only engaging in commercial free speech in using the session to introduce himself. He'd twisted no arms; those who had hired him had done so of their own free will. Presumably, Lombardo would enter the case with another lawyer and that was his right. He had no legitimate bitch.

The letter directed Rolly to serve a response in ten days. He picked up the microphone from his recording equipment and dictated a terse letter setting out his position. Eventually there'd be a hearing and the committee might even side with Lombardo but Rolly didn't care. He had the right to take the matter to a jury and felt confident a San Antonio jury would see the situation his way.

He'd ask Bill Biggers to represent him. Bill had done a good job the last time. His services came high but Rolly could afford them. He'd have more and better lawyers than the State Bar. Biggers and the rest of Rolly's team would outwork and outlawyer the opposition and bury their feeble efforts in a blitzkrieg attack that would leave no doubt about the outcome.

Rolly finished the dictation and turned to his other mail. He shook his head in amusement at the cross-action Jim McSpadden had filed against Harrigan Motors. The poor fool was really grasping at straws. Karl Abelmeyer's investigation had ruled out any possibility that a defect in the truck steering had been a factor in the accident.

To Rolly the explanation was simple: Danny Marcus had stopped at a bar between deliveries and got shit-faced drunk, then climbed back into his truck and driven it across the median into all the other cars during the storm. Under that scenario he was on the job so that the multiple layers of insurance coverage held by Alamo would apply.

Rolly had a private investigator making discrete inquiries, trying to locate the bar where Marcus had done his drinking. The testimony of other patrons from the bar would put to rest Art Kurtz's contention that Danny had gone off on an excursion of his own. Still, Art's cat and mouse confidence worried Rolly. Did he have real evidence or was he just bluffing? Rolly had served interrogatories on Art to find out who claimed to know Danny had gone off on a joyride. When Kurtz responded Rolly would take depositions and put the matter to rest.

McSpadden's cross-action against Harrigan didn't worry Rolly one bit although it did irritate him. Harrigan would come into the case with some high-powered lawyer demanding that everyone kiss Harrigan's corporate ass. Although Harrigan's efforts would be directed mainly against McSpadden, its presence in the case would complicate things. Couldn't be helped though. No saving a fool from his folly. If McSpadden wanted to waste his time and money and delude his client into thinking she had something that was his privilege.

For Rolly's part, he'd concentrate on proving Danny Marcus had at all times remained on the job with Alamo. Once that was established everything else would quickly fall into place and the case would be ripe for either mediation or trial and a brilliant resolution that would add one more chapter to the story of Rolly Sullivan's continuing mercurial success.

# 6

Several weeks after Jim filed his cross-action against Harrigan Motor Corporation he got an answer in the mail, filed by a lawyer named J. Michael Meador out of the Potts, Grossberg firm of Dallas. Like Gruen and Stillwell and Kurtz, Jacobs and Silverstein, Meador's firm occupied space in the ethereal forty story plus zone of the Dallas skyline. Along with his answer Meador had served a detailed set of interrogatories and production requests asking Jim the basis for his claim of a steering defect.

Another Dallas law firm in the case. Why couldn't he get a break? There were good insurance defense lawyers in Fort Worth. Why couldn't he draw one of them for a change? They were so much easier to work with.

The local bar had its share of jerks but on the whole its lawyers were more laid back. Fort Worth had a live and let live, you scratch my back and I'll scratch yours attitude lacking in the strident business climate of Dallas. Maybe that was why aggressive east coast insurance companies preferred Dallas lawyers.

Jim would have to go to Dallas to take depositions of the Alamo Oil people and the Harrigan people and might even have to take Laura over there for her deposition to accommodate Al Hildebrand. It seemed to Jim most of the work on a case pending in a Fort Worth court ought to be done in Fort Worth but this one sure wasn't shaping up that way.

Meador's answer had a strident tone: Jim's cross-action was frivolous and had no merit. It was outrageous to claim a defect in the Harrigan steering system which was the most sophisticated in the business. The cross-action should be summarily dismissed and Jim and his client should be required to pay sanctions in the form of attorneys' fees and costs for filing a patently false case.

"Son of a bitch," Jim muttered, his anger heightened by the knowledge that, if he struck out and lost the case, he could well end up paying Harrigan attorneys' fees and sanctions. If the trial were held today he'd lose because he had no proof of any steering defect. Any proof he could get would have to come from Harrigan itself and he sure couldn't expect much cooperation, or even honesty, from them.

Jim called Art Kurtz. "Did you get a copy of the answer to my cross-action."

"Sure did," Kurtz said.

"Who is this guy, J. Michael Meador? I don't know him."

"Doesn't that J. Michael part give you a clue?"

"It has a pretentious ring to it."

"Mike's a pretentious kinda guy."

"How old is he?"

"He's a young Turk compared to me. About forty I'd say."

"What's he like?"

"He's a big guy—a Nazi SS man in a business suit. Blond hair, tailored clothes, Rolex watch, that kind of thing."

"Can he be talked to?"

Kurtz laughed. "Hell no. He's a hardball litigator. Goes for the nuts. He's serious about those sanctions he's asking for."

"That kind, huh?"

"I'm afraid so. You drew one of the biggest assholes the Dallas bar has ever produced and that's saying something."

"Thanks for being so encouraging."

Jim spent the afternoon drafting a set of interrogatories and production requests to send to Meador as Harrigan's attorney. He asked for copies of all reports of deficiencies of the Harrigan steering system and all design modifications and recalls along with the names and titles of all Harrigan executives and employees involved with the system.

Susan did a quick job typing the documents so they could get them out that very day. Jim's answers to Meador's discovery would be due in thirty days. When Meador learned how little evidence Jim really had, he was sure to move quickly for summary judgment to try to get the case thrown out before Jim could develop it. If Jim had his own set of discovery on file he'd have a basis to demand answers to his questions and the right to take depositions of the Harrigan people before the setting of a hearing on any motion for summary judgment Meador might file.

Jim signed the interrogatories and production requests and took them to Susan for mailing.

"They look okay?" she asked.

"There's a few corrections but they don't need to be retyped."

"I'll mail them right away. What do you think you'll find out?"

Jim shook his head. "Probably not much. I know from their response to my letter they're gonna claim there's not any problem with their steering system."

"What good does all this do then?"

"They have to swear to the answers they make to these questions. That may encourage them to be a little more forthcoming. And they'll have to give me some names of their people that know about the system. That'll give me a basis to take depositions and give me a chance to get information."

The phone rang and Susan picked it up.

"Law office." She listened for several seconds. "I'll see if he's available," she said. She put the phone on hold.

"Who is it?" Jim asked.

"Laura Marcus. She says she needs to talk to you right away."

"I'll take the call in my office."

Jim went to his desk and picked up the handset. "Hello?"

"I hate to bother you Mr. McSpadden but I'm really in a bind."

"What kind of bind?"

"A money bind. I was wondering if you could talk to Houston Beneficial about paying my comp benefits."

"I can call them but it won't do any good. Joe Bob Savage will just claim Danny wasn't in the course and scope of his employment and deny the claim."

"Please at least try. I'm two months behind on the house payment and I just got a nasty call from the mortgage company."

"I'll call now and get back to you later in the afternoon."

Jim hung up and looked up Joe Bob Savage's number on his computer. In former days when he and Gene Burns and Bobby Torricelli had been together he'd frequently had cases with the Houston Beneficial senior adjuster but that was a thing of the past.

"Long time, no see," Joe Bob said when Jim had identified himself. Joe Bob's oily voice recalled his great girth, obscene, smirking mouth, and demeaning attitude toward all claimants and their attorneys.

"Yeah, it's been several years," Jim said. "I don't have much business with Houston Beneficial now that all the lawyers got run out of the comp business."

"I sure miss you guys."

"Don't add hypocrisy to your other vices."

"I mean it Jim. It's just not as much fun dealing with claimants directly."

"Why's that?"

"They whine too much."

"At least you have to listen to them now instead of me."

"That's true but I can handle them."

"I bet you can. They don't have any way to fight back."

"Life's hard ain't it? What can I do for you today?"

"I'm calling about this Danny Marcus claim."

"Oh yeah! I was surprised to see your name on that one."

"I'm handling the damage claim for his widow and told her I'd also try to help out on the comp case."

"We've already denied that claim Jim."

"I know it but I thought you might reconsider."

Savage laughed. "Don't you know me better than that?"

"This lady and her family are really suffering, Joe Bob."

"That's not my problem. Houston Beneficial is not a charitable institution."

"That's for sure."

"We pay the claims we owe and no more."

Jim felt his temperature rising. Joe Bob had always been able to piss him off. "How can you say you don't owe this one? For Christ's sake, the man was driving a company truck during business hours when the accident happened."

"We've received information from Alamo that he had gone off on a joy ride. And of course, there's also the fact that he was drunk. Comp benefits aren't due when an accident happens under those conditions."

Jim tightened his grip on the phone. "You'd better be sure you've got your facts straight Joe Bob. If you're wrong I'm gonna file the biggest bad faith case against Houston Beneficial you've ever seen. The exemplary damages for causing a widow to lose the family homestead could be huge."

Joe Bob changed his voice to a falsetto. "Oh, oh. The big bad faith wolf's gonna get me!" He switched to normal register. "You oughta know better than to throw that crap at me Jim. The Texas Supreme Court's just about wiped out bad faith actions. Besides, it's hard to argue with that blood test. We've got plenty of justification for denying the claim."

The fact Savage was right put Jim's head through the roof. "You fat asshole! You'll sing a different tune when the truth comes out."

Savage threw a gut laugh over the wire. "Same old Jim. You never could keep your cool."

"Fuck you, butthole!" Jim yelled. He slammed the phone down.

Susan stuck her head in the door, quizzing him with her eyes through her fake tortoise shell frames. "Everything okay in here?"

Jim shook his head. "Hell no. But there's nothing I can do about it. At least, not right away."

"What's the problem?"

Jim told her what Savage had said.

She shrugged. "You knew better than to try to talk to him."

"Yes I did. But it still pisses me off. Joe Bob always affects me that way."

Jim got a Seven-up from the small refrigerator in the supply room, then went back to his office. He dialed Laura's number.

"Hello?" she answered, voice hopeful.

"It's me."

"What'd they say?"

Jim kept his voice flat. "Savage won't reconsider."

Laura sucked in her breath. "What am I gonna do Mr. McSpadden? I don't want to lose my house."

"You don't have any way to make the payments?"

"Not right now. I've got a second job lined up but it doesn't start for two more weeks."

"What will you be doing?"

"I'm going to work as a night cashier for EZ Sack."

"You're gonna work all day at the bank and then half the night at a convenience store?"

"That's right."

"Those places are dangerous. What part of town is it in?"

"It's out off Seminary on the south side."

"That's a bad area. You're liable to get held up."

"I'll be in one of those enclosures with bulletproof glass."

"Somehow that's not very reassuring. Couldn't you get some other kind of work?"

"This was all I could find. I had to take it. The mortgage company's fixin' to post the house for foreclosure."

"Won't they hold off a while?"

"They say they can't. They've got to have at least one payment within the next three days."

Jim hesitated. In former times he'd have quickly advanced the money to bring the house payments current but his own income had shrunk. Between child support payments to Ellen and office expenses he just barely had enough these days to cover his personal expenses.

He needed to put all the money he could spare into the costs of the litigation and not on Laura's personal problems. But he knew she was doing the best she could and she was having a rough time. A rough time she didn't deserve. And he still had a CD or two left over from more profitable days.

"I might be able to cover the past due payments," he said. "Do you think you could keep them up after that?"

"I know I could." Relief filled her voice. "But you don't have to do that."

"Maybe not but I'd rather not have my clients living under a bridge. Can you come by tomorrow and pick up the check?"

"I'll come by at lunch."

"One more thing."

"What's that?"

"Would you try to find a different second job?"

"I'll keep looking."

Jim got the figures from Laura, then went to his bank and cashed in one of his CD's. The next day he waited for her at noon. She came into the office looking smart in a blue suit, brown hair brushed back from her forehead, subtly colored lips complementing her tanned skin.

He stood, handing her a check. As she took it, her fingers brushed his, sending an electric thrill through his body. Tears glistened in her eyes in spite of a brave smile.

"I hate having to borrow from you."

"Don't worry about it. I'll take it out at the end."

"But you don't know we'll win."

He shrugged. "If we don't I'll write it off as a business loss."

"It's still mighty nice of you."

She held his eyes with her own for a long moment. He read reams of fantasies into her look and it suddenly came to him that he loved this woman. Surely she could tell. Did she care for him? But now wasn't the time or place to find out. Her loss was still too immediate.

"I'm glad to help, Mrs. Marcus. Let's hope finances will improve with this new job."

"I'm sure they will Mr. McSpadden. I'll keep you posted."

She put out her hand. He took pleasure in the feel of her warm fingers against his own. "I'll let you know about the next step on the case in a couple of weeks."

When she had gone, Jim sank into his chair. Confused thoughts of her raced through his mind as he tried to accommodate his new feeling. Already he missed her presence, the clean, fresh scent of her perfume. He longed for her look of wry humor, the light in her eyes. Suddenly the lawsuit had a new problem: how could he objectively handle a case for a woman he had come to love?

∽

Jim walked down the stairs leading to Jernigan's Jazz Place in the basement of a renovated two-story brick building on Main Street in downtown Fort Worth. Bobby Torricelli had called late that afternoon: why didn't he and Jim and Gene Burns get together for a late dinner and some drinks for old time's sake?

Jim had jumped at the idea. He still liked his old partners. They'd had their share of disagreements over money and productivity but had always been able to work them out until the crunch caused by the collapse of their workers' compensation business had forced them to split up. Jim missed their marathon bullshit sessions over drinks and jazz music at Jernigan's.

Inside he paused waiting for his eyes to adjust to the dim light. The richly-textured tones of *All of Me*, played on a trumpet, wafted through acrid layers of blue smoke. Jernigan's didn't cater to wimps who worried about cancer.

A tall, blonde hostess approached, smiling. "We haven't seen you in a while Jim."

"I've got out of the habit of coming Billie. I'm gonna have to get in the grove again."

"I bet you're looking for Bobby and Gene."

"I sure am."

"They're right over here."

She led him through the maze of tables to one near the bandstand.

Bobby and Gene both got up as Jim approached. Tall, Roman-nosed Bobby shook his head in mock disapproval. "Oyez, oyez, oyez! Lawyer McSpadden finally arrives, late as usual."

Little Gene with a face of freckles that made him look like a teenager in spite of his faded, thinning red hair, put out his hand. "God damn it's good to see you."

Jim smiled, shaking first Gene's hand, then Bobby's. "It's good to see you bastards too."

"Ya'll ready to order now?" the hostess asked.

Bobby nodded. "Sure are."

"I'll send a waitress over."

They ordered steaks and a round of drinks. Jim sipped a Scotch and Soda, letting the effects of the alcohol and the music fuse into a mellow mood. He turned to watch the jazz group. A scholarly looking black man of around forty was doing variations on *Old Devil Moon* on trumpet, backed by an aging hippy on drums, a stringbeany, college student type on upright bass, and a balding man in his fifties playing an effectively understated piano.

"Who are these guys?" Jim asked.

"They're called the Clifton Cameron Quartet," Gene said.

"I don't remember them."

"They've been playing here on and off for a couple of months."

"They've sure got a good sound. Where are they from?"

"They're all local. Cameron's a North Texas alumnus." Gene named a school famous for its jazz musicians.

"That's the black guy?"

Gene nodded.

Bobby grinned. "Who says we don't have culture here in Foat Wuth?"

The steaks arrived and the men started eating. "This really hits the spot," Jim said. "I've sure missed this place."

"No reason we can't do this regularly," Bobby said. "Let's start trying to get together at least once a month."

"Sounds good to me."

They finished their meals and ordered after-dinner drinks. Jim sipped his Cognac, letting the aromatic fumes tickle his nose. "How are things going with you guys?" he asked.

Gene made a wry face. "About as well as can be expected."

Bobby leaned forward. "Same here. Can't say I'm crazy about what I'm doing but it's a living."

"Don't you like prosecuting crooks?"

"Sure. Someone has to do it. But it's kinda a letdown after being in practice with you guys."

Gene nodded. "That's how I feel. I'd just as soon not do the divorces but they're something people will pay for."

"I thought you were doing criminal cases," Jim said.

"I do both. About fifty-fifty."

"Bobby prosecutes them and you defend them?"

"That's right. We've already had several cases together."

"Who won?"

"We've pled 'em all so far."

"Bleed 'em and plead 'em, huh?"

"That's not the way I like to look at it."

"That's kinda how it works though."

Gene shrugged. "I guess you could say that. How about you? Can you still make a living doing injury cases?"

Jim laughed. "That's a good question. I'm keeping the doors open but not making much money."

"Didn't I see your name in the paper recently on some big case?" Bobby asked.

"It was probably about that big freeway crash in August."

"That was it. You're in that one with the great man, Rolly Sullivan."

"I wouldn't say I'm in it with him. He stole one client from me and now he's sued the one I did get."

"How'd that happen?"

Jim brought the others up to date. When he had finished, Gene shook his head. "You get yourself into the damnedest deals."

"You got that right."

Bobby snorted. "None of us can brag much about what we're doing these days. What made us want to be lawyers anyway?"

Jim smiled. "I ask myself that question a lot. I used to think it was so I could help poor people."

Gene looked away, eyes wistful. "I wanted to use the law to fight for racial justice."

Bobby laughed. "How many of those cases are you doing these days?"

Gene shook his head. "Not any. The way the courts are, they're almost impossible."

"Besides, there's no money in them," Bobby said.

Gene bristled. "That's right. And we all have to make a living."

Jim put his elbows on the table. "I still like to think I'm helping people when I take on some big corporation in a damage suit."

Bobby twisted his mouth in a knowing look. "Big business would say you're just helping yourself—that you're a limousine liberal."

Jim leaned back, spreading his hands. "Screw the bastards. I like to think of myself as kind of like Robin Hood. When I win my clients win, and part of the loot stays with me."

"How's 'ol Robin doing these days?" Bobby asked.

"Not so good. The Sheriff of Nottingham's got the squeeze on."

"That's for sure," Bobby said. "There's one good thing about being a criminal prosecutor: I get a paycheck from the county every month and I don't have to worry about any overhead."

"You're set for life then?"

"I didn't say that. I'd like to get out of law."

"Why?"

"I'm tired of lawyer jokes and all the Mickey Mouse crap you have to jack with from judges and other lawyers."

"What would you do?"

"That's the problem. I'm not trained for anything else and those house payments just keep a coming."

"I know what you mean," Jim said. "I checked on college teaching last year. I'd have to go back and get a PhD."

Bobby nodded. "Who's got time for that?"

"At least we're all surviving." Jim signaled the waitress. "Bring us another round."

They stayed in Jernigan's till after midnight listening to the music and shooting the shit about politics, hunting and fishing, courthouse gossip, and a host of other things, letting one topic flow naturally into another as the smoke haze in the room thickened and the music and booze numbed Jim's mind and gave him hope.

⤡

Rolly dialed Bill Biggers number and propped his feet on his desk as the phone rang. He looked over his tasseled loafers through his picture window at the distant San Antonio skyline.

"Biggers and Benson," answered a secretary.

"Bill Biggers please."

"May I say who's calling?"

"This is Rolly Sullivan,"

"Just a minute Mr. Sullivan," the girl said, her voice suddenly deferential. Rolly's dollars had been an important source of revenue to Biggers and Benson over the years.

"Hello Rolly." Biggers's full, self-confident voice carried the hint of a whiskey wheeze. "Haven't heard from you lately."

"I need you again Bill."

"What have you done this time?"

"What makes you think I've done something?"

"You're calling me aren't you?"

"Ronald Hobbs and his goons are after me."

"Why?"

Rolly outlined the grief counseling session Nadine had put on and how it had led to Roger Lombardo's complaint.

"Tell me again how you happened to be at the counseling session," Biggers asked.

"Nadine's a friend of mine. I asked her to set it up."

"Who fronted the money for it?"

"I did."

"How many cases did you get out of it?"

Rolly did some mental arithmetic. "I signed up three cases that night and several others later."

"Christ Rolly! How do you expect me to keep getting you out of these messes?"

"Where's the mess? I got a right to promote my services."

"I know you think so Rolly, but there's still no legal precedent that says you have the right to directly solicit accident victims and their families."

"It's just a matter of time till that's the law. This could be the case that changes things."

Bill expelled his breath. "This is gonna cost money."

"I know that. It always does."

"How much time do we have?"

"Hobbs has set a hearing next month."

"We'd better get started on it. When can we get together?"

Rolly made an appointment to see Biggers the next week.

"I know I'm a difficult client Bill," he said. "I appreciate you taking me on again."

"I'm not guaranteeing anything Rolly. It sounds like they've got pretty good evidence on you."

"Nothing you can't deal with. Work their assess off. Paper 'em to death and they'll give up just like they did on the last one."

"Don't be too sure of that."

"I've got confidence in you Bill."

"Thanks Rolly," Biggers said, in a world-weary tone. "I'll see you next week."

Biggers hung up and Rolly put the phone down. In spite of his carping Bill would do a good job. He always did. The grievance committee would hear nothing of his doubts. He'd present a solid facade of confidence in Rolly's behalf, make little Roger Lombardo look like a miserable fool, and convince the committee to dismiss the grievance. That was what he'd done last time and he could do it again.

Rolly sorted through the day's mail until he came to a notice from that jerk Jim McSpadden setting a time for taking the depositions of Alamo Oil's mechanic and Danny Marcus's supervisor. They'd be done in Art Kurtz's office in Dallas the day before Rolly's grievance hearing in San Antonio.

McSpadden was just spinning his wheels. Karl Abelmeyer had found no problem with the truck. But Rolly would have to go to the depositions and it was damned inconvenient for them to come the day before his grievance hearing. Should he try to get them put off or send his partner Pedro to the depositions? No, he decided. Best to get them over with. And Pedro didn't know enough about the case. Rolly would go himself, then come back to San Antonio that night.

He stood and walked to the window, looking out through the clear autumn air over the tops of the dark green cedars on the slope below him. He needed to take some depositions of his own in the case. Kurtz owed him answers to interrogatories he'd sent asking how Danny had deviated from the course and scope of his employment.

Kurtz would have to give Rolly the names of his witnesses. He'd take their depositions and put to rest this bullshit that Danny had gone off on a joyride. Rolly's investigator in Fort Worth hadn't turned up anyone who knew where Danny had done his drinking. Maybe Kurtz's witnesses could shed some light on that question.

A nagging worry tugged at Rolly's gut: what if Kurtz really had something? If Danny was out of the course and scope, no judgment would be collectable for more than six million dollars and that wasn't enough to take care of all Rolly's clients.

He'd have a terrible conflict of interest in trying to divide up such a small amount of money among all the catastrophic losses he represented. He'd make two million dollars and none of the clients would get anything near that much. They'd all feel sold out.

He set his jaw and turned from the window. Kurtz was bluffing and Rolly would prove it. He looked forward to deposing Kurtz's lying witnesses. But first he'd have to listen to Jim McSpadden's futile attempts to build a case and then confront the grievance committee.

He glanced at his watch: five-thirty. Time to head for the house. He'd promised to take Rae Jean out to eat. He slipped on his coat and left the office.

"See you tomorrow Maria," he said as he passed his secretary's desk.

She waved. "See you tomorrow, boss."

He drove to the loop, then south on it to Culebra where he headed toward the heart of the city. Forty-five minutes later he pulled onto the winding drive leading down an incline to his half-timbered mansion on a little creek in the heart of Alamo Heights.

He'd bought the big place for two million dollars several years earlier and spent another million renovating it. Built by a land and cattle fortune in the early years of the century, the estate had declined in recent years but the facelifting Rolly had given it had made it a show piece again.

Rae Jean was waiting for him in the living room with its dark-beamed ceiling. She rose impatiently from a couch as he came in. She had a lightly freckled complexion compounded of peaches and cream. Her light red hair piled up like a nest for some exotic bird. More striking than beautiful, she turned heads wherever she went with her pertly rounded butt and perfect small breasts.

She twisted her mouth in a sour expression. "Where have you been? Our reservations are for seven-thirty."

"That's an hour from now."

"You can't get ready that fast."

"Yes I can. Besides, it won't hurt to be late. Pierre will hold the table."

"I hate being late."

"I'll hurry." Rolly headed for the stairs.

Rolly tried not to cross Rae Jean. When she got mad her silences lasted for days and her stony face was not pleasant to behold. He knew he should have stayed married to his first wife Sandy, who had seen him through law school and borne their son, Tommy. Sandy had been a more comfortable woman than Rae Jean but dear Sandy had been going to seed for years and Rolly had craved someone younger and firmer.

A local court reporting firm had sent Rae Jean with Rolly to cover a week of depositions in the Rio Grande Valley five years earlier. They stayed at the same motel and had drinks each evening at the bar. After a few nights of that they stayed in the same room.

A year later Rolly's divorce from Sandy became final and he married Rae Jean within a month. He paid for his freedom. The two million that went to Sandy would keep her in clover for the rest of her life but Rolly had gotten off cheap.

He'd made more money since the divorce than he ever had before and Sandy didn't get any of it. Of course, Rolly was paying Tommy's tuition and expenses at the Southern Methodist University law school. Rolly put out the chickenfeed for Tommy's education as a bone for Sandy's bitterness.

At the Saint-Tropez Restaurant on New Braunfels Avenue the smells of French bread and rich cooking hung in the air. The owner, small, suave Pierre Guillon, met them at the door.

"Ah, Mr. and Mrs. Sullivan. I was afraid you weren't coming."

"Just running a little late Pierre," Rolly said. "Do you still have a good table for us?"

"Oh, of course. I would hold it all night for the Sullivans."

Guillon led them to a table screened by potted plants yet near the center of the room. They gave their orders to the solicitous waiter who brought out carefully structured dishes of veal and vegetables that looked more like artwork than something to eat.

Rolly sipped his vintage Burgundy. "What'd you do today?"

Rae Jean raised her nose in a disdainful sniff. "I went to a meeting at Constance Quimby's."

"I bet that was a lot of fun. What was it for?"

"She's planning a charity ball the middle of next month. I'm on the committee."

"I guess she wants to show off the remodeling job."

"That's it all right."

"What's the charity?"

"Some orphans' home on the west side."

"Doing her part for the poor Mexicans?"

Rae Jean nodded. "That's the way she sees it."

"Why do you get involved with these things?"

"It's expected. Besides, I enjoy it. It makes me want to laugh out loud to see her and those other old bitches carry on about how good they are."

"Do I have to go to the ball?"

"Yes you do."

"Ugh."

"You're buying a bunch of tickets too."

"Maybe I should give them to some of my clients."

"I don't think Constance would like that."

"Probably not. She wouldn't want to see anyone from the barrios there."

"It would ruin the tone of the affair." Rae Jean raised her napkin, wiping her mouth. "How's that big case in Fort Worth coming?"

"Okay so far. I'm a little worried about whether there's enough insurance."

"Some of your clients from that one could come to Constance's ball."

"That they could. I'm getting more uptown all the time."

"Constance said she heard there'd been another grievance filed against you."

Rolly straightened in irritation. He hadn't planned to tell Rae Jean about that yet. "That information's supposed to be confidential, at least at this stage."

She laughed. "Constance seems to ferret out all sorts of confidential information. She was quite catty about it. 'I do hope this new complaint doesn't cause Rolly any trouble, my dear.'"

"Goddamn old bitch."

Rolly's money and big house in Alamo Heights qualified the Sullivans for high society but its more conventional members eyed them askance. Predators all, the oil men, insurance executives, CEO's, and other big shots and their wives couldn't forget that while they preyed on the public, Rolly preyed on **them.** They tolerated the presence of Rolly and Rae Jean among them but would be glad to see them fall.

"What about it, Rolly?" Rae Jean asked.

"What about what?"

"The grievance. Is it a problem?"

He shrugged. "It's the same old thing. Someone thinks I'm not entitled to tell people what I do. Don't worry about it."

The Sullivans stayed at the Saint-Tropez until ten thirty, then drove slowly home. Rolly put the windows of the Jaguar down and savored the crisp

October air. Rae Jean snuggled next to him. The smell of her musky purfume suffused the air. She put her hand between his legs and his penis stiffened.

"You want me to have a wreck?" he asked.

She giggled. "Just keep driving." She unbuttoned his pants and put her hand inside, kneading his swollen flesh.

"Careful, or there won't be anything left," he said.

She took her hand away. "Hurry, honey. I've been thinking about it all day."

At the house Rolly opened the garage with the door opener and drove the car inside. He got out, hitched his pants up and buttoned the top button and followed Rae Jean up the stairs. By the time he got to the bedroom she stood naked before him, legs slightly spread, arms extended in invitation. Light red hair highlighted her pubic triangle.

She gave him an exaggerated wink. "Come and get it buckaroo."

He closed the door and stripped off his own clothes, leaving them in a pile on the floor. A crimson blush had covered her face and spread over her chest, blotting out her freckles. He pushed her backward onto the bed and moved over her, legs on either side of her body. His dick dragged against one of her thighs leaving a thin trail of fluid. Bending his head, he licked her erect pink nipples. She moaned, stroking his neck and ears.

He lay between her legs and entered her, pushing slowly until he penetrated. They moved together with the expertise of much practice, faster and faster, until the bedsprings creaked in cadence. The lusty noise gave them no worries since the maid slept in an apartment over the garage.

"Now honey!" Rae Jean gasped. "Give it to me now."

Bodies thrust tensely together, breath hissing between clenched teeth, they came together in a marathon spasm that left them weak and trembling. Passion spent, they lay together several minutes, covered with sweat.

"Can you do it again?" she whispered in his ear.

He shook his head. "Maybe later."

She laughed. "Only kidding. That's enough for tonight."

Later, while Rae Jean slept Rolly lay on his back next to her thinking of Nadine, her voluptuous, mature body, so expansively white in the half-light of a darkened bedroom. Why did he need two women? Did he love Nadine? For that matter, did he love Rae Jean?

His wife served as an ornament to his success but he had no depth of feeling for her. At least she was amusing to live with. He could never live with Nadine even if she weren't already married to that big, unsuspecting bozo, Bill Graves.

Nadine was best in occasional doses but he needed those doses. Maybe he could get together with her when he went up to Dallas for Jim McSpadden's depositions. But no, he couldn't stay the night. He'd have to get back to San Antonio for the grievance hearing the next day. His next session with Nadine would have to wait.

# 7

$A$rt Kurtz stood at the end of the polished marble conference table in the fifty-first story conference room of Kurtz, Jacobs & Silverstein. He beamed at Jim and the six other lawyers seated around the table. Impressive with his mane of white hair and portly demeanor, he seemed to relish his role as master of ceremonies.

Beyond the conference room's floor to ceiling windows, the mists of a chill November day blurred the outlines of the adjacent buildings. The room smelled of freshly brewed coffee. At the end of the table court reporter Bill Bittinger, sallow-faced and serious, was setting up his transcription equipment and tape recorder.

"We may not all know each other," Art said to the lawyers, "so let's go around the room and introduce ourselves and tell who we represent. I'll start us off. I'm Art Kurtz and I represent Alamo Oil Company."

Art nodded to Rolly Sullivan who cocked his head. "I'm Rolly Sullivan from San Antonio and I represent most of the victims of Alamo Oil Company's negligence."

Kurtz put on an indulgent smile. "No editorializing Rolly." Kurtz looked at a big, blond-haired man in a three piece suit who had taken a place with several empty chairs between him and Sullivan. "Tell these folks who you are, Mike."

The big man favored the others with an impressive frown. "I'm Mike Meador and I represent Harrigan Motor Company."

Looks just like he's supposed to Jim thought. He's got that go to hell look down pat. A hardball litigator. Goes for the nuts, Kurtz says. He'd get physical with you if you gave him half a chance. Or at least he'd like you to think he would. Probably plays handball and does target practice three times a week at some gun range.

At Kurtz's prompting all the lawyers gave their names and clients. Alfred Escamillo, bald and bronzed, practiced on the North Side of Fort Worth. Jim had known him for years. He had the family of Jorge Medrano, the deceased driver of the watermelon truck. Linda Fuller, a petite brunette with offices in Arlington, represented the family of Johnny Gibson, the driver of the blue pickup. Jim and pudgy Al Hildebrand, seated side by side, represented Laura Marcus as Danny's widow.

Keith Carroll, a young, earnest looking young man with dark hair and glasses, had been employed by Roger Lombardo and the other survivors of the Baer family. As was customary only the lawyers attended this preliminary round of witness depositions. The clients would come at a later time when their own depositions were taken.

The six attorneys represented all the interests involved in the case. Jim looked over the crew. Quite a menagerie. Everything from high roller, big money guys like Rollie, Mike Meador, and Art Kurtz down to solo practitioner Jim McSpadden, who was barely hanging on. He'd give the hot shots a run for their money though.

"This is your show Jim," Kurtz said. "Which witness would you like to do first?"

Jim shrugged. "Doesn't matter to me. What's best for you?"

"Let's do Marlin Reeves. He needs to get back to the terminal as soon as possible."

"Okay. Bring him in."

Kurtz left the room and returned in a few minutes with a tall, brown-haired man in grey coveralls with the Alamo Oil Company logo on a patch on one pocket.

"Have a seat, Marlin." Kurtz motioned toward a chair next to the court reporter.

Reeves sat down. Jim took his measure as Bill Bittinger swore him in. Not too nervous but he had the fish out of water look that was common to witnesses who were strangers to legal procedures. Nice, open face. Looked friendly and honest but he'd clammed up and refused to talk to Laura right after the accident. Did he have something to hide?

Bittinger finished cautioning the witness and nodded to Jim who leaned forward holding Reeves eyes with his own.

"Good morning Mr. Reeves. I'm Jim McSpadden, and I represent Laura Marcus and her family. I'd like to ask you a few questions about the day of Danny Marcus's tragic accident."

Reeves smiled. "I'll sure try to answer 'em."

After preliminary questions establishing Reeves's background Jim got down to business.

"How long did you know Danny Mr. Reeves?"

"Five or six years. Ever since he first came to work for Alamo."

"Was he a good employee?"

"He sure was. That's what made the accident so hard to understand."

"Did you ever know him to drink on the job?"

Reeves shook his head. "Not before the day of the accident."

"Did you personally see him drunk on that day?"

"I sure didn't."

"How do you know he was drunk then?"

"Just from the blood test. And Mr. Kurtz's investigation."

Jim nodded slowly. "I see. And just what did you learn from Mr. Kurtz's investigation?"

Reeves opened his mouth but Art Kurtz frowned and shook his head. "Don't get into hearsay, Marlin. Just testify to what you know about personally."

Jim turned to face Kurtz. "Alamo's claiming my client was drunk at the time of the accident. I'm entitled to ask his supervisor about the basis for that claim."

Kurtz put on a superior smile. "Anything Marlin knows about the investigation he got from me and it's protected as attorney work product. You can't ask him about it."

Jim felt his face blazing. "Art, how am I gonna know where you're coming from if you won't let me ask this witness about it?"

"It's very simple Jim. My answers to the interrogatories you and Rolly filed are due next week. In them I'll identify the witness I rely on and you can take her deposition to find out what she knows."

"Thanks for the advice."

"You're welcome."

Jim turned to face Reeves again. "Am I correct then, Mr. Reeves, that you have no personal knowledge that Danny Marcus was drunk at the time of the wreck?"

Reeves nodded. "That's right."

"And I take it you also have no personal knowledge that Danny had gone off on a joyride?"

"Well, he was overdue at the terminal."

"Other than that?"

"He'd only made one of his afternoon deliveries. We had to send another truck for the rest of them the next day."

"How many was he supposed to make?"

"There should have been four."

"Anything else that makes you think he was off on his own at the time of the accident?"

"Only what Mr. Kurtz told me."

"Again, don't get into that Marlin," Kurtz said.

Jim decided to shift gears. "Let's go over the day of the accident, Mr. Reeves. When was the first time you saw Danny on that day?"

"When he got to work around seven in the morning."

"Did you notice anything unusual about him?"

"No. He was in a good mood. He'd got tickets for a Ranger game that weekend for him and the family."

Jim straightened. Here was something Laura hadn't told him. Had she forgotten about the tickets?

"When did he leave the terminal?" Jim asked.

Reeves narrowed his eyes. "Seems like it was around seven thirty. The truck was already loaded."

"Did you see him after that?"

"Yes, I did. He came back in after lunch to reload."

"Was that unusual?"

"No. He had to reload every day to take care of the afternoon customers."

"How was he when he came back in?"

"The same. Nothing unusual about him. He was still feeling good. Joking and smiling just like he always did."

Reeves's testimony surprised Jim. He had expected sullen hostility and he wasn't getting it. Marlin had obviously liked Danny. Jim sipped his coffee, then leaned forward. "Where was he going that afternoon?"

"He had a run up into Wise County."

"When did he get started on it?"

"He logged out of the terminal just after one."

"Mr. Reeves you said earlier Danny was overdue getting back that day. When did you first become aware of that?"

"I started worrying about him around seven o'clock. He should have been through with the Wise County run and back in before then."

"Do you know when the accident happened?"

"I understand it was around six."

"Without the accident he'd have been back in by six-thirty, wouldn't he?"

"Sure. But he really should have been back in by five. He only had a few customers on that run."

"How was the weather that day?"

"Terrible. It rained hard all afternoon."

"Is it possible the storm threw him behind?"

"That's sure possible."

Jim put his hands on the table. "It's true isn't it, Mr. Reeves, that just because Danny was late doesn't mean he went off and got drunk?"

"That's very true Mr. McSpadden."

"Why wouldn't you talk about the case with Laura McSpadden at the funeral?"

Reeves nodded toward Art. "Mr. Kurtz told me he was investigating the case and I shouldn't be talking about it."

"Seems like Mr. Kurtz knows more about what happened than you do."

Reeves laughed. "I'm sure that's true."

"Maybe we oughta be taking his deposition."

"Maybe you should."

"Thank you, Mr. Reeves. That's all the questions I have today. I'll pass the witness."

Kurtz looked around the room. "Who's next?"

Rolly leaned forward with his jaw set. "Are you telling us, Mr. Reeves, that as Danny Marcus's supervisor you have no personal knowledge to support Alamo's claim that he had left the course of his employment at the time of the accident?"

Reeves nodded."That's right. I didn't see him after he left the terminal the second time."

"Do you even know the name of the witness who's making that claim?"

"No I don't."

Rolly drew back with a knowing look. "That's all I have at this time."

"Anyone else?" Kurtz asked.

J. Michael Meador moved his chair forward. "I have a few questions for you Mr. Reeves."

"I'll try to answer them."

"I represent Harrigan Motor Company. Did you know my client has been dragged into this lawsuit because of Mr. McSpadden's half-baked contention that something was wrong with the Harrigan truck involved in the accident?"

Jim's pulse pounded but he kept his voice under control. "I object to the argumentative question."

Meador turned toward Jim, eyes narrowed. "Why don't you save your objection for the judge?"

"Because the witness can't answer your question without agreeing with the way you've characterized my client's cross-action. It's an improper question."

Meador put his hands on the table, clenching them into fists. "This is intolerable. If you're going to interfere with my cross-examination, let's adjourn the deposition and reconvene it before the court."

Art Kurtz spread his arms in a soothing gesture. "Take it easy Mike. Just rephrase your question and let's go on. I think you'll find this witness doesn't have anything bad to say about your truck."

Meador turned again to Reeves. "Do you know of anything that was wrong with the truck?"

"No sir."

"How many Harrigan trucks did Alamo have?"

"Six or seven."

"Do know of anything going wrong with the steering on any of them at any time?"

"No sir."

Meador nodded. "Thank you Mr. Reeves."

"Anyone else?" Kurtz asked.

Alfred Escamillo, Linda Fuller, and Keith Carroll shook their heads.

"That's it then, Marlin" Kurtz said.

Reeves got up. He nodded at the lawyers. "Nice to meet ya'll."

Kurtz went out with Marlin and returned with the next witness. Small, shabby Elwood Lee had nicotine-stained fingers and brown, weatherbeaten skin, and wore khaki coveralls with the Alamo logo on the pocket. Looking scared to death, he took the witness chair with downcast eyes, staring at his hands on the table.

Jim asked Lee about his background. Born and raised in Fort Worth, he had worked for Alamo as a mechanic for the past ten years.

"Did you know Danny Marcus Mr. Lee?"

Elwood looked up. "I sure did."

"How did you come to know him?"

"I worked on his truck several times."

"You mean the Harrigan Motor Company truck he drove for Alamo?"

"Yes."

Jim showed Lee the truck records Kurtz had furnished describing Danny's complaints.

"Are these notes in your handwriting?" Jim asked.

Lee nodded. "Yeah."

"And did you talk to Danny personally before you made them?"

"Yeah I did."

"What did he tell you was wrong with the truck?"

J. Michael Meador half rose from his seat. "I object. Calls for hearsay."

"Go ahead and answer," Jim told the witness. "The judge'll rule on Mr. Meador's objections later when we go to court."

Lee swallowed hard. "He said he was driving down the road and the steering froze up so he couldn't turn the wheel."

"How many times did that happen?"

"He brought it in twice within two months."

"Was his complaint the same each time?"

"Yeah."

"What did you do to check it out?"

"Both times I drove the truck myself, got down under it, put it on the rack, tested it every way I knew how."

"Could you tell what was causing the problem?"

Meador slapped the table. "I object to the form of the question. You're assuming there was a problem."

Jim clenched his fists, then relaxed. There was no point in arguing with the asshole. He was right on this one. "I appreciate your pointing out my error Mr. Meador. I'll rephrase the question. Did you find a problem, Mr. Lee."

The little man shrugged. "I didn't find nothin'."

"Did you have any idea what might have caused the steering to stiffen up as Danny had described?"

Meador hit the table again. "I object. The question calls for speculation."

Jim stared at Meador. "We certainly wouldn't want the witness to speculate would we?"

"No we wouldn't."

Jim beamed a reassuring smile at Lee. "Just tell what you know."

The witness shrank down in his chair. "Like I said, I didn't find nothin'."

"Did you think Danny really was having trouble with the steering?"

"I object, invites speculation," Meador intoned.

"Go ahead and answer," Jim said.

"Danny thought somethin' was wrong but I couldn't find it."

End of the road, Jim thought. Nothing else to ask. "I'll pass the witness."

Meador leaned forward, fire in his eye. "Mr. Lee, I understand Alamo has six or seven Harrigan trucks."

"We got six of 'em."

"Did any of the other drivers ever complain about a steering problem with any of them?"

Elwood shook his head."No."

"Do you know of there ever being any problem?"

"They broke down sometimes."

"But I'm talking about steering problems. Were there ever any steering problems with the Harrigan trucks?"

"Not that I know of."

"And as one of the mechanics you'd know if there had been any trouble wouldn't you?"

"Probably would."

"Thank you Mr. Lee. That's all the questions I have."

Kurtz looked at Rolly. "Any questions?"

"I think Mike's covered everything," Rolly said.

"Anyone else?" Kurtz asked.

The other lawyers shook their heads.

Kurtz smiled. "You're through Elwood."

Lee frowned. "Did I do okay Mr. Kurtz?"

"You did just fine. Go on back to the terminal."

When Elwood Lee had gone Kurtz smiled at the other lawyers. "What's the next act in this circus counselors?"

Rolly stuck out his chin again. "I need to depose your mystery witness."

Kurtz laughed. "I think you'll be interested in what she has to say. You'll get her name next week."

"How soon can we set up her depo?"

"Pretty fast. How does your calendar look about three weeks from now?"

"I'll call you in a couple of days and let you know."

"I'll get it all set up as soon as we pick a date."

The attorneys and court reporter started packing up to leave. Mike Meador walked around the conference table to where Jim and Al Hildebrand stood. He set his briefcase on the table. "How soon can you get my client out of this charade?" he asked without offering to shake hands.

Jim stepped back, returning Meador's icy stare. "I'm not quite ready to do that Mr. Meador."

"I don't see why not. It oughta be pretty obvious to you after Elwood Lee's deposition that you don't have a case against Harrigan."

"I need to take Gerald Forbes's deposition."

"You *what*?" Meador asked, incredulous.

"To take Gerald Forbes's deposition."

"He's the president of the company. He doesn't have time to jack with you."

"Isn't he familiar with the truck design?"

"Sure he's familiar with it. Lots of people are familiar with that design. Several of the engineers can tell you all about it."

"But I want to ask Mr. Forbes."

"Well, I'm not about to agree to that. And I'll tell you another thing. If you don't let me out of this lawsuit in pretty short order, I'm filing a motion for summary judgment and sanctions. How would you like to pay the thirty thousand dollars in legal fees my client's already incurred?"

Jim laughed. "You must be kidding. There's no way you could have done more than a few thousand dollars worth of work at this point."

"You can bet I'm not kidding. We take these cases seriously even when they're patently frivolous. The costs and fees mount up quickly. And my client shouldn't have to pay to fight a case it shouldn't have been dragged into in the first place."

Jim nodded slowly. "So that's the way it's gonna be. Well, I tell you what Mr. Meador, you go ahead and file your motions and I'll file my notice to take Harrigan's deposition. We'll get a hearing and let Judge Ferreira decide what I can and can't do."

Meador looked at the floor, lips pressed in a hard line. "Don't say I didn't warn you." He grabbed his briefcase, spun away, and left the room.

Al Hildebrand chuckled. "Same old Mike."

"Is he always that big a turd?"

"Always."

Jim and Hildebrand left the conference room and headed across the reception area toward the elevators.

"Mike's right about one thing," Hildebrand said.

"What's that?"

"We didn't get much out of the depositions today."

"I didn't really expect to."

"What's next then?"

"I want to see what Art's mystery witness says about Danny. Then we'll get a hearing with Judge Ferreira and have it out with Meador."

"I hope you know what you're doing."

"So do I."

∞

Rolly met Bill Biggers in the hallway outside the large conference room in the old Bexar County courthouse where the initial hearing of Roger Lombardo's grievance against Rolly was scheduled. A hearty-looking man with a high-domed bald head, substantial jowels and an overhanging gut, Biggers advanced as Rolly came off the elevator.

He took Rolly's arm. "Let's talk a minute."

Rolly allowed himself to be led to the end of the hall where they sat on a bench.

"How does it look?" Rolly asked, nervous in spite of his strong sense of self-justification.

Biggers shrugged. "No way to tell. It's not good though. We know they're out to get you."

"Is Lombardo here yet?"

"They're talking to him now. He was scheduled half an hour before you."

"Don't I get to hear what he has to say?"

Biggers shook his head. "Not the way they're doing these hearings these days. They talk to the complaining party first, then the accused lawyer."

"Seems like I oughta be able to listen to him."

"You'll get to listen to him all right, if they decide to sustain the grievance. We'll end up in court and he'll be the main witness against you."

Rolly leaned forward, arms across his knees. What a nuisance. He'd done nothing wrong—just given the accident victims a chance to get a good lawyer. Now he had to waste his time with this farce.

"What's likely to happen today?" he asked.

"Probably nothing. They won't make a decision right away. This is just an investigative hearing. Later, if they find just cause for the grievance they may recommend a sanction."

"What do you think they'll want?"

"No way to tell. Could be anything from a reprimand to disbarment."

"The dirty bastards!"

Hobbs smiled. "I know what you think but there's some real danger for you in this complaint. How would you feel about accepting a reprimand? That wouldn't hurt you much."

Rolly twisted his mouth. "Fuck 'em. I'm not agreeing to anything."

Bill nodded. "That's what I thought you'd say."

Down the hall the door of the conference room opened and little, grey-haired Roger Lombardo stepped out, followed by the grievance committee chairman, Ronald Hobbs, a tall man with a hatchet-thin, self-righteous face. He was chief of the litigation section for a glitzy downtown San Antonio law firm of sixty attorneys. Lombardo looked toward Rolly and Bill Biggers. His face colored and his mouth tightened in a bitter line. He turned away and walked to the elevators.

Hobbs nodded to Biggers. "We're ready for you now."

Rolly followed Bill into the conference room. Several folding tables had been set up at the front. Behind them sat the members of the Texas State Bar grievance committee for San Antonio and the surrounding area. Hobbs took a seat in the center of the group. He and five others made up the committee. All but one of the six members were lawyers.

Biggers had given Rolly the names of the committee. Rolly knew three of them besides Hobbs: Lewis McKinley, a black general practice lawyer; Juan Saenz, like Rolly a personal injury lawyer but with a much more modest practice; and Anthony Lakewood, a big firm lawyer who represented commercial interests. Clyde Cantrell, a dentist appointed by the State Bar president to represent the lay point of view, and Alice Wilson, a woman lawyer who did mostly divorce work, rounded out the committee.

It had more lawyers who represented the little guy than business and insurance attorneys but that fact gave Rolly little comfort. In some ways lawyers with people-oriented practices resented him more than the others did. Rolly and Biggers took seats on the opposite side of the table from the committee members. Hobbs studied some documents on the table for several seconds then looked up, face stern.

He looked at Rolly. "Good morning Mr. Sullivan. It's nice to see you again." His voice held ironic overtones.

Rolly presented a disarming smile. "Good morning Ronald. I'm glad to be here."

Hobbs continued. "We've just heard from Roger Lombardo who filed the complaint against you. He's made a very serious charge that you violated Disciplinary Rule 7.03 by directly soliciting the victims of an accident for representation. His allegations, if proven, would also support a criminal indictment for barratry under Section 38.12 of the Texas Penal Code. Our function here today is to take evidence for an investigation to determine if there is just cause to proceed further."

Bill Biggers cleared his throat. "Rolly understands the charges against him Ronald. He's here to answer your questions."

Hobbs flashed an icy smile. "Very well then. I'll ask the first one. Mr. Sullivan, how did you come to be present at a meeting that was promoted by psychologist Nadine Graves as free grief counseling for the victims of a multiple vehicle traffic accident?"

Rolly thought it best to be brazen. "I sponsored the session."

Hobbs drew himself up. "What do you mean, you sponsored it?"

"Just that. I asked Mrs. Graves to provide the session and I paid for the costs of the hotel meeting room."

"Did you also put her up to writing letters to all the victims informing them of the session?"

Biggers spoke quickly. "Could you use a little different phrasing Ronald? Suggesting that Rolly 'put someone up' to something suggests a bias on the part of the committee."

Hobbs smiled. "We surely don't want to show any bias. Just tell us Mr. Sullivan, did you ask Mrs. Graves to write those letters?"

"We talked about it."

"You approved then?"

"Sure. No one would have come if they hadn't known about it."

Dentist Clyde Cantrell, a fleshy man with a perspiring red face, raised his hand.

Hobbs nodded to him. "Yes, Dr. Cantrell?"

The doctor held his hands out, palms facing. "Let me get this straight Mr. Sullivan. You paid for the room, asked Mrs. Graves to invite the people, and then used the session to promote your services?"

"I wouldn't put it that way," Rolly said. "It was basically a free counseling session. At the end I covered some of the legal aspects of the wreck and some of the folks decided to employ me to represent them."

"How many of them did that Mr. Sullivan?"

"Three families signed contracts that night and several others employed me later."

The dentist stared at Rolly. "Don't you know you're not supposed to directly solicit accident victims?"

Rolly returned Dr. Cantrell's look. "That isn't what I did."

"What would you call it, then?"

"Providing a free service and being there if they needed me."

Cantrell leaned back, shaking his head.

Anthony Lakewood raised his patrician head with a look of cold disdain. "Mr. Sullivan we've just heard from the complaining witness who told us he went to your session in good faith to share his sorrow with others who had suffered losses only to be greeted with a closing pitch from you worthy of the crassest used car salesman. Weren't you ashamed to represent your profession in that way?"

Again Biggers spoke. "I know this is an informal session but I really think we should stay away from argumentative questions."

Lakewood put on a thin smile. "I'll withdraw that question and ask another. Mr. Sullivan, how can you justify this kind of conduct?"

Rolly seethed with contempt for this holier than thou hypocrite. How many business clients had he massaged away from other attorneys through questionable means during his career?

With difficulty Rolly kept his voice cordial. "It's easy Tony. There's nothing wrong with a tasteful presentation of the legal aspects of the case coupled with an opportunity for the people to discuss their options. There was no hard sell involved. I think the presentation I made at Mrs. Graves's counseling session falls under the protection of the United States Constitution as commercial free speech."

"That's your opinion?"

"That's my opinion."

Biggers put his hands on the table. "We'll be glad to provide the committee a brief on that point."

Lakewood turned to Bill with a look of disgust. "I appreciate that offer Mr.

Biggers. However, I already have my own opinion on the limits of commercial free speech. We've considered the issue before."

Bill assumed a sincere look. "All we can ask is that you keep your minds open."

Lakewood laughed. "We'll look at anything you have to show us."

Hobbs beamed a questioning look at the other committee members. Juan Saenz was staring uncomfortably at the table top. He'd sent cases to Rolly in the old days and they'd always gotten along together. Lewis McKinley and Alice Wilson shook their heads.

"I think we understand the facts," Hobbs said. "We'll adjourn this hearing at this time and issue a decision in several weeks."

Hobbs and the other members rose and started gathering their papers and briefcases. Rolly followed Biggers into the hall.

"That didn't go so good did it?" Rolly asked.

Biggers smiled. "No it didn't. You're not gonna win this grievance at this level."

"Juan Saenz won't want to find against me."

"He's just one man. And even he may feel the evidence compels them to take action."

"Thanks for your confidence."

"I didn't promise you anything and you're entitled to the straight truth."

"I appreciate that Bill. I don't give a damn what they do. Screw 'em. We'll see 'em in court."

"That seems to be where we're headed."

Rolly left the courthouse, got his Jaguar from the private parking slot he maintained and drove toward the office. The attitude of the grievance committee didn't surprise him. Promoting Nadine's counseling session had been a calculated risk. Rolly had known he'd get little sympathy if there was a complaint and a complaint like Lombardo's had been predictable.

But things weren't as cut and dried as the good members of the committee believed. It was true that no United States Supreme Court case stated directly that in-person, uninvited solicitation of accident victims was justified and protected as commercial free speech.

On the other hand, no case from the nation's highest court had said such contacts weren't protected and the court's cases dealing with attempts to restrict lawyer advertising suggested strongly, at least to Rolly, that lawyers had a right to approach accident victims and offer their services. Until the United States Supreme Court said he couldn't do it he'd continue to contact accident victims directly even if he had to put his license on the line. The grievance committee could bite his butt.

At Zarzamora and Culebra Rolly impulsively turned to the right and drove several blocks north on Zarzamora toward the site of the office he and Pedro had opened together almost twenty-five years earlier. They'd both come out of the Bexar County District Attorney's office full of confidence in their talents and ready to set the world on fire. Time had borne out their ambitions. The firm of Sullivan and Ávila had achieved success beyond the dreams of most lawyers.

Rolly slowed as he approached the now-dilapidated strip center where they had started out. It had been a nice, fairly new line of shops in those days. Now, trash drifted across the rutted, chug-holed parking lot. The signs above the storefronts needed painting. A tacquería occupied the space where Rolly and Pedro's office had been. María Elizondo's quincianera botique still had the corner slot but Jorge Gonzalez's small auto parts store had folded and its window displayed a For Lease sign in English and Spanish.

A lump formed in Rolly's throat as he recalled the struggle of the early days, all the cases, large, small and medium-sized, they'd handled over the years. They hadn't really come too far. For all their success they were still outsiders and would never be part of the respectable legal community. That was fine. Rolly liked it like that. The fatuous bastards could stuff it. He'd succeeded in spite of them and they hated him for it.

He passed the strip center, turned at the next corner, and drove through busy mid-afternoon traffic toward the office. He thought of his father whose troubles had led Rolly to follow the law. Mike Sullivan of Newark, New Jersey, had come to San Antonio in the army and had been stationed at Fort Sam Houston where he was a diesel engine specialist.

Small like Rolly with an angular jaw and red complexion, Mike married a local girl and stayed in San Antonio when his enlistment was up. He got a job servicing diesel trucks for Bill Miller Peterbilt and worked there fifteen years. Rolly's mother Sarah, small and blonde, was the daughter of a cabinet maker and a cashier in a dry goods store.

The Sullivans had five children. Rolly was the oldest. They lived in a modest home on a shaded street in an old neighborhood several miles east of the downtown. A normal working class family, they had no particular worries except Mike's occasional drunken bouts and infidelities until the accident.

Rolly remembered his mother's face when the call came in.

"Oh my God," she'd said, voice anguished, her prematurely lined face ashen.

"What is it, mama?" Rolly, a precocious sixteen year old, asked when she put the phone down.

"Your dad's been hurt. We gotta get to the hospital."

Rolly helped bundle the four smaller kids in the car and they drove to the Santa Rosa Medical Center where Mike lay near death from head and spinal injuries. A co-employee had failed to set the brake on a truck and it had rolled from a hydraulic lift, striking Mike in the back and hurling him across the room into a post. Rolly remembered camping out in the hospital visitor's room for several days until the outcome was determined: Mike would live but would never walk again.

Worker's comp paid a paltry sixteen thousand dollars, all that was owed under the law of that day for a worker who was permanently disabled. Eventually Mike came home to sit embittered in his wheelchair while the family finances went to ruin. In spite of Sarah's double shifts at the greasy spoon where she worked as a waitress, they lost everything. They moved into a cramped low rent apartment when the bank foreclosed on their home.

It had seemed incredible to Rolly that nothing could be done. His father had been hurt through no fault of his own and all Bill Miller Peterbilt owed was the sixteen thousand dollars paid by its worker's comp carrier. Rolly decided to study law so he could learn how to make a difference for people like his father.

He'd done well in the Saint Mary's Law School. Its degrees didn't have the prestige of those from the University of Texas or SMU or east coast institutions like Harvard and Yale but the small school on the west side of San Antonio enjoyed healthy respect in the Texas legal community.

He'd been the editor of the law review and close to the top of his graduating class. Many top business-oriented law firms around the state had interviewed him but the idea of working for any of them turned his stomach. He wasn't about to betray his principles and go over to the enemy.

Instead, he'd taken a job with the Bexar County District Attorney's Office where he'd broken in as a lawyer prosecuting crooks for everything from petty theft to murder. But personal injury work drew him like a magnet. After a few years he and Pedro had opened their storefront office.

In the ensuing time Rolly had won hundreds of recoveries for injured workers that exceeded by many times the pittances they had received from worker's compensation insurance. He couldn't always make a difference. Sometimes the liability just wasn't there or there was no deep-pocketed insurance company or business concern liable to pay. But he'd made a big difference for a lot of people, to his immense satisfaction and personal profit.

As he approached the office he cleared the grievance from his mind. Biggers would do a good job and Rolly was prepared for a long fight. In the meantime he'd concentrate on what he did best: preparing and trying personal injury cases. Sometime this week Art Kurtz would have to reveal his mystery witness in Richaud versus Alamo Oil Company.

Kurtz had referred to the witness as a woman. Was she going to claim to be Danny's girl friend? What could she say that would take Danny out of the course and scope of his employment with Alamo so Alamo's reinsurance coverage wasn't liable? Rolly would waste no time in scheduling her deposition. He had to know what she'd say before he did anything else.

∽

On the weekend after Thanksgiving Travis sat beside Jim in the pickup as they drove on Highway 180 west of Mineral Wells. The weeks since Jim's last visitation weekend had passed quickly with all the work on Laura's case and Jim's turn had come around again. He'd spent Thanksgiving day alone in the town house watching football and feeling sorry for himself. Today he and Travis would belatedly celebrate the holiday with Jim's parents at Possum Kingdom Lake.

A spell of misty, raw weather had given way to a crisp Saturday with a cloudless blue sky and bright sunshine enhancing the contrast between the evergreen cedar trees on the hills and the somber browns and yellows of range grasses along the road.

"How you coming on your Eagle?" Jim asked.

"Pretty good. I only need six more merit badges."

"When you think you'll get it?"

Travis shrugged. "I dunno. Maybe next spring."

Travis's advancement to the Eagle rank had been a hope of Jim's for several years.

"You have to work at it, son or it'll never happen."

Out of the corner of his eye Jim saw Travis's look of irritation.

"Scouts is kinda boring these days dad."

"It'd be a shame not to make Eagle, having come this far."

"I do want to do it but basketball season's coming up. I'll be too busy the next couple of months."

"When's the first game?"

"We've got a tournament in two weeks."

"Is it at Cottonwood Springs?"

Travis nodded. "Yes."

"I'll be there. I want you to do good with your basketball. It may be your ticket to college. I'll help you with the merit badges after basketball season, if this big case I'm working on doesn't swallow me up."

"What kind of case is it?"

As they drove Jim told Travis about Laura's case, the problems he was having with it, and the uncertainty of success. He turned and drove north through a series of sweeping hills to the town of Graford, then turned west again. Twenty minutes later he pulled onto the park road that ran onto the peninsula, an area of high ground that had been inside a bend of the Brazos River before the river had been dammed between a line of cliffs to form Possum Kingdom Lake.

Now the lake snaked back from the dam for many miles, first penned between the twisted cliffs, then broadening into a wider expanse of clear water. They passed a series of bait shops, marine stores, and other roadside business, then a pioneer cemetery. At the peninsula's narrowest point the road ran along a ridge and the land fell away to the lake on either hand.

Beyond the ridge Jim turned onto a narrow road running through a thicket of cedars to a series of lake houses, some imposing, substantial structures, others modest cabins. At the end of the road he pulled into the driveway of the small house with wood shingled exterior where his parents had lived since their retirement.

As Jim and Travis got out of the car Jim's father came out to meet them. A large man, Lloyd McSpadden had sandy hair streaked with grey and a red complexion.

"Ya'll have a good trip out?" he asked.

Jim nodded. "Real good."

Lloyd grinned at Travis. "You ready for some fishing?"

"Can we eat first?"

"You bet. Your grandmother's got it almost ready."

In the living room with knotty pine walls, the smell of roast turkey filled the air. Jim's small, white-haired mother, Rose, came in from the kitchen, wiping her hands on her apron.

She hugged Travis. "You're getting taller all the time. When you gonna stop growing?"

"Don't know grandma. Not for a while I hope. I need two more inches to play college basketball."

"Don't I get a hug?" Jim asked.

She hugged him. "I've always got a hug for my little boy."

Jim kissed her on the cheek.

"How's that turkey coming?" Jim's father asked.

"Everything's ready. Come on in and let's eat."

Rose had fixed a full Thanksgiving dinner with turkey, cornbread dressing, homemade cranberry sauce, mashed potatoes and giblet gravy, and pumpkin pie. As always it seemed strange to Jim to have the holiday meal the weekend after Thanksgiving but they had followed this procedure since Jim's divorce.

Travis and his mother always spent Thanksgiving with her family. With Jim their only child it didn't inconvenience his parents to alter the Thanksgiving schedule. It saved a frantic rush to shuffle Travis between families on Thanksgiving day. After dinner they all helped clear the table and wash the dishes.

Lloyd put the last dish back in the cabinet. "Now let's go fishing."

Rose frowned. "Ya'll gonna run off and leave me by myself?"

"Don't worry mama," Jim said. "Take a nap. Plenty of time to talk this evening."

She laughed. "Just kidding. Get out of here and give me some peace."

Jim and his father and son walked down a gentle slope to the boat dock where a pontoon boat with a gay canopy lay in a slip. Jim carried a cooler with beer and soft drinks and Travis carried the rods and tackle boxes. On board Lloyd started the motor and backed the boat from the dock. A soft breeze from the south rippled the water.

Lloyd turned the boat and advanced the throttle and they knifed their way across the lake. Jim pulled a bottle of Pearl out of the cooler, popped the cap, and took a drink. The beer tasted good.

A jumble of half-submerged large rocks marked the approaching shoreline. Between them, the bare branches of long-dead trees, drowned when the lake was formed, thrust upward like arms. Lloyd killed the motor and tied the boat to one of the limbs.

Silently they baited their lines with purple-hued artificial worms. Jim cast his line between two of the dead trees near shore and slowly retrieved the worm with no effect, then tried again. Travis fished parallel to the line of trees, keeping his line well away from the snags, while Lloyd put his worm almost into the maze of brush, jerking it lightly to keep it from sinking and snagging. A red-tailed hawk sailed above them.

After twenty minutes with no strikes Lloyd pulled in his line. "I'm gonna move down to the next inlet."

Jim and Travis reeled in their lures and Lloyd started the motor. As they moved slowly parallel with the shore Travis reached in the cooler and pulled out one of the Pearls. He looked at Jim who shook his head.

"Better not. Wouldn't want to contribute to the delinquency of a minor."

"I'll take that," Lloyd said.

Travis handed the beer to his grandfather then got out a Pepsi for himself. Lloyd stopped the boat near a group of dead trees beside the channel where a small creek entered the lake.

He tied the boat to a snag. "Almost always catch something here."

This time Lloyd caught a several pound bass on his first cast. His line stiffened with the strike and the fish quickly broke water.

"Don't let him get tangled in the trees," Travis said.

Lloyd smiled. "You trying to tell me how to fish?"

Expertly, he played the fish away from the branches to the side of the boat where he lifted it with a net.

He held it and took the hook from its mouth. "This one's a nice eatin' size." He tossed it in the live well between the seats.

Travis had stopped to watch his grandfather land the fish. Now he cast again, almost into the branches of the dead tree they had tied up to. Carefully, he jigged the worm up and down, then let it sink slowly. The line suddenly tightened and Travis flicked his wrist to set the hook in the way Jim had taught him.

The fish broke the water in a tight curve, its body bent in frantic contortions, the white of its belly in contrast with the dark scales of its back.

"That's a good 'un," Lloyd said. "Don't let him get in the trees."

Travis kept his eyes on his line. "You tryin' to tell me how to fish?"

Lloyd laughed. "I'll shut up." He drank from his beer.

Travis played the fish to the side of the boat and Jim slipped the net under it.

"He'll go five or six pounds," Jim said.

His father nodded. "Mighty nice bass."

They stayed in the creek mouth for another hour and all of them caught fish, though Travis's big one was the best of the day. Finally in late afternoon, they headed back for the house. The live well held eight or ten bass which they'd clean before they went into the house for holiday conversation. It was shaping up to be a great weekend.

∽

Late the next afternoon Jim pulled into the driveway of his former home and parked near the front door. He walked with Travis up the walk. Ellen met them at the door.

"Ya'll have a good time?"

Jim nodded. "We sure did."

"How're your mother and father?"

"Just fine."

"That's good. I need to talk to you."

"What about?"

Ellen looked at Travis. "We need to visit a while honey."

124

"See you later dad." Travis went into the house.

"What's the deal?" Jim asked.

Ellen's green eyes assumed the sincere expression she affected when she wanted something. "I need more child support Jim."

He shook his head. "I'm having trouble making the payments already."

"Oh come on. You always made good money. Think of Travis. I need to get him a car."

"I thought the real estate business was booming."

"It is. I'm doing fine. But it's only fair that you do your part."

Jim chopped the air with his hands. "Christ Ellen, You don't know how bad things are for personal injury lawyers these days."

"I can't believe you can't afford a car for your son."

"Is that what you want? A car for Travis? I might could do that. But give me a couple of months. Things are really tight right now."

Ellen folded her arms. "Okay Jim. I'll wait two months. I'd sure rather work this out than have to go back to court. But I'm gonna need more monthly child support too. Cars are expensive to operate."

"They damn sure are. I'm having trouble keeping my own running. But I'll do something in about two months."

Her eyes softened. "I'm sorry to have to bother you with this."

"Think nothing of it," Jim said, tight-lipped.

As he drove toward his town house, all the good feeling of the weekend left him. He couldn't even have a holiday with his son without his ex-wife dunning him for money. Money he didn't have. But he'd show her. One way or another he'd get Travis a car. And in the process he'd find the money to fund Laura's case against Harrigan Motors, even if he had to kiss all his hard-earned savings goodby.

# 8

Rolly studied Norvella Poteet while court reporter Bill Bittinger swore her in. She sat at Art Kurtz's conference table, a small, scrawny woman with coarse black hair streaked with grey wearing a print dress covered with large red roses on a saffron background. All the lawyers in the case clustered around the table. Court reporter Bittinger sat poised at his stenograph machine, ready to report the deposition.

Outside the tall windows the late autumn sun shone brightly but Rolly's mind wasn't on the good weather. What did this woman know and why had Kurtz identified her as the witness who could prove Danny had got drunk and abandoned his job? She sure didn't look like anyone's girlfriend. Danny had undoubtedly been drunk but under what circumstances? The investigator Rolly had hired had scoured the bars of Fort Worth for information and learned nothing.

"Good afternoon," Rolly said in a charming tone.

The woman looked up, eyes suspicious. "Afternoon," she said, her voice cracked and hoarse.

"Is it Miss or Mrs. Poteet?"

"I'm a Mrs."

Rolly nodded. "I thought so. Mrs. Poteet, I'm Rolly Sullivan, and I represent a number of people who have suffered as a result of the accident involved in this lawsuit. I'd like to ask you some questions about it."

"I don't know nothin' about it."

Rolly straightened. "What do you mean?"

"I don't know nothin' about the wreck."

"You must know something about it or we wouldn't be here."

"What I know is, that man was in my place the afternoon it happened."

"What man?"

"Marcus."

"How do you know it was him?"

"Seen his picture in the paper afterward."

Rolly sipped his coffee. The woman sounded confident, almost belligerent.

"Where is your place Mrs. Poteet?"

126

"Up north of Decatur off Highway 287."

"What kind of place is it?"

"It's a little bar and café."

So that was it. Rolly's investigator had struck out because Danny hadn't done his drinking in Fort Worth.

"I thought Wise County was dry."

Norvella laughed. "Most of it is. But we got one wet precinct and that's where my place is."

"Had you ever seen Marcus before that day?"

She shook her head. "Sure hadn't."

Rolly leaned forward, capturing her eyes with his. "You mean to tell me you can positively identify a man who you'd never seen before just by his picture in the paper?"

"That wasn't all."

"What else was there?"

"He had that Alamo Oil patch on his uniform."

Across the table Jim McSpadden's face had turned red. He was no poker player. He was sure a big, goofy looking son of a bitch with that two-tone beard and wispy blond hair. And he oughta do something about his wardrobe. That sports coat had seen better days.

Rolly didn't show his feelings. He kept his face impassive. Mustn't let the witness know she had him just about convinced she knew what she was talking about. Besides, she hadn't hurt him, yet. Everyone knew, or should know, that Danny had been drinking somewhere. Why not up in Wise County?

"How'd Marcus get there?" Rolly asked.

Norvella shrugged. "Don't know."

"You didn't see his truck?"

"It might've been parked out on the highway. I didn't look."

"Tell me everything that happened from the time he came in the door until he left."

Mrs. Poteet leaned forward, elbows on the table, with a look of satisfaction. She was plainly enjoying the limelight.

"It was about two o'clock and raining cats and dogs. Mr. Marcus came in and took a seat at a back table. I asked did he want a menu and he said no, just bring him a beer and a hamburger."

Rolly held up his hand to stop her. "What kind of beer?"

The witness wrinkled her forehead. "Don't remember. Seems like it was Lone Star."

"Go on."

"Well, he finished that one in about three minutes and I give him another when I brought out his hamburger. He put a bunch 'a change in the jukebox and set there for two hours drinking 'em as fast as I could bring 'em out."

"What kind of music did he play?"

"Country music. That's all I got."

"How many beers did he drink?"

"Eight or ten."

"Then he left?"

"Yep. The rain was still coming down but he got up, made a call on the pay phone, then come up to the register and paid his bill. Kinda grinned at me and said he had to get going because he had a hot date in Fort Worth."

Rolly's mouth tightened. Here was the testimony that could beat him—the testimony Kurtz was relying on.

"What time was this?"

"Right around four. Maybe a little after."

"What kind of shape was he in?"

"He was stumblin' a little and not talkin' straight but he wasn't too bad."

"Did he say anything else about the date?" Rolly asked.

Mrs. Poteet shook her head. "Nope."

"Didn't say who it was with?"

"Nope."

Rolly paused. This witness explained how Danny had got drunk and that didn't hurt Rolly. Rolly needed for him to be drunk. But he didn't need him abandoning his route to chase after some woman. Norvella Poteet sure didn't have any details but just the fact that Danny got drunk, said he had a date, and then went back to Fort Worth without finishing his Wise County deliveries could sink Rolly's ship. How could he get to her?

"How many people were in the bar that afternoon?" he asked.

Norvella looked down at the table. "Don't remember. Not many. It was a week day and all that rain kept 'em away."

"Was there anyone else there?"

"I'm sure there was but I don't remember who."

"Don't you have some regulars? Some people who are in every day?"

"Maybe not every day but several times a week."

"Who are some of them?"

"Billy Potter comes in pretty often."

"Who else?"

"Jack Cline and Dan Arnold."

"Anyone else?"

"Those are the regulars."

128

"But you don't remember if any of them were there when Danny Marcus was?"

The witness narrowed her eyes. "Seems like Billy was there part of the time."

"How would I get hold of him?"

"Just come up to the place. I'll show you where he lives."

"Thanks Mrs. Poteet. I'll have my investigator drop by. He'll want to talk to the other regulars, too."

Rolly asked a few more questions, saw he wasn't getting any useful information, and passed the witness.

Kurtz looked around the table with a smug smile. "Who's next?"

McSpadden held up his hand. "I have a few questions for this witness."

"Go ahead Jim."

Rolly saw that the tips of McSpadden's ears still flamed red. Look out big shot, Rolly thought. You can't ask good questions if you're not in control.

McSpadden put his hands on the polished conference table. "Mrs. Poteet, I'm Jim McSpadden, and I represent Danny Marcus's widow. Are you saying that, on the day of the accident, he had a date with another woman?"

Mrs. Poteet shrugged. "All I know is what he said—that he had a hot date."

"And you have no idea what he meant by that?"

"Oh sure. I thought he meant he was going to meet somebody."

"But you don't know who it was?"

"That's right."

McSpadden leaned back in his chair, and the color in his face subsided. "Have you shared this information with the police?"

"Nope, sure haven't."

"Why not?"

"Wasn't no need to. The man's dead. Ain't gonna be no charges against him."

"How did you come to contact Mr. Kurtz?"

"I read in the paper he was Alamo's lawyer. I thought he'd like to know what happened."

"But you didn't think the police would like to have the same information?"

"Didn't seem to be no need to call them."

"Don't you think they'd be interested in why a bar owner would knowingly serve a customer enough beer to get him drunk and then let him get out on the highway with no warning to other motorists?"

"I didn't take that man to raise."

"Did you know you might be liable to all the accident victims for serving a customer that much beer?"

Mrs. Poteet vented a nervous laugh. "I don't have no insurance. If they win, I'll just give 'em the bar. Maybe they'll have better luck with it than I have."

"You said Danny drank eight or ten beers and was stumbling when he went out?"

"He wasn't all that bad. I bet he did some more drinkin' on the way back to Fort Worth."

McSpadden frowned. "You don't know that do you?"

"No I don't. But he had to have to be as drunk as he was at the time of the wreck."

"So he wasn't drunk when he left your place?"

"I'd say he was just happy."

McSpadden nodded. "I see. He was just happy on eight or ten beers. Is it possible he didn't really drink that much?"

Norvella looked relieved. "Sure. I didn't count 'em. Eight or ten was just an estimate."

McSpadden leaned forward, eyes judgmental. "How much are you being paid for your testimony here today?"

Art Kurtz held up his hand. "Hold on before you answer that Mrs. Poteet. I'm going to object to the implication the witness is testifying in return for money."

Rolly thought McSpadden might be onto something. Norvella Poteet looked like the type who'd be in it for the money.

"I'll rephrase the question," McSpadden said. "Are you being reimbursed for your time and expenses here today?"

Norvella nodded. "Mr. Kurtz said he'd pay my travel expenses and for the time away from my place."

"How much does that come to?"

"Five hundred dollars."

"Does your bar bring in that much every day?"

"Not during the week. But it hurts to have to close it down for a whole day."

"I see. Thank you Mrs. Poteet. I'll pass the witness."

"Who's next?" Kurtz asked.

"I'll go next," Mike Meadors said. The big man looked like a fashion ad in his subtle grey suit and bright tie.

"Mrs. Poteet, the fact is that Danny Marcus was in no shape to drive an eighteen wheeler loaded with gasoline or anything else when he left your bar, isn't that true?"

130

"I don't know that's what he was driving."

"Whatever he was driving he shouldn't have been out on the road should he?"

Norvella shrugged. "All I know is, he drunk a lot of beer."

"And you told us that was eight or ten beers in two hours, didn't you?"

"That was just an estimate."

"But it's what you remember?"

"I guess so."

"And Marcus really shouldn't have been driving after that, should he?"

"I guess not—but I didn't know that at the time."

"Thank you Mrs. Poteet. That's all I have today."

Art Kurtz smiled at the witness. "Mrs. Poteet, why did you call me about this accident?"

"Because I thought Alamo Oil would like to know what happened."

"Have you told these lawyers everything you remember about that day, to the best of your recollection?"

"Yes sir."

"And however much beer Danny Marcus had, you do recall him saying he had a date in Fort Worth as he was leaving?"

"I object. Leading question." McSpadden said.

Kurtz acknowledged the objection with a nod. "Go ahead and answer."

"Yes he did. He definitely said that."

Again, Kurtz looked around the room. "Anyone else have any questions?"

Alfred Escamillo shook his bald head. "All mine have been covered."

Linda Fuller, Keith Carroll, and Al Hildebrand all nodded.

"That's it then," Kurtz said. He looked at his watch. "It's only four. Ya'll can all get out of here ahead of most of the traffic."

Clear of downtown Dallas Rolly drove toward Fort Worth on the old turnpike. Norvella Poteet was a problem for him. Danny Marcus had driven his truck back to Fort Worth from Wise County, following a route that would take him back to the Alamo terminal in Parker County. Those facts pointed toward a man who, though drunk, had been doing his employer's business.

On the other hand he had not completed his route and Norvella would testify he said he had a date. The jury could rely on those facts to find Danny had abandoned his work. Her testimony would make the case much harder and would just about guarantee it couldn't be settled.

At least what she said wasn't conclusive. There was still plenty of room for the jury to believe Danny was still working at the time of the wreck. Rolly would have to convince them that was the truth.

Could Jim McSpadden help him on that point? What kind of witness would Mrs. Marcus make on her husband's behalf? Rolly didn't like the idea of dealing with McSpadden. He was a loose cannon with his half-baked claim there had been something wrong with the truck but he had asked some good questions today.Rolly would have to talk to him eventually. In the meanwhile Rolly would have his investigator do some snooping around up in Wise County. Maybe some other witness from the bar would remember things differently.

He checked his watch. Almost five. Nadine wasn't due at the Worthington until eight or nine. Plenty of time for him to go by Angelo's barbecue joint and do some drinking of his own before their session in the hotel room. He'd drive back to San Antonio in the morning.

∽

"Did you know Danny had tickets for a Ranger game the weekend after the wreck?" Jim asked Laura Marcus several days after the Norvella Poteet deposition.

She sat across from him in his office, wearing jeans and an open-collared white blouse. He had asked her to come in that afternoon to talk about developments in the case and to answer the interrogatories J. Michael Meador had sent.

Laura shook her head. "No I didn't. Who said he had them?"

"Marlin Reeves. He said Danny was talking about taking the family to the game before he went out on his Wise County run."

Tears rose in Laura's eyes. "That was so like him. He was always surprising us with something like that."

"We took the deposition of Alamo's mystery witness a couple of days ago."

"Who is she?"

"A lady who owns a bar up north of Decatur. She says Danny came in during the rain, drank eight or ten beers, and left, claiming he had a date with some woman in Fort Worth."

Laura laughed. "That's incredible."

"It sure seems that way. But I have to ask you this. Is there any chance Danny had a girlfriend?"

Laura shook her head. "No way Mr. McSpadden. I'd know if something like that had been going on."

"Are you sure?"

"Yes I am."

Her confidence reassured Jim. Norvella Poteet had to be wrong. Could she have Danny confused with someone else?

"What kind of beer did Danny drink?" Jim asked.

"Coors Light. Sometimes Bud Light."

"Didn't drink Lone Star?"

Her brown eyes smiled. "Sure didn't. Couldn't stand that stuff. Said it tasted like old inner tubes."

"This lady said he was drinking Lone Star."

"That wasn't Danny then."

"Did he like country music?"

She twisted her mouth. "He listened to it, just like we all do. You can hardly get away from it."

"But would he play it on a juke box?"

"No way. He liked older rock and roll."

Jim shook his head. "The whole thing's a big mystery. Danny was acting okay back at the terminal but the blood test from the wreck shows he was drunk and now this woman comes forward to corroborate that he drank a bunch of beer, except it doesn't sound like she's talking about Danny."

"How does all that stack up for me?"

"Not good. I don't know how to refute her testimony."

Laura leaned across the desk, putting her hand on Jim's arm. "You believe me don't you?"

He nodded. "I believe you. But I don't know how to convince a jury we're right."

"What's the next step?"

"I want to take the deposition of Harrigan Motor's CEO and see what he can tell me about the truck steering. But their lawyer, Meador, won't agree to it. We're gonna have a hearing with the judge in a couple of weeks."

Laura's eyes softened. "I've really got you into something haven't I?"

He laughed. "Yes you have."

Jim got out Meador's interrogatories and started going over them. Normally he would have had Susan do this job but Meador was mean as a snake and he'd want to take Laura's deposition, sooner or later. There was no point in giving him ammunition with some answers that weren't just exactly right.

Most of the questions dealt with the history of the Marcus family, where they lived, their education and work experience, and other background matters, but a few of them zeroed in on critical areas.

"Question twenty-two asks if Danny had ever been convicted of a crime," Jim said. "He hadn't been, had he?"

Laura shook her head. "No."

"He didn't have any DWI's?"

"No. Nothing."

"They're gonna do everything they can to bolster that blood test. Are you sure he didn't have a drinking problem?"

"Yes. I told you he didn't drink except socially. He wouldn't drive if he'd had more than one or two."

"Who drove home after the Ranger games?"

"I did."

They slogged relentlessly through Meador's questions. Susan put her solemn face in the door just after five.

"I'm going home, boss. Need anything else?"

"No thanks Susan. We've got everything under control."

"See you tomorrow then." She locked the office door behind her.

Just after seven Jim and Laura finished the drudgery.

Jim leaned back in his office chair. "That oughta do it. I can't think of anything else we need to cover tonight."

Laura looked at her watch. "I'd better get on home. The kids'll be expecting me."

"They're probably hungry."

She laughed. "I'm the hungry one. They'll have eaten by now. I left a casserole in the refrigerator."

Jim had a sudden impulse. "Would you like to have dinner with me?"

She smiled. "I would but I'd better not."

"Why? Those kids can take care of themselves for a few more hours."

"I hate to leave them alone."

"We won't be very late. You deserve a break."

She looked down, eyes thoughtful. "I guess it wouldn't hurt. What did you have in mind?"

"This place downtown has good steaks and live jazz."

"I can't make a night of it."

"I know. I won't keep you out too late."

Laura laughed. "You're pretty persuasive. I'll call and tell them I'm gonna eat before I come home."

Jim slid the phone on his desk toward her. Half an hour later they parked on the street near Jernigan's Jazz Place. Jim escorted Laura to the steps leading down to the cave-like club. She walked ahead of him down the stairs, tall, almost regal, brown hair curling around her slender neck. He was just taking a client to dinner but it seemed much more than that.

In the club the hostess, Billie, smiled as they came in. "Good to see you again Jim. Table for two?"

"Yes. Ya'll have a band tonight?"

"Sure do."

"Who is it?"

"Clifton Cameron and his group."

"When do they start?"

"In about fifteen minutes."

Billie took them through the smoky room to a table against the far wall. They ordered draft beer and the charbroiled steaks that were the specialty of the house from a cryptic waitress with a face lined with hard living. She brought them frosted mugs topped with foam.

Laura buried her nose in her mug and took a drink, then set it down. "That's sure good."

Jim nodded. "There's a lot of pleasure in a cold beer."

"You must be a regular at this place."

"I used to be. I haven't been coming much lately."

"Why'd you stop?"

"I used to come here with my partners. A couple of times a month, we'd come over here and have dinner after work and stay till the place closed. When the partnership broke up, we didn't feel like doing it any more. We got together here for the first time in several years a few weeks ago."

"What caused the breakup?"

"Economic pressure. The personal injury business has been hard lately. We just couldn't bring in enough money any more."

"Sounds like a pretty rough time."

"It was."

She sipped her beer again, then set the mug down. "You're not married are you?"

"I was but I'm not now. How did you know?"

"It's just a feeling I had. When was the divorce?"

"About two years ago."

"All this bad stuff happened about the same time?"

He nodded.

"I'm not the only one with problems," she said.

"Mine are nothing to yours. My wife wasn't killed."

"You still lost her though. Did you love her?"

"Yes I did."

Laura smiled, brown eyes gentle. "Do you still see her?"

"Just when I have visitation with my son."

"How old's he?"

"Sixteen."

"That's just one year older than Eddie."

"How's Eddie doing?"

She shook her head. "I wish he'd smile more. He used to be so happy."

"How about your daughter?"

"She's sleeping better but she still wakes up with nightmares."

"I don't guess they'll ever get over it completely."

"Some things you're not supposed to get over."

Jim looked away toward the bandstand. Clifton Cameron and the group were setting up. The layers of blue smoke cast them in a surreal image. The leader, Cameron, dark brown and sad-eyed, played a snippet from *Bugle Call Rag* on his trumpet; the ragged drummer fired off a warmup routine.

"What about you?" Jim asked.

She shrugged. "I'm still taking it one day at a time. Having the kids to worry about actually makes it easier."

"I know it's hard having to mess with this lawsuit on top of everything else."

"It's important to me," she said, voice intense. "I need to know what happened for my own peace of mind."

"We may never get the truth."

"I know that. But I've got to see it through."

"Don't let it consume you," he said. "It's an important case but it shouldn't control your life."

She spread her hands on the table. "I've got to prove Danny didn't do what they're claiming."

He put his hands over hers. "We may not be able to do that."

"I've got to try."

The waitress brought their salads: romaine lettuce, tomatoes, cucumbers and olives, with a roll of hard bread on a wooden platter.

"Ya'll want another round?" she asked.

Laura shook her head. "Just bring me a glass of water."

"I'll have another beer," Jim said.

At the bandstand Clifton Cameron took the microphone and introduced the group, then led them into an uptempo rendition of *In the Mood*. The crisp notes of Cameron's trumpet bounced off the old plaster walls filling the place with sound.

"How do you like the music?" Jim asked.

"It's nice but I don't listen to jazz much."

"What do you really like?"

"Rock and Roll. Something with lots of blues in it."

"Like ZZ Top?"

She nodded. "That's it."

"I like that too."

"Danny and I went to one of their concerts once. It was great."

The waitress brought them platters filled with steaks and baked potatoes. While they ate the band cycled through a series of jazz classics. On some of the numbers, a slender young black woman with a jubilant smile provided vocal. Jim and Laura were far enough from the bandstand they could still talk.

"Is the law practice really that bad?" Laura asked.

Jim smiled. "It's probably not as bad as I think but there's no doubt the personal injury business is in a slump."

"What happened to cause it?"

"I'm not really sure. Bad publicity, tacky advertising, and too many lawyer jokes. To say nothing of an intense anti-lawyer publicity campaign by business and insurance groups."

"I thought lawyers made a lot of money."

"Some of them still do."

"You sound bitter."

"That's because I am."

She regarded him with solicitous eyes. "What made you want to get into personal injury work anyway?"

He laughed. "I'm asking myself that question a lot these days. To be honest it was a combination of idealism and greed. I thought I could help the little guy and not charge unless I won. And in the process I'd make big bucks."

"And that hasn't worked out for you?"

"There's been times in the past when I did pretty well but I've never been in any danger of getting rich."

"This case of mine must be a problem for you. It sure doesn't look like a money maker at this point."

He put his hand on her arm. "Don't worry about it. I can handle it."

"You'd have been better off with some of Mr. Sullivan's clients."

Jim laughed. "I was supposed to get one of them."

"What do you mean?"

"That guy Richaud was going to come in and see me but Sullivan got to him first."

She leaned forward, eyes shining. "Are you sorry you didn't get him?"

Jim pondered the question. He'd been depressed for days when Richaud had hired Sullivan. That case had seemed a surefire cure for Jim's legal blues. But now he'd come to share Laura's passionate belief in the justice of her cause. And then there was Laura herself. He'd have been against her if he'd taken Richaud's case.

Jim caught her eyes with his own. "No, I'm not sorry. Not sorry at all."

The band launched into a slow, dreamy version of *Am I Blue*. The young woman vocalist sang with her eyes partly closed, projecting the sad mood of the song. A spotlight knifing through the layers of smoke cast her expressive face in sharp relief.

"Laura, would you dance with me?" Jim asked.

She smiled. "Sure."

They moved onto the dance floor. Jim wanted to hold her close but circumspectly kept a distance between them. He took pleasure in the firm feel of her waist under his fingers, her fragrant hair, and solemn brown eyes. They danced slowly without words until the song ended.

Back at the table Laura looked at her watch. "I'd better be going." Several tears ran down her cheeks.

"I'm sorry," Jim said. "I didn't mean to upset you."

She raised her chin. "You didn't upset me. It just seemed strange to be dancing with someone. I haven't gone out since Danny died."

"I wanted to make you feel better."

"You did Jim. This has been good for me. But I'd better be getting home."

They drove back to the office where he located her car on the parking lot. He got out and opened the door of the pickup for her.

She put her hand on his arm. "Thanks for everything."

"I'll call you about the case in a couple of days."

With a pensive smile she turned to her car. As Jim drove through the streets of the west side toward his town house, he saw the neons of the roadside signs, the passing traffic, the darkened buildings, with new eyes. Laura's sadness held him at bay. He could not express the love he felt while her grief was still so fresh but his feeling for her had filled him with a new and welcome gladness.

Around ten o'clock the next day Susan buzzed Jim on the intercom. "You'll never guess who wants to talk to you."

"It must be Joe Bob Savage. He's decided to pay Laura's claim."

"Guess again."

"I give up. Who is it?"

"Rolly Sullivan."

Jim laughed. "What can the great man want with me?" He punched the blinking button. "Hello?"

"Jim?"

"This is Jim McSpadden."

"This is Rolly. I wanted to talk about our case." Sullivan's voice oozed with charm. He had to be wanting something. There was no reason for him to call otherwise.

Jim's fingers tightened around the phone. "What's there to talk about?"

"I know we're more or less on opposite sides but we do have some common ground."

"Not the way I see it. If you win, my client loses."

"That's true all right. It's pretty obvious her husband was drunk and that was the main cause of the accident. That's a burden you have to bear."

"I don't think so Mr. Sullivan. It was out of character for him to get drunk like that. There's been some mistake."

"Now how are you going to prove that Jim?" Sullivan spoke with a condescending tone.

"I don't know but I'm damn sure gonna do it."

Sullivan laughed. "Good luck Jim. But I didn't call to argue. As I said, we do have some common ground."

"What's that?"

"For me to win I have to prove the accident was Danny Marcus's fault but that he was still in the course and scope of his employment. You have to prove the accident wasn't his fault and something was wrong with the truck.

"Now I don't think you have a case against Harrigan. My engineer looked the truck over very carefully and there wasn't anything wrong with it. PILE doesn't have a record of steering problems with Harrigan trucks.

"So I can't agree with your theory of what happened and you can't agree with mine. But it's to our mutual advantage for Danny to have been on the job. If the jury believes he was chasing after some woman we're both sunk."

Jim found himself nodding. "That much is true."

Sullivan continued. "I really have some doubts about this Poteet woman. I think Marcus was in her place and probably drank all that beer but I doubt if he said anything about having a date."

"I can understand why you'd think that way," Jim said. "That's the way you need things to be. I think she's wrong about the whole deal."

"We'll just have to agree to disagree about the drinking. I think Marcus just took a break on a rainy afternoon and overdid it before getting back on the road. Did he have a history of alcoholism?"

"No he didn't."

"How do you know?"

"My client told me he didn't."

"You sure she knows everything there is to know about his drinking history?"

"I think she does but just to be sure I checked the court records. There's nothing on Danny. At least not in this county."

"Well, I'll ask her about that when we take her deposition. But look Jim,

I need to talk to Mrs. Marcus before the deposition. I need to know her slant on this girl friend business."

"I can tell you that. She says he didn't have a girl friend. She'd know if he had."

"I'd expect her to say that. But I'd like to meet her—to see what she's like so I'll know what kind of impression she'll make."

"In other words you want to figure out how to discredit her on the drinking but make her believable on the girl friend?"

"I don't want to attack your lady at all," Sullivan said. "I just want to form my own judgment about her."

Jim paused. Rolly wasn't fooling him. All this good guy stuff was a bunch of crap. He'd never have called Jim if he wasn't worried. There was a lot of satisfaction for Jim in that. Sullivan needed his help. How could Jim turn the situation to his advantage? Sudden inspiration seized him.

"Look Rolly," Jim said, deliberately abandoning his formal tone, "what you say is true. We do have a lot of common ground. It's to our mutual advantage to prove a defect in the truck steering. You haven't even sued Harrigan yet. If I prove a defect on the truck that'll exonerate Danny Marcus and kill your case against Alamo Oil. I'll win and you'll lose.

"I'll make this deal with you. I'll let you talk to Mrs. Marcus if you'll sue Harrigan and help me prove what was wrong with the truck. That way we both win and you don't have to attack my client."

Sullivan answered in a patient, sorrowful tone. "I can't do that Jim. There's no way there was anything wrong with the truck. If I sue Harrigan, it'll just weaken my case against Alamo. I owe it to my clients not to do that."

"I understand your position Rolly. Now you understand mine. I don't have all the clients you do. I only have one client in this case and I owe it to her to protect her in every way I can from undue harassment. You'll just have to wait and talk to her on the record."

"I'm sorry you feel that way, Jim. I'll look forward to Mrs. Marcus's deposition. Of course, I may not be so gentle as if I'd been able to talk to her first."

Jim laughed. "Forewarned is forearmed. I'll be talking to you."

When they had hung up Jim sat at his desk, hands behind his head. He was enjoying Rolly's twisting on the horns of his dilemma. Jim hadn't expected him to join the case against Harrigan although Jim would have welcomed the help even from Rolly.

The many dollars he could have contributed would have eased the financial burden on Jim. But there was no way he would let Sullivan have a preview of Laura's testimony without something in return. Rolly should have known better than to ask.

The next day Jim spent the morning calling insurance adjusters trying to settle cases to get some money flowing. He had several car wrecks that were ripe for settlement. They weren't high damage files but the income would get him through the next several months.

He'd just settled a sexual harassment case for a woman who'd been fired from her job because she wouldn't sleep with the boss. The company had claimed she was fired for inefficiency but enough witnesses had come forward to establish the real motive. The settlement wasn't a home run but would provide some funds Jim could earmark for the expenses of the Marcus file.

Every day he worked on a variety of matters to keep the pot boiling but Laura's case had become his consuming interest. He'd have preferred to work on it full time but had to do other things to sustain himself. He couldn't stay in the fight if he couldn't keep the office open.

Just after lunch Bobby Torricelli called him. "You got time for a beer after work?"

"Sure. Where should we meet? Jernigan's?"

"Let's go to Greasy's this time. I've a yearning for one of his hamburgers. I've got something I need to run by you."

"How about a preview?"

"It'll wait till this afternoon. 6:00 okay?"

"Sure."

Jim left the office at 5:45 and drove out the Jacksboro Highway to a seedy dive run by a big porcine man who always looked like he'd been working on cars. Grease stains splotched his grey jumpsuit and ingrained dirt darkened his oily face. The outside sign said the bar was Moran's Place but everyone called it Greasy's. Inexplicably, it had become a favorite watering hole for the downtown legal community.

Jim parked on the gravel parking lot and went inside. Bobby sat at a booth near a decrepit pool table, nursing a Pearl Beer. Greasy's wasn't a place where you drank anything fancy. Jim slid into the seat across from Bobby.

Greasy came over from the bar. "What'll it be?"

"One of those'll be okay." Jim nodded toward the Pearl.

The bartender turned to get the beer. Jim surveyed the angular face of his former partner. The wrinkles of maturity had begun to give it character. Grey hair now salted Bobby's temples, tempering his bronzed Mediterranean good looks.

"How goes the battle in the DA's office?" Jim asked.

Bobby smiled. "It's pretty hectic these days. I just got promoted to Chief Felony Prosecutor. I get a little more money and a lot more responsibility."

Greasy set a beer bottle on the table. Jim took a pull from it, then put it down. "You're looking pretty prosecutorial all right. What's this deal you wanted to ask me about?"

Bobby leaned forward, lowering his voice. "It's about that case you've got with Rolly Sullivan. Richaud versus Alamo Oil.

"What about it?"

"You were telling me you were supposed to get the husband of one of the victims and ended up with the truck driver's widow instead."

"That's right."

"Did you ever figure out what happened?"

Jim shrugged. "Sullivan got to Richaud before he could talk to me. That's all I know."

"I know the score."

"And what's that?"

"Sullivan and a psychologist named Nadine Graves put on a counseling session at the Worthington and invited all the accident victims and their families who Sullivan thought had good cases. After the session, Richaud and a bunch of others signed up with Sullivan."

Jim shook his head. "The dirty bastard! I figured it was something like that. But where'd you get your information?"

"The father of one of the woman killed in the wreck was highly offended. He filed a grievance against Rolly in San Antonio but he didn't stop there. Several days ago he presented evidence to the Tarrant County Grand Jury. They're fixin' to indict your friend for barratry."

Jim smiled. "I thought Grand Jury proceedings were secret."

"They are. But those of us in the inner sanctum have a pretty good idea what's happening."

"What puts you in that group?"

"I've been picked to prosecute the SOB." Bobby leaned back with a satisfied smile.

Jim's brain churned. Barratry—direct solicitation of legal business by lawyers—had recently been upgraded by the Texas Legislature to a felony. Rolly could get a long jail term. Was this development good or bad for Jim? Rolly might get what he deserved but the criminal prosecution could delay the damage suit and prevent a prompt and fair trial. Jim's complex, difficult case had just become even harder.

"I'm not sure I like this," he said.

Bobby nodded. "I know what you mean. But we've got to strike while the iron's hot. The grand jury's more likely to indict when the information's fresh. It's time to put a stop to the type of tactics Sullivan uses to get cases."

"Are you sure you can stay up with him? He'll work your ass off. And he's got more money to spend on the case than you do."

"We know that. We're prepared for a tough fight. But we're in the right and we've got to do it."

"I hope you nail him."

Bobby leaned across the table, face serious. "I may need you to testify."

Jim drew back. "Why?"

"To show how you didn't get Richaud's case."

"He never got in to see me. He was never a client."

"He never had a chance to be one. Not with Rolly in the picture."

Jim considered what Bobby was asking. Sullivan ought to be prosecuted, no doubt. But Jim had to get along with him in order to handle Laura's case. How could Jim complain about not getting Richaud's case in the barratry prosecution, while representing Laura's interest?

"I don't see how I can help you Bobby. I've got a bad conflict of interest."

Bobby nodded. "I guess you do at that. You'd be complaining about not getting a client who's now adverse to you and saying you'd rather have his case than the one you did get. We'll have to prove the case another way."

"Sorry Bobby."

"That's okay. You've got your client to think of."

They washed down a couple of Greasy's unsanitary looking hamburgers with another round of beer and continued talking, first about Sullivan and the case, then about old times in their former law office. Later, Jim drove toward home, mulling over what Bobby had told him.

Sullivan's indictment, while deserved, would not be a welcome development because of the complications it would cause but it shouldn't affect Jim's side of the case. He'd just continue with the game plan he'd already laid out.

The next step would be the hearing at the end of next week before Judge Ferreira to determine if Jim could take the deposition of Gerald Forbes. Surely the key to the case lay behind Forbes's cold blue eyes.

# 9

"Mr. Sullivan?" The man on the phone had an officious voice tinged with contempt.

"This is he," Rolly said.

The man gave his name. "I'm with the sheriff's office," he said. "I have a warrant for your arrest."

Anger and fear gripped Rolly. "What for?"

"Something called barratry. The grand jury in Fort Worth indicted you yesterday."

"The bastards."

The deputy laughed. "I didn't have nothin' to do with the indictment but I do have to arrest you. You want to come in or should I come out there?"

"Let me call my lawyer."

"Okay Mr. Sullivan. You do that. But I gotta arrest you sometime today."

"I'll come in. My lawyer will make the arrangements."

Rolly took the deputy's number, then called Bill Biggers.

"What's going on Rolly?" Bill asked.

"The shit just hit the fan."

"What do you mean?"

"I've been indicted in Fort Worth."

"God damn! When?"

"Yesterday. I just got a call from a deputy who wants to arrest me. Can you check it out?"

"You got his number?"

Rolly gave Biggers the number, hung up, and walked to the window. He stared at the San Antonio skyline in the distance. He and Biggers had talked about the possibility of an indictment but Rolly hadn't thought it would really happen. There was a lot of talk about indicting lawyers for soliciting cases but usually no action.

Rolly was ready for the bastards. Neither the bar nor the legislature had any right to tell him what to do. He'd use this indictment to vindicate himself.

Half an hour later Biggers called back."I've got everything worked out."

"What do you mean?"

"You don't have to go downtown. You can turn yourself in tomorrow in Fort Worth."

"Boy, what a deal!"

Biggers laughed. "It's not as bad as it sounds. I talked to the DA who's handling the case. You'll be arraigned and we can make bail at the same time."

"I won't have to go to jail?"

"Not yet. Of course, you will if you're convicted."

"But that's not gonna happen."

"I can't promise anything."

"Why'd I get indicted?"

"Your friend Roger Lombardo took the case to the grand jury."

"The little jerk. Are you going with me to Fort Worth?"

"I've already made the reservations."

The next day Biggers parked the big Cadillac he had rented in a lot half a block from the Tarrant County Justice Center, a boxey ten story structure with ornate trim of green-painted metal. Rolly walked with Biggers toward the building. Vans from several television stations, their dish antennas extended many feet in the air, were parked along the curb. An assemblage of media people with cameras and microphones clustered on the steps.

"You reckon those sharks are looking for me?" Rolly asked.

Biggers nodded. "If there's not some sensational criminal trial going on, you're probably the bait."

"Lucky me."

As they started up the broad steps to the entrance doors the media mob pressed forward. A big, red-faced man led the pack. He thrust a microphone forward while the camera operators trained their lenses on Rolly.

"What's your comment on this indictment Mr. Sullivan?" Redface asked.

Biggers stepped in front of Rolly, looking bland and confident. "I'm Bill Biggers and I represent Mr. Sullivan. My client's done nothing wrong. We're sure he'll be found not guilty."

Redface put his chin forward. "Is it true Rolly put on a fake counseling session to get clients?"

Biggers shook his head. "No, that's not true. It was a legitimate counseling session designed to help the accident victims."

"Why was Rolly there?"

"We'll tell you all about that at the trial."

A slim woman with straight blonde hair and a tight mouth pushed in front of Redface. "What about that kickback scheme in San Antonio, Mr. Sullivan? Did you make a deal to pay a bondsman for referring you a case?"

Biggers stared at the woman. "If you've done your homework, you know that grievance was dismissed. My client was completely exonerated. Excuse us, please."

Biggers pushed past the media pack and Rolly followed in his wake. He was dying to talk to the bastards but wisdom dictated that he let Biggers earn his keep.

Inside, they went through the metal detector by the door under the watchful eyes of several sheriff's deputies. Rolly had been through such stations hundreds of times without a thought, but now it seemed the lawmen scrutinized him hostilely as though he had already been convicted.

Media people followed them onto an elevator, followed by a random pack of citizens headed for the upper floors. The sour smell of sweat filled the air. Rolly moved back against the wall behind the bulk of his lawyer but the red-faced man and tight-lipped woman from the assault on the steps crowded against him on either side.

"Has any plea deal been offered?" the man asked.

"What do your clients think of these charges?" queried the woman.

Biggers turned, snarling. "Mr. Sullivan has no comment."

Rolly kept quiet. On the seventh floor he followed Bill into Criminal District Court 10 with the media people pushing in behind. Rolly felt helpless and out of control. He was riding the coattails of his lawyer just like his clients rode his coattails during court proceedings.

The young, sandy-haired judge sat on the bench, incongruous in his somber black robe. A thickset woman with greying hair and a gun strapped to her side officiated as bailiff from her desk at the side of the room. At the counsel table a tall, dark-complexioned man with a hooked nose got up and came toward them. He met them at the rail.

"Mr. Biggers?" he asked.

"That's me," Bill said. "And this is Mr. Sullivan." He nodded toward Rolly.

Ignoring Rolly, the dark man put out his hand to Bill. "I'm Bobby Torricelli."

Biggers shook Torricelli's hand. "Good to meet you."

The young judge spoke into his microphone. "Mr. Torricelli, are you about ready to proceed?"

Torricelli turned to the court. "Yes your honor."

"I've got to go to my office for a telephone conference," the judge said. "I'll convene the arraignment hearing in ten minutes." He left the bench and exited through a back door.

Rolly sat with Biggers while Torricelli talked to several lawyers at the back of the courtroom. Rolly spotted Jim McSpadden among them. What was he doing here? What happened in this case wouldn't affect the civil damage suit.

The judge soon reentered, followed by a serious-looking young man wearing thick glasses who slipped into a chair at the court reporter's desk.

"All rise, please," said the bailiff.

With a collective shuffling of feet, the people stood.

The bailiff spoke again. "Oyez, oyez, the 10th Criminal District Court of Tarrant County, Texas is now in session, the Honorable Winston Hewitt presiding."

Judge Hewitt nodded to the people. "Thank you. Please be seated. Are we ready now, counsel?"

"Yes your honor," Torricelli said, walking to the counsel table.

"I'll call cause 10-310923, The State of Texas versus Rollin Sullivan. Mr. Torricelli, I'll ask you to read the indictment."

Biggers got up. "We'll waive the reading, your honor."

"Very well. Mr. Sullivan, do you understand the charge against you?"

Rolly stood. "Yes your honor." He resented the authority of this young ass of a judge. A burden of shame lay heavy on him. The stink of this case would always dog him even if he were acquitted. But fuck the bastards. He wouldn't let them get him down.

"How do you plead?" asked the court.

"Not guilty."

The judge made a notation in a book on the bench. "I've entered your plea of not guilty, Mr. Sullivan, and I'll set your bond at ten thousand dollars. You are ordered not to leave the state and to keep the court advised of your whereabouts. This case will be tried in about two months. I'll advise your attorney of the setting date later. Do you have any questions?"

"No your honor."

"In that case this hearing is adjourned."

"All rise please," intoned the bailiff, and everyone in the court got up as the judge left the bench.

Biggers and Rolly then went to the clerk's office where they posted the bond. They pressed through the crowds in the hall to the elevator. On the street, they walked to the sheriff's office in a nearby building where Rolly was fingerprinted, then drove in the Cadillac toward the airport.

"That didn't take very long," Biggers said, with satisfaction. "Maybe we can get an earlier flight."

"The sooner we get back to San Antonio the better I'll like it," Rolly said.

Biggers grinned. "Is Fort Worth beginning to get on your nerves?"

"You might say that."

"There's one good thing about this indictment."

"What is it?"

"I talked to Ronald Hobbs about the situation. He says the grievance committee will put everything on hold until after the trial."

"What's good about that?" Rolly asked. "They'll just fire it back up if I'm acquitted. Between the indictment and the grievance, the assholes have two shots at me."

Biggers shook his head. "I don't think so. If you're convicted, they've got you and there's no point in going forward with the grievance. But if you're acquitted, reviving the grievance will look like beating a dead horse. If the jury doesn't convict you, it'll look mighty petty for the committee to try to sustain the grievance. They'll have to dismiss it."

"I see what you mean. Everything's riding on this trial then."

"That's the way I see it."

At the airport they turned in the car and boarded a flight for San Antonio. When the plane had climbed to its cruising altitude, Rolly stared through the window at the billowing tops of the clouds under them as he reviewed the happenings of the day.

The mean looking newswoman on the elevator had asked what his clients thought of this indictment. The first order of business back in San Antonio would be to find out the answer to that question.

He got to the office by midafternoon and pulled the green Jaguar into its parking place. Inside, he asked Maria what messages had come in.

"Al Richaud's called twice. He sounded pretty upset."

"What'd you tell him?"

"Just that you'd call him as soon as you got back in."

"Get him on the line now."

Rolly headed for his office. Richaud was the strongest client in the lawsuit against Alamo Oil. His case had the most appealing facts. Rolly winced every time he thought of Richaud viewing the blackened bodies of his wife and children in their burned-out car. That evidence would be dynamite with the jury.

A decisive businessman, Richaud had built a string of submarine sandwich shops into a profitable little empire. Stubborn and opinionated but well-spoken, with the stocky build of an aging athlete, he would make a good witness. That was why Rolly had listed his name first in filing the case. He planned for Richaud's testimony to set the stage for all his other evidence. It was essential for Rolly to retain this client's confidence.

Maria called on the intercom. "Mr. Richaud on line one."

Rolly picked up the phone. "How're you doing, Al?"

"I don't know Rolly. You tell me. What's going on with this indictment?"

"It's nothing to worry about."

"Are you sure? I don't see how I can go to trial with a lawyer who's in jail."

"I'm not going to jail."

"The news reports sound pretty bad."

Rolly laughed. "They always do. Look Al, you were at the session with Nadine. Did you think I did anything wrong?"

"I thought you were pretty sneaky, getting us all in there for a counseling session, then making a pitch to get our cases."

"But did you think it was wrong?"

"No. No I didn't. I've never had a case like this before and I pray to God I never will again. I didn't know who to get for a lawyer. My pastor referred me to somebody but I have no idea how good he was. I never even talked to him. I knew you were what I needed as soon as I heard your presentation."

"Will you come to court and tell the jury how you felt about the session?"

"I'll do anything I can to help."

"You might leave off that part about it being sneaky."

"That's just between you and me."

"Good. Now stop worrying about the indictment. With testimony from you and some of the other clients, there's no way for us to lose."

"I'm with you all the way. This late in the game I have to be."

Rolly hung up and turned to his computer where he brought up the file of the case. He started typing strategy notes for Bill Biggers. In spite of the confidence he'd projected to Richaud, he had misgivings about this indictment. He knew he was right but how could he and Biggers overcome Roger Lombardo's outraged testimony and get their position across to the lawyer-haters who were bound to end up on the jury?

∽

Large, bald-headed Judge Charles A. Ferreira looked over the edge of his raised desk at the lawyers assembled at the counsel tables before him. Jim sat with a disheveled Al Hildebrand at one table and J. Michael Meador, in his three-piece pinstriped suit, fancy watch, and gold jewelry, leaned back in his chair at the other. Next to him Malcolm R. H. Witherspoon, a young Turk from Meador's firm with a high, intellectual forehead and a superior smirk, poured over a case notebook.

The other lawyers had not attended. This fight was between Jim and J. Michael. Red-haired Sally Gregory was adjusting her court reporter's stenotype machine and the bailiff, squat Juan Vasquez, kept order from a desk at the side of the room.

The judge pulled his microphone forward. "Counsel, I have before me Mr.

McSpadden's motion to take the deposition of Gerald Forbes and Mr. Meador's response in opposition, which includes a motion to rule for costs and for attorney's fees. I'll hear from Mr. McSpadden first."

Jim stood and walked to the podium. "Thank you, your honor. Mr. Forbes is the CEO of the defendant, Harrigan Motor Company. I've tried to find out what caused the steering on the Harrigan truck involved in this case to jam but with no success. I believe Mr. Forbes knows something about it and that I ought to be allowed to depose him."

Judge Ferreira held up his hand. "Let's stop right there, Mr. McSpadden. I'd like to hear Mr. Meador's response to what you've just said."

Jim sat down and Meador walked to the podium, every blond hair in place, his face red with indignation.

"May it please the court, your honor, this request of Mr. McSpadden's is simply outrageous. We've already taken the deposition of the Alamo Oil Company mechanic who worked on the truck.

"He says there was nothing wrong with the steering. There's just no doubt the husband of Mr. McSpadden's client caused this accident. Mr. Forbes is a busy man. There's no point in requiring him to answer questions that dozens of lower level people could respond to."

Judge Ferreira leaned forward, eyes thoughtful. On first acquaintance he appeared to have no sense of humor but those who knew him well looked for a certain subtle smile that demonstrated his ironic understanding of all things legal and political. He kept himself aloof from the legal community he served but had a reputation for intellectual honesty and scrupulous fairness.

"What you say does concern me, Mr. Meador. This court does not favor apex depositions of CEO's filed for harassment, or just as fishing expeditions."

Meador nodded. "That's exactly what this is, your honor. An unjustified apex deposition. That's why I'm asking that permission be denied. In light of the lack of evidence against my client, I'm also asking that Mr. McSpadden be required to post a bond to guarantee Harrigan's costs in the case and to pay our attorney's fees for being here today."

The judge turned a penetrating look on Jim. "What's your response, Mr. McSpadden?"

Jim walked back to the podium with a queasy feeling.

"Your honor, it's a little misleading for Mr. Meador to say that the Alamo mechanic testified there was nothing wrong with the steering. He did say he didn't find anything wrong but he also testified the driver had reported malfunctions on several occasions of the sort that would account for this accident."

"But you can't prove anything specific?"

"Not at this time, your honor. That's why I need to take Mr. Forbes's deposition. I haven't taken any depositions of Harrigan personnel yet."

"Why Mr. Forbes? Couldn't Harrigan designate someone else? Some senior engineer, for example?"

"I don't believe any of them would know what Mr. Forbes knows."

"That doesn't make sense, Mr. McSpadden. I certainly would expect design engineers to know more about a product than the president of the company."

Jim put his hands palms down on the podium. "As a general rule I'd agree with that, your honor, but in this case, Mr. Forbes personally supervised the design of the truck."

"Do you have any evidence of that?"

Jim pulled the brochure on the M-5000 Loadmaster from an accordion file. "May I approach the bench, your honor?"

"Yes you may."

Jim walked forward and handed the brochure up to the judge, turned to the inside cover where Forbes's picture appeared along with the glowing description of how he had participated in the design of the truck. Judge Ferreira read the page and the corners of his mouth curved in that faint smile Jim had learned to look for.

"Have you seen this brochure, Mr. Meador?" the judge asked.

"I don't know, your honor."

The judge turned to Jim. "Show this to Mr. Meador."

With a feeling of impending triumph, Jim took the brochure and put it in front of Meador, who quickly scanned it.

"Yes, I've seen this before."

"Doesn't it pretty strongly support Mr. McSpadden's argument?"

Meador stood. Even the tips of his ears were red. "I don't believe so, your honor. What goes in a promotional brochure doesn't always give the full picture of who knows the most about a product. There are other engineers who know a lot more about this truck than Mr. Forbes."

"But you do agree it says he personally supervised this design?"

"Yes, your honor."

"Thank you, counsel, you may be seated."

Meador sat down, and Jim took his place at the counsel table next to Hildebrand.

His honor assumed a judicious demeanor. "In light of the fact that Mr. Forbes supervised the design of this truck, I'm going to grant Mr. McSpadden's motion. However, I'm going to direct that the deposition be taken in Chicago and that it not exceed four hours in length. I order the parties to cooperate in setting it up as soon as possible."

J. Michael stood. "What about my motion for costs, your honor? Shouldn't he have to pay my expenses for going to Chicago?"

Judge Ferreira shook his head. "The parties will pay their own costs in connection with the deposition and the motion to rule for costs is denied. However, I'll revisit the issue of attorney's fees at a later time. Mr. McSpadden, I'm going to give you a chance to make your case but if your cross-action turns out to be groundless, your client may end up paying Harrigan's attorney's fees."

Jim nodded. "I understand, your honor."

The judge studied the court file in front of him, then looked up. "There are a lot of damages in this case but the accident facts aren't complicated. It seems to me we should be ready to try this matter late this spring. I'll be setting it in May and notifying all counsel of the date. Is there anything further we need to take up today?"

Jim and J. Michael shook their heads. "No, your honor."

"Do ya'll think it'd help for me to order mediation?"

"No, your honor," said J. Michael. "There's no way I'm gonna pay Mr. McSpadden much of anything and I doubt if Mr. Sullivan and Mr. Kurtz can get together, either."

"Very well then. We'll have a trial. That's what the courthouse is for. This hearing is adjourned."

As the attorneys walked toward the rear of the courtroom, Meador sidled up beside Jim. "Our attorney's fees are up over a hundred thousand dollars now," he said. "They'll be double or triple that if we have to try the case. Why don't you just let Harrigan out now and save everyone a lot of trouble?"

Jim stopped and turned to face Meador. "You ready to pay my client a couple of million dollars?"

Meador sniggered. "Don't be ridiculous."

"Screw you, then. I'm looking forward to visiting with Mr. Forbes."

"You stupid fool! You're gonna be sorry you ever heard of this case."

A red rage swept through Jim's brain. "Go to hell asshole!"

Meador raised his fists and Hildebrand quickly stepped between them. "Just stay cool, Mike."

With an angry shake of his head, Meador headed toward the elevators with a shocked Malcolm R. H. Witherspoon in tow. Hildebrand pulled Jim into a conference room.

"It won't help to get in a fight with the bastard."

Jim's hands shook. "He pisses me off every time I see him."

Hildebrand laughed. "Mike affects people that way."

They walked together to the elevators. Outside the courthouse they shook hands and Hildebrand headed for his car for the drive to Dallas. It was nice that the Dallas lawyers had come to Fort Worth for a change.

As Jim drove toward his office he started planning the questions he would ask Gerald Forbes. He'd control himself in Chicago better than he had today. No point in spoiling such a good opportunity with a fist fight. With great satisfaction he remembered the look of chagrin on J. Michael Meador's face when the judge made his ruling. It had been a great day.

∾

Jim stood next to Al Hildebrand in the waiting area of their American Airlines gate at O'Hare Airport. Where the hell was Jamal? Jim had called him the night before and he had promised to meet them at the gate.

"You think your guy's stood us up?" Hildebrand asked.

Jim shrugged. "Don't know. Let's wait a few more minutes."

"We can always get a taxi."

"I think he'll be here."

From down the busy concourse a bearded man in a blue suit approached. Dark glasses concealed his eyes. He stopped across the waiting area from them, reached inside his suit jacket and pulled out a small placard. He looked warily up and down the concourse, then held the placard over his chest. "Jim McSpadden," it read.

Jim walked quickly through the milling passengers. "Is that you, Jamal?"

The bearded man smiled. "Yes boss."

"I was about to give up on you."

"Sorry boss. Had to move car."

Jim introduced Al Hildebrand who shook Jamal's hand with a look of skeptical amusement. The three started walking toward the terminal.

"I didn't recognize you with that beard, Jamal," Jim said. "And what happened to your cap?"

Jamal favored him with a sad look. "I have a lotta trouble boss."

"What kind of trouble?"

"Cops give me hard time. They know me too good now. I gotta look different, move car all the time."

"Why's that?" Hildebrand asked, eyes puzzled.

"Jamal doesn't have a taxi license," Jim explained.

"Oh I see."

In the Lincoln, now repainted a dark, shiny green, they headed for the southside. Dirty snowbanks lined the freeway and the pavement was wet with melted ice and snow.

Hildebrand shook his head at the stark scene. "I'm glad I don't live here."

Jim nodded. "The only snow I like is on Christmas cards."

"It's okay on the ski slopes."

"But not where you have to live."

Jim opened his briefcase and pulled out the Harrigan manual on the Loadmaster. He'd had a conference with Nick Stavros and he'd talked again to Walter Ellis in Billings and Ernest Starnes in Tupelo about the accidents involving their clients. He had lots of questions for Gerald Forbes.

"What do you think we'll find out today?" Hildebrand asked.

"I don't know. I know from my last trip up here that Harrigan's having problems but I don't know what they are."

"I sure hope we get some answers."

"So do I. I don't know how I'm gonna prove the case if I don't get something from Forbes."

Jamal turned to look at them over the back of the front seat. "You guys some kinda big shots?"

Jim laughed. "No way Jamal. We're just a couple of honest lawyers."

"I thought you were truck driver."

"That was last time. This time I'm a lawyer."

At the Harrigan headquarters Jamal pulled up to the gatehouse guarding the visitors' parking lot. A grim looking guard asked their business and waved them through. They pulled into a parking space and Jim and Hildebrand got out, briefcases in hand.

"Wait here Jamal," Jim said.

Jamal frowned. "How long?"

"It'll be around four hours."

"You pay now?"

Jim shook his head. "I'll pay you a hundred bucks when we get back to the airport. That was the deal. A hundred bucks for half a day."

Jamal's face took on a resigned look. "Okay boss. I'm waiting."

On the second floor of the headquarters a secretary with greying hair ushered them into a palatial waiting area. Brocaded sofas and chairs stood on an oriental rug surrounded by polished hardwood floors. Oil portraits of all the Harrigan CEO's, back to old Patrick Harrigan, the founder of the company, lined the walls. A young woman with straight black hair sat on one of the sofas with court reporting paraphernalia on a luggage cart next to her.

"Please sit down gentlemen," the secretary said. "Can I bring you some coffee?"

154

"Sure," Jim said. "Make mine black." He looked at the court reporter. "Are you from Steinmetz Reporters?"

She nodded. "Yes sir."

"I'm Jim McSpadden. I get the bill for today's performance."

"I'll set up as soon as I can," she said.

Jim sat on the edge of his chair, intimidated by the opulence around him in spite of his contempt for it. At the far side of the room, raised gold lettering identified Gerald Forbes's office. Al picked up a *New Yorker* from a coffee table and started leafing through it. They weren't waiting for anyone else; Rolly Sullivan and the other lawyers representing accident victims didn't believe Jim had a case against Harrigan and had opted not to come.

The deposition had been scheduled for two, but that time passed with no movement of the gold-lettered door. At two-fifteen Jim started fidgeting. According to Judge Ferreira's order the deposition was supposed to conclude at six.

Jim turned to Hildebrand. "I wish we could get started. They're on my time now."

Hildebrand laid the magazine down. "They're sending you a message Jim. They don't have to march to your drum."

Jim got up and walked over to the secretary's desk. "Could you remind Mr. Forbes we're out here?" he asked.

The woman shook her head. "I'm sorry sir. He gave strict orders not to disturb him. You'll just have to wait."

Fuming, Jim returned to his seat. At two thirty-three, the door to Forbes's office opened and J. Michael Meador came out, followed by Forbes and Doug Spivak. Jim and Al stood up.

Meador put on a chilly smile. "Did you have a good flight?"

Jim concealed his irritation. "Just fine. Can we go ahead and get started?"

"Sure." Meador turned to the court reporter. "Just go on in and set up by Mr. Forbes's desk."

The girl pushed her cart toward the office door. Forbes stepped up and shook hands with Jim and Al. He wore a charcoal grey suit with a bright yellow tie and regarded them with a look of tolerant amusement that said he was too big a man to be worried by this kind of petty harassment. His cold blue eyes locked with Jim's, narrowing as though he were trying to recall their brief exchange of looks in the cafeteria many months before.

Meador motioned toward Spivak. "This is Doug Spivak. He's familiar with the quality control on the Loadmaster. He's been helping us with the documentation."

As they shook hands Spivak bent a questioning look at Jim. "You sure do look familiar Mr. McSpadden. Have we met before?"

Jim decided to evade the question. "We may have,Mr. Spivak. You look familiar to me too."

"You don't mind if Doug sits in do you?" Meador asked. "He can help us with locating the documents."

"That's fine," Jim said.

Meador checked his watch. "We'd better get started. We need to get out of here by five o'clock."

Jim raised his head. "What do you mean, five o'clock? The order says I have till six."

Meador smiled. "I thought it was five."

Jim jerked open his briefcase, pulled a copy of the order out, and handed it to Meador.

J. Michael shook his head. "Son of a gun! It does say six. I'm sorry but Mr. Forbes can't stay past five. He has a meeting downtown."

Jim spread his hands in frustration. "We're already half an hour late. We were supposed to start at two."

"I thought it was two-thirty."

"Check the order."

Meador looked at the document. "Right again, Jim. Well, can't be helped. You've still got two and a half hours. I think that'll be plenty of time to find out what Mr. Forbes knows."

Jim had carefully planned his deposition around questions directed to Forbes's background, followed by many pages of technical questions provided by Nick Stavros about the functioning of the Loadmaster. Four hours had not been too much time for the material he had to cover. Now he'd have to hurry.

He shrugged. "Let's get started, then. But if I don't finish we may have to come up here again."

Meador shook his head. "That shouldn't be necessary Jim. You've got plenty of time."

As Jim and Al followed the others into the office Jim spoke softly under his breath. "Goddamn jerk!"

Hildebrand nodded.

Gerald Forbes sat behind his big mahogany desk, arms folded, mocking Jim with his ice-blue eyes, his mouth twisted in a superior smile. Through the windows behind him, the Chicago skyline spread out in the distance above the snowy roofs of the southside.

On one side of Forbes, sour, red-faced Doug Spivak officiated over a file box of documents and on the other, J. Michael Meador glowered, hostile-eyed.

Jim sat in a chair in front of the desk and Al took a place on a nearby sofa. He was here to observe and wouldn't ask any questions.

The court reporter swore the CEO to tell the truth and Jim started his questioning. Quickly, he established Forbes's family and educational background, then covered his work experience. He had graduated from the University of Chicago and worked for Ford and GM before coming to Harrigan. With the company for more than twenty years, he had been CEO for the last five.

"And how much are you paid at present?" Jim asked.

Forbes shot an irritated look at J. Michael. "What does that have to do with anything?"

Meador leaned forward, thumping the desk. "Mr. Forbes's compensation is absolutely immaterial. Move on to something else."

Jim stood his ground. "I think I'm entitled to ask about that as part of his general background."

Meador shook his head. "No you're not. Ask him about something else."

Jim bowed his neck. "Mike, you've already cut an hour and a half off my time by pretending you didn't know what the order said. If you're gonna interfere further by limiting my questions, I think we'd better continue this deposition and go back and get some ground rules from Judge Ferreira."

"That's just fine with me." Meador started gathering papers off the desk.

Forbes put his hand on Meador's arm. "It doesn't matter that much Mike. My compensation's a matter of public record anyway. I just can't see what it has to do with anything."

Meador shrugged. "Let's get on with it then."

"How much are you paid Mr. Forbes?" Jim asked.

"Six point two million a year not counting stock options."

"And how much are they worth?"

"It varies. There weren't any, last year."

"Why was that?"

Forbes's face turned red. "It wasn't a good year."

"How are you going to do this year?"

Meador put clenched fists on the desk. "Really Jim, you're out of line now. Get off this subject or let's shut it down."

Jim affected a sweet smile. "I'll withdraw that question Mike." He looked at Forbes again. "How does your pay compare with other CEO's in the auto industry?"

"It's nothing compared to GM, Ford, and Chrysler."

"I'm sure that's true." Jim turned to another subject. "Mr. Forbes, the notice for this deposition included a subpoena for all the records on the design of the M-5000 Loadmaster along with any records of customer complaints, recalls, and modifications. Have you brought those with you today?"

Forbes nodded toward Spivak. "Doug's got that all organized for us."

For the next hour Jim asked Forbes about the design and construction of the Loadmaster while Spivak handed the CEO the documents he needed to respond. Just after four o'clock Jim launched his most important round of questions.

"Mr. Forbes, what role did you have in the design of the Loadmaster power steering?"

Forbes put on a modest smile. "I was principally responsible for that design."

"What's so great about it? What makes it better than other power steering systems?"

"It represents a state of the art refinement. Conventional power steering systems react to pressure on the wheel to apply force to assist in making the turn. In our system a sophisticated computer measures the rate of the turn and applies just the right amount of pressure in precision increments."

"How is that better?"

"It gives the driver a level of control unheard of a few years ago. It's as easy to turn one of our trucks as it is to turn a small car."

"Sounds pretty impressive. What problems have you had with the system?"

Forbes cocked his head. "None, really."

"No recalls?"

"None. It's been the most trouble-free design change we've ever had."

Jim asked about the accidents in Montana and Mississippi and Spivak pulled out investigative files on each of them and handed them to Forbes. Forbes testified that after studying the police reports and doing some in-house tests, Harrigan Motors had concluded both accidents were due solely to driver inattention.

J. Michael Meador looked at his watch. "You about through Jim? It's almost five."

Jim forced a friendly tone. "Just a few more questions Mike." He caught Forbes's eyes and held them. "Are you telling me you've had no problems at all with this steering system?"

Forbes met Jim's stare. "That's right Mr. McSpadden. That's what I'm telling you."

"And there've been no situations in which you concluded the steering could bind and freeze under certain conditions?"

"No there haven't."

"And anyone who says there have been situations like that is lying?"

Forbes eyes displayed a glimmer of doubt. "I can't imagine anyone saying anything like that."

"What if some Harrigan employee says you've been having troubles of that kind?"

Forbes's face tightened. "They'd be talking about something they knew nothing about."

"You're sure of that?"

"Absolutely sure."

Jim flipped his briefcase closed. "That's all I have for today." He leaned across the desk, extending his hand. "Nice to meet you Mr. Forbes."

Forbes returned a firm handshake. "My pleasure Mr. McSpadden."

Jim turned to Spivak, grinning. "Real good to see you again, too Doug."

Spivak drew back, eyes wide. "Now I remember. You're that damn truck driver!"

Jim smiled. "You mean 'ol Tex? Yep, that's me."

Mike Meador frowned. "You haven't been snooping around here talking to my client's employees without permission have you, Jim?"

Jim shook his head. "Not since I sued Harrigan, Mike. Let's just say Doug and I had a friendly little game of pool while I was doing the presuit investigation."

Meador looked at Spivak then at Forbes. "We'd better talk about this."

Jim nodded. "Yeah, I wish ya'll would talk. And if you find you've failed to tell me something I'm entitled to know, be sure to give me a call." He turned to the door.

"Do you know something I don't?" Al asked Jim as they drove with Jamal back toward the airport.

"Not anything solid."

"Were you pulling a bluff in there then?"

"Not entirely. This little guy, Rusty, who was in the pool game with Doug Spivak and me, did say they'd been having trouble with the steering system. Trouble was, he didn't know the details."

"Our ox is still in the ditch then."

"Yeah, but we've got 'em worrying a little."

"You think you've got enough to keep 'em in the lawsuit?"

"I don't know Al. I sure hope so. Forbes is lying. If we can keep Harrigan in the case, I'll figure out a way to prove it at trial."

"I'd say we were hanging by our fingernails."

# 10

Three days after Gerald Forbes's deposition, J. Michael Meador served Harrigan Motor Corporation's motion for summary judgment on Jim. Supported by Gerald Forbes's affidavit that Harrigan's steering system was free from defects, the motion asked that Laura's case against Harrigan be dismissed and that Harrigan be awarded one hundred and thirty thousand dollars in attorneys' fees because the claim was without basis and frivolous.

Judge Ferreira had signed an order setting the motion for hearing in a month. Jim would have until seven days before the hearing date to file opposing affidavits. If the judge thought Jim's affidavits had merit, the court would overrule the motion and Laura's claim would stay in the case. Otherwise, her claim would be dismissed and costs and attorneys' fees would be assessed against her.

She would remain a defendant as representative of Danny's estate and Al Hildebrand would defend her against the claim for Danny's negligence. Alamo's insurance company, United of Rhode Island, would pay any judgment against Danny up to the six million dollar policy limits. Alamo's reinsurance policy would pay anything over six million up to five hundred million dollars but only if Danny had not abandoned his job and gone off on a joy ride.

Jim called Laura on the phone. "Meador filed that summary judgment I've been expecting."

"What are our chances of beating it?"

"Not good. I didn't get much out of Forbes's deposition and it's gonna be hard to convince the judge you have a claim."

"What happens if the judge grants the motion?"

"You'll owe over a hundred thousand dollars now and maybe a lot more if the jury finds Danny was negligent but not on the job."

"What do they want?" Laura asked. "My house and kids?"

Jim laughed. "They can't get the kids, and the house is exempt as homestead. You can wipe out the judgment with a bankruptcy."

"What's their point then?"

"Rolly's just after the insurance and Meador knows he'll never collect attorneys' fees from you."

"Just do the best you can and let's see what happens."

"I'm working on it now. I'll plan to file your answer and opposing affidavits in about two weeks. The hearing's on February 28."

Later that day Jim called Nick Stavros. "I need your help, Nick."

"What's up?"

"Harrigan's filed a motion for summary judgment and I have to controvert it with an expert affidavit that something was wrong with the truck."

"I don't see how I can help you Jim. Not with what I have right now."

Jim had expected Nick to be cautious. He would damage his reputation if he gave an opinion that wasn't supported by the facts.

"What else do you need?" Jim asked.

"Something that would allow me to credibly criticize the truck."

"Can't you base your opinion on what L. T. Tinsley says?"

Nick's sarcasm flowed over the line. "You mean that crazy old bastard who says the hand of God swept the truck off the road?"

"When you take off the religious spin, what Tinsley says is that Danny Marcus was driving along at a normal rate, not weaving or speeding, and his truck suddenly made an abrupt swing to the left and went through the median fence."

"Yeah, but that blood test shows Marcus was double drunk and it's not unusual for someone in that condition to lose control that way. Weren't you gonna take a deposition at Harrigan Motors?"

"I did that several days ago."

"What did you find out?"

"Nothing new. The Harrigan CEO designed the system and claims they haven't had any problems with it."

Stavros spoke in a reluctant tone. "I'd like to help Jim. That's what you hired me for. But there's just not enough to go on."

Jim drew in his breath. "I was afraid you'd say that. Let me see what else I can come up with."

"Give me some ammunition Jim. I've got to have some basis for what I say."

Jim hung up and sat thinking so hard his head hurt. It looked like the end of the road. Nothing else to do. Best to just call Laura and tell her. Why keep up false hopes? But he'd sleep on it and see if some inspiration came during the night. If not, he'd bail out tomorrow.

Maybe he could get Meador to forego attorneys' fees if he just dismissed the claim. He didn't look forward to humbling himself in that way but he owed it to Laura to protect her from a judgment if he could. He lay awake worrying half the night, slept late into the morning, then stumbled into his clothes and drove reluctantly to the office.

Susan shook her head when he walked in. "You look like hell. What's the problem?"

"Looks like I'm gonna have to let go of the Marcus case and I'm not looking forward to telling Laura."

"I can sure understand that. You did get a call about that case. You might want to call this guy before you call her."

She handed him a slip. Rusty Day in Chicago. Rusty Day. That had to be little Rusty from Slim's Truck Stop.

Jim took a cup of coffee to his office and called the number.

"Do you know who I am Mr. McSpadden?" Rusty asked.

"I sure do. Has your pool game got any better?"

Rusty laughed. "No, but it looks like I'm gonna have lots of time to practice."

"Why's that?"

"I just quit my job at Harrigan."

"What for?"

"It was because of you."

"What'd I do?"

"You told Mr. Forbes and Doug Spivak at that deposition last week that I said we were having trouble with the Loadmaster steering."

"I didn't use your name."

"Doesn't matter. Doug knew who you were talking about. He told me he'd break my head if I talked to you again. I told him to go screw himself. He grabbed me by the shirt and slapped me, so I quit."

"I'm sorry Rusty."

"Don't be. I'm tired of Doug's bullshit anyway."

"Why are you calling me?"

"Because I don't like how they're doing you. There is some trouble with the Loadmaster steering. I don't know what it is but I know they're worried about it."

"Gerald Forbes claims there's nothing wrong."

"He's lying Mr. McSpadden. Doug told me himself he'd had meetings with Forbes and some of the other bigshots about it."

Jim tightened his grip on the phone. "You sure you don't know what the problem is?"

"I don't know what causes it but I do know it can cause loss of control. Doug let that slip one night when he'd drunk a bunch a beer. He got to talking about some wreck in Montana that happened because the steering froze."

"Forbes claims that wreck was caused by driver error."

"That's not what Doug told me."

Jim's brain pounded. Rusty hadn't told him anything he didn't already know but coming from someone who had worked for Harrigan the information might carry some weight, both with Nick Stavros and with Judge Ferreira.

"Would you make an affidavit about this for me?" Jim asked.

"Sure. I want to help all I can. Harrigan shouldn't get away with what they're trying to pull. But I can't swear to the details—just that there is a problem."

"That's all I can ask."

Jim got Rusty's address, then hung up and called Nick Stavros.

"I've come up with something Nick."

"What is it?"

"One of the Harrigan employees just called me. He's willing to sign an affidavit that Harrigan's having trouble with the steering system and that the problem can cause loss of control."

"How can he do that and still work there?"

"He just quit. He's mad as hell at 'em because they've been hassling him."

"Does he know the technical cause of the problem?"

"No. He was just an assembly line worker. But he can swear that they're lying about having no trouble."

"I dunno Jim. It's still pretty thin."

"I know it is Nick. But it's all I got. If you assume, based on this guy's testimony, that there is some defect in the steering, that it caused the wreck up in Montana and that it does cause loss of control and put that with an affidavit from L. T. Tinsley that Danny was driving normally before his truck suddenly veered to the left, won't that do it?"

"I guess so," Stavros said. "I guess I could honestly sign an affidavit that, under those circumstances, a defect in the steering was probably one of the causes of this accident."

"Thanks Nick. I'll get the affidavit to you in a couple of days."

∽

Jim and J. Michael Meador sat side by side in front of Judge Ferreira's big desk while the judge reviewed Jim's response to Meador's motion for summary judgment. He put the documents down and leaned forward, clasping his hands and favoring Jim with a faint smile.

"That's a pretty creative answer Mr. McSpadden."

"I'm a creative guy."

The judge nodded. "I'd say so. I'm trying to figure out if there's enough substance here to justify keeping you in the case."

"My affidavits do show there's a problem with the truck that could account for this accident."

Judge Ferreira looked at Meador. "What do you say?"

Meador raised his hands in a gesture of frustration. "I'm at a loss for words, your honor. I've seen a lot of half-baked summary judgment responses in my day but nothing to compare to what Mr. McSpadden's filed. He claims there's some mysterious problem with the steering but he can't tell us what it is. He's got the affidavit of a disgruntled employee claiming the scuttlebutt around the plant is there's something wrong and the affidavit of a hired gun engineer who claims this unknown defect caused this accident. And that opinion's based in part on an affidavit from another witness who told our investigators that the hand of God pushed the truck off the road."

Judge Ferreira turned to Jim. "Do you think this testimony raises enough evidence to take your case to the jury, Mr. McSpadden?"

"Yes I do, your honor. I'd have more facts if Mr. Meador's client weren't hiding the ball on me. Rusty Day's affidavit clearly states the steering problem's common knowledge around the plant but Gerald Forbes swore on his deposition he knows nothing about it."

"He can't get to the jury on that balderdash, your honor," Meador said. "My client's entitled to get out now and recover attorney's fees for this patently false claim."

Slowly the judge shook his head and Jim exalted that he had prevailed, at least for today.

"I hear what you're saying Mr. Meador, but I'm going to deny your motion. There's a clear conflict between what Rusty Day says and what Gerald Forbes says. I believe that raises a fact issue precluding summary judgement. I'm not saying I'd submit the case to the jury without more proof but I'm not going to kick Mr. McSpadden's client out of court at this point."

J. Michael's face flamed. "Your honor, why should my client have to put up with this charade?"

Judge Ferreira raised his hand. "That's enough Mr. Meador. I'll decide what constitutes a charade in this court. Your motion's overruled. I'll look forward to seeing you for the trial along with everyone else on the 18th of May."

Meador bent his head in submission, his lips a thin white line. "Very well, your honor."

"Thank you your honor," Jim said.

The judge shook his head again. "You may not thank me in the end. I'll revisit this issue at the close of the testimony in the trial. If I haven't heard a lot more evidence to support your claim than I've seen today I may well grant a directed verdict against your client. If I do that I'll also award Harrigan substantial attorneys' fees."

It was Jim's turn to bow. "I understand, your honor."

In the hall by the elevators Meador turned to Jim, his lips curled. "Since we're blessed with a judge who won't follow the law, I'd better start getting ready for trial. When can I depose your lovely client?"

Jim stifled his anger. "Just about any time Mike. Call me about some dates in the middle of March."

"I'll fax you a list this afternoon."

Meador turned abruptly and walked toward an open elevator. Jim held back. He couldn't stand the thought of being close to J. Michael for eight or nine stories. He got a cup of coffee in the lawyers' lounge.

Back at the office he called Laura and gave her the good news. Then he called Rusty Day.

"How'd it go Mr. McSpadden?" Rusty asked.

"I'm still alive. The judge overruled their motion. But I need more evidence. I still need to know what the problem is so my engineer can tie it into this accident."

"I'll ask around and see what I can find out."

"Call me if you learn anything. And good luck on finding a new job."

"I already got one. I'm working as a security guard in an apartment building. A free apartment's part of the deal."

"I'm glad you found something so fast."

"So am I. I'll call you as soon as I can."

Jim spent the rest of the afternoon planning his strategy. Only eleven weeks to go and lots of things to do. There'd be several rounds of depositions and preparation of his trial exhibits. He needed to do some more investigation. He still didn't have an answer to the blood test showing Danny was drunk. He needed to talk to the people who were in Norvella Poteet's place the day of the accident.

Suddenly, time seemed too short. At this point pre-trial excitement should drive him to the extra effort to get the case ready. But the fact he lacked proof of the defect in the steering system cast a damper on his spirits. Rusty Day was the key. If Rusty didn't come through, Jim could spend the next two and a half months of his life working on this case and end up with a directed verdict. And by that time, bankruptcy would be staring him in the face.

❧

On the first day of his trial for barratry, Rolly sat next to Bill Biggers at the defense table. Young Judge Winston Hewitt presided from the bench. Prosecutor Bobby Torricelli stood at the podium projecting a tone of outrage as he examined Roger Lombardo about Nadine's grief counseling session. A crowd of media, lawyers, and other courthouse types filled the spectator's seats.

"How did you learn about the counseling session?" Torricelli asked.

Roger, small with curly grey hair, leaned toward his microphone. "I got a letter from a psychologist named Nadine Graves."

"What did it say?"

"She expressed sympathy for what had happened and invited me to come to a free grief-counseling session at the Worthington with other accident victims."

"Did that idea appeal to you?"

"Yes it did." Lombardo passed his thumb and fingers over his eyes, wiping away tears. "I'd just lost my daughter and her husband. I couldn't sleep at night thinking how they'd burned to death and it broke my heart to hear my two-year-old granddaughter keep asking for her mama. I needed to share my problem with other people who'd suffered similar losses."

"You went to the session?"

"Yes I did."

"How did it go?"

"Everything was all right at first. Mrs. Graves made a good presentation and got us all to talking. It made me feel better to hear other people voicing the same feelings I had."

"What happened after that?"

Lombardo's voice shook as he answered. "She finished the session and introduced Rolly Sullivan."

"Why did that bother you?"

"It didn't at first. He started talking about our legal rights and I thought wasn't that nice of him to take his time to volunteer this information but the longer he talked, the more obvious it was the whole session was just a subterfuge for him to make a pitch to get our cases."

Biggers started to get up as though he were going to object, but settled back in his seat. "No point in making it any worse," he whispered to Rolly.

Torricelli drew himself up tall and swept the jury with his eyes, then turned again to Lombardo. "Did Mr. Sullivan's conduct offend you?"

Lombardo raised his voice. "You bet it did. Here I was in the worst time of my life and all Sullivan could think about was profiting from my misery."

Biggers rose from his chair. "I object to the last part of the answer, your honor. It's non-responsive."

Judge Hewitt shook his head. "Overruled."

166

Biggers sat down, whispering again to Rolly. "I'm gonna just let him talk."

Rolly nodded. He glanced at the jurors. Tears streaked the cheeks of several on the front row. A man in the back stared forward, arms folded. Things didn't look good for Rolly.

Torricelli continued. "Mr. Lombardo, did you call Mr. Sullivan before the session and tell him you wanted to talk to him about your case?"

"I certainly did not."

"Did you even know who he was?"

"I'd read about him in the paper."

"But did you recognize him at the meeting?"

"Not until Mrs. Graves introduced him."

"Did you encourage him in any way to talk to you about your situation?"

"I did not."

Torricelli looked toward the jury again. "I'll pass the witness."

"Cross-examination Mr. Biggers?" Judge Hewitt asked.

"Yes your honor." Biggers walked to the podium and stood behind it, Buddha-like, smiling at Lombardo. "Mr. Lombardo, you are a plaintiff in the litigation arising from this accident?"

"That's right. I sure am."

"And you have a lawyer representing you?"

"Yes I do."

"And there's nothing wrong with having a lawyer, is there?"

"No."

"Why did you think you needed one?"

"I don't know enough about the law to represent myself."

"At the counseling session, what did Mr. Sullivan tell you?"

Lombardo looked down at the desk in front of him, eyes narrowed. "He told us what he thought the insurance companies would do and said we needed a lawyer to deal with them."

"How long after the session did you employ your own attorney?"

"About a week later."

"Isn't it fair to say you followed Mr. Sullivan's advice in hiring your lawyer?"

Lombardo shook his head. "It wasn't like that at all. I was going to get one anyway."

"But you did employ an attorney of your choice within a week of hearing Mr. Sullivan's presentation?"

"Yes."

"And in talking to you, Mr. Sullivan never said he had to be the lawyer you hired, did he?"

"It was obvious he wanted it to be him."

"But he never said it had to be, did he?"

"No."

"Thank you Mr. Lombardo. I'll pass the witness." Biggers left the podium and walked with dignity back to the counsel table.

"Any further questions Mr. Torricelli?" Judge Hewitt asked.

"Yes, your honor." Torricelli approached the podium. "Mr. Lombardo, how did you feel when you left Mr. Sullivan's grief counseling session?"

Lombardo put clenched fists on the table before him. "Like I'd been used for Mr. Sullivan's personal advantage."

"Thank you." Torricelli looked at the judge. "The prosecution rests."

Judge Hewitt glanced at the clock on the back wall of the courtroom. "We'll take a fifteen minute break and reconvene at 2:45."

"I have a motion to present, your honor," Biggers said.

"I'll take that up in chambers with the lawyers."

The jury filed out and Biggers and Torricelli followed the judge. Rolly knew Biggers would make a motion for directed verdict and dismissal of the case, which would be duly overruled. They'd have to put on testimony to have a chance of winning. Rolly turned to go out for the break.

Jim McSpadden stood by the rear door of the courtroom talking to several other men. His beard needed trimming and he wore the same seedy sports coat Rolly had seen before. What was the jerk doing here? Coming to gloat over Rolly's problems?

As Rolly walked toward the rear door, a tall, red-haired young man crossed the courtroom toward him. Rolly hugged the boy, then held him at arm's length. His son had his mother's height and Rolly's own big jaw.

"You didn't have to come over here, Tommy," Rolly said.

"I thought you needed the moral support."

"This is no big deal."

"What do you mean, no big deal? They're trying to send you to prison."

"But they're not gonna do it."

Tommy smiled. "Anyway, I'm here. How's it going?"

"Did you hear that last witness?"

"Sure did."

"He's the main guy against me."

"He sure sounded upset."

"He is that. But no sweat. We're gonna beat 'em. How's school going?"

"Everything's in good shape."

"Don't cut classes over this trial."

"I won't. I got permission to be out today and tomorrow."

Tommy would graduate from SMU next year and come into practice with Rolly and Pedro. That is, if Rolly didn't go to jail.

Aside from Rae Jean, his son was all the family Rolly had that counted. His embittered father had died in a nursing home ten years ago and his mother hadn't lasted long after that. His brothers and sisters had scattered to the winds. He exchanged Christmas cards with them and that was about their only contact. They were different kinds of people, with different agendas.

Rolly and Tommy left the courtroom and bought coffee from a machine in an alcove in the hall. McSpadden came out and Rolly walked over to him, hand extended.

"I wouldn't think my problems would interest you so much Jim," Rolly said.

McSpadden shook his hand. "What happens here will sure have an effect on me."

"How's that?"

"It'll be hard to get our case to trial in May if you get convicted."

Rolly laughed. "Don't worry about it. I'm not gonna get convicted. And even if I am, we'll appeal. I'll still be able to handle the case."

"I don't see how you can with all the adverse publicity you'll get."

"Are you pulling for me to win then?"

McSpadden shook his head. "I can't really say I am. I think the way you got these cases was wrong."

Rolly nodded. McSpadden's attitude didn't surprise him. No doubt he was jealous. He wished he had all the cases. That way he could buy a new sports coat.

"Sorry you feel that way Jim. But don't worry. One way or another, we'll go forward."

"At least I'm still in it."

"Yeah, I saw where Meador's summary judgment got overruled. But there wasn't anything wrong with that truck steering."

McSpadden's face reddened. "Don't be too sure about that."

Rolly laughed. "If there's one thing I'm sure of, it's that nothing was wrong with that truck."

The bailiff came to the door of the court room and called into the hall. "Judge wants to get started again."

Rolly walked back into the courtroom and took his place at the defense counsel table. He and Biggers had discussed trial strategy the day before. Should Rolly testify? No, they had decided. Torricelli would hammer away at Rolly's motivation in setting up the counseling session. Charming as he was, he'd look like a jerk if he testified.

The prosecution had called Nadine as a witness earlier that day. She'd put everything in the best possible light for Rolly but still had to acknowledge that he asked her to set up the session and paid her for it. In spite of his confident predictions to Tommy and Jim McSpadden, Rolly knew Torricelli had proven a clear violation of the barratry statute. Biggers was going to have to earn his pay to win this one.

"Call your first witness, Mr. Biggers," Judge Hewitt said.

Biggers gripped the sides of the podium with his big hands. "I'll call Odell Wyatt."

With four blacks on the jury, Biggers and Rolly had decided to play the race card early. Thin and sad-faced, Wyatt stopped to be sworn, then took the witness stand. Biggers asked his name and established that he was the father of badly burned Demetria Wyatt.

"How did you learn about the meeting, Mr. Wyatt?" Biggers asked.

"Got a letter from Mrs. Graves."

"What'd it say?"

"To come to a counseling session at the Worthington."

"Did you go?"

"Yes I did."

"What appealed to you?"

Wyatt spread his hands. "I was just about wore out with going to the hospital, seeing my little girl laying there, burned so bad she'd never be the same. I needed to talk to someone about it."

"Did the session help?"

Wyatt nodded. "It sure did. I felt a lot better at the end."

"Did you stay for Mr. Sullivan's part of the program?"

"Yes, I did."

"And I believe you hired him to represent you and your family that same night?"

"I sure did."

"Any regrets about that decision?"

"No sir."

"Did it offend you for Mr. Sullivan to offer his services?"

Wyatt shook his head. "It sure didn't."

"Had you had time to look for a lawyer before that, Mr. Wyatt?"

"Naw. I'd been thinking about it, wondering who I'd get but I hadn't had time to do nothin' about it."

"What was your attitude about Mr. Sullivan's presentation?"

"I was glad he came. I could see he was a real good lawyer and it saved me the trouble of going out and looking for one."

"Thank you. I'll pass the witness."

Torricelli came to the podium, a friendly look on his face. "Mr. Wyatt, have you ever been involved in a litigation before?"

"What do you mean, litigation?"

"A case like this."

"I had a little car wreck claim that settled out of court."

"But have you ever had a case that went to trial?"

Wyatt shook his head. "No sir."

"Did you know that it was against the law for a lawyer to directly solicit accident victims like Mr. Sullivan did?"

Biggers pushed himself up. "I object, your honor. The judge defines what the law is, not Mr. Torricelli."

"Sustained," Judge Hewitt said. "The jury will disregard the question."

Score one for our side, Rolly thought.

Torricelli stepped back, looking down as though in thought, then moved to the podium again. "Is it fair to say, Mr. Wyatt, that you aren't very familiar with how the law works?"

"Sure. That's true."

"And you just don't know what the rules are, do you?"

"No I don't."

Torricelli looked up at the judge. "I have no further questions for this witness."

One by one Biggers called Rolly's clients to the stand. They all testified how glad they were that Rolly had made his presentation and expressed their great satisfaction with how he was handling their cases. For the most part, Torricelli left them alone. He was smart enough not to attack people who'd suffered like they had. In each case he did establish that they didn't know what a lawyer could lawfully do in contacting potential clients.

Biggers closed with his most sophisticated witness. Wearing a conservative blue suit, Al Richaud projected solid dependability.

"Were you offended by the fact Mr. Sullivan offered to talk to the accident victims about representation?" Biggers asked.

Richaud shook his head. "No I wasn't."

"Did you feel coerced in any way?"

"I sure didn't. I didn't have to talk to Mr. Sullivan. I could have left at any time."

"And did Mr. Lombardo have that same option?"

"He not only had that option, he exercised it."

Biggers finished his questions and Torricelli went to the podium for cross-examination. "Mr. Richaud, who instituted the contact between you and Mr. Sullivan?"

"I did." Richaud said.

Torricelli drew back. "Isn't it true you wouldn't have talked to him if he hadn't made a pitch for your business?"

"I might have. I was getting ready to try to find a lawyer and he's the best in this state."

"But you wouldn't have talked to him that night."

"No, I suppose not."

"So he instituted the contact between you?"

Richaud shook his head. "I wouldn't say so. I chose to talk to him."

Torricelli gave up. "That's all my questions."

∽

Rolly sat next to Biggers at the counsel table, sweating the jury verdict. Across the room, Torricelli leaned back in his chair with the front two legs off the floor, hands behind his head, frowning at the ceiling. A few spectators still lingered in the courtroom. The jury had been out for six hours and for the first time, Rolly thought he had a chance to win.

All his clients had stood by him and Biggers had done a good job in closing argument. Where were the victims here? Biggers had asked. No one was complaining except Roger Lombardo and he hadn't really been hurt. He was in the lawsuit, with a lawyer of his own choosing. And Rolly's clients had an attorney of their choosing. One they had gained through the counseling session. What harm had been done?

But Bobby Torricelli had done a good job, too. How Rolly's clients felt about their attorney wasn't the point, he'd told the jurors. The law didn't permit lawyers to directly solicit accident victims and there was a good reason for that rule. Grieving people who need attorneys should find them in their own way and not be subject to shameless sales pitches by hucksters like Rolly. The lawyers who play by the rules shouldn't lose out to the ambulance chasers.

Shameless sales pitches. Hucksters. Ambulance chasers. Those words stung Rolly to the quick. What did a criminal law hack like Torricelli know about high dollar personal injury law? How could he know how important it was in a case like Richaud versus Alamo Oil for the accident victims to get the right attorney quickly before the insurance companies got the best of them?

Rolly had no illusions about how the public felt about lawyers and he'd watched the jurors as Torricelli made his argument. He'd seen it hit home with some of them and expected a quick guilty verdict. Fast verdicts usually favored the prosecution in criminal cases and the insurance companies in civil damage cases. It took longer to do right than it did to do wrong. But six hours of deliberation on a simple question of guilt or innocence meant difference of opinion and that was good for the defense.

Two knocks suddenly sounded on the door of the jury room. Torricelli swung forward, bringing his chair legs to the floor with a sharp crack. Rolly's stomach flipflopped. Despite all his years of waiting for juries, cold excitement still gripped him at everything they did. He lived and died by their actions, especially in this case where his career hung in the balance. Did the knocks mean they'd reached a verdict?

Cora Kendrick, the thickset woman bailiff, walked to the jury room door and went inside. In a few seconds she came out holding a piece of paper in her hands.

"Oh my God!" Biggers said. "A note."

The bailiff took the paper back to Judge Hewitt's chambers. Minutes later the judge entered the courtroom in his robes and ascended the bench. Media people and spectators flooded in from the hall.

The judge held the paper in front of him. "The jury has sent out a note, which I'll read," he said. "'Your honor: we are unable to reach a verdict and appear to be hopelessly deadlocked. Please tell us what to do next.'"

Relief contended with disappointment in Rolly's mind. Verdicts in criminal trials had to be unanimous. The jury's failure to reach a decision would mean he wouldn't be convicted today but the State could retry him at a later time.

Judge Hewitt looked at the lawyers. "I hate to call it this soon. I'm going to ask them to deliberate further."

"I'd appreciate it, your honor," Torricelli said.

Biggers stood. "For the record, your honor, we oppose further deliberation. The note says the deadlock is hopeless. I don't believe the court should intimidate the jurors into doing something they wouldn't do on their own. I move for a mistrial."

"Overruled at this time," the judge said. "I'm gonna give 'em another shot at it."

Biggers leaned toward Rolly. "I'd like for them to find you not guilty but you know when the judge presses them like this, it usually goes the other way."

Rolly nodded. "All things considered, at this point, I'd settle for a mistrial."

After a coffee break the jury deliberated for two more hours then sent out another note. They were still split in the same way and there was no chance of agreement.

Judge Hewitt looked at Torricelli. "I'm gonna grant Mr. Biggers's motion."

Torricelli shrugged. "So be it, your honor."

The judge called the jury in and dismissed them. He thanked them for their service and told them their time had not been wasted despite their failure to reach a verdict. They had contributed to the integrity of the process and that was what was important.

As the jury filed out, Biggers went over to talk to Torricelli while Rolly and Tommy walked into the hall. The media people crowded around, cameras and mikes thrust forward.

"What do you think of the mistrial, Rolly?" asked the red-faced man.

Rolly smiled. "I'm disappointed the jury didn't reach a decision but I think the fact they couldn't shows just how weak the state's case is."

A scrawny reporter with an acne-scarred face pushed forward. "Will the state offer you a plea deal now?"

"I don't know," Rolly said. "But it doesn't matter. There'll be no deal as far as I'm concerned."

Gradually the media throng got their footage, their pictures, and their statements, and melted away.

Rolly turned to Tommy. "Thanks for coming over."

"I had to dad."

"Looks like I'll have to do it again."

"I'll be here for the next one, too."

Biggers came around the corner smiling. "It's been a pretty good day for us," he said.

Rolly shook his head. "I'd say just so-so. They've still got a shot at me."

"Yeah, but they're not gonna take it."

"What do you mean?"

"Torricelli and I talked to the jurors. They were split six to six. Torricelli said if he couldn't do any better than that he'd just let the case go. He's got a backlog of murderers and rapists he needs to try instead."

"He's disappointed today. He may change his mind tomorrow."

"I don't think so. I think he's serious. He's gonna move for dismissal. Your case really does have a pretty low priority compared with other things they handle."

"That's good," Rolly said. "I guess that means Ronald Hobbs and his boys on the grievance committee will fire up again and try to get me in San Antonio."

Biggers shook his head. "I talked to our friend Ronald a couple of days ago. He told me they'd go forward with the grievance if you got convicted but not otherwise. He's not into beating dead horses."

Rolly stuck out his hand. "Thanks for another good job, Bill."

"You're welcome Rolly. I wasn't sure we could come out on this one but we did. Just one more thing."

"What's that?"

"Don't bitch when you get my bill."

∽

Jim sat with Bobby Torricelli at Dirty's. Bobby stared into space, mouth set firmly.

"I'm sorry," Jim said.

Bobby slapped the table top with his palm, rattling the beer bottles. "I thought I had the son of a bitch."

"You never can tell what a jury will do."

"I had six of 'em convinced but the other six screwed me. That foreman was mad as hell at 'em. He walked out shaking his head."

"Rolly's clients all said they loved him."

"That's what did it all right. Couldn't they see they were helping a guilty bastard get off?"

Jim shook his head. "Either couldn't see it or didn't care."

"It might've helped if you'd testified."

Jim laughed. "I don't think so. My bitchin' would have sounded like sour grapes."

"But Rolly stole one of those cases from you."

"Not exactly. I'd never talked to Richaud."

"But that's so damn chickenshit."

"Life's chickenshit."

Bobby drained his beer and set the bottle down. "Oh to hell with it. Fuck it. I got better things to do than jackin' with a bastard like Rolly Sullivan. I'm gonna get back to dealing with dangerous criminals instead of little sneaks like him." Bobby turned to the bar. "Hey, Dirty! Bring us another round."

∽

Rolly bawled out the words of *Honkeytonk Angels* as he steered the green Jaguar down Highway 281 southwest of Fort Worth. The speedometer read ninety. He'd decided to take the scenic back way to San Antonio. The willows and elms were leafing out and redbuds brightened the underbrush beside the road. The road led through creek bottoms and over the crests of low, sweeping hills. He stopped singing and nudged the car up to one hundred.

He'd had a wonderful time with Nadine the night before. They'd celebrated his mistrial with a big barbecue dinner at Angelos, taken in a movie, and finished off with a marathon of lovemaking in Rolly's top floor suite at the Worthington. His dick stirred at the remembrance of her large, pendulous breasts swinging in his face. It was lucky for Rolly that her husband traveled so much.

What had made that damn fool, Torricelli, think he could convict Rolly Sullivan? Enough of the jurors had recognized his right to promote himself that the prosecution had been a futile gesture. Rolly pressed the accelerator, taking the car up to one ten, then one twenty.

He crested a hill. At the bottom, in a hollow by a creek, a black Texas Highway Patrol car waited, ass-end pointing its radar beam right at him.

"Shit!" Rolly said.

The cruiser's lights came on and it started pulling toward the road. Should he stop or put it to the floor? The police car was a full-sized sedan, not one of the small high performance types. In sudden decision he stomped the gas and whizzed by the officer at one twenty five.

He'd gone over two hills before he saw the police car again. Just as he topped a rise it appeared briefly in his rear mirror, about half a mile behind him on the crest of a hill. Then Rolly shot down into another creek bottom. Just beyond a bridge over the creek, a ranch road veered to the left. A paved road. Dirt or gravel wouldn't do because of the dust.

Smoothly, Rolly applied the brakes, taking care not to leave any skid marks and then accelerated onto the ranch road. Anxiously, he watched his rear view mirror until he cleared a small hill and went down the other side. The police car had not come into view. He pulled to the roadside, cut the motor, and lowered the windows. If the officer guessed right, Rolly's ass was history.

Seconds later, the police car roared by on the main highway, siren wailing. Rolly pulled back onto the ranch road and drove along it on it at a sedate pace for several miles until he came to an intersecting highway. Had the trooper guessed what he'd done and turned on this road? No way to know but life wasn't meant to be too safe. He turned east and headed back for the interstate. It would be best not to travel 281 any more today.

An hour later, with no unpleasant encounters, he rejoined the interstate at Temple and lost himself in the crowd of semi's and other traffic. He'd proven once again that he was bullet proof. Now, it was time to get into high gear on Richaud versus Alamo Oil. His Fort Worth investigator was still interviewing witnesses in Wise County. It was time for Rolly to get up there and talk to them himself.

# 11

The lawyers in Richaud versus Alamo Oil sat shoehorned in Jim's tiny conference room for Laura's deposition. The room had a close, unpleasant feel. They were starting late, at six o'clock, because they had deposed two of the accident victims earlier in the day at Kurtz's office in Dallas.

Laura sat next to Jim, pale and vulnerable-looking, wearing slacks and a white blouse. He hated the thought of throwing her to the wolves but the other attorneys were entitled under the rules to depose her prior to trial. At the end of the table, court reporter Bill Bittinger finished rolling a paper tape into his equipment and nodded to J. Michael Meador.

"Ready to go Mike," Bittinger said.

Meador leaned toward Laura, his face set in hostile lines. "State your name please."

He took her through the family history, where she and Danny had been born and raised, where they'd gone to school, the names and birthdays of their kids. He already had all this information from the interrogatories Laura had answered but conventional wisdom dictated asking it again so the deposition would read like a book—a book about the Marcus family.

Over the last several weeks all the other parties had been deposed in their lawyer's offices as part of the preparation for the trial, now only five weeks away. Lawyers didn't like surprises and detailed depositions prior to trial helped prevent them.

The intensity of the effort had turned Jim inside out. One by one, he'd listened to the victims describe what the accident had done to them and their families. He'd heard Al Richaud's gruesome account and of the psychiatric counseling his young son required.

Odell Wyatt and Roger Lombardo had detailed their personal versions of the catastrophe as had Dr. Mary Shaw and Rhonda Carter and the other survivors of Ruby Walthall. Now it was Laura's turn and Jim feared for her. Could she stand up to the gut-wrenching questions the lawyers would ask?

Hildebrand had offered to let Jim use his conference room since Jim's was really too small for this crowd but pride had prevented him from accepting the offer. It was easier for Laura to come to his office. If the bastards wanted to depose her, they could do it on his turf. Trouble was, Meador's hostile, overbearing face leered at Laura from only a few feet as he asked his questions. Jim wished there were more distance between them.

Meador took her through Danny's work history, then put his elbows on the table, the tips of his fingers touching. "Mrs. Marcus, I'd like to turn now to your husband's drinking problem."

Laura's face reddened. "He didn't have a drinking problem."

Meador smiled. "Wouldn't you call it a drinking problem when someone gets drunk and drives a tanker truck through a fence?"

"Don't argue with her Mike," Jim said. "Just ask her what she knows."

"Thanks. I'll do that very thing. How much did your husband drink Mrs. Marcus?"

"Not very much. Just a few beers at the ball games."

"Are you sure about that?"

"Yes."

"How do you account for the fact that a witness saw him drink eight or ten beers in a bar up in Wise County on the day of the accident?"

"That witness is wrong."

"You're sure about that?"

"Yes."

"He didn't ever drink when he was with his girlfriend?"

Laura raised her chin. "He didn't have a girlfriend."

"I guess you wouldn't know about that, would you?"

Jim slapped the table. "She's answered your question Mike. Go on to something else."

"I'll be glad to. How many DWI's had your husband had Mrs. Marcus?"

Jim sucked in his breath. Meador wouldn't have asked the question if he didn't have something. The other lawyers leaned forward, heightened interest in their eyes. All except Rolly who affected a bored look.

"None," Laura said.

"What if I told you he did have a DWI prior to the accident?"

Laura's voice shook. "I'd say you were lying."

"We'll see about that." Meador pulled a document from his briefcase and handed it to the court reporter. "Mark that, please."

Bittinger marked the paper as an exhibit and handed it back to Meador who handed it across the table to Laura. "I'd ask that you study the document I've just handed you and tell us if you can identify it."

Jim looked over Laura's shoulder at the paper. His stomach sank as he read it. Under seal of one of the criminal courts the record advised that one Daniel Murkus had been put on deferred adjudication for driving while intoxicated a year and two months before the wreck in August.

A note at the bottom advised he had completed the adjudication period and the case had been dismissed. Jim had checked the records for DWI's but hadn't thought to look for similar names. Trust J. Michael and his staff to be thorough. The misspelled name and the fact the charge did not count as a final conviction accounted for why the newspapers hadn't picked up the DWI at the time of the accident but the record clearly identified Danny.

Laura's lips trembled. "There must be some mistake. This isn't Danny."

Meador smiled. "It's got his address and birthdate, doesn't it?"

"But the name's wrong."

"Only the spelling. There's no doubt this DWI involved your husband Mrs. Marcus."

Jim clenched his fists under the table. "Are you asking questions or testifying?"

"I'm just trying to clear up why Mrs. Marcus didn't tell me about this DWI in her interrogatory answers. I'd hate to think she lied about it."

Tears ran down Laura's cheeks. "I didn't know. I just didn't know."

"So you admit this is your husband?"

"I guess it must be."

Meador nodded. "That's obvious, Mrs. Marcus. And isn't it also obvious that a man who would keep something like this from his wife might not tell her about his secret girlfriend?"

"Don't answer that question," Jim said. "It's argumentative."

Meador stared at Jim. "She'll have a lot harder questions to answer when we get to trial." He turned to Laura again. "How does it feel to be the wife of a man who killed eight people with his drunken driving?"

She put her hands to her face, sobbing. Blood fury ran through Jim's brain, extinguishing reason.

"You goddamn asshole!" he shouted.

He sprang from his chair, sending it crashing into the wall behind him, and threw himself across the table at Meador, driving his fist into J. Michael's patrician nose. Meador shook his head, sending a shower of blood to either side. Laura pushed away from the table and stood to the side, tears streaking her cheeks.

Anger replaced surprise in Meador's eyes and he charged, driving his fist into Jim's mouth. Tasting blood, Jim struck again, catching Meador's eye with a looping punch. Hildebrand moved in front of Jim and pushed him back from the table.

"Get hold of yourself, man. Think what you're doing."

Across the table, Kurtz and Sullivan held Meador on either side.

"Let me go," he yelled, trying to shake loose.

"Take it easy Mike," Kurtz said and Meador stepped back, glowering at Jim.

"You just screwed up big, McSpadden. You'll be off this case so fast it'll make your head swim."

Jim shot him the finger. "Fuck you asshole!"

Meador started forward again but Kurtz and Sullivan pulled him back.

"Just calm down Mike," Kurtz said. "I think we've done enough deposing for today. Let's all go home and have another run at this another time."

Sullivan handed Meador a paper towel from the coffee tray and he wiped the blood from his face. "I'm not coming back here again."

Portly and wise-looking, Kurtz nodded. "That's fine, Mike. Suit yourself. But for now, let's go home."

"I can't get out of this dinky little place fast enough."

Meador stuffed papers into his briefcase while Bill Bittinger disassembled his court reporting equipment and the other lawyers gathered their things. Laura leaned against the wall, her face wan and miserable.

Meador stormed out ahead of the rest. In a few minutes, Jim saw the other opposing lawyers out. Rolly Sullivan turned at the door. With a wink he shook Jim's hand.

"Way to go, Jim. I don't blame you for hitting the bastard."

Al Hildebrand stayed. His gravy-stained tie hung askew. "Looks like my main role in this case is keeping you from fighting J. Michael."

Jim grinned. "You fell down on the job tonight."

"You were too fast for me. We need to talk about this DWI that Meador's come up with but Laura's too upset to do it now."

"I'll call you tomorrow."

Hildebrand left. Jim locked the door of the office and went back to the conference room. Still sitting at the table, Laura had her compact out and was wiping streaks of mascara from her cheeks with a Kleenex.

She looked up at Jim, anger in her eyes. "Do I have to face that man again?"

"Probably. But we'll do it in Hildebrand's conference room so you'll have more distance. Next time we'll be ready for him on that DWI."

"I didn't know about it."

"That was obvious. Can you remember how Danny might have got one?"

She nodded. "I've been thinking about it. A little over a year ago, he went to a bachelor party for a friend and didn't make it home. We had a big argument. I told him he could at least have called but he said he fell asleep on a sofa and didn't wake up till morning."

"I guess he didn't want you to know he got arrested."

"He was like that. Is this DWI a problem?"

Jim sat next to her. "It could be. It isn't really a big deal. He was put on deferred adjudication, fulfilled the court's conditions, and the case was dismissed. It doesn't count as a conviction."

"Can Meador talk about it in court?"

"Maybe. He might be able to get it in as evidence of a pattern of conduct, especially since we denied Danny'd ever had a problem."

"But I didn't know." She covered her face with her hands. "What a nightmare!"

Tears brimmed in Jim's eyes. Laura didn't deserve this hassle. Not on top of everything else. He put his arm around her shoulder and pulled her to him.

"Don't cry," he said.

She buried her face in his chest and he held her, loving her for the pain she had endured. She looked up and they kissed; her tongue probed his mouth, hurting him slightly as it passed over the wound left inside by Meador's blow. Jim got up, took her hand, and pulled her to her feet. They pressed their bodies together. He ran his hands over her buttocks.

"I love you Laura," he said.

She shook her head. "Don't say that."

Jim led her through the empty offices to the waiting room where she faced him, desire in her eyes. He unbuttoned her blouse and pushed it over her arms, then unfastened her brassiere and let it fall to the floor. He cupped her small breasts in his hands, then ran his tongue over her nipples. She stepped back, loosened her belt, and let her skirt drop around her ankles.

Seconds later, they stood naked before each other. Her tall, taut-stomached figure projected an almost unendurable sensuality. He turned off the lights and pulled her down onto a couch and they made love in the half-light of the darkened office. Later, they lay entwined as the sweat cooled on their bodies. She put her hand on the cut on his lip.

"Does it hurt much?"

He shook his head. "Doesn't amount to anything."

"What will the judge do?"

"Don't know. I'm sure we'll have a hearing. Meador'll get all the mileage out of it he can."

She put her head on his shoulder. "It seems funny being with a man again."

"Are you sorry?"

"No. It was going to happen, sooner or later."

"I meant what I said."

"About what?"

"I love you."

She laughed. "Don't be silly." She got up and started putting on her clothes.

Half an hour later Jim drove toward his town house with the scent of her perfume still on his skin, the feel of her head against his chest strong in his memory. He didn't mind the throbbing of his cut lip and scarcely thought of the bad turn the case had taken. The feel, the look, the joy of Laura possessed him.

∽

Judge Ferreira looked over the edge of the bench at the lawyers assembled before him, his face stern. Jim sat alone at one table while J. Michael and his pupil, the high-domed Malcolm R. H. Witherspoon, occupied the other. J. Michael didn't need Witherspoon's legal help with this hearing; he had probably come as an unlikely bodyguard.

Jim had a fat lip but Meador sported both a swollen nose and a greenish-black ring around one eye. Meador had moved for monetary sanctions and asked that Jim be disqualified from further participation in the case.

The judge cleared his throat. "I've studied Mr. Meador's motion and Mr. McSpadden's response. I must say I find what has happened disgusting. Attorneys should be professional enough that there should never be any question of violence during a deposition.

"I'm going to admonish both of you in the strongest possible terms to avoid anything like this in the future. I'll refer any further physical confrontation between the two of you to the appropriate grievance committee."

Meador raised his hand. "May I be heard, your honor?"

"Yes Mr. Meador."

J. Michael stood. "I would never have hit Mr. McSpadden if he hadn't hit me first."

Judge Ferreira rocked slowly in his swivel chair. "I'm aware Mr. McSpadden struck the first blow, Mr. Meador. And for that reason I'm going to fine him five hundred dollars, payable immediately."

Jim let out a breath of relief. He couldn't really spare five hundred dollars right now but the sanction could have been so much worse.

Meador's face showed his disappointment. "What about my motion to disqualify, your honor?"

"I'm going to deny that motion. It wouldn't be fair to Mr. McSpadden's client to deprive her of his representation at this late date. I expect both of you to work together with no further problems. And Mr. Meador, I will tell you that

I have read the deposition transcript and it demonstrates considerable provocation on your part. In the future I expect you ask proper questions and not to bullyrag the witnesses."

"I'm entitled to test their credibility, your honor."

The judge shook his head. "What you did with Mrs. Marcus went well beyond that. Don't test my patience by arguing about it."

Meador lowered his head. "Yes, your honor."

Jim waited while the judge left the bench and Meador and Witherspoon cleared the courtroom. He had no desire to exchange pleasantries with either of them in the hall. He'd go right to the clerk's office and pay his fine. He was the real winner of this skirmish. Smashing Meador's face had been worth every penny.

∽

Rolly sat at his desk the Monday after Laura Marcus's deposition in Fort Worth, taking pleasure in recalling what had happened. Jim McSpadden was kind of goofy but not a bad guy. Rolly had a more favorable opinion of him now. On the other hand, J. Michael Meador represented the kind of lawyer Rolly despised; the kind he had fought all his life.

He'd enjoyed seeing the blood fly when McSpadden hit Meador in the face. Laura Marcus didn't deserve Meador's contempt even if her husband's drunkenness had caused the accident. Besides, Meador's vicious stupidity had interfered with Rolly's game plan. He'd learned about Marcus's earlier DWI and planned to save the evidence for trial.

Forewarned, McSpadden would be ready now. He seemed awfully protective of Laura. Was he fucking her? Probably so. Rolly approved. He'd do the same in McSpadden's place.

The intercom buzzed and Rolly pushed the button. "Yes?"

"Mr. Pritchard on line five," Maria said.

Rolly had hired laconic Bud Pritchard to investigate the case in Fort Worth and Wise County. He'd proved his worth by getting copies of the court papers on Danny Marcus's DWI. What else did he have?

"Hello Bud."

"How ya doin' Rolly?"

"Pretty good. What you got?"

"I talked to those witnesses at that bar up north of Decatur."

"What'd they say?"

"Cline and Arnold said they weren't in the place that day but Billy Potter remembered your guy. He backs up Norvella Poteet. Says Marcus came in, got

183

shit-faced drunk over a couple of hours, and left, claiming he had a hot date in Fort Worth."

" 'Course, I need for Marcus to be drunk," Rolly said, "but I damn sure don't need him running off after a woman. If he was awol from his job, I'm down to only six million in coverage."

"I know."

"What's Potter like?"

"A little, rat-faced guy. The kind you wouldn't trust with your wallet. And he's thick with Norvella. When I went in the bar and told her who I was she called him on the phone and he came running."

"You think he's lying?"

"Sure do."

"How do we prove it?"

"I been workin' on that. After I talked to Potter I hung around outside, asking other customers about Marcus."

"What'd you find out?"

"Most of 'em didn't know anything one way or another but finally, this big guy pulled up in one of those tandem gravel trucks. I caught him before he went in and he told me he did remember Marcus. Norvella came to the door and gave us a dirty look but we got in his truck and I got a recorded statement."

"What'd he say?"

Pritchard outlined what the gravel truck driver had told him and Rolly knew he had to talk to the man in person. Two days later he flew to the DFW Airport, rented a Chrysler Imperial, and headed to the northwest toward Wise County. He had talked to the trucker on the phone and gotten directions to his place.

Spring rains had visited the area, bringing out a profusion of wild flowers on the face of the prairie. The red and yellow of Indian blanket vied with yellow daisies and pink primroses, and tall, showy plumes of skyrockets thrust up from the sides of the ditches.

North of Decatur he spotted Norvella Poteet's bar on the access road to the highway. It occupied an old white frame shed with half the paint gone. Norvella's Place—Beer and Hamburgers advised a sign at the roofline. Next door a Diamond Shamrock station solicited travelers with rows of pumps, a convenience store, and several truck repair bays.

Following the trucker's directions he turned on the next gravel county road. In a mile and a half he turned at a mailbox onto a chugholed private road that led to a blue and white mobile home on cinder blocks, stark and lonely in the middle of a pasture. A large Mack truck attached to a gravel-hauling trailer sat beside the mobile home.

As Rolly got out of the Imperial, a lethargic hound lying in the shade of the mobile home struggled to its feet and came toward him, showing its teeth and growling. He got back in the car. The trailer door opened and a huge man came down the metal steps. About thirty-five, broad with massive arms straining the sleeves of his T-shirt, he had to weigh at least three hundred.

"Come on out. He don't bite," he called.

Rolly left the car again and walked toward the big man. The dog slunk back to his shady place. Rolly put out his hand.

"Mr. Cooley?"

"That's me, but call me Tank." Cooley surrounded Rolly's hand with his. "Come on inside."

They sat at a Formica-topped table in the tiny kitchen.

"You live here by yourself?" Rolly asked.

Tank shook his head. "Nope. Got a wife and two kids. Kids are in school, wife's at work."

"How's the gravel business?"

"It's good. I'd be working today if I wasn't talkin' to you."

Rolly took the cue. "I'll sure pay for your time."

"I figure I could of made three hundred bucks."

"Really?"

"You bet. They're repavin' a section of the interstate north of Dallas. We been haulin' till after dark every day."

"I'll write you a check when we're through."

"I'd rather have cash."

"Cash it'll be then."

Rolly pulled out a transcribed copy of the statement the investigator had taken and turned on a small tape recorder. He put it on the table between Cooley and him.

"I wanted to go over the things Bud Pritchard covered with you," he said.

"What do you want to know?"

"Do you actually remember seeing Danny Marcus in Norvella's Place on the day of the accident?"

"I seen a pretty big guy in a shirt with an Alamo Oil patch on it sittin' at a back table by hisself."

"What do you mean, pretty big? Big as you?"

Cooley laughed. "Ain't nobody big as me. Naw, not that big, but a good-sized man."

"When did you first notice him?"

"When I come in. The rain had shut down the job I was working so I come home early. Figured I might as well have a few beers, so I went to Norvella's."

"How many people in the place?"

"Not many. Norvella and Billy and half a dozen others. I stayed most of the afternoon and the place never did fill up."

"Did you talk to Marcus any?"

Tank shook his head. "Naw. I got to jawin' with Norvella. She's the only one I talked to."

"Is she a friend of yours?"

"Not 'specially. I don't like her much. She's a sleazy bitch but she makes good hamburgers and her beer's cold."

"Did Marcus drink any beer?"

Cooley looked out the window, massive forehead wrinkled in concentration. "I didn't notice but he probably did. Most everyone who comes in there has a beer or two. I know he had a hamburger and some chips."

"But you can't say how much he drank?"

"Nope. Just didn't notice."

"Did he play the jukebox any?"

Tank shrugged. "Might have. Didn't notice."

"Who left first, you or Marcus?"

"He did. I was talkin' to Norvella at the register. He got up, made a call on the pay phone, then come up to pay his bill."

"What'd he say?"

"Nothin' much. Just asked for his ticket and paid it."

"Was he drunk?"

"He wasn't stumblin' or nothin' but he might 'a been drunk. I really couldn't tell."

"Did he say anything about having a date?"

Tank scratched the back of his neck. "I didn't hear him say nothin' like that."

"Were you there the whole time he was paying his bill?"

"Yep."

"And he didn't say he had a hot date?"

"Not that I heard."

Rolly paused. He'd covered everything on the statement Pritchard had taken. Cooley didn't clearly remember that Marcus was drunk but Rolly didn't need him for that. What Cooley could do was to refute Norvella's claim that Marcus had a date with some woman, and that was critical to Rolly's case. What else did he know?

"Did you ever see the Alamo Oil truck?" Rolly asked.

Tank wrinkled his forehead again. "It wasn't parked in front of the bar. Might 'a been on the truck stop parkin' lot."

186

"But you didn't see it?"

"Naw, sure didn't."

Rolly looked over the statement and the notes he had made in the margin. "I guess that's just about it. Can you think of anything we haven't talked about."

"Not that happened that day."

"What do you mean? Did you see Marcus another time?"

"Naw. That was the only time I seen him. And after that he was dead. But Norvella and Billy was talkin' about him a coupla weeks later."

"Tell me about that."

Tank leaned back and the metal frame of his chair complained. "I was in there at lunch grabbin' a quick hamburger. Norvella was up at the register readin' the paper. She called Billy over and told him she'd seen somethin' about that truck driver that was killed. They put their heads together and started lookin' at the paper and then Norvella said they could make some money off this deal."

"Did you know what they were talking about?"

"No. Just that they was talkin' about Marcus."

"What paper was it?"

"The *Star-Telegram.*"

"About two weeks after the accident?"

"About that."

Rolly looked out the window at the sunny field under the cloudless spring day. What had happened two weeks after the accident? What had Norvella and Billy Potter been talking about?

"Norvella sure seems to see a lot of Billy," Rolly said.

Cooley nodded. "I think they're shackin' up."

"Isn't there a Mr. Poteet around somewhere?"

"I ain't never seen him."

"Anything else you can think of?"

Tank shook his head. "Nope. I told you all I know."

Rolly pulled out his wallet and handed Tank three crisp one hundred dollar bills. "Thanks for talking to me. I may need you to testify in a couple of weeks. You gonna be around?"

"Sure. If you pay me for my time."

Back on the highway Rolly headed for the Diamond Shamrock truck stop. He'd just see if anyone there knew anything. Wasn't any point in trying to talk to Norvella or Billy. He already knew the story he'd get from them. But a visit to the *Star-Telegram* newspaper morgue in Fort Worth was in order. Maybe he could figure out what had piqued Norvella's interest in the case by going through old issues of the paper.

Midway through the first week in May, Jim called Rusty Day in Chicago. "You found out anything for me?" Jim asked.

"Nothing yet Mr. McSpadden but I'm working on it."

"Cut out that Mr. McSpadden stuff. Call me Jim."

"I still think of you as Tex."

"You can use Tex or Jim but not Mr. McSpadden. You got any leads?"

"Not yet. I been going in Slim's after work several times a week trying to catch someone drunk enough to talk and let something slip but Doug's pretty well warned 'em not to talk to me. Even when they're drunk, they just walk away. And he caught me in there the other day and started pushing me around till that guy, Joe, who owns the place, made him quit."

"Be careful Rusty. He's a lot bigger than you are."

"Don't I know it though."

"Doesn't sound like you're gonna get anything out of Slim's."

Rusty laughed. "You're probably right. Doug's poisoned the water there. I'm gonna start eating lunch in the cafes around the plant and keep my ears open."

"Even if you don't find out anything new, I'm gonna need you to testify in this trial. I want the jury to know Harrigan's not leveling with 'em about their problems."

"Just send me a ticket and I'll be there."

"Thanks, Rusty. Keep track of your time. I'll see that you get paid for it eventually."

"Don't worry about that, Mr. McSpadden."

"Jim."

"Okay, Jim."

That evening after Susan left, Laura came to the office from her shift at the bank. She told Jim she had a new second job as a cashier in a Jiffy Dan convenience store on the west side, away from the high crime danger that had worried him. She worked eight to twelve p.m., four days a week. Between the two jobs she didn't have much time for anything else. He hadn't seen her since her deposition several weeks earlier.

She sat across the desk, elegant in a beige business suit. He studied the soft lines of her face, remembering their lovemaking on the couch.

"You gonna wear that outfit to the Jiffy Dan?" he asked.

She shook her head. "It's too classy for that place. I'll go home and change to my jeans."

"I won't keep you long. I just wanted to go over our game plan for the trial."

"I'm not looking forward to it."

"I know."

"Have our chances improved any?"

"Not really. My guy in Chicago hasn't come up with anything new. All we've really got is his testimony that Harrigan has problems with the steering. But their CEO's gonna swear under oath that's not true."

"We haven't made any progress, have we?"

"No, but we'll give it our best shot."

For the next half hour they went over the depositions in the case, the interrogatories they had answered, and all the other things she might be asked about.

Around six-thirty, Laura looked at her watch. "I'd better get going. Don't want to be late."

Jim nodded. "We've covered everything we need to, for now. We'll need to get together with Al Hildebrand one more time the weekend before the trial."

"What do I tell them at work about this trial?"

"It's scheduled to start the 18th of May and my guess is it'll last five or six weeks."

"Do I have to be there the whole time?"

"Unfortunately yes."

"Do you think I can work my night job?"

He shook his head. "Don't even think about it. You wouldn't get enough rest. And you've still got to take care of your kids."

"I guess you're right. I may lose both my jobs over this."

"Talk to your bosses. I'll write letters to them if it'll help."

"I think the bank will give me a leave of absence but Jiffy Dan probably won't be so understanding."

"You gonna be able to meet your expenses while you're off?"

"I think so. I've saved a little since last fall and I can hold out."

"Get on to work, then. You might as well make money while you still can."

He followed her to the front door of the office, admiring the grace of her walk, the curve of her neck. She turned at the door and he drew her to him, smelling her perfume, feeling the warmth of her body.

"Whatever happens, I want to see more of you."

She put her cheek against his chest. "You've been good for me, Jim, but I'm not sure what I feel for you. Let's give it some time until this trial's over."

"The trial won't make any difference in how I feel about you."

She looked up, tears in her eyes. "I know that."

He kissed her. "Good night Laura."

"Good night."

He watched her walk down the hall to the elevators, then went back to his desk where thoughts of her vanquished his resolve to work on the case. He daydreamed for half an hour, shoved the file away in disgust, and went home.

In the days that followed he spent most of his time at the office in pretrial preparation. He knew Rolly Sullivan, Kurtz, and the others considered him a minor player without a chance to win, but he owed it to Laura to be ready.

Al Hildebrand represented her in defense of the case against Danny but Jim and he had agreed Jim would take the lead on her part of the case. United of Rhode Island thought Danny would surely be found liable and was reconciled to paying its six million under the basic coverage and its umbrella.

The company was banking on Kurtz to get a jury finding Danny had left his employment at the time of the wreck so all they'd owe would be the six million. Essentially, Hildebrand had been hired to hold Laura's hand. An aggressive, conscientious lawyer, he didn't see his role as so limited and would use anything he or Jim could find to improve Laura's chances.

In his heart Jim knew he'd never get to the jury on Rusty Day's testimony something was wrong with the steering. Rusty just didn't know enough. A directed verdict dismissing Laura's claim against Harrigan was almost a sure thing. Still, Jim would see the case through, do the work, and spend the money to bring little Rusty down from Chicago. Lightning might strike and give him the breaks he needed.

Trouble was, he'd been working so much on this case he'd neglected the few others he had. He'd borrowed heavily to meet office expenses and couldn't keep things going much longer. He lay awake nights, stomach churning, as he contemplated the possibility of bankruptcy by the end of the summer. But each day he doggedly dragged himself to the office for another round of what seemed futile preparation.

On the Friday at the end of the first full week in May with the trial one week away, Gene Burns called Jim at the office.

"How about taking a break and having dinner and a few drinks with Bobby and me at Jernigan's tonight?"

Jim started to decline. He'd planned to spend the whole weekend in drafting jury instructions and trial motions. But he didn't really have that much to do and he needed to distance himself from the work before it put him under. He could take Friday night and Saturday off and work all day Sunday.

"What time ya'll gonna do it?" he asked.

"Around eight. We won't stay too late."

"I'll be there."

That evening Jim sat with Gene and Bobby at their usual table against the wall, listening to Clifton Cameron and his group while they waited for their steaks. The slender singer with the infectious smile launched into a wistful rendition of *Tenderly*.

Jim looked at Gene. "Haven't seen much of you lately. What've you been doing?"

Gene twisted his mouth in self-depreciation. His faded red hair and incongruous freckles gave him the look of an aging juvenile delinquent. "I'm just trying to keep my office running. How about you?"

"I've been so tied up on this Alamo Oil case I haven't had time for anything else."

"How's it coming?"

"Not good. The trial'll take over a month and we're probably gonna lose."

Torricelli snorted. "I can sure sympathize. I still haven't got over what the jury did with your friend Rolly."

"You could have tried him again."

"Oh sure. And probably with the same result. It just wasn't worth it."

Jim laughed. "I guess we're just a bunch of losers."

"Not all of us," Bobby said. "Gene beat me on one two weeks ago. Everybody whups up on me these days."

"What kind of case?"

"A DWI negligent homicide. Gene's client got three sheets in the wind, busted a red light, and killed a nice old man and his wife."

Gene shook his head. "Be fair now Bobby. That's not exactly true. My guy ran the red light but he wasn't drunk."

"Oh, come on, Gene. You may have sold the jury on that bullshit but we both know he was drunk. According to witnesses, he was weaving all over the road and had run two other lights. The investigating officers smelled alcohol on him and there was a mess of empty beer cans in the car."

"Did they do a breath test?" Jim asked.

Torricelli shook his head. "Couldn't. He was out cold with a head injury so they sent him to the hospital in an ambulance but they did a blood test there."

"And it was negative," Gene said in triumphant tone.

"There was some kind of screwup. There's no way that man hadn't been drinking."

Gene shrugged. "Maybe not Bobby. Maybe not. But the blood test made for enough doubt the jury found him not guilty."

Bobby's dark face turned bitter. "You got a free one on me, just like Rolly Sullivan."

During the interplay between Burns and Torricelli Jim's pulse had quickened. "Who did the blood test?" he asked.

"E. M. Daggett Hospital," Bobby said.

"When did this wreck happen?"

Bobby looked at Gene. "It was back in August wasn't it?"

"That's right."

Jim put his hands on the table. "This sure sounds like the reverse of the problem with my driver in Alamo Oil. It was out of character for him to drink on the job but the blood test shows him double the legal limit. You reckon Daggett got the blood tests mixed up?"

Bobby laughed. "I wouldn't be surprised at anything those bozos did but I don't know how you'd prove it."

"I'd sure like to know if the two accidents were on the same date."

Gene's face assumed a guarded look. "You couldn't tie the two things together even if they were."

"Relax Gene," Jim said. "Your guy's already been found not guilty. He can't be tried again."

"That's true. But there's still a civil case pending. He's not my favorite client but I can't help you."

"Why don't you like him?" Jim asked.

"Still owes me money and says he's not gonna pay. Told me after I'd got him off that I overcharged him."

"You don't have to get involved," Bobby said. He looked at Jim. "You gonna be in the office in the morning?"

Jim had changed his mind about taking the day off. "Yes, I'll be there."

"I'll check the file and send you an email."

"What's this guy's name?"

"Homer Dorfenweider."

"That's easy to remember."

The rest of the evening, Jim could hardly keep his mind on his friends. This could be the break he'd been needing. A mixup in the tests would account for false reports on both men, showing Danny drunk when he was wasn't, and Gene's client sober when he was drunk. Around ten, Jim made his excuses and went home. He now had a reason for going to work in the morning.

When he got to the office the next day an email message from Bobby told him Dorfenweider's wreck had occurred on the fifteenth of August, the same day as the Alamo Oil accident. Dorfenweider had gone to the hospital around 11:00 p.m., while the big freeway crash had been in the afternoon, but blood samples from the two wrecks had undoubtedly been in the E. M. Daggett lab at the same time.

But how could he prove a screwup had occurred? Natty little  Delbert Dillow, the lab supervisor, had a government bureaucrat's uncanny knack for stonewalling. He'd just claim his department never made mistakes and both tests were correct.

Bobby closed his email window and returned the computer to the home page of pricklypear.net, his internet service provider. What would happen if he put the name Dorfenweider on one of the internet search engines? He knew he couldn't isolate anything with meaning searching with Smith or Jones but Dorfenweider was unusual enough something might turn up.

Not all the search engines looked for the same things. His best bet would be to use Dogpile, a site that searched many different search engines for their best results. He pulled the keyboard forward and made the proper entries. When the scrappy pooch logo of the Dogpile site came up he entered the name of Gene's ungrateful client and waited, full of hope.

**12**

Jim sat with Laura and Al Hildebrand at a temporary table next to the bailiff's desk as they watched Rolly preparing to question the jury panel on the first day of the trial of Richaud versus Alamo Oil. Ordinarily, one counsel table for the plaintiffs and one for the defendants sufficed but this case involved more than twenty-five different parties and nine lawyers. A stuffy feel pervaded the courtroom, contributing to an atmosphere of suspicion and hostility.

Rolly and Al Richaud had the place of honor at the main counsel table of the plaintiffs while Art Kurtz sat with Marlin Reeves at the central defense table. Reeves was serving as Alamo Oil's corporate representative. Linda Fuller, Alfred Escamillo, and Keith Carroll, the lawyers representing the remaining plaintiffs, shared a table behind Rolly.

Mike Meador and Malcolm Witherspoon sat behind Kurtz with Doug Spivak who represented Harrigan Motors. Meador had advised the judge that Gerald Forbes would come down from Chicago when Jim started his part of the case.

Bailiff Juan Vasquez had jammed Roger Lombardo, Odell Wyatt and his daughter, and all the other plaintiffs onto the spectator's benches in one section of the courtroom. The fifty- person jury panel occupied the remaining two sections.

Judge Ferreira rocked in his swivel chair behind the bench. He had sworn the panel in, advised the panel members of the ground rules, and had them state their names, addresses, and occupations. Now, Rolly was starting his voir dire—the questioning process that would determine which of them were selected. He had turned the podium around toward the prospective jurors and all the lawyers and parties inside the bar had also turned to face them.

He stepped up to the podium, his square face friendly but serious. "Good morning ladies and gentlemen." His voice held rich intonations of confidence and good will that instantly put the confused, resentful mob at ease.

He launched into a folksy introduction that set the stage for the points he would make and the questions he would ask the panel. He was Rolly Sullivan from San Antonio and had practiced law down there for about twenty-five years. Had any of the people on the panel heard of him?

Ten or twelve hands went up and Rolly called on one of the volunteers, a man in khaki pants and a sports shirt. From the jury information cards Jim saw he worked on line in the General Motors plant in Arlington. Rolly was smart to call on him instead of the banker in the immaculate pinstripe who'd likely be unsympathetic.

"Mr. Kendal, how'd you become acquainted with me?"

Rolly called the man's name with confidence and without looking at any notes. With a sense of awe Jim realized Sullivan had memorized the last names and seating positions of the entire panel—all fifty of them—in the thirty minutes since the bailiff had handed the panel list to the lawyers. It was a feat Jim would never have attempted for fear of getting a name wrong.

Kendal smiled like Rolly's long-lost friend. "I read where you got someone around a hundred million down in South Texas last year."

Frowning, Art Kurtz stood. "Your honor, I object to Mr. Sullivan going into his past successes. I'd ask that his questions be confined to what personal knowledge the jurors may have of him and not to what they may have read or seen on the media."

Judge Ferreira stopped rocking. "I sustain the objection. Mr. Sullivan, just ask if they know you."

Rolly turned to the judge with an obliging smile. "Yes, your honor."

He questioned the others who had raised their hands. None of them knew him personally. Kurtz's objection had stopped him before he went very far but he had used Kendal to make the point that he was a high dollar lawyer with at least one person on the panel who thought well of him.

With his facile face somber, he described the accident. Had any of the panel members heard of it? Again, hands went up and Rolly asked what each person knew. Most of them had seen news coverage of the wreck but one man had come on the scene while the fires were still raging. Jim knew he would be excused for cause. His personal knowledge of what had happened might interfere with his objectivity.

With subtle craft Rolly conveyed the enormity of the catastrophe as he asked the panel members what damages they could award. Could they award Al Richaud damages for the physical pain and suffering his wife and daughters had suffered as they burned to death? Did anyone on the panel object to that kind of damages? Could they award Al damages for his own mental anguish sustained from seeing the bodies of his loved ones in the car at the scene? Could they award Demetria Wyatt mental anguish and disfigurement damages for the burn scars she would always bear?

Over a period of several hours Rolly went over what he expected to prove for each of his clients. In a routine case a lawyer was lucky to get forty-five minutes for his whole voir dire but this was not a routine case and Rolly had a lot of folks to cover. When he finally concluded and sat down Jim had the sense that Rolly was in control, the panel loved him, and he would be very hard to beat.

True, several conservative types had expressed reservations about the amount of the damages but there weren't that many of them. Rolly had undoubtedly duly noted who they were and could get rid of them with the peremptory challenges the law allotted him to use as he saw fit.

The lawyers for the remaining plaintiffs followed Rolly, echoing his sentiments with "me too" enthusiasm. They were all sure the jury that was selected would be as fair to their clients as those of the great Rolly Sullivan.

The voir dire of the plaintiffs' lawyers took all the first day. At five-thirty, Judge Ferreira called time and excused everyone for the night. Jim approached the door of the courtroom at the same time as Doug Spivak. Jim stood aside and made a sweeping motion with his hand.

"After you Doug."

Glowering and red-faced, Spivak held back. "Fuck you, Tex."

With a smile Jim preceded Spivak through the door. Outside the courthouse Jim walked with Laura and Al Hildebrand toward the parking lot.

"What do you think?" Laura asked.

Hildebrand shrugged. "It's about what I expected. Rolly did a good job of laying out his position but what he says isn't evidence."

"It was sure impressive how he memorized all those names," Jim said.

Hildebrand twisted his mouth. "It's a good trick but there's no substance to it. I don't think it'll make much difference."

Jim kept his disagreement to himself. Anyone so focused he could memorize an entire jury panel and still successfully juggle all the other things he had to do in a voir dire was bound to look like he had a leg up on the other lawyers.

Kurtz opened the next morning. His shock of white hair and rumpled but expensive-looking suit gave him a grandfatherly, dependable look. Solemnly, he told the jury panel he was Art Kurtz of Kurtz, Jacobs, and Silverstein in Dallas. He had the onerous task of representing Alamo Oil Company, a large corporation. But a corporation was just a collection of people making decisions very much like individuals made in their own families. And the people of a corporation were entitled to the same fair consideration as individual parties.

Did anyone think Alamo Oil should be liable just because it had a lot of money? None of the panel raised hands. Did any of them think it should be liable just because it had the nerve to appear in a Fort Worth courtroom with a Dallas lawyer? Several of the people laughed and Kurtz smiled.

He said of course they didn't think like that because that would be wrong and he was sure the panel members would be just as fair to a big corporation with a Dallas lawyer as they would to an individual. And the evidence would show in this case that Alamo should not be liable at all because its driver had gotten drunk on duty and gone off on an excursion of his own.

Did anyone think a company should be liable for the actions of a driver who was not taking care of company business? Again, no hands. Kurtz nodded. He was sure the jury ultimately selected would be fair and would look forward to working with them. Beaming a reassuring smile at the panel, he sat down.

Jim's turn to shine had come. As attorney for Laura as cross-plaintiff he had no case against Alamo Oil and Judge Ferreira had deferred his presentation until after Kurtz's. Now, the time had come to tell the people why Danny should not be liable and why Harrigan Motors should pay Laura and her family many millions of dollars.

With his heart in his throat he went to the podium. He told the people he had the privilege to represent the widow and children of Danny Marcus. They'd already heard about Danny from Rolly Sullivan and Art Kurtz who both said his criminal negligence in driving a gasoline tanker while intoxicated had caused the accident. Kurtz even said he was using the Alamo truck for a joyride at the time of the accident.

Jim's job was to show the jury a different Danny Marcus, a devoted family man who, far from being on a drunken joyride, had been on his way to the Alamo terminal. From there he had planned to go home so he could present his wife and family with tickets to a Rangers game. Were there any people on the panel who could not keep an open mind and go into the trial just as prepared to believe Jim's version of the facts as Rolly's or Art Kurtz's?

A brown-haired man in his mid-forties on the third row held up his hand. Jim checked his seating chart and notes. Bill Winkler. Married with two pre-teen children, taught math in a middle school. "Yes Mr. Winkler?"

He stood. "I've got an open mind all right, Mr. McSpadden, but what about that blood test?"

"That's certainly a problem for us but we plan to bring you testimony showing that the test was wrong. Can you wait until you hear all the evidence before making up your mind about it?"

"I'll sure try to." Winkler sat down.

Now Jim had to confront the weakest part of his case. With trepidation, he made his pitch.

"Ladies and Gentlemen, we expect the evidence to show that this accident happened not because Danny Marcus was drunk on duty but because the steering on the Harrigan Motor Company truck he was driving jammed, causing the truck to veer to the left and go through the median fence into the vehicles involved in the collision on the other side of the road.

"We will bring you evidence that similar accidents had happened with other Harrigan trucks on at least two occasions, coupled with testimony from a former Harrigan worker that Harrigan is covering up the problems with its steering system. Our automotive engineer will testify that, based on these facts, in his opinion, a defect in the steering caused the wreck.

"I must tell you that we don't have specific testimony about the nature of the defect because Harrigan has concealed that information. And that brings me to this question: Could you consider the possibility that a defect in the truck steering caused the accident even if you didn't know specifically what the defect was?"

Jim singled out Betty Alkek, a woman airline pilot. Early fifties, greying blonde hair, married to another pilot. She had impressed Jim as a tough nut, likely to be skeptical.

"Ms. Alkek, could you make a finding like that?"

The pilot stood, face twisted in doubt. "I'd have a hard time with it if I didn't know the nature of the defect."

"But what if we proved to you that the reason we didn't have that information was because Harrigan was withholding it?"

Mike Meador pushed himself up, face furious. "I object, your honor. Mr. McSpadden is asking her to speculate about the evidence."

Judge Ferreira pulled his mike forward. "I'll overrule that objection but I'll remind the panel members that what the lawyers say is not evidence and that Mr. McSpadden's contentions should not be considered for any purpose without sworn proof that they are true."

"Thank you, your honor," Jim said. He looked at Betty Alkek. "Could you find there was a defect under those circumstances?"

She nodded. "If I thought the only reason you didn't have proof was because they were withholding the truth, I'd find in your favor."

"Thank you Ms. Alkek."

So far so good. He'd planted the seed for the jurors to believe Rusty Day when he testified. But Jim still had a hard burden. Betty Alkek had made the proper response but her face registered extreme skepticism. As he went through the rest of his voir dire, he felt he was swimming upstream. He sensed the whole panel considered his version of the facts very unlikely.

Couldn't blame them, really. The police report, the blood tests, much of the anticipated testimony, all supported the proposition Danny had been drunk and derelict in his duty. But Jim had set the stage for the bombshells he planned to throw when it came his turn and the jurors would remember then what he was saying now.

J. Michael followed Jim. He approached the podium with righteous fire in his eye. He told the panel his client had been dragged into this lawsuit by Jim McSpadden who had not one shred of evidence to demonstrate any defect in the Harrigan truck. If the jury exonerated Harrigan, were there any on the panel who could not award the company substantial attorney's fees and costs for being wrongfully brought into the lawsuit? No hands went up. Meador thanked the panel and took his seat.

The judge gave the lawyers fifteen minutes to make their strikes. Jim, Hildebrand, and Laura hurried to a conference room.

"What do you think of the panel?" Jim asked Al.

"I'd say it's pretty conservative, just like you'd expect in Fort Worth or Dallas."

"Any gut feelings about who we should strike?"

"What about that school teacher?"

Jim shook his head. "I want to keep him. He's worried about the blood test but I think that'll put him on our side when we prove it's wrong." He looked at Laura. "What do you think?"

She laughed. "You guys are the experts."

"Let's keep him." Hildebrand said.

Jim nodded. "We oughta keep Betty Alkek for the same reasons."

"She's a mighty tough lady."

"She'll be tough for us if we convince her."

"Let's go with her, then."

Quickly, they worked through the jury list using the peremptory challenges allotted by the judge to strike the prospective jurors they judged least favorable. Back in the courtroom Jim handed his list of strikes to bailiff Vasquez who took it back to the court's chambers.

With all the lawyers and parties in the courtroom, Judge Ferreira called the names of the twelve selected to try the case. The pinstriped banker didn't make the cut. Jim and Hildebrand had struck him and Rolly and the other plaintiffs probably had as well. Kendal, the GM worker who'd responded to Rolly earlier hadn't survived either. Either Kurtz, Meador, or both of them had axed him. Bill Winkler and Betty Alkek were on the jury. They hadn't made the other lawyers nervous enough to strike them.

The mix wasn't bad: seven women, five men. Six whites, three blacks, two hispanics, and a lone Korean. Occupations ranging from blue collar to middle management and professional: a diesel mechanic, a janitor, a registered nurse, a credit manager, a Baptist preacher, the airline pilot, the teacher. On the whole, they were a satisfactory lot.

Judge Ferreira excused the panel members who weren't chosen, gave the jury instructions not to talk about the case, and excused everyone for the rest of the day. Rolly would start his evidence in the morning. With a feeling of accomplishment in having survived so far, Jim celebrated with a Mexican dinner and a movie.

∽

Jim watched as Officer Albert Wilson sat in the witness box, eyes distant with remembrance, recounting the way the wreck had occurred.

"I knew we had a big problem as soon as those watermelons tumbled all over the pavement."

At the podium Rolly asked, "had anyone been seriously hurt at that time?"

Wilson raised his muscular forearms, palms up. "I don't know Mr. Sullivan. I don't think so. It was a pretty big mess with all those cars piled into each other but I didn't see anything that looked real bad."

"What happened next?"

"I called for help on the radio and then the tanker crashed through the fence and exploded."

"What'd you do then?"

"Got back on the radio, then got over there as quick as I could. But there wasn't anything I could do. I just had to stand there and watch."

"Could you tell why Mr. Marcus lost control of the tanker?"

Wilson shook his head. "I couldn't see a reason for it."

Sullivan leaned forward, gripping the edges of the podium. "Mr. Tinsley, one of the other witnesses expected to testify says he was traveling behind Marcus and it was like the hand of God swooped down and swept him off the road. Did you see anything like that?"

Wilson smiled. "Mr. Tinsley told me that but I didn't see it."

"Would you have noticed if something like that happened?"

"I sure think so."

Rolly molded his face into a judgmental frown. "Are you familiar with how alcohol affects the way people drive?"

"Yes, I am."

"Was Marcus's driving what you'd expect from someone who was drunk?"

Jim got to his feet. "I object, your honor. He's leading the witness and inviting him to speculate about something not in evidence."

"Sustained," Judge Ferreira said. "The jury will disregard the question."

Rolly twisted his mouth in a condescending smile. "Thank you, your honor. We'll present evidence in a few minutes showing that Mr. Marcus was drunk."

"Excuse me, your honor," Jim said, "but I object to Mr. Sullivan's statement. He's not a witness."

Judge Ferreira drilled Rolly with a stern stare. "Sustained. The jury will disregard the statement. Just stick to the evidence Mr. Sullivan."

"Yes, your honor."

Rolly went over the rest of the accident facts with Officer Wilson, then sat down. Kurtz asked a few questions, then Jim's turn came.

"Officer Wilson, did you see the tanker as it was approaching the accident scene?"

"Yes, just briefly. I was mainly watching that mess on the other side of the highway."

"As the truck approached the scene, what did it look like?"

Wilson shrugged. "Like any normal truck, just coming straight down the road."

"Wasn't speeding or anything?"

"Didn't seem to be."

"How did it move when it left the road?"

"It just suddenly veered to the left and went through the fence."

Jim leaned forward over the podium. "To someone traveling behind the truck, could it have looked like something swept it sideways off the road?"

Wilson's eyes narrowed. "I suppose so. It left the road pretty fast."

"Thank you officer." Jim sat down.

Rolly walked back to the podium. "Did you see anything come in contact with the truck to cause it to leave the road?"

"No."

"Not the hand of God or anything else?"

"No."

"That's all. Thank you officer."

Wilson came down from the witness stand and left the courtroom.

Judge Ferreira looked at Rolly. "Call your next witness."

"I'll call Elaine Jones."

A studious-looking middleaged black woman in blue slacks and white blouse, Elaine Jones testified she worked as a lab technician at the E. M. Daggett Hospital lab.

"Were you the technician who tested the blood of Danny Marcus for alcohol content?" Rolly asked.

Ms. Jones nodded. "Yes I was."

"Was the test accurately and properly done according to your usual procedures?"

"Yes it was."

"And what did it show?"

Jim stood. "I object, your honor. A proper predicate has not been laid for this witness to testify as an expert and a proper chain of custody has not been shown for the blood sample."

"Sustained," Judge Ferreira said.

Methodically, Rolly went over the witness's qualifications and the procedures under which the blood sample had come into her hands, then asked again for the test results. This time the judge overruled Jim's objection.

Ms. Jones looked at the paperwork in front of her. "It showed that Mr. Marcus's alcohol blood content was at the level of .21 grams per 100 milliliters of blood."

"And what is the level that creates a presumption of intoxication?"

".1 grams per 100 milliliters."

"So Mr. Marcus was more than twice as drunk as the law allows?"

"That's right."

"I'll pass the witness." With a satisfied smile at the jury, Rolly took his seat.

The judge looked at Kurtz. "Any questions?"

Kurtz shook his head. "No, your honor."

"Anyone else?"

Jim stood up. "Yes, your honor." He walked to the podium. "Ms. Jones, when did you first see the blood specimen you've identified as being from Mr. Marcus?"

The witness laughed. "I can't remember things like that. Sometime on the day the test was done."

"But you don't specifically remember when you first saw it?"

"Sure don't"

"Who drew the specimen?"

The witness looked at her paperwork. "Mr. Lee in the medical examiner's office."

"I see. How did the test sample get to the lab?"

"A courier from the medical examiner's office brought it in and someone in our office signed for it."

"Who was that?"

"Mr. Dillow."

"That would be Delbert Dillow, your supervisor?"

"Yes."

"How do you know the sample you tested came from Danny Marcus?"

"The paperwork says it did."

"But you have no personal knowledge that this blood came from him?"

"No I don't."

"Is it fair to say, Ms. Jones, that since Mr. Dillow signed for the sample, he's the one who gave it to you?"

"Yes."

"Thank you Ms. Jones."

Jim sat down. He'd used his questions to make the point that the sample had passed through the grimy hands of Delbert Dillow before it got to Ms. Jones. Jim had wanted to ask her about the sample from Homer Dorfenweider but he knew she wouldn't remember it without the paperwork. Besides, he didn't want her to go back to Dillow with the news Jim was interested in Dorfenweider. It would be best not to forewarn either of the creeps.

∽

Late on Friday afternoon at the end of the fourth week of trial, Rolly sat across the table from Art Kurtz in a small conference room across the hall from Judge Ferreira's courtroom. Rolly's last witness had just testified. The other plaintiffs would present their cases next week. Only Rolly and Kurtz were in the room. The judge had released everyone for the weekend but Kurtz said he wanted to settle the case so Rolly had stayed to talk. He'd hear what Kurtz had to offer but there wasn't much chance of settlement. Not at this point.

His clients had all testified strongly and Nadine had underscored their emotional damages with her psychological assessment. Life would never be the same for Al Richaud and his son, for Demetria Wyatt and her friends, for Rhonda Carter, Mary Shaw, and all the families. Kurtz and United of Rhode Island couldn't argue with their damages. The jury's verdict would reflect the morbid horror of death and disfigurement from fire but Rolly needed to trigger findings making the insurance company liable for the full amount.

Kurtz regarded Rolly with a look of benevolent good will. "I've never been in a case before where the damages might exceed the reinsurance."

"I'm glad you recognize your exposure."

Kurtz smiled. "I didn't say I had that much exposure. I said I recognized the nature of the damages."

Rolly shrugged. "What's the difference?"

"There's a lot of difference. The jury may well award you and the other plaintiffs five hundred million or more but all you'll get will be six mill if they find Marcus was on a joy ride."

Rolly looked at his watch. Kurtz was wasting his time. "Is that what you wanted to tell me? That I oughta take the six mill? I told you no on that a long time ago."

"Be reasonable Rolly. Of course I don't expect you to take six million, although I think that's all you're gonna get. Especially after Norvella Poteet testifies."

Rolly returned Kurtz's self-satisfied look with one of his own. "You may be surprised by what Norvella has to say."

"What do you mean?"

"I don't think she told the truth on her deposition."

Art had a good poker face but Rolly thought he saw a line or two of doubt in it.

"What do you mean?" Kurtz asked.

"You'll find out soon enough."

"Come on now, Rolly. If you expect me to discount Mrs. Poteet's testimony you're gonna have to level with me."

Rolly shook his head. "I'm not gonna telegraph my trial plan. You say you know the case is worth more than six mill. How much are you prepared to offer today?"

"Twenty million dollars for your clients and the other plaintiffs."

Rolly stood. "That's mighty generous of you, Art, but no thanks."

"That's not my final offer."

"Maybe not, but it's so damn cheap I don't want to respond. Let's talk again after Norvella testifies."

Kurtz pushed himself up. "Okay Rolly. But I think you're making a mistake."

"We'll see about that."

Rolly rode down the elevators with Kurtz, then walked toward the Worthington. He'd talk to Kurtz again after he cross-examined Norvella.

∽

Jim thought Norvella Poteet looked even more scrawny than when she gave her deposition. Over the past several days the other plaintiffs had put on their cases. Now it was Kurtz's turn to lead the defense effort and he had called Norvella as his first witness. She sat in the witness box wearing a faded dress covered with large roses. It looked like the same dress she had worn before. Limp, greasy looking hair framed her sallow face.

"What time did Danny Marcus come in your place?" Kurtz asked.

"It was around two in the afternoon."

Kurtz took her back over her deposition testimony. In the midst of a heavy rainstorm Danny had come in and sat at a back table in her bar drinking beer and listening to the jukebox for two hours, made a phone call, then left the place in exceedingly drunk condition.

"Did he say anything about where he was going as he was leaving?"

Jim had been waiting for this question. He got up. "I object, your honor. He's calling for hearsay."

The judge looked at Art. "How about that Mr. Kurtz? Sounds like hearsay to me."

Smiling, Art shook his head. "I anticipated that objection, your honor. May we approach the bench?"

"Yes you may."

Jim, Kurtz, Rolly and the other lawyers crowded around the bench. Kurtz spoke in a low voice only the lawyers, the judge, and the court reporter could hear.

"This testimony is hearsay, your honor, but it is still admissible as a statement against interest. Mrs. Poteet will testify Mr. Marcus said he was leaving the bar to meet a woman. Since an excursion of that sort was adverse to his employment, he wouldn't have said it if it weren't true."

Judge Ferreira turned to Jim. "Do you agree that's what the testimony will be?"

"Yes, your honor."

"Then I'll overrule the objection."

Jim followed the other lawyers back to the counsel tables. Kurtz had done his homework. Jim hadn't caught him napping.

Art went back to the podium. He swept the jury with his eyes, then turned to Norvella. "I'll ask again Mrs. Poteet. As Mr. Marcus was leaving, did he say anything?"

"Yes he did."

"And what was that?"

"He said he was going to Fort Worth to have a hot date with a woman."

Kurtz drew himself up in triumph. "I'll pass the witness." With a satisfied smile he went back to the counsel table and took his seat.

Rolly approached the podium, carrying a large Styrofoam board with wrapping paper covering its front. He regarded Norvella with a sorrowful, pitying look.

"Mrs. Poteet, I'm Rolly Sullivan. You remember me, don't you?"

She nodded. "Yes I do."

"And you remember when you gave your deposition in Mr. Kurtz's office last fall and you were asked how you came to contact Mr. Kurtz about the accident?"

"Yes."

"And you told us you read about it in the paper and thought he might like to know what happened in your place?"

"Yes."

Rolly looked at the jury, raising his voice slightly. "Where in the paper did you read about the accident?"

Norvella's eyes widened and she drew back her thin shoulders. "It was front page news for several days."

"But I'm asking where you read about it."

"I read all the stories about the wreck."

"Are you telling this jury it was the news stories that prompted you to call Mr. Kurtz?"

Sudden confusion swept Norvella's face. She hesitated, then answered in a defensive tone. "Yes I am."

Rolly regarded her with a steady look. "That's not true, is it Mrs. Poteet?"

"Yes it is!"

With a theatrical air Rolly removed the wrapping paper and turned the front of the Styrofoam board toward Norvella. Jim, Al, Art, and the other lawyers got up and moved to the side of the courtroom so they could see. It was a blowup of a newspaper page from the personals section of the classified ads with a red box drawn around one small ad.

"Have you ever seen this before?" Rolly asked.

Norvella looked down. "Yes I have."

"What is it?"

"That's the ad Mr. Kurtz put in the *Star-Telegram*."

Rolly looked toward Kurtz, shaking his head as if he couldn't believe what he was hearing. Kurtz's face flared red under his snowy thatch.

"How do you know this is Mr. Kurtz's ad?" Rolly asked.

"Because it's got his phone number."

"How do you know it's his number?"

"Because I called him at it."

"How did you come to see this ad?"

"I read the personals every day."

"Why do you do that?

"No tellin' what you might find there."

Rolly nodded. "I'm sure that's true. Would you please read the ad to the jury?"

Norvella squinted as she read in a halting voice. "Anyone having knowledge of the whereabouts of Alamo Oil driver Danny Marcus during the afternoon of August 21st call 214-555-0089 for a substantial reward."

"Thank you Mrs. Poteet." Rolly lowered the poster and stood it against the podium, pointed toward the jury. The other lawyers returned to their seats. "And when did you see this ad?" Rolly asked.

"About a week after the wreck."

"And isn't it true that it was the ad and not the news stories that prompted your call to Mr. Kurtz?"

Norvella spread her hands. "It was both of them. I'd seen the news stories and I knew Marcus had been in my place that day. When I seen the ad I knew I should call."

One of the jurors on the back row sniggered. Jim glanced at the jury box. Betty Alkek was looking down with an amused smile. Several of the others were grinning. Rolly was doing a great job. This testimony would help Jim as much as it would the plaintiffs.

Rolly compressed his mouth into a solemn line. "The ad mentions a reward, Mrs. Poteet. Did that have anything to do with your call to Mr. Kurtz?"

"I would of called anyway."

A few titters from the jury box subsided with a stern look from the judge.

"How much was the reward?" Rolly asked.

"One thousand dollars."

"I see. And I believe you're being paid for your time here today, aren't you?"

"Sure. I'm losing business back at my place."

"And that rate is five hundred dollars a day?"

"That's right."

"Let's see, Mrs. Poteet. You got a thousand dollars up front, five hundred for the day of the deposition, and five hundred for being here today. That's two thousand dollars so far. Is that all?"

"There was another five hundred for a conference in Mr. Kurtz's office."

"Oh, was there, now?"

"Yes there was."

"When did you first decide that Mr. Marcus was on his way to a date when he left?"

Kurtz got up, his face telegraphing his chagrin. "I object, your honor. She didn't testify that she ever decided anything like that."

Rolly looked at the judge. "This is legitimate cross-examination, your honor."

"Overruled," said the judge.

"When did you decide that Mrs. Poteet?" Rolly asked again.

"He did say it. I swear he did."

"You're sure about that?"

"Yes."

"Thank you Mrs. Poteet." He sat down.

Judge Ferreira looked around the room at the lawyers. "Who's next?"

Lawyers Escamillo, Carroll, and Fuller shook their heads. Jim knew why they had no questions. They couldn't improve on Rolly's cross-examination. But Jim had some points to make. He got up and moved forward.

"Mrs. Poteet, you've testified Danny Marcus was drunk when he left your place. Do you remember testifying on your deposition that he was just happy?"

Norvella glowered. "Yes, but you confused me."

"How did I do that?"

"You acted like someone was going to sue me over the deal."

"How do you know they won't?"

"Mr. Kurtz says no one can do nothin' if I just tell the truth."

"When did he tell you that?"

"After the deposition."

"You testified you read all the newspaper accounts of the wreck. Did you read that the blood test showed that Danny Marcus was drunk?"

"Yes."

"If it turned out there was a mistake and the blood test was wrong, would that change your opinion?"

She shook her head. "Mister, I deal with a lot of drunks in my business. I know one when I see one and Mr. Marcus was drunk. There's no doubt about it."

Jim put on a disgusted look. "That's all the questions I have of this witness." He went to his seat.

Laura whispered in his ear. "She's sure cocky for a liar."

∽

Rolly and Kurtz sat in the conference room during the break after Norvella Poteet's testimony. Kurtz had partially rehabilitated her with some friendly questions on re-direct. Yes, she said, she had claimed the reward and she was being reimbursed for her time but that didn't change her testimony.

She wouldn't tell a lie before God for a few thousand dollars. Danny had been in her place, he had got drunk, and he had said he was on the way to meet a woman. Rolly had watched the jurors while she testified. Their stony faces said they weren't buying her story.

Rolly looked across the table with a cynical smile. "There's no telling what you'll dredge up when you advertise a reward in the personal section of the classifieds."

Kurtz slapped the table. "God damn it Rolly! She's telling the truth."

"Why'd you pull a trick like that?"

"None of us would ever have known where Marcus had been if I hadn't."

"Maybe not. But she didn't come across too good once she admitted to seeing that ad."

"That was my fault," Kurtz said. "I should have asked her about it on direct."

"You were hoping I didn't know about it."

"That's right. I should have known better. How *did* you know about it?"

"Found it by going through back issues of the paper."

"Why'd you do that?"

"Just a hunch I had." Rolly put his hands on the table. "I think Norvella's telling the truth about some things. Marcus was in there. And he did get drunk. The blood test proves that. But that deal about going to meet a woman was something she made up to tell you what you wanted to hear."

"I don't agree with that," Kurtz said, "but I'm prepared to increase my offer."

"How much, Art?"

"Forty million for all the plaintiffs."

Rolly shook his head and pushed back his chair.

"What do you think it's worth, then?" Kurtz asked.

"We could probably do business at three hundred million if the other plaintiffs were reasonable."

With a sad look Kurtz shook his head. "You must be insane."

Rolly got up and headed for the door. "There's still some more testimony you need to hear."

# 13

On the morning scheduled for the beginning of his presentation of testimony Jim got to the courthouse early, got a cup of coffee from a machine in the break area and rode the elevator up to Judge Ferreira's courtroom. Kurtz had concluded his case the day before with Elwood Lee's testimony about maintenance of the Alamo Oil tanker trucks. Jim had subpoenaed Delbert Dillow as his first witness and he wanted to be there when the little man arrived.

When Jim got off the elevator just after eight, Rolly Sullivan stood by the door of the courtroom, smiling.

"Good morning Jim. You can't get in yet. Door's still locked."

"Morning Rolly. I'm looking for one of my witnesses."

Rolly put his hand on Jim's arm. "Can we talk a minute?"

What could the great man want? "Sure Rolly."

Jim allowed himself to be led into the conference room. "What's on your mind?" he asked.

Rolly put on an earnest look that made Jim want to keep his hand on his wallet. "I've got two witnesses I'd like to put on out of order."

Jim boiled with resentment. "Christ Rolly, can't you wait till I'm finished?"

"I don't know your trial plan," Rolly said, "but I do know you need to prove Marcus wasn't off on some joy ride, just like I do. These witnesses will do that for you."

"You've already done a pretty good job on that, Rolly. Nobody's gonna believe Norvella Poteet after the workout you gave her."

"Maybe not, but there's still some doubt about it. These two guys can clear everything up. It'll work better for both of us to put 'em on now instead of waiting for it to come back around to me."

"Give me a preview of what they're gonna say."

Jim listened with growing excitement as Sullivan outlined the expected testimony. Rolly's proposed evidence would be a perfect introduction to Dillow's testimony. Delbert would just have to cool his heels for a while.

"Okay," Jim said. "You're on. I'll tell the judge I'm agreeing to let you put some testimony on out of order. Now, I'd better find my witness and tell him he's gonna be tied up longer than I thought."

"Thanks, Jim."

"Thank *you*, Rolly."

Around 8:30, Dillow came scurrying off the elevator, his face pinched with irritation. He wore a black bow tie with white polka dots and his wire-rimmed glasses gave him the look of an aging subversive.

Jim stepped forward. "Mr. Dillow?"

The small man stopped. "I'm Delbert Dillow."

"I'm Jim McSpadden, the one who subpoenaed you."

"What's this all about Mr. McSpadden? I thought Ms. Jones's testimony would answer all your questions."

"I didn't call Ms. Jones. She was Rolly Sullivan's witness."

"But why do you need me? You have no idea how inconvenient this is. I have a lab to run."

Jim recalled Dillow's arrogance when he had tried to talk to him before. Now he knew the bluster had a purpose. Delbert had something to hide.

"There are some things Ms. Jones didn't know about, Mr. Dillow."

Dillow drew back, eyes guarded. "What things?"

"I don't want to have to go over them twice. Let's save the discussion for when you testify."

"How soon will you call me?"

"Not right away. Something's come up."

"You mean you dragged me down here with a subpoena and you're not even ready to put me on?"

"That's about the size of it. At nine o'clock, the judge will swear you in. Then you'll need to sit out here in the hall until we finish with some other witnesses."

"This is intolerable."

"Sorry 'bout that, Mr. Dillow. Can't be helped. Just have a seat until court starts."

Glaring daggers and shaking his head, Dillow sat on a bench next to the courtroom door while Jim retreated into the now open courtroom, not even trying to suppress his satisfied smile.

Promptly at nine, Judge Ferreira took the bench. The jury was waiting in the jury room. At Harrigan's counsel table, Gerald Forbes sat next to Michael Meador, blue eyes cold and superior.

The surly Doug Spivak had rotated back to Chicago on the corporate jet the night before. Jim had overheard Doug joking with Meador about the VIP treatment. It seemed he wasn't highly enough placed in the company to ride the jet very often but his involvement in this case was important to Forbes because of his quality control expertise.

"Are you ready to proceed Mr. McSpadden?" his honor asked.

Jim stood. "I've agreed to let Mr. Sullivan put on two witnesses out of order but I do have a witness who needs to be sworn first."

"Bring him in."

Jim walked to the door and called Delbert in. He walked through the gate in the rail and approached the bench.

"Raise your right hand and be sworn," said the judge.

"Can I ask a question first?" Delbert asked.

"Go ahead."

"Mr. McSpadden has just told me he's not ready for me yet. Is there any way I can go back to work until I'm to be called?"

The judge looked at Jim. "What's your feeling about that, Mr. McSpadden?"

It didn't fit Jim's game plan for Delbert to go back to the lab. "Your honor, Mr. Sullivan assures me his witnesses will be short. We'll be ready for Mr. Dillow before noon."

"You'd better just plan to stay with us, Mr. Dillow," the judge said. "We'll get you out of here as soon as possible."

With bad grace Delbert allowed himself to be sworn and retreated to the hall. Rolly went to the podium.

Art Kurtz got to his feet. "Before Mr. Sullivan starts, I'd like to know who these witnesses are."

Rolly turned, smiling at Kurtz. "William Cooley and Joe Masters."

"I object, your honor," Kurtz said. "I don't believe either of these men is on Mr. Sullivan's witness list."

Rolly didn't wait for the judge to speak. "Do you have my third amended list?"

Kurtz sifted through a mound of papers in front of him. "Yes I do."

"Look about three quarters of the way down the tenth page."

Kurtz shuffled the pages and his face fell. "Oh, I see them now. But I still object. The information on these two new witnesses is sandwiched in among a listing of medical records custodians. I didn't notice names had been added. I haven't had a fair opportunity to interview these people."

"Are the names, addresses, and phone numbers there?" the judge asked.

"Yes, your honor."

"And how long have you had this list?"

"About six weeks."

"Overruled. Bring in the jury."

The jurors filed in and the judge nodded to Rolly. "I'll call William Cooley," he said.

Bailiff Vasquez went to the courtroom door and called into the hall. "William Cooley."

A huge man in his thirties came in. He wore oversized khaki pants and a Hawaiian sports shirt with a pattern of bright red and yellow flowers.

"Come forward, please," the judge said.

Cooley came inside the rail, swore to tell the truth, and went to the witness box, turning sideways to get his massive legs through the narrow opening. He plopped into the witness chair, barely fitting between the arms.

"Are you William Cooley?" Rolly asked.

"That's my name but everyone calls me Tank."

Several jurors laughed and the judge shut them up with a quick sweep of his head.

Rolly bent forward over the podium. "You and I have met before, haven't we?"

"Yep, sure have."

"What's your occupation?"

"I'm a gravel truck driver."

"Are you one of those guys who comes down the highway at ninety miles an hour, running everyone off the road?"

"That's me."

"And how much do you make doing that?"

"Anywhere from two to four hundred dollars a day. But I don't work all the time."

"And I've agreed to pay you three hundred a day for your time off work?"

"That's right." Cooley grinned at the jury.

Jim admired the way Rolly had handled Tank's expenses. The jury was far more likely to forgive Tank for his cheerfully acknowledged greed than Norvella, whose avarice in responding to Kurtz's ad had been so carefully concealed.

"You know Norvella Poteet?" Rolly asked.

"Sure do. Go in her place all the time."

"Were you there the afternoon Danny Marcus came in?"

"Yes I was."

"I'll ask you whether or not you were near the cash register when he paid his bill?"

"I was."

"What, if anything, did he say as he was leaving?"

"Nothing that I heard. Just paid his bill and left."

Rolly compressed his face into a solemn look. "Did you hear him say anything about having a date with a woman?"

"Sure didn't."

"And what was his condition?"

"You mean was he drunk?"

"Yes."

Tank shrugged. "Mighta been. He'd been in there a good while. But like I said, he didn't say much so I couldn't really tell."

"Thank you Tank. That's all I have." Rolly took his seat.

Kurtz took his turn with cross-examination.

"Are you sure you heard everything Mr. Marcus said while he was paying his bill?"

Tank shrugged. "It's possible he said somethin' else and I just didn't hear it."

"Could he have said something about having a date?"

"Anything's possible. All I know is, I didn't hear it."

"Did you see him go use the phone before he came to the register?"

"Yeah, he used the phone," Tank said.

"And it's possible he used it to make a date with a woman?"

"Could have. I didn't hear what he said."

Al Hildebrand whispered in Jim's ear. "Why doesn't Rolly object? Kurtz is calling for pure speculation."

Jim cupped his hand over his mouth so his voice wouldn't carry. "Don't worry. Rolly knows what he's doing. At least as far as this testimony's concerned."

Judge Ferreira excused Tank Cooley and Rolly asked for Joe Masters.

Vasquez called into the hall and a razor-thin man in grey coveralls with a Diamond Shamrock logo on the pocket entered the courtroom. A thin nose split a weatherbeaten face accented by iron-grey eyebrows. The judge swore the witness in and he took the stand.

"State your name," Rolly asked.

"Joe Masters."

"How are you employed, Mr. Masters?"

"I work at a Diamond Shamrock in Wise County."

"Is that the one that's next door to Norvella's Place?"

Masters nodded. "Yes it is."

Jim looked around him. He knew what was coming because Rolly had given him a preview. The people in the courtroom were leaning forward. All fidgeting and clearing of throat had ceased. Suspense charged the atmosphere.

Rolly continued. "Do you recall the day of the big freeway accident in Fort Worth last August?"

"Yes I do."

"Did you see the Alamo Oil Company truck involved in the accident on that day?"

"Yes, but I didn't know it was the same truck at the time."

"When did you first realize it was the same one?"

"When you came by the station and talked to me a couple of months ago."

"Tell the jury the circumstances under which you were involved with this truck."

Masters turned to the jury, gesturing with his thin hands. "The driver brought it in in the middle of a rain storm. He'd run over something in the road and had a flat on one of the outside duals and the inner dual was losing air. Asked me could I fix 'em and I said sure, if he had a couple of hours 'cause I had to wait on other customers and those duals are a mess to work on anyway."

Jim glanced at Kurtz. He looked like a deflated balloon and Jim almost felt sorry for him. But he had this coming for what he'd tried to pull with Norvella.

"Did you fix the tires?" Rolly asked.

Masters nodded. "Sure did."

"What did the driver do while you were working on his truck?"

"Said he was going to Norvella's to get a hamburger. I told him to call me in a couple of hours."

"Did he do that?"

"Sure did."

"And when he came back and got the truck, did he say anything about having a date with a woman?"

Masters twisted his mouth in a negative. "All I remember is he had some baseball tickets he was taking to his wife."

"And could you tell if he'd been drinking?"

Masters shrugged. "I couldn't tell. He didn't act drunk to me. But he might have had a few. Really couldn't say."

Rolly turned, smiling at Kurtz. "Your witness."

Kurtz made a half-hearted effort at cross-examination but Masters testimony had too much the ring of truth to invite attack. When Jim's turn came he hammered at the point Danny had not seemed to be drunk. Then J. Michael Meador took a turn. Wasn't it possible Danny was drunk? Maybe, Masters said, but you couldn't prove it by him. Jim welcomed J. Michael's examination. It fit in well with what Jim had coming.

Finally, all the lawyers were through, Judge Ferreira excused Masters, and called a break. Jim slipped into the hall ahead of the crowd to tell Delbert Dillow he'd be the next witness.

∞

In the hall, Rolly grabbed Kurtz by the sleeve, grinning. "Still think he wasn't in the course and scope?" he asked.

Art shook loose. "He may have been but he sure wasn't acting like a drunk man."

"But we know he was drunk. The blood test proves that. And he did drive his truck through that fence."

"Could you take a hundred million?" Kurtz asked. "That's the limit of my authority."

Rolly shook his head. "Too little, too late, Art. Let's roll the dice."

∞

"Mr. Dillow, to what extent are you personally involved with the testing done in your lab?" Jim asked.

Dillow glared down from the witness stand. "I don't do the tests myself."

"Do you know how to do them?"

"Of course. I've done them all many times. You don't get to be the supervisor without knowing how to do the tests."

"But you weren't personally involved in the testing of Danny Marcus's blood?"

Dillow shook his head. "No. That's why I can't understand why I'm here."

Jim turned to the judge. "I object to the non-responsive answer, your honor."

"Just answer the questions you're asked, Mr. Dillow, and we'll move along faster," Judge Ferreira said.

Jim held Dillow's eyes with his own. "Did you even handle the sample, Mr. Dillow?"

"I don't think so. I certainly don't remember it."

"Did you know Elaine Jones testified she got the sample from you?"

"Did she?"

"Yes. Does that refresh your recollection?"

Dillow vented an uneasy laugh. "Mr. McSpadden, I really don't recall handling that sample."

"But would it be unusual for you to do so?"

"No. Occasionally, when the courier from the medical examiner's office comes in, I sign for the samples and then give them to the technicians for testing."

"And you may have done that in this case?"

"Yes."

"And it's possible you handled other samples that night in the same way?"

"It's possible."

Jim pushed himself back from the podium, pausing before the first loaded question.

"Did you recognize the names on any of the samples that came in that night?"

Dillow's head jerked slightly and a shade of confusion passed over his eyes but he recovered quickly. "No, I didn't."

"You're sure about that?"

"Yes."

Jim drew a paper from a file. "I have here a list that shows all the names that pertain to the samples that came into your lab for blood alcohol tests that day. I'd like to read them and see if you're familiar with any of them."

"All right."

"Artis Fletcher?"

Dillow shook his head. "No."

"Danny Marcus."

"I know who he was."

"But only because of this case?"

"That's right."

"Irene Escobar?"

"No."

"Homer Dorfenweider."

"No."

"Thank you Mr. Dillow." Jim looked over his shoulder at Al Hildebrand. "I'm ready for the computer."

Al walked to the side of the room and rolled a computer on a cart with a large monitor into position where Dillow and the judge and jury could all see it.

Rolly stood. "Judge, I object to this procedure. I haven't seen this video yet."

Jim smiled. "This isn't a video. I want to ask Mr. Dillow about something on the internet."

"I still object. You should have listed it as an exhibit."

"But it doesn't have a tangible form. I can't make an exhibit out of a web site." Jim turned to the judge. "I just want to ask Mr. Dillow about some of the things on this site. I'll be brief."

The amused look in Judge Ferreira's eyes showed Jim had piqued his curiosity. "Since there's no exhibit I'll overrule the objection."

Hildebrand strung a telephone extension line along the floor and plugged it into the modem. Jim turned on the computer and loaded the windows operating system and the internet browser. He brought up the pricklypear.net and entered an address. A display of multi-colored graphics took shape on the screen, identifying the web site as Homer's Cozy Home Page.

Jim looked up at Delbert. "Have you ever seen this display before?"

Wary-eyed, Dillow shook his head. "No I haven't."

At the plaintiff's table, Rolly popped up again. "I renew my objection, your honor. I fail to see the relevance of this charade."

"Where are you headed with this Mr. McSpadden?" the judge asked.

"Just bear with me a minute, your honor. I'll connect everything up."

"No more than a minute," said the court.

Jim clicked the mouse for the next part of the display and a page of text appeared, identifying the web site of Homer Dorfenweider who lived on Primrose Circle and worked for Lockheed Martin as an engineer.

"Are you sure you don't know Mr. Dorfenweider?" Jim asked.

Delbert's face had lost color. His polka-dot tie bobbed on his Adam's apple.

"Did you understand my question?"

"Could you repeat it?" Dillow asked in a low voice.

"Do you know Homer Dorfenweider?"

"Yes," Dillow said, voice barely audible.

Jim clicked the mouse again and a page of pictures appeared with Homer's proud announcement that they were shots of his family.

"Can you identify the man in the picture at the bottom of this display?" Jim asked.

"It's me," Dillow admitted.

The picture displayed him with a blond child on each knee. Homer's caption identified the Dorfenweider twins with their loving maternal grandfather, Delbert Dillow.

"So you are the father-in-law of Homer Dorfenweider?"

"Yes."

"Why did you say you didn't know his name when I read it a few minutes ago?"

Dillow twisted in the witness chair. "Was that one of the names you read?"

"Yes it was."

"You read so fast. I didn't recognize it."

Jim panned the jury with a disbelieving smile which several of the jurors returned. He turned back to Dillow.

"In any event, he is your son-in-law?"

"Yes, he is."

"And you did handle the sample of his blood that night, didn't you?"

Rolly got up. "I object again, your honor. Mr. Dorfenweider's not on trial here."

The judge looked at Jim, eyebrows elevated.

"I'm entitled to test the accuracy of the lab procedures, your honor. Dorfenweider's test was done the same day as Danny Marcus's."

"Overruled."

"Did you handle the sample, Mr. Dillow?"

"I don't remember."

Jim pulled a packet of papers from his file and located the lab report and other documentation on Homer Dorfenweider that Bobby Torricelli had given him.

"May I approach the witness, your honor?"

"You may."

Jim handed the papers to Delbert. "Is that your signature on the receipt, Mr. Dillow?"

"Yes."

"So you did handle the sample?"

"Apparently so."

"Did you know at the time that the blood had come from your son-in-law?"

"No. I didn't notice the name."

"Did you know Mr. Dorfenweider was recently tried and found not guilty of negligent homicide due to driving while intoxicated?"

"Yes, I heard about that."

"And did you know this blood test that you handled supposedly established that he wasn't drunk?"

Delbert looked down, eyes evasive. "I really didn't follow the trial that close."

Rolly jumped up again. "I must object, your honor. What does this have to do with Danny Marcus?"

"Overruled."

Jim moved a step closer to the witness. "Would you tell the jury what the test on Homer Dorfenweider showed?"

Delbert looked down at the paper in his hand. "It was negative for blood alcohol."

"And that means it shows Mr. Dorfenweider hadn't been drinking at all on the evening in question?"

"That's right."

"That was the evening of the day of the big freeway wreck involving Danny Marcus?"

"Yes."

"And what did Danny Marcus's test show?"

"As I recall, his blood alcohol level was around .2."

"How much beer would a person have to drink to get up to that level?"

Delbert shrugged. "Depends on a lot of things."

"But it would have to be more than two or three?"

"Oh yes. The Marcus test indicates a substantial level of consumption."

Jim moved back to the podium, then turned to Dillow with judgmental eyes. "Isn't it a fact, Mr. Dillow, that you switched the samples before giving them to Ms. Jones so that the test in the name of Danny Marcus actually pertains to Homer Dorfenweider?"

Delbert's face turned red. "That's a damn lie!"

The judge banged his gavel. "One more outburst like that and I'll hold you in contempt. Just answer Mr. McSpadden's question."

Delbert turned to the judge, waving his hands. "The answer is no. I would never do such a thing."

Jim stepped back from the podium. "I'll pass the witness."

The judge looked at Kurtz. "Any questions?"

"No, your honor."

"Anyone else?"

No one spoke up.

"May this witness be excused?" asked the judge.

Jim shook his head. "I'll have some more questions for him after the next witness."

The judge turned to Dillow. "You'll need to wait in the hall until you're recalled."

Slowly, Dillow left the stand and headed for the courtroom door, shoulders slumped.

"Call your next witness," Judge Ferreira said.

"I'll call Homer Dorfenweider."

Dillow's head jerked up and he stopped for a second, then walked quickly toward the door. Jim followed Dillow. It wouldn't do for him to have a word with his son-in-law before he testified.

Jim reached the courtroom door just behind Delbert and followed him into the hall. A young blond man in his mid to late twenties with a sly, conceited face sat on one of the benches.

"Hello Delbert," the young man said. "What's going on? I just got subpoenaed down here out of the blue."

Dillow opened his mouth but Jim stepped around him. "Mr. Dorfenweider?"

"Yes?"

"The judge is ready for your testimony."

"What testimony? I don't know anything about this case."

"Just come on in, please."

Dorfenweider looked at Delbert who shrugged and shook his head.

Jim held the door for Homer and he walked through. With a bewildered look, he took the oath and entered the witness box. Rolly leaned forward on his counsel table, feverish of face, obviously wanting to object, but unable to come up with a good reason. Jim had carefully included Homer on his witness list.

Jim took Homer through the introductory questions. He was Homer Dorfenweider, worked at Lockheed, had a nice family, and Delbert was his father-in-law. Then Jim cut directly to the business at hand.

"Mr. Dorfenweider, I believe you were involved in an accident last August?"

"What does that have to do with this case?"

"Just answer the question, Mr. Dorfenweider," Judge Ferreira admonished.

"Yes I was." Homer said.

"And you were charged with negligent homicide due to driving while intoxicated as a result of that accident?"

Rolly almost leapt from his chair. "I object, your honor. Irrelevant, prejudicial, has nothing to do with this case."

Judge Ferreira looked down thoughtfully at the lawyers. "In light of the previous testimony from Mr. Dillow, I'm going to overrule your objection."

With hands spread in exasperation, Rolly sat down.

"That's true, isn't it?" Jim asked Dorfenweider.

"Yes that's true."

"And it's also true that you had been drinking that night?"

Homer hesitated, face fiery red and streaming with sweat. "I decline to answer on the basis the answer might tend to incriminate me," he said.

"But you've been found not guilty, Mr. Dorfenweider. You can't be tried again and therefore can't incriminate yourself."

"There's still a civil case pending."

Jim looked at the judge. "Could the witness be instructed to answer?"

"I instruct you to answer," the judge said. "Under the circumstances, you have no privilege against self-incrimination. The privilege doesn't apply to the civil matter unless it could lead to a criminal prosecution and it can't in this case since you're already been tried and found not guilty."

"What about perjury? I could still be tried for that."

"What about that, Mr. McSpadden?" the judge asked.

"He didn't testify in the criminal case, your honor. He relied entirely on the blood test and the presumption of innocence."

His honor turned back to Dorfenweider. "Is that true?"

"Yes, your honor."

"Then you can't be guilty of perjury unless you commit it here today. Answer the question."

Homer's face took on a calculating, evasive look.

"I wasn't drunk."

"But you had been drinking?"

"Yes, a little."

"How much is a little?"

"Two or three beers."

"Can you explain why the remains of two six packs were strewn around the floor of your car?"

"I don't believe it was that much."

"Isn't it true you really don't remember?"

Rolly got up. "Objection. He's arguing with the witness."

"Sustained. Stick to the facts, Mr. McSpadden."

Jim affected an earnest look. "Could it have been more than two or three beers?"

Homer shrugged. "Maybe four. No more."

"And the accident occurred when you ran a red light and hit another car?"

"I had the green."

"And the old couple in the other car died in the wreck."

"Yes."

Jim looked up at the judge. "That's all I have, your honor."

Rolly left Homer alone. Jim knew there was no way for Rolly to cross-examine without making things worse for himself. Jim walked Homer to the door and waved Delbert back into the room. The jurors followed him with accusing eyes as he went back to the box. Jim got right to the point.

"Mr. Dillow, would it surprise you to learn that your son-in-law just testified he had been drinking on the night in question?"

Dillow stared at Jim, defiant-eyed. "Yes it would."

"You mean he's never told you he was drinking that night?"

Delbert looked down at the desk top. Jim knew how his mind was working. What had Dorfenweider testified? There was no way for Delbert to know.

"We may have discussed it," the little man finally said.

"And he may have told you he'd been drinking?"

"He may have."

"And even two or three beers would have shown up on the blood test, wouldn't they?"

Delbert studied his hands as though they were abstract art.

"Did you hear me, Mr. Dillow?"

Delbert looked up, eyes distant. "Yes, I heard you."

"What's your answer?"

"You're quite right, Mr. McSpadden. Any amount of alcohol would have shown up."

"You do understand, don't you, that you are under oath and may be charged with perjury if you lie?"

"Yes, I understand that."

"Bearing that in mind, I'm going to ask you again. Did you switch those samples?"

Dillow looked down for long seconds, then raised his eyes in a sad look. "Yes."

The quick rumble of voices filled the courtroom as jurors, spectators, and parties shared their opinions. Jim turned to Laura with a thumbs up sign. Tears coursed down her cheeks but she was smiling.

Judge Ferreira banged his gavel. "The court will come to order." Gradually, the din subsided. "Proceed, Mr. McSpadden."

"Why, Mr. Dillow? Why did you do it?"

"Homer's a good man," Dillow said, eyes moist with tears, "but he'd already had one DWI. With another one, tied in with a fatal accident, he was in for a lot of trouble."

"So you just took things into your own hands?"

"Didn't seem like it would hurt anything. Marcus was dead, and he couldn't be charged with a crime. It wouldn't bring the old couple back to life to put Homer in jail."

"So the truth is that Danny Marcus's test proves he hadn't been drinking at all and Homer's test was the one that showed the .21 blood alcohol level?"

"That's right."

"Thank you, Mr. Dillow." Jim turned and walked back to the counsel table. He sat down and put his arm around Laura who sobbed on his shoulder.

"What do you think now, Rolly?" Kurtz crowed in the conference room.

Rolly shrugged. After all his years in court, there wasn't much that could surprise him but he'd had no foreboding that the blood test might be wrong. Had he failed to avail himself of the intuition that usually served him so well?

"McSpadden put one over on both of us," he said.

"That's right," Art agreed. "But it helps me. I bet you'd take fifty million now."

Rolly shot him the finger. "Screw you Art. Drunk or sober, Marcus was negligent and it's now set in concrete that he was on the job for Alamo Oil when he ran through that fence. You're on line for all the damages the jury will award for eight people burned alive in their cars and ten or twelve others horribly scarred."

Kurtz nodded. "You've got a point there and that's why I'm not pulling the one hundred million offer. Let's put this case to bed and let McSpadden see if he can nail Harrigan Motors for his widow lady."

"No Art," Rolly said. "I can't do that. There's no way that truck was defective. Marcus's negligence was the only cause of this wreck. McSpadden doesn't have a prayer. And the case is still worth at least two hundred million for the plaintiffs."

Kurtz shook his head. "There's no separating a fool from his folly."

Rolly flipped his finger again. "Fuck you, Art!"

On the ground floor of the justice center, Jim and Al got cups of coffee and stepped out on the shaded walkway for some fresh air and a place to talk alone. The July temperature stood at over one hundred but the searing heat felt good to Jim after the cool, close stuffiness of the courtroom. It was Friday, and he'd be glad to get the day over so he could unwind over the weekend and prepare for his assault on Harrigan Motors on Monday.

Al set his coffee on a ledge and tucked in his shirt tail. "You gonna put Tinsley on?"

Jim nodded. "He's due here any minute."

"You sure it's a good idea?"

"I don't know but he's the only one who saw the accident from behind Marcus."

"He's so crazy."

"I know. But we're only halfway where we need to be. We've proved

Marcus wasn't drunk and Rolly proved he wasn't on a joyride. Now we've got to convince the jury he wasn't negligent."

"But we also have to convince 'em there was something wrong with the truck. Tinsley says the hand of God pushed it through that fence."

"Nobody's gonna believe that. The point is, he'll testify there wasn't anything wrong with Danny's driving."

When they got back to the courtroom, L. T. Tinsley was waiting in the hall. He smiled when he saw Jim, showing his uneven teeth. He wore black slacks, the seat shiny from wear, and a wrinkled white dress shirt.

"How you doing son?" he asked.

"Fine, Mr. Tinsley. We'll get you in and out of here as quick as we can."

"I'll appreciate it. I got to go down to Mansfield and get a freezer this afternoon." His face turned solemn. "Remember, now—I'm not gonna swear to nothin'. I don't hold with swearin'."

After the jury filed in, Jim called Tinsley up and the judge gave him the oath in the way Jim had requested.

"Do you affirm to tell the truth, the whole truth, and nothing but the truth?"

Tinsley hesitated. "Is that anything like swearin'?"

"No, Mr. Tinsley."

"Then I agree to it."

Tinsley testified he had been on his way to Weatherford to pick up a used refigerator for his appliance business when the accident happened. Danny Marcus had passed him at a moderate speed and pulled four or five car lengths ahead of him.

"Did you see the pileup on the other side of the road?" Jim asked.

Tinsley scratched his bulbous red nose. "Yeah, I seen all those cars come together."

"Did you see the watermelons on the road?"

"Not till later. It was raining cats and dogs."

"What happened next?"

The old man's eyes widened and he stared at the far wall of the room. "The hand of God came down through the sheets of rain and pushed that truck through the fence, into the wickedness on the other side."

Jim glanced at the jurors. Most of them focused on Tinsley with stony-faced intensity but Betty Alkek displayed a supercilious smile. Jim really couldn't blame her. How to make Tinsley more credible?

"You mean that's what it looked like when he went through the fence?"

Tinsley shook his head. "There weren't no lookin' to it. The hand of God came down like judgment and pushed him through the fence."

Best to let the description alone. "Did Mr. Marcus do anything to cause the wreck?"

"He must of. God wouldn't have smote him like that for nothin'.'"

"But did you see anything about his driving that caused the accident?"

"Nope. He was just goin' down the road driving normal when God swept him into the others and purified them all with His holy fire."

The angry murmur behind Jim told him the families of the accident victims didn't appreciate Tinsley's take on what had happened. It would be best to close down this witness.

"Thank you Mr. Tinsley. That's all I have."

J. Michael Meador got up from his place next to Forbes, imposing in his dark pin-striped suit and bright tie, blond hair carefully molded into place. He had left off his gold chains for the trial. Probably didn't want to look too slick to the jury.

He walked to the podium, regarding Tinsley with a friendly smile.

"Mr. Tinsley, I'm Mike Meador, and I represent the folks who made the truck Mr. Marcus was driving. Could you see anything wrong with it that caused this accident?"

Tinsley shook his head. "Wasn't nothin' wrong with the truck. God pushed it through the fence, that's all."

Solemn-faced, Meador nodded. "I see. What did the hand of God look like?"

Tinsley stared ahead, eyes fearful. "Like a strong dark shadow in the rain."

The suggestion of a smirk passed over Meador's face. "Mr. Tinsley, do you have your driver's license with you?"

"Sure do."

"May I see it, please?"

Tinsley drew back. "What for?"

"I want to ask you some things about it."

Partially rising, the old man pulled a ragged wallet from his rear pocket and took out a card. Meador walked to the witness stand and took it from him.

"I see this license requires that you wear glasses when you drive."

"That's what it says."

"Do you have any glasses?"

"Nope. Sure don't."

"Why not?"

"I see plenty good with the eyes the good Lord gave me."

"So you weren't wearing glasses when the accident happened?"

"Nope. Wasn't no need of it."

Meador drew himself up to full height. "Are you telling this jury that, in the midst of a heavy rainstorm, you could clearly see something you call the hand of God come down on the freeway even though you weren't wearing glasses as the law requires?"

Tinsley's face grew somber and his lips trembled. "I know what I saw. Wasn't nothin' the matter with my eyes."

J. Michael handed Tinsley's license back with a sarcastic smile. "The fact is, Mr. Tinsley, that you didn't see any hand of God at all. All you saw was a truck driver lose control of his truck and drive it through the fence and across the median. Isn't that true?"

Tinsley stood, clenching his fists. "Mock not the messenger of the Lord, most miserable of men. I saw the Lord smite all those sinners, just like he'll smite you for your wickedness."

Judge Ferreira banged his gavel. "That's enough, Mr. Tinsley."

The old man turned, staring. "Oh, you false judge! You accursed hypocrite! Beware! The day of judgment is at hand."

The judge called to the bailiff. "Could you please help Mr. Tinsley find his way out of the courtroom?"

Vasquez came to the witness stand, took Tinsley by the arm, and led him from the room. His honor turned to the lawyers, smiling.

"I assume there was no further cross-examination?"

"No, your honor," several of them said in unison.

Meador took his seat with a triumphant smile. The court announced the noon recess and excused the jurors. He asked the lawyers to stay. Everyone rose as the jury filed out.

"Be seated, folks," Judge Ferreira said. "A little problem's come up that we need to discuss. Juror number seven, Reverend Martin, told me this morning one of his close friends died last night. He needs some time off to be with the family and he needs Monday off to preach the funeral."

Rolly raised his hand.

"Yes, Mr. Sullivan?"

"I think the court should accommodate the man. We won't have a very happy juror if we don't."

"That's the way I see it," Judge Ferreira said. "I'm gonna call a recess until Tuesday."

The judge's decision suited Jim perfectly. Rusty Day had been scheduled to testify Monday. Jim had planned to fill in the Friday afternoon with some testimony from Laura but his presentation would flow more smoothly if he called her after Rusty. Now, Rusty could start Tuesday and Laura could follow.

Jim, Al, and Laura held a quick conference in the hall. "I shouldn't have called Tinsley," Jim said.

Hildebrand laughed. "Don't blame yourself. At least he got across the idea Danny wasn't driving dangerously before the accident."

"Yeah, if the jurors believe he could see that far."

"What's next?" Laura asked.

"I'll call Rusty Day and tell him he won't testify till Tuesday. But I'll still have him come on down on Sunday. We can use the extra day to get him ready."

"There's sure a lot riding on his testimony," Hildebrand said.

"He'll make us or break us," Jim said. "But one thing's for sure. There's a lot better chance the jury will believe the truck was defective now that we've proved Danny wasn't misbehaving."

"What are our chances now?" Laura asked.

"Twice as good as they were before this last week but still not worth a damn."

She put her hand on his arm. "Get some rest Jim. You look like you need it."

He smiled. "Don't worry. I'll be over Tinsley by tomorrow and ready to give 'em hell on Tuesday."

# 14

That evening Jim propped himself up on the bed in his town house and called Rusty on the bedside phone.

"You all set to come down here?"

"Sure, but something important's come up."

"What's that?"

"When you took Forbes's deposition, did you notice an older secretary outside his office?"

Jim's mind formed the image of the woman, stern-lipped, guarding the boss's office. "Yeah, I remember her. A real dragon lady."

"That's the one."

"What about her?"

"Forbes fired her."

"What does that mean?"

"She was quite a bit more than a secretary."

Jim shifted the phone from one ear to the other. "You mean they were having an affair?"

"For years and years. But it's over now. Forbes got rid of her and brought up the girl from the front desk downstairs."

"I remember her, too. No doubt Forbes would consider her an improvement. But how does this fit in with my case?"

"Millie Thomas—that's the old secretary—she's very bitter. She's been talking trash about Forbes in the bars."

"In Slim's?"

"Hell no. Slim's ain't her kind of place. She goes for nice cocktail lounges."

"How'd *you* find out what she was saying?"

Rusty laughed. "Some of the guys from the plant said she was shooting her mouth off in the Silver Slipper so I gutted up, put on a suit, and went in there a couple of nights ago."

"You talk to her?"

"Yeah. She was pretty drunk. She knew I'd been snooping around trying to find out about the Loadmaster steering. She'd heard Doug and Forbes talking about it. I bought her a couple of drinks and she opened up pretty good."

Jim's pulse picked up. He swung himself to the edge of the bed and sat up. "Does she know what's wrong with the system?"

"No. They've been more careful than that. But she does know where the file's kept. What's more, she had a key to the file drawer and she gave it to me."

"And I guess you just walked right in there and got the file?"

"I tried to do that last night."

"What happened?"

"I thought I could get past security with my old ID but Doug had 'em looking for me. They ran me off. Said they'd call the police if I tried again."

"So where does that leave us?"

"We need for someone the security boys don't know to get in there at night, use the key, and just walk out with the file."

Jim tightened his grip on the phone. "Are you saying I should do something like that?"

"I don't know how else you'll ever get it. If you try to subpoena it, Doug and Forbes'll trash it and claim it never existed. It'll be their word against Millie's and she's just a rejected lover. Besides, she doesn't know what's in it."

"I see what you mean."

Jim wanted to keep his law license and stay out of jail. Burglary could lead to a bad result in both those areas. But he sure needed that file. Could he find a private investigator in Chicago who'd do the job on short notice? No. He didn't know anyone to ask.

Harrigan Motors owed him the material. He'd asked for information on the steering system problems in discovery and they'd stonewalled him. What they were doing was against the law. He'd just be setting things right. And he couldn't win just on Rusty's testimony. Bottom line was, he had to have that file.

"How can I get in there if you couldn't?" he asked.

"I've got you covered there," Rusty said. "I found a name tag from the janitorial service lying in the hall a few weeks before I quit. It looks pretty official. You can put on some grey coveralls and walk right in."

"Won't security check my driver's license?"

"Not unless they've changed procedures since I left. They let the maintenance guys in if they're wearing name tags."

"Are they picture ID's?"

"Yes."

"Do I look anything like this guy?"

"Not really. Your skin tone's much too light."

"Christ, Rusty! What do we do about that?"

"Bring me a passport photo from one of those little booths you see in malls. I've already taken the ID apart and I know a place I can get it re-laminated."

"Did anyone ever tell you that you have a criminal mind?"

Rusty laughed. "My ex-wife used to accuse me of that."

Jim hesitated, considering other potential problems.

"How do I get in Forbes's office?" he asked. "It might be locked."

"Millie gave me a key to it, too."

"She's really mad, isn't she?"

"She wants to get the bastard."

"So do I." Jim took a deep breath."This is crazy, Rusty, but what time do I do it?"

"Tomorrow night would be good. That's when they do their heavy duty cleaning. They'll be lots of maintenance guys in the building."

"I'll be up in the morning, then."

"You want me to meet you at the airport?"

"Naw. Just give me directions and I'll be at your place around noon."

∞

Jamal pulled the Lincoln to the curb in front of the seedy apartment building Rusty had given as his address. A facade of dingy yellow brick stretched several stories into the south Chicago sky. The straggly hedge and paint peeling from the window frames told the world the place was not a desirable address.

Jim opened his door. "Wait here. I'll be a while."

"Okay, boss." Jamal slouched down in his seat and turned up his tape of Arabic music.

According to Rusty the apartment provided him as part of his compensation for serving as security guard had its own entrance on the side of the building. Jim walked around the building through an fetid alley littered with trash and found the door. Jim knocked twice.

In several seconds Rusty opened the door. "Come on in Tex," he said.

He wore khaki work pants and a white T-shirt, and had lost weight since Jim last saw him. His coarse brown hair hung in tangles over his forehead and dark hollows underscored his eyes. He'd sure need to look better before he testified. Jim followed him into a room furnished with a threadbare brown couch and chairs.

"How long you been divorced?" Jim asked.

Rusty laughed. "I know what you're thinking. Place looks pretty bad, don't it? No woman's touch here, that's for sure. It's been two years now."

"Any kids?"

"Two. I get to see 'em once a month when my child support's current. I been having trouble keeping up with it since I quit working for Harrigan."

"Visitation's not supposed to depend on child support."

"Tell that to my ex." Rusty motioned toward one of the chairs. "Have a seat."

Jim sat down.

"Want a beer?" Rusty asked.

"No, need to keep my head clear."

Rusty picked up a can of Miller Lite from a table and drank from it.

"Let's see this ID you got for me," Jim said.

Rusty took several squares of paper and material from a scarred coffee table in front of the couch and handed them to Jim. "Careful. It's all in pieces."

The ID said the bearer was Cleo Perkins and worked for Mistletoe Cleaning Service. The photo displayed a middleaged black man with a grizzled goatee.

"You bring a new photo?" Rusty asked.

"Yeah." From his shirt pocket Jim pulled a photo he'd made in a booth in a mall on the way to the airport.

Rusty studied the picture. "It'll do fine."

"Do you think I look like a Cleo?"

"Maybe not, but you're about the same age. You'll just have to get past security before they have time to think about it. Gimme the card and I'll go around the corner and get it laminated. While I'm gone, you can try this on." He picked up a grey jumpsuit from the floor and handed it to Jim. "It's new but I've washed it twice so it won't look like it."

Rusty left and Jim tried on the jumpsuit. It was a fair fit except for being a little short in the legs but he'd brought his work boots, so he'd look all right. In half an hour Rusty returned with the re-laminated card. Jim looked closely at it. There were no signs it had been taken apart.

"I think this'll work," he said.

"That guy outside in the Lincoln belong to you?" Rusty asked.

"Yep. That's my driver."

"He's starting to attract attention."

"Is that a problem?"

Rusty nodded. "Doug's been keeping an eye on me. He's figured out where I live and I've seen him drive by a couple of times before. Wouldn't want him to wonder who that guy is."

"That could be a problem, all right. Spivak's been back in Chicago all week. Forbes took his place at the trial."

"Why don't you cut your driver loose till tonight?"

"I was going to have him take me to a motel."

Rusty spread his arms, grinning. "You don't need a motel. You can stay here."

Jim glanced at the decrepit couch.

"Don't worry," Rusty said. "I'll sleep out here. The bed's not too bad. Only a few roaches and no bedbugs."

"I don't mind the couch," Jim said. "It would be pretty handy for me to stay here. I've got us both on the same flight in the morning."

"Okay then. Tell your guy to get out of here and come back around eight o'clock."

Jim left the apartment and walked around the building. Jamal still sprawled behind the seat, cap pulled over his head. He'd put the windows down and was sharing the wail of his music with the world. Three black kids leaned against the wall of the apartment, staring at the shiny green Lincoln and its exotic occupant.

Jim went up to the window. "Hey Jamal!"

With a shake of his head, Jamal straightened. "What boss?"

"Don't need you any more till eight o'clock. Let's get my overnight bag out and then you can go see if you can get some other fares."

"Still two hundred dollar, boss."

"What do you mean?"

"That's the deal. Two hundred dollar for all day."

Jim threw his hands in the air. "Don't worry about it. You'll get your money. Just get my stuff out of the trunk and get out of here."

"Okay boss."

Jamal opened the door and got out. Shoulders slumped, he extracted Jim's bag from the trunk, then got back under the wheel.

"Eight o'clock Jamal."

"Okay boss." He started the car and drove away, tape still blaring.

Back in the apartment, Jim and Rusty mapped out a game plan for the evening. Rusty would stay at the apartment. It wouldn't do for him to be seen around the plant. He drew Jim a map of the layout, showing the door where he'd enter and the route to take to Forbes's office.

When they had finished Rusty turned up the television and changed it to an afternoon talk show. A couple of right-wing goons with angry, knotted faces were arguing that defense of American ideals would justify the assassination of various deserving politicians. Many in the live audience agreed with them.

Jim watched the show in an attempt to keep his mind off the evening's activities but his stomach knotted, and sweat drenched his shirt. Should he go through with the plan? He was equally unready to die or go to jail but both possibilities loomed before him.

On the verge of telling Rusty he couldn't go through with it, he thought of Laura. He'd done a good job of establishing that Danny hadn't been drinking but the only way he could prove a defect in the truck steering was through Rusty and Rusty didn't know much. Besides, even if the jury believed Harrigan had a problem with the Loadmaster steering system, that didn't prove the defect was a factor in the accident.

To win, Jim had to give Nick Stavros enough ammunition to prove Laura's case. Jim would be throwing the game away if he didn't try for that file. With this thought he steeled his mind to what he must do and tried again to absorb himself in the inane antics of the talk show folks.

Around six-thirty Rusty opened a couple of cans of chili, and Jim forced himself to eat half a bowl. Immediately, heartburn set in compounding his bad feeling. He lay on the couch trying to relax but every muscle in his body seemed in knots. Finally, the time came to go.

Rusty shook his hand at the door. "Be careful Tex."

"Don't worry, I'll see you in an hour or two. Or at least I hope I will."

"Good luck."

Rusty closed the door and Jim walked toward the front of the building. The sun lay low to the west, casting long shadows of buildings across the streets. The Lincoln sat waiting at the curb. Jim wore the grey coveralls Rusty had given him and had already pinned the bogus name tag over one pocket.

Jamal raised his eyebrows as Jim got in. "You going to work boss?"

"You might say that."

"What kind of job this?"

"I'm gonna do a little housecleaning."

Jamal twisted his face in suspicion. "Some kinda crooked deal?"

Jim shook his head. "Don't worry about it."

"I don't want no trouble."

"There won't be any. All I need you to do is drive to the Economy Ritz. I'll walk from there. You can wait in the restaurant. I won't be very long."

"Sure boss?"

"Sure."

Fifteen minutes later they swung into the drive of the Economy Ritz and stopped in front of the restaurant. Through the large windows, Jim saw the people in the booths drinking their coffee and eating the predictable fare.

"Go in and get something to eat," Jim said. "I'll be back in about an hour."

Jamal frowned. "You gonna be okay, boss?"

"Yes. Don't worry."

234

With a downward wave of his hand Jim turned and walked to the corner. The setting sun had turned the western sky pink behind the sad old houses and the streets lay in heavy shadow as darkness descended on the city.

Jim clenched and unclenched his fists as he walked toward the plant. He studied every car that passed, hoping Doug Spivak wouldn't spot him. There was no reason for Doug to be around the plant so late on a Saturday night but Jim's apprehensive mind still expected him.

He stopped for a red light across from the plant, studying the hulking brick buildings through the passing traffic. All of them blazed with lights. The night shift would be assembling Harrigan trucks in the larger buildings while the maintenance crew cleaned the smaller headquarters.

The light changed and Jim crossed the street, stomach churning. He tried to assume a natural, nonchalant air as he approached the small security shed he had to pass to get through the fence.

"How ya doin'?" he asked the impassive guard.

The man pushed a paper on a clipboard toward him."Pretty good. Hot enough for ya?"

"Plenty hot for me. We could sure use some rain."

"That's for sure."

Jim saw the paper was a sign-in sheet. He pulled a pen from his pocket and signed Cleo Perkins, with a flourish, then turned and walked toward the headquarters building.

"Don't work too hard," the guard called after him.

"Don't worry," Jim said over his shoulder.

So far so good. Maybe he was meant to be a maintenance man. He could take up the job once he got out of prison. He ascended the steps of the building, took a deep breath, and opened the double front doors. No one was in the reception area.

Halfway down the hall to the right an oriental man was vacuuming the carpet. The sound of the motor rose and fell as he moved the cleaner back and forth. Jim had memorized the route to take to Forbes's office on the second floor. He'd go down the left hall, then up the stairs at the end instead of taking the elevator. Less chance of running into someone. He turned and walked down the hall, bouncing with false confidence as he tried to look like he belonged there.

Midway to the stairs he spotted a men's room. Bladder uncomfortably full, he turned and went in. A middle-aged black man in a grey jumpsuit stood next to the sinks, emptying the built-in waste receptacles.

Jim walked to the urinal and relieved himself, then went to rinse his hands. The man turned toward Jim, a plastic bag of trash in his hands. He had a grizzled goatee. Jim's eyes traveled to his name tag. Cleo Perkins, it read.

The real Cleo eyed Jim's tag. "I didn't know they was two of us."

Nonchalantly, Jim rinsed his fingers. "I just started a few days ago."

"I knew I hadn't seen you before."

Jim could almost feel Cleo's mind working as he stood there, suspicious-eyed, pulling on his beard.

Jim smiled. "That's sure a coincidence. It's good to meet you but I better get back to work."

"Yeah, I guess you better."

Jim walked quickly to the door and hurried down the hall, then up the stairs. He'd have to work fast. No telling what Cleo would do if he connected Jim to the name tag he'd lost. On the next floor he could see the length of the hall. No one in sight.

He practically ran to the door of dark wood that led into the executive offices. He put his hand on the knob, pulled, and the door came open. No one was in the room. All the past Harrigan CEO's stared down from their lighted frames. The lamps on the tables shone on the polished hardwood floors. A buffing machine stood against the wall next to the gold lettered door of Forbes's office.

Jim crossed the floor to the door and tried to open it, but it was locked. He pulled the key Rusty had given him from his pocket. It went into the lock smoothly but wouldn't turn it. Damn. Forbes had anticipated trouble and changed the lock. Jim tried the other key, the one Rusty said went to the filing cabinet, but it wouldn't even go in. Beaten. Best to get out while he still had a chance.

Jim tensed as the door to the hall opened. He crouched, ready for a sprint for freedom. A pretty young Mexican girl came in pushing a cart holding a canvas bag half filled with trash. Jim straightened, grabbed the buffer, and pulled it toward Forbes's door.

"How you doing?" the girl asked.

"Pretty good. But I need to get in here to buff." He waved his hand toward the door.

"I'll let you in."

She pulled a ring of keys from her uniform pocket, selected a shiny new one, and opened the door.

"Thanks."

Jim flipped on the overhead lights and pulled the buffer through the door. He plugged it into a wall socket and started buffing the floor while the girl collected the trash.

"I'll lock it later," she said, nodding as she left the room.

As soon as he heard the door into the outer hall close, Jim stopped the machine. He closed the office door and turned to the elegant wood filing cabinet next to Forbes's massive desk. Bottom drawer, Rusty had said. Jim pulled on it but it was locked. Would the key fit or had Forbes changed that lock too?

Jim slid the key into the lock and turned it. It caught for a split second, then turned. He pulled the drawer open and thumbed through the files. Toward the back he found what he was looking for: a thick brown accordion file marked Loadmaster Steering.

He pulled the file from the drawer and put it on Forbes's desk. He'd just look at a few of the documents to make sure of what he had before he left. Before he could open the flap he heard the door from the reception room into the hall open and footsteps of several people on the hardwood floor.

Quickly, he closed and locked the file cabinet, then crouched behind Forbes's huge desk with the accordion file of documents under his arm. The footsteps approached the door to Forbes's office. Jim crawled into the legspace under the desk. Lucky it was so big. Plenty of room, even for Jim. And the front of the desk came all the way to the floor.

The office door opened and footsteps sounded on the floor. They approached the desk and stopped in front of it. Could the people hear the thumping of Jim's pulse?

"Was he in here?" asked an officious voice.

Not Spivak, and that was good. Probably a security guard.

"Yes." Jim recognized the voice of the Mexican girl. "He said he needed to buff the floor. I let him in."

"You should have known better."

"He had a name tag."

"Yeah, my name tag," the real Cleo Perkins said. "The one I lost a couple a months ago. Only now, it has his picture on it."

"What'd he look like?" asked the authority voice.

"Big man, had a beard, blond hair. About my age."

"That sound like the same guy, Maria?"

"That's him."

Jim kept still, muscles knotted. The slightest sound would betray him. Would they look under the desk?

"Well, you'd better get back to work," said the one Jim took to be the guard. "Can't think what he'd be after. No cash around here and he'd never get anything very big through the gate. I'll tell the guys to be looking for him."

Jim heard the three people leave the room. Someone turned the lights out and locked the door. He crouched beneath the desk in the dark, listening to the receding footfalls. Gradually, his eyes adjusted to the darkness.

When silence again ruled, he crawled from beneath the desk. Light filtering through the blinds gave him a dark view of the room. He wouldn't turn on the overhead lights. Someone might spot them from outside. No way to look at the documents in the folder. Best to just get out of the place.

Carrying the file in the crook of one arm, he walked to the door. The handle turned but a deadbolt held the door in place. He felt for a release knob but all his fingers found was an inside lockface. The door could be unlocked from either side but it took a key to do it. Wasn't that some kind of fire code violation? An academic question.

Surely Forbes had an escape route. Jim went to one side of the room and walked into an executive rest room with no other exit. On the other side of the big office an unlocked door led into a short hall with another door at the end. But the far door was locked and had no release knob.

Back in the office, he went to the window and pulled the blinds up. The window accessed an old-fashioned hinged fire escape with a counterweight that kept the free end off the ground. This route held promise. Jim found the lock securing the window and released it, then raised the window. Gingerly he stepped onto the platform of steel slats.

Fifty yards away the lights of one of the large assembly buildings flooded the lawn. He saw no one but knew there were bound to be periodic patrols, especially with the alarm he'd caused. To the right the lawn led to a tall privet hedge just inside the perimeter fence of the compound. A good preliminary goal.

He stepped onto the fire escape stairs. With a horrible grating and creaking they descended as his weight overcame the counterbalance. Had to get out of here before the noise brought security. He took the steps two at a time, almost losing his balance as the bottom impacted the ground. He hit the grass running, finding speed he didn't know he still had.

He reached the hedge, dove into it, and pushed his body through the scratching twigs until he reached the fence. He looked back across the lawn. Two security guards, one tall, one short, came running around the far side of the headquarters buildings, flashlights stabbing the air. The fire escape had gone back up and presented an innocent appearance.

"What the hell was that?" the tall one asked.

"Dunno," said the other.

They inspected the ground with their lights. "Here's the deal, Bill," said the short one, voice tense. "Look at these marks in the dirt. Someone's come down the fire escape."

Both of them looked up toward Forbes's office. "That window's open," Bill said. "He's been in there."

Both men flashed their lights around. "Don't see anyone around here," shorty said. "We'd better report this and check the office."

The men walked back around the building. Jim studied his surroundings. On the other side of the fence a sidewalk ran along a busy street. That was where he needed to be. How to get there?

He stood. Stretching his arms above his head, he could touch the top of the chain link fencing but three parallel strands of barbed wire ran above that. He had nothing to cut it with. He'd seek another route. On his knees he crawled along in the space at the bottom of the hedge where it didn't meet the fence. He came to a corner and turned it.

Straight ahead, at a distance of twenty-five or thirty yards, the hedge ended at the gate. The security guard sat in a metal chair in front of his shed. Jim froze. His crawl space lay shadowed by the hedge from the spotlights on the headquarters building but noise and movement could still attract attention.

For long minutes, he lay still. The guard showed no signs of moving. He kept drinking from a mug in his hand. All that coffee. Didn't he need to take a piss? The man seemed glued to the chair. Jim heard footsteps behind him and looked around. A woman and a little boy came walking along the sidewalk. Christ, this was all he needed. He put his head down, trying to blend with the ground.

"How much further, mama?" the little boy asked.

"Not far," the woman said, irritation in her voice.

"I'm tired."

"We're almost home."

They drew abreast of where Jim lay. The fencing rattled against the posts. Jim looked up to see quizzical eyes staring at him.

"Mama! There's a man in there."

"No there isn't, honey."

"Yes there is."

The woman bent over. Shock twisted her face as she spotted Jim on the ground. He put his finger to his lips.

"Shhh."

She screamed, snatched up the child, and ran toward the guard shack. The time had come for action. Jim pushed through the hedge and got to his feet, then edged toward the gate.

The guard stood as the woman approached. "What's wrong ma'am?"

"There's a man in the hedge." She pointed in the direction she had come.

"You'd better show me."

She led him along the sidewalk toward where Jim had been. Jim walked along the other side of the hedge to the driveway, slipped through the gate, and started walking along the sidewalk in the opposite direction from the others.

Pretty damn slick. Now he looked like any other pedestrian. And he still had the accordion file.

"There he goes," piped the little boy.

"You there! Stop!" yelled the guard.

Jim broke into a run. He looked over his shoulder. The security guard was pursuing, gun drawn. The man stopped and aimed. Jim bent low. The guard fired and the bullet zinged against a lamppost, then smashed the windshield of a passing car. The car accelerated past the guard and out of the area.

At the next corner a red light had stopped the cars on Jim's street and a steady stream of traffic was crossing from both directions on the intersecting four lane road. Jim ran behind one of the speeding cars. The following car braked and swerved and he continued into the path of a Budweiser truck. A blast from its horn encouraged him to greater efforts, and he reached the center of the road.

He glanced back at the corner he had left. The security guard had holstered his gun and raised his handitalkie to his face. Reinforcements would be coming. Jim turned to the remaining lanes. He waited until a slower car passed, then ran behind it. A red Camaro approached at devilish speed.

Jim pushed his legs to their limit and cleared the road just ahead of the Camaro. His momentum carried him to the curb where he tripped and fell sprawling to the sidewalk, still clutching the file. He scrambled to his feet and ran.

Halfway up the next block, he ducked into an alley between two commercial buildings and looked back. The light had changed and the guard had resumed his pursuit. Jim ran down the alley, turned at the next street, and turned into the driveway of a house where he crouched behind a car, badly winded, pulse racing.

Seconds later the man passed him in a slow trot. Jim waited several minutes, then turned back down the alley he had come out of. He made a wide detour of several blocks, then walked down an intersecting street to the area of the Economy Ritz.

Jamal lay sprawled asleep in his Lincoln in front of the restaurant. Jim pulled open the door on the passenger side.

"Wake up Jamal! Let's get out of here!"

Jamal jerked upright, then stared at Jim. "What happened boss? You look like hell."

"Don't worry about that. Let's go."

Jamal turned the key, then backed out of the parking space. Jim surveyed his damage. The phoney name tag hung askew and a jagged tear ran down one leg of his jumpsuit. His face and arms stung from numerous scratches.

240

One hip ached. He'd be lucky if he could walk tomorrow. But he had the accordion file.

"Where to boss?"

"Back to the apartment."

As they drove through the streets of the south side, Jim reconsidered his plans. He had the file but he'd been detected. Doug Spivak would probably be notified. He'd know the file was gone. He knew where Rusty lived and that he was scheduled to testify on Tuesday. Doug was likely to come looking for them. Jim checked his watch. 9:30. It had taken an hour and a half to get in and out of the Harrigan plant. Too late now to get a flight to DFW tonight.

Jamal pulled up in front of Rusty's apartment building.

"Wait here," Jim said.

Still carrying the file under one arm, he walked through the dark, malodorous alley to Rusty's door. Light leaked through the closed blinds of a single barred window, casting bleak stripes on the trash-littered pavement. Jim knocked and waited but no one came.

"Hey, Rusty!" he called softly.

No answer.

He knocked again, harder, and the door swung partly open. In his partial view of the room, he saw sock feet at odd angles to each other protruding from the end of the couch.

"Rusty?" Jim stepped into the room.

The little man sprawled on the couch with a round hole in the center of his forehead and the back of his head blown away. A gun lay on the floor, several feet from his outstretched hand. Jim took a step back, shaking. Poor Rusty. He'd never see those kids again. Beyond the body the door leading into the central hall of the building stood open. Was the killer waiting there? Spivak, or someone else? No way to know. Maybe just neighborhood violence. Had to get away. Couldn't help Rusty now.

Jim's overnight bag lay in a chair next to the couch. He grabbed it and backed into the alley. He pulled the door closed, ran to the front of the building, and piled in next to Jamal.

"Let's get out of here."

Jamal started the engine. "What's the matter boss?"

"Let's go!"

As they pulled away from the curb, a stocky man wearing a ski mask came running down the steps of the apartment building. He leveled a gun and fired and the bullet splintered the rear window, then went out through the windshield between Jim and Jamal, leaving a spiderweb of radiating cracks.

Jamal floorboarded the accelerator and swung the car around the corner as the man fired again. The round ripped through the rear of the car. Face tense, Jamal drove several blocks at seventy miles an hour, then slowed down.

He turned accusing eyes on Jim. "You said no trouble, boss."

"I didn't plan this."

"You pay?"

"Don't worry. I'll fix everything."

"You pay *now!*"

"I don't have enough money with me."

"How can I trust you?"

"You know who I am. Get some estimates and send 'em to the office."

Jamal stared at the cracked windshield, tears in his eyes. "How'm I gonna work, boss?"

Sudden anger swept over Jim. "Quit whining. My friend's lying dead back there and all you can think of is your goddamn car."

Jamal turned, mouth slack."Dead?"

"Dead."

"Sorry boss. You gonna call police?"

Jim shook his head. "They'll get there soon enough. I don't have time to talk to 'em now."

"That's good boss. Where you going now?"

"The O'Hare Hilton."

Forty minutes later Jamal pulled up in front of the fortress-like hotel at the center of the cluster of airport terminals. Jim opened his door and got out.

"Send me your estimates Jamal. Don't worry. I'll take care of the car."

"Okay boss. You be careful."

In the hotel Jim found a restroom, washed the blood from his face and arms, and combed his hair. Then he limped to the front desk. The clerk viewed Jim's torn clothing with dubious eyes but checked him in after verifying his credit card. In the room, Jim collapsed on the bed. His flight left at ten the next morning. Still lots to do before he could sleep.

He forced the sad vision of Rusty's body to the back of his mind and opened the flap of the file. As he read the documents, the pieces of the puzzle fell quickly into place. He'd need Art Kurtz's help and officer Wilson's to get the evidence into shape where Nick Stavros could use it.

Just after midnight, Jim called Kurtz's home number.

"Hello?" Kurtz growled.

"Hello Art. This is Jim McSpadden."

"Why the hell are you calling so late?"

"How'd you like to win the case?"

Kurtz laughed."Don't be silly. I'll be happy to hold the damages under two hundred million."

"You can do lots better than that. You can win. We both can win. But we need each other's help."

"What the hell are you talking about?"

"Just listen."

For the next ten minutes, Jim told Kurtz what he had.

"God damn, Jim," Art said when he'd finished. "How'd you get that material?"

There was no point worrying Kurtz with the details.

"I had some help from my guy here in Chicago."

"What do you want me to do?"

Jim quickly outlined what he needed. "Think you can handle that?"

"You bet. I'll see you tomorrow afternoon."

Jim hung up, then made calls to Nick Stavros and Al Hildebrand. Both said they'd meet him at the Alamo Oil Company terminal west of Fort Worth the next afternoon. Kurtz would take care of notifying Officer Wilson. His arrangements complete, Jim threw himself on the bed fully clothed and quickly fell into exhausted sleep.

The next morning a ray of sun slanting through the partly opened drapes woke him at seven o'clock. With renewed horror, he recalled Rusty's open, expressionless eyes, the neat round hole in his forehead, his blood and brains on the cushion. Should have called the police. But then, there'd have been questions. No way to get back to Fort Worth and finish the trial. Couldn't stand to go through it again. Time enough later for apologies to Chicago's finest.

He showered, shaved, had breakfast in one of the hotel dining rooms, then checked out. In the terminal every man seemed a threat. Was that sandy-haired one with the red tie really reading the paper or was he looking at Jim? Spivak must know Jim had the Loadmaster file. Had that been him at Rusty's apartment?

Jim checked in at the gate and waited for his flight, scrutinizing every new arrival to the area. When the gate attendant called the flight he shuffled into line and crowded onto the plane with the other passengers. He expected Spivak to show up any minute and take one of the remaining seats but the moveable ramp pulled away and the plane started taxiing for the runway with no sign of Doug's angry red face.

At the DFW Airport he found his pickup in the parking garage and headed for home. He'd just have time to change clothes and fix a sandwich before heading for the Alamo terminal. As he drove into the maze of circling streets around the Ridglea Country Club, paranoia overwhelmed him. He'd best check out the lay of the land before going home.

He parked beside the road two blocks from his town house, grabbed the precious accordion file, and walked into a tree-filled gully that ran between two legs of the golf course. He'd jogged over this turf many times. Where the jogging trail came up out of the gully he slowed and stopped behind a screen of bushes.

The midday sun bounced brightly from the white brick of the town house. The doors appeared secure and no cars waited on the street beyond. Looked like the coast was clear. But as Jim turned to go back to his car, a white Chevrolet rounded the corner and came slowly along the street. Through the tinted side windows Jim saw that a large man was driving but the dark glass obscured his features.

The car stopped briefly at Jim's drive, then moved away. Some innocuous person looking for an address or Doug Spivak looking for Jim? No way to tell. He'd skip the stop at home and go directly to the Alamo terminal. Then he'd need to find a motel. He couldn't go home until the evidence was in. Then he'd have the bastards and they'd leave him alone.

# 15

Rolly sat next to Al Richaud at the counsel table, waiting for all the parties to assemble for the final round of the trial. A murmur of voices rose from his clients in the benches behind him. At Harrigan Motor Corporation's table, J. Michael Meador sat huddled with Gerald Forbes and Doug Spivak. The three men wore solemn, angry faces.

All things considered, Rolly was in pretty good shape. Through Delbert Dillow, McSpadden had established that Danny Marcus hadn't been drunk at the time of the accident but Rolly had put him clearly still on the job. Alamo would be liable for the full damages. Drunk or sober, Marcus's actions had caused the accident. The jury was sure to return a huge verdict.

Rolly turned as the rear doors of the courtroom opened. Jim McSpadden entered, followed by Laura Marcus, Al Hildebrand, and Art Kurtz. McSpadden looked like hell. He walked with a limp and scratches covered his face. Dark pockets hung under his eyes. He looked like a man who'd spent the weekend in the gutter.

As McSpadden started placing papers on the counsel table, Meador got up and walked over to him. Face set in implacable anger, he handed Jim a document.

"Here's a motion to start your day. We'll need to have a hearing on it before you start your evidence."

McSpadden responded with a curt nod. "That's just fine, Mike."

Meador returned to his table while McSpadden read the motion. A bitter smile played over his lips.

The door behind the bench opened.

"All rise, please," intoned Bailiff Vasquez and all got to their feet as Judge Ferreira took the bench.

"Good morning ladies and gentlemen. Counsel, are we ready to bring in the jury?"

Meador stood. "Not quite, your honor. I filed a motion that needs to be heard first."

"Let's get on with it then."

"I'd suggest we do it in chambers, your honor."

"Why?"

"It's a motion to disqualify Mr. McSpadden because of some things he did over the weekend."

Judge Ferreira looked at the bailiff. "Tell the jury we'll be in recess for twenty more minutes."

With all the lawyers crowded into his chambers, Judge Ferreira studied Meador's motion. He looked at McSpadden.

"Have you read this?"

"Yes, your honor."

"There are some extremely serious allegations here. What's your response?"

"To which allegations, your honor?"

"Let's start with the claim you pilfered a file from Mr. Forbes's office in Chicago over the weekend. Is that true?"

"I wouldn't use the word pilfered."

"But you did break in and take the file?"

"I didn't break in."

"Let's not play games, Mr. McSpadden. Did you go in Mr. Forbes's office without permission and take a file?"

"Yes."

Rolly leaned forward in his chair, caught up in the excitement. What the hell was going on? McSpadden was in deep shit. Was he going to screw up Rolly's case by causing a mistrial? Maybe the judge would just dismiss the case against Harrigan and let Rolly continue.

Judge Ferreira raised his hands."What on earth possessed you to do a thing like that?"

"All I did was take a file they held back in discovery. A file that should have been produced months ago."

The judge turned to J. Michael."What about that, Mr. Meador?"

Meador shook his head."That file's privileged, your honor. It deals with a problem that has nothing to do with this accident. A problem that was fixed long ago. That's why it wasn't produced. We've filed charges against Mr. Meador with the Chicago police. I expect a warrant to be issued for his arrest sometime today."

"You have the file, Mr. McSpadden?" Judge Ferreira asked.

"Yes I do."

"You'd better let me see it."

McSpadden handed the court a thick brown accordion file. The judge opened the packet and started looking at the documents. The lawyers sat silent and immobile. The tension in the room gripped Rolly along with the rest. Sweat streaked his face. What was in that file, that McSpadden would risk his career and even his liberty to get it?

Judge Ferreira put the papers back in the file and laid it on the desk then blistered J. Michael Meador with his angry eyes.

"Mr. McSpadden may have burglarized Forbes's office but you've committed a far worse offense."

Meador drew back with a contrived look of shocked disbelief. "What's that, your honor?"

"You've lied to the court about these documents. They are plainly responsive to Mr. McSpadden's discovery and highly relevant. You filed discovery responses claiming this stuff didn't exist."

"We certainly didn't intend to do that, your honor. We held the documents back on the good faith belief they didn't pertain to this case."

The judge shook his head."Have you even seen this file, Mr. Meador?"

Meador hesitated."No, your honor. I'm going on what my client's representatives tell me about it."

"That's what I thought. You'd better have a look." Judge Ferreira selected several documents from the file and handed them to J. Michael.

Rolly studied Meador's face as he read the material. His color receded and his mouth curled in a sickly expression. Finally, he looked up.

"Your honor, I had no idea this material existed."

"I'd like to think that's the truth, Mr. Meador."

"It is, your honor."

"Then that means your client's people have lied to you. Did you say they've made a complaint to the Chicago police about Mr. McSpadden?"

"Yes they have. After all, he did break into Gerald Forbes's office."

The court nodded."I don't condone that and I don't have any control over what the Chicago police do but I think you'd better tell Mr. Forbes he's looking at some formidable sanctions for holding back this material. I'm thinking of several million dollars."

"I'll talk to him about the charges on Mr. McSpadden."

"You do that. And I'll take what he does on those charges into consideration when we talk about the sanctions against Harrigan."

Rolly sure didn't like the lay of the land. The whole landscape of the trial was changing. That file must be dynamite. Its contents couldn't do him any good. Had to try to make some waves. He raised his hand.

"Yes, Mr. Sullivan?"

"Your honor, I'm in the dark about what's going on and I'm sure that's true for the other plaintiffs too."

Keith Carroll, Alfred Escamillo, and Linda Fuller all nodded, their faces tense and perplexed.

"This stuff doesn't really concern you," said the judge. "None of you have claims against Harrigan."

"But this evidence could affect our case against Alamo Oil. Shouldn't we at least be privy to these documents?"

Judge Ferriera laughed. "I'm pretty sure you're fixin' to find out all you want to know about 'em and then some. I don't want to keep the jury waiting any longer." The judge looked at Jim. "Are you ready to proceed with testimony, Mr. McSpadden?"

"Yes, your honor."

"Let's get going then. The motion to disqualify is overruled."

Back on the bench Judge Ferreira had Bailiff Vasquez bring in the jury. The twelve filed in, some with impassive faces, others with irritated looks. Rolly knew they were wondering about the delay.

"Sorry to keep you waiting," said Judge Ferreira. "We had a matter of law we had to clear up before we could start." He nodded to McSpadden. "Call your next witness."

McSpadden stood at the podium. Rolly saw several jurors studying his appearance. He sure didn't look his best this morning.

"I'll recall Officer Albert Wilson," McSpadden said.

The bailiff brought Wilson in from the hall and he took the stand. He projected integrity and dependability with his compact, muscular build and open features. McSpadden took him through a few preliminary questions, reminding the jury who Wilson was, then focused his questioning on the past several days.

"Did you receive a call from Mr. Kurtz early Sunday morning?"

Wilson nodded. "Yes I did."

"What did he ask you to do?"

"He wanted me to check out the police car I was driving at the time of the accident and meet him at the Alamo Oil Company terminal west of town that afternoon."

"Did he tell you why he wanted you to do that?"

"He said you and him wanted to run some tests."

"Were you able to get the car?"

"Yes I was. It was out of service. I called my supervisor and made the arrangements."

McSpadden paused, sipping from a glass of water at the podium. Rolly looked at the jury. McSpadden had their attention. They didn't know what was going on but they were all watching Officer Wilson. Rolly didn't know where McSpadden was going yet but he had a bad premonition.

"Did you meet me and Mr. Kurtz and some other folks at the Alamo terminal?" McSpadden asked.

"Yes I did."

"And did you cooperate in running some tests with us?"

"Yes."

"And did we make a video of the tests you participated in?"

"Yes you did."

McSpadden looked up at the judge. "At this time, your honor, I'd like to take Officer Wilson through the video we made."

Meador stood. "I object, your honor. We're entitled to preview any re-enactment of the accident so we can object before it's shown to the jury."

"This isn't a re-enactment, your honor," McSpadden said. "I just want to take the officer through the tests we did step by step."

Meador waved his arms. "But your honor! Surely we're entitled to preview this testimony. We asked for test results and videos months ago."

McSpadden leaned forward, clutching the top of the podium with both hands. "Judge, we couldn't do these tests until we got the steering material—material they never did furnish voluntarily."

With a faint smile, the judge leaned back in his chair. "I'll overrule the objection."

Al Hildebrand took a video cassette from his counsel table and put it in the courtroom's VCR. He wheeled a large monitor on a cart into a position where both the judge and jury could see it, then turned a second monitor screen toward the other lawyers and the plaintiffs sitting beyond the rail.

Hildebrand handed McSpadden the remote control and he started the tape. The video had been taken from an elevation looking down on a police car parked beside a strip of asphalt paving. McSpadden stopped the tape.

"Is that your police car, Officer Wilson?" he asked.

"Yes it is."

"Were you in it when this video was taken?"

"Yes."

The tape started again. From the left, a large gasoline tanker truck with Alamo Oil Company in large letters on its side appeared, moving slowly.

"Is that the same make, model, and year of truck as was involved in the accident?" McSpadden asked.

"Yes."

The truck advanced along the strip of paving until it was even with the police car. Suddenly it veered across the roadway away from the car at a forty-five degree angle and came to a stop. McSpadden stopped the tape, leaving the images of the truck and police car on the screen.

He leaned forward with one hand on each side of the podium. "Officer Wilson, I'll ask whether or not the movement the truck made across the roadway just now was similar to what happened with Danny Marcus's truck last August?"

Wilson nodded. "It was very similar, except Marcus was going a lot faster."

"Was there any particular thing you did in the video we've just seen at the time the truck veered off the roadway?"

"Yes there was."

"And what was that?"

"I pressed the button on my microphone."

The people in the courtroom seemed to collectively exhale pentup breath and a low, excited rumble of voices came from the plaintiffs' benches. Rolly's stomach knotted from the impact of the testimony but with his streetfighter's self control he kept his face non-committal. He glanced at Richaud. His client's face betrayed the grim realization of a serious problem.

"Let's have order," said the judge, banging his gavel. The noise subsided.

McSpadden continued his questioning. "At the time of the accident, did you make any radio transmissions?"

"Yes I did."

"And were those transmission made just before the truck went out of control?"

"Yes. I'd just reported the first accident on the radio when the truck went through the fence."

McSpadden stepped back from the podium. "I'll pass the witness."

"Any cross-examination?" asked Judge Ferreira.

Meador shook his head.

The judge looked at Rolly. "Mr. Sullivan?"

Rolly tried to think of some brilliant ploy he could use to destroy this testimony but there wasn't any. He shook his head.

"Anyone else?" asked the judge.

None of the other lawyers took the bait.

His honor turned again to McSpadden. "Call your next witness."

"I'll call Nick Stavros."

Urbane-looking in a form-fitting suit and tasseled loafers, Stavros took the stand. Rolly remembered their encounter during the trial in Corpus Christi several years earlier. He had demolished Stavros that time. The jury had rejected his testimony that the Ford involved in the accident was not defective and awarded Rolly's clients millions based on Karl Abelmeyer's testimony that it should not have exploded when the train hit it. This time Stavros was in the driver's seat.

McSpadden took the witness through the qualifying questions, then asked about the tests run over the weekend.

"This last Sunday, did I supply you with a packet of technical information on the Harrigan Loadmaster?"

Nick answered in his grating tone. "You did."

Stavros testified that the packet contained two reports of accidents involving Loadmaster trucks in Montana and Mississippi, test data generated by Harrigan, several engineer's reports, and a memorandum summarizing the situation.

"Did you observe the test Sunday afternoon when the Harrigan Loadmaster owned by Alamo Oil pulled suddenly to the left as the police officer activated his radio?" McSpadden asked.

"Yes I did."

"Do you have an opinion of why that happened?"

"Yes."

"Would you please give the jury that opinion."

Rolly glanced at J. Michael Meador. He was staring blankly at the top of his counsel table. He obviously wasn't going to do anything.

Rolly got up. "I object, your honor. Mr. Stavros hasn't been shown qualified to give an opinion. There's been no proper predicate for this testimony."

The judge shook his head. "Overruled."

Stavros turned to the jury, punctuating his testimony with hand movements. "It's my opinion that radio frequency interference from the police radio overloaded the computer in the truck steering system, causing it to react as if it had received a signal to turn the truck to the left."

"And what is that opinion based on?"

"It's based on Harrigan's own technical data. As a result of the tests they did after the accidents in Montana and Mississippi they found that, under certain circumstances, improperly adjusted radios operating at public safety frequencies can generate spurious frequency emissions that interfere with the Loadmaster power steering computer."

"Based on that same data, do you have an opinion as to why the Harrigan truck driven by Danny Marcus went out of control?"

Stavros nodded. "It was the same cause. I had the radio in the car Officer Wilson was driving on both occasions tested yesterday. It is misadjusted to the point it produces the kind of spurious emissions that cause the problem."

Even through this dry, technical testimony, all the jurors were leaning forward, faces bright with sudden understanding. A smiling Art Kurtz caught Rolly's eye. Rolly looked away. No point in giving the asshole any satisfaction.

McSpadden leaned forward on the podium, face intense. "Did Harrigan Motor Corporation take any corrective action in response to this information?"

"Yes they did."

"What was it?"

"They changed the filtering and shielding on current production models so spurious signals can't get into the power steering computer."

"But did they do any recalls to fix trucks already on the road?"

Stavros shook his head. "They did not."

"Did they say why?"

Nick held up a document. "It's all in this memorandum. Gerald Forbes and one of the other senior engineers decided the two earlier accidents were flukes and unlikely to recur. They opted not to do a recall because of the expense. They concluded the cost of paying some claims would be less than the cost of the recall. Since they were concealing the problem, in most cases the cause of any accident would be assigned to driver error."

McSpadden went to the witness stand and took the memorandum from Stavros. "I'd like to make this an exhibit, your honor."

"Have the court reporter mark it," said Judge Ferreira.

With the memorandum marked and admitted, McSpadden handed it to the first juror who started reading it.

"That's all I have of this witness," McSpadden said.

Meador made a half-hearted effort to cross-examine Stavros. How could he be sure a radio signal caused a malfunction when he didn't run his tests until a year after the accident? Couldn't there have been substantial changes in the radio in Officer Wilson's car during the intervening time? How did Stavros know the truck used in the tests would behave the same way as the one in the accident?

Stavros conceded he couldn't be certain but a computer malfunction due to radio interference was ninety percent likely to be the cause of the wreck. J. Michael gave up and sat down.

Rolly came to the podium for his questions. Did Stavros recall having made a detailed examination of the truck involved in the accident just a few weeks after the wreck? Yes, Nick recalled that. And wasn't it true he couldn't find anything wrong with the truck steering at that time? Yes, but the steering had been badly damaged in the wreck and Nick hadn't had the advantage of Harrigan's own testing, which showed the problem. Rolly realized he wasn't making any headway and retired.

"Call your next witness," said the judge.

McSpadden limped to the podium. "I'll call Gerald Forbes as a hostile witness."

Forbes raised his head, eyes wide with anger. He bent toward Meador and whispered in his ear. Meador shrugged, shaking his head, and Forbes walked to the stand and took the oath.

McSpadden skipped the preliminaries. "Mr. Forbes, you remember giving your deposition in Chicago last winter?"

Forbes nodded. "Yes I do."

"Do you remember telling me at that time there were no problems with the Loadmaster steering and that Harrigan's tests established there were no defects?"

"I don't recall that."

McSpadden nodded slowly, smiling. "Well, let's see if we can refresh your memory." He turned through the deposition booklet on the table in front of him, then looked up at Forbes.

"On page 162, you said 'there have never been any defects in the Loadmaster steering system.' On page 165, you said 'all the accidents reported to us turned out to be due to driver error.' Do you recall making those statements, Mr. Forbes?"

Forbes stared his hatred at McSpadden.

"Did you understand my question?" Jim asked.

"Yes."

"What's your answer?"

Forbes folded his arms across his chest. "I decline to answer on the grounds the answer might tend to incriminate me."

McSpadden turned to the judge. "Your honor, could you instruct the jury on the effect of Mr. Forbes's invoking of the Fifth Amendment?"

Judge Ferreira cleared his throat. "Ladies and gentlemen of the jury, you are instructed that the witness has a right to invoke the privilege against self-incrimination. In a criminal case, you are not allowed to draw any conclusion from the failure of the witness to testify but where the privilege is invoked in a civil case such as this one, you can draw whatever conclusions you think warranted, including the conclusion that the answer would be unfavorable to the witness."

"Thank you, your honor," McSpadden said. "Mr. Forbes, was it your decision not to order a recall to fix the radio interference problem due to the cost?"

"I decline to answer the question for the reason previously stated."

McSpadden asked a series of questions hammering home the fact Forbes and others had done exactly what their memorandum said—made a cold-blooded, calculated decision to play games with the safety of the public in an effort to save money. Forbes took the Fifth Amendment on every question. Rolly knotted his fists under the table. Forbes was pounding the nails in Harrigan Motors' corporate coffin but Rolly and his clients would be buried along with the company.

Finally, McSpadden concluded his questions, completing the carnage. The other lawyers opted not to cross-examine Forbes. Grey-faced and shaking, he sat down.

"Call your next witness," said the judge.

McSpadden turned triumphant-eyed to his client. "I'll call Laura Marcus."

∽

Jim sat between Laura and Al Hildebrand, waiting for the jury verdict. Behind the rail, Odell Wyatt and Rhonda Carter were talking in hushed voices. No rule of silence had been invoked but the atmosphere of anticipation in the stuffy courtroom seemed to call for subdued speech. At Alamo Oil's table, Art Kurtz leaned back in his chair next to lanky Marlin Reeves. Art had his hands folded across his big gut with the air of a man who had no worries.

It was just after six p.m. The jurors had been deliberating for eight hours. Would they finish tonight or go home and come back in the morning? The tension was beginning to wear on Jim. The longer they went, the better for Laura, unless they hung up. Quick decisions usually favored the defense, especially in complicated cases like this one. Jim didn't expect a defense verdict but he never allowed himself to celebrate until the jury came in.

Laura had made a good witness. She hadn't cried, and that was good. Jim didn't like for his clients to cry on the stand. He'd seen too many jurors nod in supercilious disbelief at such displays. She'd dispassionately described her marriage to Danny, his relation to their children, his sense of humor, the vacations they'd taken, the shared special moments, and everything that went into a healthy, functioning family.

Meador had opted not to cross-examine. Apparently, he wasn't as proud of Danny's DWI conviction now that Jim had established that Danny wasn't drunk at the time of the accident.

Jim glanced toward the Harrigan table. Meador was sitting at the end, far from the glowering Doug Spivak and Gerald Forbes. Jim could tell J. Michael just wanted this to be over. He'd had his nose rubbed in it about as much as he could stand for one trial and wanted to get back to Dallas so he could work up the huge bill he'd present to Harrigan's insurance company. Defense counsel got paid the same, win, lose or draw.

Rolly sat with an unhappy looking Al Richaud. Sullivan was affecting a cocky, jaunty look Jim was sure he didn't feel. The testimony against Harrigan had destroyed Rolly's theory about what had happened. He'd made the best of the situation in closing argument, contending that Stavros's theoretical evidence of a malfunction in the Harrigan steering system didn't provide the most logical explanation of the accident.

The most credible evidence in the case established that Danny had passed L. T. Tinsley at an excessive rate of speed in the rain, hit a slick spot, and rammed through the fence into the other cars. Danny's negligence had caused the crash, not some unestablished malfunction of the truck steering. Jim didn't think the jury would buy Rolly's glib argument but he couldn't be sure. Just like Meador, Jim needed this case to be over so he could let his tired mind and body rest.

Laura patted his hand."You've had a hell of a time the last several days."

He smiled. "I hope I never have another trial like this. How're you doing?"

"Okay. But when this is over, I'm gonna go home and sleep for twenty-four hours straight."

"Will you be able to sleep even if we lose?"

"We're not gonna lose. You did too good a job for that."

Bailiff Vasquez appeared in the door to the hall leading to the jury room. All eyes turned toward him.

"We have a verdict," he said.

Jim's stomach flopped and a nervous charge ran through his body. Showtime. Chairs and feet scraped and people cleared their throats. Judge Ferreira entered the courtroom, drawing his robe over his shoulders. He ascended the bench and Vasquez brought the jury in. None was smiling. Was that good or bad?

The judge looked at the jurors. "I understand you've reached a verdict?"

They nodded.

"Who is the foreperson?"

Betty Alkek, the greying blonde airline pilot, stood. "I am, your honor." She held up the charge.

Vasquez took the sheaf of papers to Judge Ferreira who leafed through them quickly. "It appears you have a unanimous decision. I'll now read your answers."

Jim leaned forward, elbows on the table, tight with anticipation.

"Did the negligence of Danny Marcus cause the occurrence in question? And you've answered no."

Jim squeezed Laura's hand. He felt the trembling of her body. Danny had not been at fault. They had won. The rest of the verdict was predictable. The jury exonerated Alamo Oil Company, then found the negligence of Jorge Medrano, the watermelon truck driver killed in the wreck, and Johnny Gibson, the deceased driver of the blue pickup, had contributed in causing the accident.

Behind Jim, the plaintiffs represented by Rolly and the other lawyers were silent. Jim knew the disappointment and anger they must be feeling. The wreck wasn't the fault of the parties their lawyers had sued. There would be no recovery for any of them.

Judge Ferreira moved on to the questions concerning the Loadmaster truck. Had Harrigan Motor Corporation marketed an unreasonably dangerous product? Yes, said the jury and the defective condition of the Harrigan truck was ninety percent responsible for the accident. The negligence of Medrano and Gibson had contributed the remaining ten percent.

Keeping his voice level, the judge read the answers to Laura's damage questions. Ten thousand dollars for funeral expenses. One million dollars for Danny's lost earnings. Twenty million dollars for Danny's conscious pain and suffering. Five million dollars for Laura and her children's loss of Danny's companionship and support. And finally, a whopping one hundred million dollars in exemplary damages to teach Harrigan a lesson for playing with people's lives to save money. Grand total: $126,010,000.00, a huge verdict in anybody's book.

Judge Ferreira thanked the jurors for their service and excused them.

Jim turned to Hildebrand. "Let's try to catch 'em on the way out."

Al pushed his chair back. "Yeah, I'd like to see what they thought about it."

Al, Jim, and Laura hurried to the back of the courtroom. By the door, Rolly's clients clustered around him while he explained the verdict. Alfred Escamillo, Keith Carroll, Linda Fuller, and their clients stood by listening. All wore long faces. Al Richaud looked down at the floor, face tense with anger and disgust.

Jim felt sorry for them. If their lawyers had filed cross-actions against Harrigan they would have won, too. Escamillo, Carroll, and Fuller had followed Rolly's lead to their detriment. But Jim really couldn't blame them or Rolly either. A week ago, who would have predicted this outcome?

Jim walked into the hall just in time to see the backs of J. Michael Meador, Gerald Forbes, and Doug Spivak as they retreated into the elevator. Didn't they want to talk to the jury?

Jim stood with Al and Laura by the door that led into the jury room. Art Kurtz came into the hall from the courtroom, broad, genial, and silvery haired.

"You sure did a good job, Jim, and saved my bacon in the process."

Jim put on a mock frown. "It's more than you deserved after the way you manipulated Norvella Poteet's testimony."

"Sorry 'bout that. A poor boy's gotta do the best he can."

"You redeemed yourself in helping set up the tests."

The jury room door opened, and the jurors started coming out. Jim shook hands with the preacher, Martin.

"We appreciate your service, Reverend."

Martin smiled. "We just did what was right." He nodded to Laura. "Good luck to you, Mrs. Marcus."

Tears shone in Laura's eyes. "Thanks for your help."

The preacher raised his hand in salutation and moved toward the elevators. Betty Alkek and the brown-haired teacher, Bill Winkler, came through the door, followed by a knot of other jurors.

"Ya'll feel like talking about the case?" Jim asked.

Alkek smiled. "Sure."

"Did ya'll have any trouble reaching a decision?"

"No. Not after you proved what really caused the wreck."

"What if we hadn't had that evidence?"

Winkler took a step forward. "I think we'd have had a lot of trouble with it. We all had a lot of sympathy for Mrs. Marcus, once you proved her husband wasn't drunk but the accident still looked like his fault."

Betty Alkek nodded.

"That's pretty much the way we saw it," Hildebrand said. "We knew we needed to prove what was wrong with the truck to win."

"How did you get that material?" Winkler asked.

Jim shook his head, laughing. "That's too long a story to tell here."

"It was obvious they held it back on you. I hope that exemplary damage award sends 'em a message."

Jim nodded. "It's a message it'll be hard for 'em to ignore."

After more handshaking, congratulations, and good wishes to Laura from the jurors, the last of them went to the elevators. With a departing wave to Jim, Art Kurtz followed them. As Art and the jurors entered the elevator, Gene Burns got off, freckled face bright with excitement.

He approached, hand extended. "Congratulations, Jim. I just finished up a long divorce hearing on the next floor and one of the bailiffs came in with the news. What an incredible victory!"

Jim shook Gene's hand. "Thanks."

"Seems to me a celebration is in order. Let's go on over to Jernigan's and have dinner and a few drinks. I'll see if I can round up Bobby."

Jim started to beg off. His bruises and strained muscles were complaining. But sudden exhilaration banished his fatigue. They had won a great victory. One like this wasn't likely to come along again soon. He owed it to his friends to accept their congratulations.

He looked at Laura. "You feel like going?"

She smiled. "One drink's liable to put me under the table."

"Oh come on. We don't have to stay long."

"All right," she said. "I'll call the kids to tell 'em the good news and that I'll be a little late."

"How about you, Al?" Jim asked.

Al shook his head. "Got to get back to Dallas. Ya'll enjoy the drinks. I'll call you tomorrow."

An hour and a half later Jim sat at Jernigan's with Laura, Gene and Bobby Torricelli. The waitress had just cleared the plates from the table. Jim had slipped his hand into Laura's. The warm, dry feel of her skin exhilarated him. With his other hand he lifted a snifter of Cognac, savoring its fiery fragrance.

Bobby slapped the table gently, dark face elated. "I wish I'd been there to see Rolly's face when he realized the accident wasn't Danny's fault."

"He didn't let it show much," Jim said, "but I could tell he knew he'd been had."

"And those Harrigan guys. You proved their story was a complete fabrication."

"They didn't look too happy."

"I bet they didn't," Gene said. "Wonder what the stockholders will think of this deal?"

"Probably won't set well with them."

The Clifton Cameron Quartet started up a slow rendition of *Stardust*.

"Let's dance," Jim said, and he and Laura rose together and eased onto the dance floor.

She put her cheek to his. "What a day!"

"A good one, for a change."

"Yes. It's been a good one. But when I think about losing Danny, this victory seems pretty hollow."

He felt the wetness of her tears on his cheek and longed to fill the gap of her loneliness.

"He was a good man, Laura. The way you and your kids feel about him tells the whole story."

They danced slowly for several minutes, clasped closely together.

He drew back, studying her sad, tear-stained face. "You remember what I told you before the trial?"

She cocked her head with a wan smile. "What's that?"

"I love you."

She touched his lips with her fingers. "Hush!"

He shook his head. "I can't help it, Laura. Will you see me again?"

"Of course."

"I don't mean about your case."

"I know what you mean. Yes, we can see each other."

He held her close again. "Just give me a chance," he whispered.

Later, when they had said goodby to Bobby and Gene and he had kissed her at her car and sent her home, he drove out the West Freeway toward his town house. He passed the accident site, marked by new fencing along the median.

"We did it Danny," Jim said. "We won the son-of-a-bitch. For her. And for the kids. And I'll take good care of her if she'll have me."

It seemed as if Jim had actually known Danny. He felt his presence here, at the place where he had died. The big man's spirit seemed to fill the cab of the pickup. Poppycock, Jim told himself. The dead didn't visit the living. But for all that, Danny seemed to be there, infusing Jim with his benign sanction.

He left the freeway and made the turns that took him home. He pulled the pickup into the drive and got out. What a great day. The win of a lifetime and a chance at Laura's love. It seemed he couldn't fail.

He put the key in the lock, opened the door, stepped inside, and turned on the lights. Across the room, Doug Spivak regarded him balefully from the depths of the recliner, a large-bore revolver leveled at Jim's belly.

"Close the door, Tex. You're letting out all the AC."

Jim kicked the door shut behind him, his thoughts suddenly focused totally on survival.

# 16

"To what do I owe the pleasure of this visit?" Jim asked.

Spivak sighted down the barrel of the revolver at a spot in the middle of Jim's chest. A thick silencer covered the gun's snout.

"Don't get smart-ass with me, Tex."

Prickles of fear ran over Jim. Had to play for time. He spread his hands.

"What do you want?"

Spivak laughed. "I want you, Tex."

"What for?"

"Because you're an asshole."

"Does doing my job make me an asshole?"

Spivak shifted forward in the recliner, bringing his feet to the floor. "It's the way you did it. All that snooping around in Chicago, pretending to be a trucker."

"It was the only way for me to find out what I had to know."

"You should have stuck to your own business."

Jim shook his head. "No point in arguing about it, Doug. Shooting me's not gonna do you any good."

"Yes it will. I got to shut you up. They're already looking for me."

"Who is?"

"The Chicago police."

"What for?"

"Don't play dumb. You know damn good and well."

"Because of Rusty?"

Spivak nodded. "I called the office after the trial. They said the police want to talk to me."

"That doesn't mean anything. They'll be talking to lots of people. How could they know?"

"Good thinking, Tex. You're a smart fella. They probably don't know anything. And I mean to keep it that way."

"What do you mean?"

"You're the only one who saw me besides your driver and I doubt he can identify me."

"But with that ski mask, I didn't know it was you."

"I couldn't be sure of that," Spivak said. "Besides, now you do know."

Jim had not moved from his position just inside the front door. To his right the door to the hall leading to his bedroom stood open. He'd never make it. Spivak would drill him before he went two feet.

"Why'd you have to kill Rusty?" Jim asked.

"I didn't want to. He forced me."

"Oh yeah. Pulled the trigger himself."

"I just wanted the Loadmaster file back but when I went in there for it, he grabbed his gun. He'd been my friend for years."

"Rusty didn't have the file."

"I figured that out when I saw you had it."

"Why didn't you shoot me in the room?"

"I went in the hall when I heard you at the door. I came back to the hall door just as you were going out. I thought I'd catch you at the front of the building but you were too fast for me."

"You've sure got yourself in a mess, Doug."

Spivak laughed. "The way I see it, you got me into it. But I'm getting ready to fix that." He looked at the gun in his hand.

Had to keep him talking. "Why did Harrigan play games with the steering system? Couldn't you have done a recall?"

Spivak shook his head. "The company's in bad shape. A recall of that size would have busted it. 'Course that's not important now. Harrigan's done for."

"Insurance will pay the claims."

"Yeah, but that won't help customer confidence. The last thing Forbes did before going back to Chicago was to fire me. He blames me for not controlling the damage."

"He's such a nice guy."

"He's a bastard. Always has been. But he was my meal ticket. Now we're both finished."

"Why make things worse by killing me?"

"It won't make things worse. It'll give me a chance. Without you they can't connect me to Rusty's death."

"Don't you think they'll figure out pretty quick who did it?"

Spivak looked around him. "You've got some nice things here, Tex. Nice TV, nice stereo. I bet you've got some money on you, too. It'll be pretty easy for the police to see burglary as the motive."

"You've got it all figured out, don't you?"

"Yes I do. And the only thing I've been doing wrong is being too mouthy about it. I did want you to know what was happening. There's a lot of satisfaction for me in that. You took my life so I'm taking yours. But the time for talking's over."

Spivak raised the gun, resolve in his eyes.

Jim looked beyond Spivak toward the door to the kitchen. "Shoot officer!"

The ploy worked. Spivak glanced over his shoulder and the barrel of the gun wavered. In that instant Jim slipped through the door to the hall. The gun popped twice spitefully but both shots missed. Heart racing, Jim ran down the hall to his bedroom and blocked the door closed with a chair. From the hall, Spivak fired through the door and the round hit the far wall.

Jim threw himself on the bed, rolled to the far side, and jerked open the drawer on the bedside table. He felt the reassuring grip of his .38 Special. Hoped it was loaded. He rolled away from the drawer and trained the gun on the door just as Spivak kicked it open. Doug's squat, thick body jumped through the opening. He swung his revolver toward Jim.

Jim fired and Spivak jerked from the force of the round just as he pulled the trigger and his shot went wide. His arm drooped toward the floor. Gritting his teeth, he raised it, struggling to train the gun on Jim. Twice more Jim fired and Spivak fell forward. Torrents of blood soaked the carpet. His gun had fallen free and lay several feet from his outstretched hand. Raising his head, he reached for it. Jim rolled to his feet and kicked it away.

Spivak looked up, eyes filled with hate, lips curled.

"Asshole!" He spoke in a hoarse whisper.

His head flopped to the floor, blood poured from his mouth and his eyes lost their focus. Sick at his stomach and trembling like a man with a high fever, Jim went to the bedside telephone to call the police.

∽

Rolly walked slowly back to the Worthington after the trial. His clients had really given him a hard time. Why hadn't he sued Harrigan, Richaud and the others had asked. Then they all would have won. He'd tried to explain how improbable the case against Harrigan had seemed but they weren't buying it. McSpadden had sued Harrigan. Why hadn't Rolly?

Fuck 'em all. What the hell did they know about it? Harrigan was all McSpadden had. That's why he'd sued the company. He'd gotten incredibly lucky. Rolly had said he could still sue Harrigan in a new lawsuit. No statute of limitations had run. They'd talk about it, Richaud said, acting as spokesperson for the group.

Rolly stood on the corner across from the hotel waiting for a light. He'd sue Harrigan for them if they wanted him to. If not, screw 'em. He didn't need 'em. With all his millions in the bank, one case more or less didn't make much difference. He crossed the street and entered the Worthington lobby.

The money didn't matter but the loss still stung him to the quick. He hated to lose. Especially to a second-rater like McSpadden. But he had to admit, the man had done a good job getting the stuff on the Loadmaster steering. Rolly had never even imagined a problem like that could have caused the accident.

In the room he peeled off his wrinkled suit and headed for the shower. He'd drive back to San Antonio tomorrow but tonight, Nadine was coming by. They'd eat somewhere then copulate copiously. Rolly was never too tired or out of sorts for sex.

While he was toweling off, two gentle knocks sounded at the door. Rolly wrapped the towel around him and walked into the living area. As he opened the door, the words of greeting stuck in his throat. Bill Graves, not Nadine, stood there smirking at him. The man was huge with a big bald head and ham-like arms straining his tight black T-shirt. His right arm sported an American flag tattoo with the words Semper Fi under it.

"Expecting someone Rolly?" Graves asked.

"Not particularly, Bill. What brings you here?"

Graves swung his arm, backhanding Rolly in the jaw and knocking him to the floor. The towel fell from his body.

"You know why I'm here, you goddamn little weasel."

Rolly pushed himself to his feet. Graves took him by the arms and shook him till his balls slapped his thighs. The big man slammed him backward into the wall. His head indented the plaster and he slid to the floor.

"I'll teach you to screw my wife you little piece of shit."

From his spot on the floor, Rolly contemplated the situation. Wouldn't do for him to fight Bill. It would be like giving the man a license to kill. Had to placate him.

Rolly raised his arm in supplication. "Take it easy Bill. I won't see her again."

Graves snorted. "You sure won't, that's for sure."

A chill ran over Rolly. "You haven't hurt her, have you?"

"No. Not much. She'll have a fat lip for a day or two but I wouldn't say she was hurt. What I did do was have a talk with her. I've had a private investigator watching her the last month so when she said she was going to the store tonight, I knew better. We've been married a long time and we're not about to get divorced at this late date. She's promised not to have anything more to do with you."

"That's good Bill. That's just as it should be. Can I get up now?"

"Sure Rolly. Any time you're ready."

Rolly put his back against the wall and pushed himself up. As soon as he was upright, Grave hit him on the chin and he slid down again.

"On second thought, I like you a whole lot better on the ground, you sniveling little shyster."

A man in a blue suit appeared in the open door of the room. His eyes took in the situation.

"I'm with hotel security. What's the problem here?"

Graves turned, smiling. "There's no problem. No problem at all except that Mr. Sullivan has a headache. Maybe you could get him some aspirin."

Graves headed for the door and the security man grabbed his arm.

"Just a minute, sir. I'll have to ask you to stay until I determine who's responsible for the damage."

Graves shook loose. "Talk to Mr. Sullivan about it. I'm sure he'll take care of everything."

Shaking his head to clear it, Rolly stood. "Let him go," he said. "I'll pay."

The man stepped toward Bill. "You'll still need to stay."

"Fuck you asshole," Graves said. He turned and went out the door.

"Let him alone," Rolly said. "The man's crazy. I'll handle the situation."

"You sure, Mr. Sullivan?"

Rolly nodded. He'd had enough hassle for one night. Now it was time for damage control. He picked up the towel and wrapped it around him.

"Just let me get some clothes on and we'll get this straightened out."

The next morning Rolly slept late, then rolled out of bed slowly, nursing his sore spots. He'd spent half an hour in the hot tub after the security man left but felt like hell in spite of it. He ate a quick breakfast and checked out, then headed the green Jaguar down I 35 toward San Antonio.

South of Temple he flew by a state trooper at 85 miles an hour. The lights came on and the small, high-performance Camaro pulled in behind Rolly. Son of a bitch! This was all he needed. Should he try to outrun the cop? No. That car was probably as fast as his. He'd only make things worse. He pulled to the side of the road. By the time the cruiser had stopped, Rolly stood behind his car, driver's license and insurance papers ready.

The officer approached, tall and professional in his neatly pressed grey uniform and big white hat.

"What's the big hurry, sir?"

"No hurry, officer. Just wasn't watching my speed."

The cop studied Rolly's battered face. "Who got hold of you?"

"It's a long story."

"I bet it is. That car of yours sure looks familiar. You ever travel over on Highway 281?"

Rolly remembered his escape several months earlier. Was this the same officer? "I go that way sometimes but it's been a while."

The officer grinned. "I bet it has. I'm afraid you'll have to come with me, sir."

"Can't you just write me a ticket?"

"We prefer to dispose of charges on the out-of-county drivers the same day. You can pay the fine or post bond."

Irritated, Rolly shrugged. "Should I follow you?"

"No sir. You'll need to leave your car here."

"I can't do that. Someone'll mess with it."

"There isn't any choice, sir. I can't afford to let you get back in a fast car like that until we get this matter taken care of."

An hour later Rolly paid a two hundred dollar fine and court costs to a surly old justice of the peace who presided over court in his suspenders in the back of a roadside convenience store. No point in posting bond. In this county he'd have to pay the fine sooner or later. The officer drove Rolly back to where they'd left the Jaguar. It was gone.

Sick anger clawed at Rolly's gut. "I told you someone would mess with it."

Solemn-faced, the cop shook his head. "Son of a gun! You were right. It's probably on its way to Mexico by now. There's folks down there will pay a premium price for a car like that."

Rolly clenched his fists. "Hope your insurance is good."

"What do you mean? I didn't steal the car. Besides, I'm immune."

Rolly forced himself to shut up. The cop was right. Both the State of Texas and its officers were largely immune in a case like this. Rolly's own insurance would have to buy him a new Jaguar. Two hours later, with a police report duly filed, Rolly resumed his journey in a rented Chevrolet. He pulled into San Antonio late in the afternoon and drove directly home.

As he pulled into the drive of the half-timbered mansion, he glanced at his watch. Seven o'clock. Just a little over twenty-four hours since the verdict. He'd have to explain to Rae Jean how he got beat up. He'd tell her three villains attacked him in a bar. That ought to do the trick. Then he could take a hot shower and go to bed. He might not get up until the next afternoon.

He stopped by the front door and headed for the house. No luggage to bring in; it was gone with the Jaguar. As he approached the front door, a sallow-faced man in a suit stepped from behind a hedge.

"Mr. Sullivan?"

"Yes. Who the hell are you?"

"I'm with the constable's office. Got some papers for you."

Rolly quickly scanned them. Rae Jean was suing him for divorce. She had hired one of the meanest junk yard dog lawyers in San Antonio and alleged incompatibility and adultery as grounds. Bill Graves had spread his poison well. Rolly's eyes filled with angry tears. Life was suddenly so unfair.

"Can I go in and get a few things?" he asked the process server. "My car and luggage got stolen on the way up."

The man shook his head. "You can't go in, sir. You're under a restraining order. There's a hearing date next week. You can ask the judge then for a time to get your stuff."

"I know the drill officer. It's just that I have nothing with me."

"I'm sorry, sir. You can't go in."

Rolly looked toward the house. At the living room window, the curtain was pulled back and Rae Jean stared out at him, face spiteful and vindictive. This was gonna cost him. He'd made most of his money since he'd married her and she'd be entitled to at least half of it. Probably more.

Rolly shot her the finger. "Dirty bitch!" he yelled.

"You'd better leave, sir," said the officer. "You're just making matters worse."

Rolly got himself under control and turned, smiling. "Thanks for that good advice."

He walked quickly to the Chevrolet, got in, and backed from the drive, almost hitting Constance Quimby's BMW as she pulled up in front of the house. Come to commiserate with Rae Jean. That was fine. The two bitches deserved each other. Rolly would head for the office where he could use the bedroom and bath he'd included in the construction plans for just such emergencies. Tomorrow, he'd call Bill Biggers and start working on this latest problem. Down but not out, he'd survive to fight another day.

∽

Two weeks after the trial Jim sat in his office studying new cases that had come in. News of his success had spread and lawyers who hadn't talked to him in years were calling, wanting to refer files to him. Susan stuck her head in the door, skinny face mock-solemn behind her horn-rimmed glasses.

"Joe Bob Savage is here," she said.

Jim leaned back in his swivel chair, folding his hands over his belt. "Have him come in."

Joe Bob had put on weight that he could ill afford. It bloated his body like excess profits inflated the coffers of the insurance company he worked for. He squinted at Jim through the lard-lined caverns of his eyes. Drops of sweat stood on his forehead.

"How you doing, Jim? Long time no see."

Jim motioned toward a chair. "Just fine Joe Bob. What brings you my way?"

"I got a check for you."

"What for?"

"Mrs. Marcus's worker's comp funeral and death benefits."

"Aren't you a little late?"

The big man vented an uneasy laugh. "I don't think so. Wasn't any reason to pay before."

Jim nodded. "Do you have any idea of the misery you caused my client by not paying these benefits? She had to borrow money for the funeral and go back to work to save the house."

Savage looked down. "I know, Jim. But I can't be giving away the company's money. It sure looked like we didn't owe it until you proved what really happened."

" 'Course, you get it back out of what we recover from Harrigan."

"I know that. I just wanted to show good faith by tendering payment."

"But you still expect to get it back when we get paid?"

"Of course."

Jim shook his head. "Keep your damn money then. There's no point in taking it if we have to pay it back. Besides, I'm still thinking about a bad faith lawsuit against you for not paying when the money was due."

"That wouldn't be justified, Jim."

"Maybe not, but it's an intriguing idea."

"You won't take this check, then?"

Jim shook his head. "No. You can cram it up your fat ass, as far as I'm concerned. But thanks for coming by."

Savage rose ponderously. "No need to be abusive, Jim."

"Yes there is. It makes me feel better."

When Savage had gone, Susan came back in the office. "Al Richaud's on line one."

Al Richaud. Should Jim talk to him? Why not? Jim grabbed the phone. "Hello Mr. Richaud. This is Jim McDonald."

"I need an appointment, Mr. McDonald."

"What happened to Rolly?"

"He no longer represents me or any of the others. We all want to talk to you about handling our cases."

"Rolly could sue Harrigan for you."

"I know that. But we want you, Mr. McDonald. You're the one who got the evidence and you've already proved what you can do with it."

"Has Rolly given you a release?"

"Yes. Said it didn't matter to him, we could get who we wanted."

"When would you like to come in?"

After he'd made the appointment and hung up, Jim got up and stood at the window, looking at the strident traffic on the freeway. Things were sure looking up. There was some justice in the world after all.

∽

Jim and Laura stood on the front lawn of his parents' house at Possum Kingdom watching his father's speedboat making a wide wake on the lake. Travis sat behind the wheel and Eddie Marcus waved to them from the water skis the boat was towing.

Laura put her hand in Jim's. "They're getting to be good friends."

"Yes they are," he said. "I was worried they wouldn't."

The front door banged and Kim came out with a tray in her hands. "Try some of these stuffed jalapeños."

Jim took a bite. "You can just leave those out here."

Laura laughed. "Don't you think your mother and father might like some?"

"That's okay," Kim said. "There's another tray in the kitchen." She put the peppers on a picnic table.

"Thanks Kim," Jim said.

With a quick smile she retreated to the house. Jim and Laura walked to the water's edge and sat on the bleached, twisted limb of a dead cedar. On the lake the speedboat turned, following the roughhewn cliffs along the far shore. The late August sun glistened on the choppy waters.

"It's been a good day," Jim said.

She leaned against him. "Yes it has."

"Have you thought any more about it?"

"About what?"

"You know."

"Oh that." She looked across the lake toward the mesquite, cedar and prickly pear growing in profusion at the top of the cliffs. "Yes, I've done a lot of thinking."

"Have you made up your mind?"

She nodded. "Yes I have."

"Will you marry me, then?"

She put her hand to his cheek and kissed him. "Yes, Jim. I'll marry you."

Standing, he pulled her to her feet and they embraced. "You won't be sorry," he said.

268

"I know I won't," she whispered.

As they walked together toward the house, sudden joy welled up through Jim. He had a place in the world again.

# POSTSCRIPT

Jim McDonald and Laura Marcus married and bought a one thousand acre ranch on the western edge of the Cottonwood Valley. Eventually Jim settled the remaining claims against Harrigan Motors for three hundred and fifty million dollars.

With the help of his long-time attorney, Bill Biggers, Rolly Sullivan worked out an eighty million dollar divorce settlement with his wife, Rae Jean. She continues to reside in the mansion in Alamo Heights where she and her friend, Constance Quimby, are frequent hosts to charity events. Rolly's son, Tommy, came into practice with him and recently won his first million dollar verdict in a products liability case involving defective air bags in a pickup. Ronald Hobbs and the San Antonio grievance committee are investigating allegations that the Sullivans unlawfully solicited the case through an ambulance attendant who got a kickback from their fee.

Bobby Torricelli successfully prosecuted Gerald Forbes for negligent homicide in the deaths of the nine killed in the Fort Worth freeway crash. Forbes is now serving a five year sentence in a Texas prison. Torricelli also prosecuted Delbert Dillow for perjury in connection with his testimony in the Harrigan civil case. Dillow received a two year probated sentence but lost his job as supervisor of the E. M. Daggett Hospital lab.

Harrigan Motors took bankruptcy and went out of business. Its assets were acquired by the Arirang Heavy Equipment Company of Pusan, South Korea. Arirang is making construction equipment for the American market in Harrigan's former plant in Chicago.

Art Kurtz recently went on senior status with the Kurtz, Jacobs & Silverstein firm. He still maintains an office and conducts frequent seminars for the firm's aspiring young attorneys.

As a result of the Harrigan Motors loss, its insurance company pulled all its business out of the Potts, Grossberg, firm, and the firm terminated J.

Michael Meador as a partner. He now works as house counsel for Houston Beneficial Insurance Company, defending it against worker's compensation claims before the Texas Worker's Compensation Commission with the sage advice of its senior adjuster, Joe Bob Savage.

Al Hildebrand was promoted to section chief in the Gruen & Stillwell firm and now supervises the work of five younger attorneys.

Jamal El Ibrahim changed his name to Jimmy Abrahams and bought a limousine service in Chicago. Several of his cousins and his wife's brothers now work for him. A Chicago television station recently featured him in a documentary on the entrepreneurial spirit among recent immigrants.